I0655441

War of the Lesbian Zombies

LESBIAN ZOMBIES, THE MILITARY AND POLITICIANS MAKE STRANGE BEDFELLOWS

By George S. Naas

Golden Publishing Company · Lakewood, CO
2021

This is a work of fiction. Names, characters, places, and incidences are either a product of the author's imagination or are used fictitiously. Any resemblance to any actual person, living or dead, events, or locales is entirely coincidental.

Edited by Terry Wright – TWB Press
www/twbpress.com

Cover art by G. S. Naas
Cover model images licensed at shutterstock.com

Published by
Golden Publishing Company, Inc.
PO Box 150425
Lakewood, CO 80215
USA

ISBN: 978-1-736247-80-8

Chapter One

Brenda sat in the cafeteria at Memorial Hospital in New London with a fresh cup of coffee while waiting for Robert to come in and tell her that Maggie had delivered their baby. She hoped the news would be good, that mother and baby were healthy and doing fine.

After adding cream to the coffee, she slowly stirred it and watched the black coffee turn to a delicious brown. When she took the plastic stir-stick out of the cup, she accidentally dropped it on the floor. Reaching down to pick it up, she looked at an obese woman sitting at the next table. Her barrel legs and varicose veins reminded Brenda of her days waddling about in a similar body.

I used to look like her.

She'd been miserable back then, and even though her fiancé had told her she was beautiful, she'd clung to the hope that he really loved her and that they were actually destined to be married. When it turned out he'd only wanted her money and his ex-wife, the betrayal had cost him dearly.

She supposed his bones were still where she'd left them, baking white in the Nevada desert with a boulder on his head, which would make a nice tombstone: "Here lies John Marshall: He cheated the wrong woman and got his brains bashed in."

My Goddess, look at all that's changed in the last thirteen months. I died in Haiti, made a bond with Loa, the Lesbian Goddess of the Universe, and came back in this beautiful body, a body to die for...and many foolish men had done just that.

She chuckled and sipped her coffee, ignoring the buzz of conversation around her, the clatter of plates, and the ding of the cash register.

After John Marshall, there came Big Bad Brooklyn Daddy. That pimp thought he was tough because he could slap women around. Maggie was his number-one girl. She'd carried her bruises like badges of disgrace.

The Goddess Loa felt pity for her and sent me to be his executioner. His beating heart felt hot in my hand as I took the first bite. After all, I am a zombie.

She couldn't take credit for the killings in Mexico. The drug cartel's demise was purely the work of her very own deadly sister Maria. She was the Sisterhood's Mexican-born senorita, more beautiful than a twirling Cantina dancer, clacking her castanets and stomping her feet.

On the other hand, the demise of the entire Heinrich SS gang in Brooklyn was more of a Sisterhood affair.

Lastly, turning a violently abusive husband into mason jars of dogfood was all Chloe's idea, the blue-eyed blonde beauty who wore her lesbianism like a beauty pageant sash. Girlie Dog, their adopted Jack Russell Terrier with the personality of a Toy Poodle and the ferocity of a Hungarian Wolf hound, was very appreciative of the high-protein meals that gushed from an industrial-sized meat grinder in the garage. It would undoubtedly be employed in the future, as there were many deserving male candidates on the wrong side of the *#MeToo* movement.

Brenda's musings were interrupted by a voice on the intercom. *"Miss Brenda Ayler, please go to room 327 on the maternity floor."*

Her heart lurched. Robert was supposed to meet her here in the cafeteria. She set down her coffee cup. *Something must've gone horribly wrong.*

She rushed to the elevator, stepped inside, and pushed the number three button. As the elevator doors closed, a hand stopped them, beautifully manicured nails, pearl white on ebony fingers, smooth and young. Monica's hand. The doors opened to reveal the Sisterhood: Monica, Jackie, Maria, Chloe, Donna, Melinda, and sweet little nine-year-old Caroline, their expressions a mix of concern and joy.

"What is wrong?" Monica asked as they all piled aboard.

Brenda hit button number three. "I don't know."

"We were in the lobby, heard the page."

Caroline hugged Brenda. "Is something wrong with the baby?"

With a smile, Brenda looked down at Caroline. "We don't know yet, sweetie, but I'm sure your little sister is beautiful."

"And I'll be her big sister."

The elevator jerked to a stop, and the doors opened to a cacophony of wailing babies. Nurses hustled about. The door to room 327 was closed. Brenda pushed it open, cautiously, her senses on full alert for any dread and despair lurking in the room.

A beaming Robert turned from his wife's bedside. "Come in. Come in."

Caroline pushed by and led the way inside. "I want to see the baby." She jumped on the bed where Maggie held the bundled infant. "Is she okay?"

Maggie beamed. "She's wonderful."

The Sisterhood gathered around the bed. Jackie asked, "What name did you decide on?"

"Zoey." She held up the baby to Brenda. "Wanna hold her?"

Brenda held Zoey and gazed into her beautiful blue-gray eyes, which shifted from face to face above her. She seemed much more alert and curious than a normal three-hour-old infant. *Yep. She's a smart little baby, all right. No doubt about it.*

"My turn," Maria said.

Brenda carefully situated the bundle in Maria's arms.

"She's so tiny."

Melinda tickled Zoey's chin. "I really like your name, little one. In ancient Amazonian culture, Zoey means *from death comes life*."

Zoey fidgeted and whimpered.

Caroline got up on her knees. "I think she's hungry."

"She's going to be so spoiled." Maria handed Zoey back to her mother.

Maggie brushed the nipple of her left breast against Zoey's lips, and the baby suckled in earnest.

Caroline watched intensely. "How does she know what to do?"

Maggie said, "It's a mystery of life, honey."

While everyone watched Zoey and Maggie, Robert took Brenda's hand and pulled her aside. "Maggie told me how you healed my spinal cord when I was paralyzed. One kiss. She said you gave me a virus, and she gave me a pill to counter the side effects, like the virus would make me some kind of super stud. Who me? But I believed her, and now we have our sweet little girl." He bent to Brenda's hand and kissed it. "If you ever need anything, just ask. I'll be there for you."

Brenda stroked Robert's cheek. "I'll remember that."

A nurse walked in. "Okay, folks. The party's over."

Caroline looked dejected. "No. I wanna stay."

"Sisters..." Brenda announced, "Maggie needs to get some rest."

After saying their goodbyes and each kissing Zoey's forehead one more time, the Sisterhood made their way outside to the parking lot, chattering like a gaggle of teenage girls.

Jorge, Jackie's chauffeur, from his seat in the limo, saw them coming and had to quit playing with himself, an oversexed side-effect of the lesbian zombie virus he'd contracted during an orgy with the sisters at the pool. He tucked himself away, got out of the limo, and opened the rear door.

As the women piled in, Brenda stopped Jackie and Monica. "You two are riding with me. Girls, we'll see you back at The Ranch." She tossed Jackie a key fob, after all, it was her Mercedes. "You drive." The strawberry blond bombshell was probably the richest woman in New York City. She was sixty-five years old but didn't look a day over twenty-one, thanks to a kiss from Brenda's lips and a massage with a happy ending.

While Jackie drove, Brenda rode shotgun and pondered what would come next for the Sisterhood. She needed more sisters, more money for the foundation, and a clear path to women's equality in this country.

Monica, seat-belted in the back, tapped Brenda's shoulder. "What is so secret our sisters cannot hear what you have to say?" Monica's Haitian accent and perfect enunciation wasn't her only endearing trait. She gave the saying *Black is Beautiful* a lofty new high bar.

Brenda got down to business. "I want to throw another Black Friday Party, but I know the girls aren't going to like it."

"A bunch of drunk, smelly men? What is to like?"

"They've got money and connections, and we need to broaden our scope. Besides, it's been a while—"

"That's a lot of work, Brenda," Jackie put in. "Just thinking about it makes me hungry. Let's stop at that diner up ahead, the one with the dilapidated sign. Max's Diner."

Brenda groaned. "You're kidding. Look at the place. It's a dump. I'm not *that* hungry."

"It's the only restaurant for miles, and I can't wait to get back to Long Island to eat."

Monica leaned forward. "I am hungry, too."

Jackie laughed. "That's two votes to one, Brenda. You lose."

"Okay. I guess I wouldn't mind a bowl of soup."

Jackie turned the car into a weed-infested parking lot, home to one lonely Jeep. The restaurant seemed a good prospect for crime-scene tape and a *This Property Condemned* sign nailed to the front door.

Brenda huffed. "We better lock the car or it might not be here when we get back."

The sisters got out and walked into the restaurant. The tile floors suffered from wax buildup, and the booth-seats exposed their foam innards through cracks in the faded black vinyl.

Monica whispered, "This place is old as Haitian Voodoo."

Jackie stopped at a sign that read: *Please wait to be seated.* "It's not busy so they should be able to get us in."

A man's voice boomed from the kitchen. "You better not be holding out on me, bitch."

A woman's voice cried, "I didn't take the tip money, Max."

"Look at that. You got customers waiting."

Rushing from the kitchen, the waitress spotted the sisters. "Sit anywhere you like."

They picked a booth by the kitchen door.

The waitress promptly came back with three menus. "Sorry about my boss. He thinks everyone is ripping him off."

While Monica and Jackie studied the menus: "Chicken fried chicken looks good," Monica stated. Jackie responded with, "I need red meat."

Brenda wasn't thinking about food. She was inspecting the waitress who now delivered three glasses of water. *Five-foot-four inches tall, a bit dumpy, and no wedding ring. I just love her light brown hair and those tired eyes that have the look of pure innocence.*

"What can I get you, ladies?" The nametag pinned to the

slope of her left breast read: *Lilly.* She had her pad and pen ready. "Pan-fried trout is our specialty. Max is making some for himself right now."

Brenda read Lilly's mind: *"Please hurry. Max is in a bad mood. If I don't find the missing tips, my ass is grassed."*

Jackie handed Lilly her menu. "I'll take a blood-rare hamburger with fries and a beer, if you have one."

"There's one in my Jeep you can have at no charge."

"That's very nice, Lilly. I'll give you a big tip."

Monica decided to go with, "Chicken fried chicken."

"And you, ma'am?" She was looking at Brenda.

"Lilly," Max shouted from the kitchen. "Get your ass in here."

Brenda leaned back and felt an errant spring stab her shoulder blade. "Lilly, I can't decide. I should first check the kitchen and confer with the chef—"

"Brenda," Jackie cut in. "Let it go."

After sliding off the worn seat, she stood and looped her arm around Lilly's shoulders. "Come on, honey. Introduce me to Max."

Monica said, "Brenda, bad idea."

"Please, ma'am," Lilly begged. "Don't say anything. Max will take it out on me when you leave. He has a terrible temper...beats me something awful. I'll show you the bruises. You don't want to end up like me."

"Okay. Show me. Turn around."

"Not here. Max will see—"

"Okay, then.. Where's the restroom?"

"Around that way." She pointed.

Making a left turn toward an all-gender restroom, Brenda glanced back to see her sisters looking at her with arms folded and lips pressed tight. "We still want to eat, you know." That came from Jackie.

Brenda pulled Lilly into the restroom and closed the door. "Turn around."

Lilly didn't move. "Ma'am, please. I-I'm afraid of you."

"There's nothing to fear. Do what I say."

She turned around.

Brenda unzipped the back of Lilly's waitress dress and pulled it open, revealing black and blue splotches on her ivory skin.

Brenda ground her molars and angrily zipped up the dress. "Why do you keep working here? Your boss should be in prison."

"Max...well...he's my husband."

Brenda scowled. "You're not wearing a ring."

Lilly bowed her head. "It's not something I'm proud of."

"Ever think of getting away from him? A battered women's shelter, a tent on the sidewalk, a blanket in the gutter? Anywhere is better than this—"

"If I ever leave him he'll..."

"He'll what?"

"He'll kill me." That came out with a sob.

"We'll see about that. Stay here until I come for you."

Shaking, Lilly managed, "Max is *not* going to like you butting into his affairs. He'll beat you too."

"We'll see about that, as well." Brenda left in a huff, stormed to the kitchen, and kicked open the door.

"I'm looking for Max."

A six-foot-plus bruiser stepped up, king-size belly, arms covered in tattoos of dragons and busty women, buzz-cut gray hair and scraggle on his chin. He crossed his arms and glared at Brenda. "What can I do for you, Red?"

As Brenda stalked up to him, she read his mind: *"I hope she wants to party with me, but knowing my luck, she's probably here to complain about my cooking."*

Brenda scowled at him. *Oh, I'm going to party with you, all right, Max, but not in the way you're thinking. But first I'm going to stroke your womanizing ego.* She stopped in front of him and looked up into steely eyes that had no soul. "Lilly told me the cook was a real stud."

"Lilly said that?"

"Sure did."

"Where is she?"

"Somewhere safe, for now. What's that you're cooking?" She indicated the spitting pan on the stove.

"Pan-fried trout. My specialty."

"That grease sure looks hot."

"What do you want, Red?" The bully in his voice came out.

Brenda looked back and saw Jackie and Monica at the door, watching and waiting for the inevitable. It wasn't long in coming.

Brenda turned the trout over with her bare fingers then showed him her scalded flesh, let him watch it heal.

His bully bravado turned to horror. “What the hell?”

Reading his mind, Brenda thought this prick would actually run and hide. The coward. She reached for the hot pan handle, picked it up, and dumped the trout and grease on the floor. As Max turned to flee, he tripped over the trout and fell facedown in the hot grease. Screaming like a scalded lobster, he tried to get up but Brenda slammed her foot on his back and bashed his head with the frying pan.

“Are you ever going to beat Lilly again, you fat creep?”

“No. I’ll never touch her again. I swear.”

The frying pan was cooling down. “Stand up, you pig.”

Struggling to his feet, he slipped on the grease and fell again. “Lady—”

“Get up.”

When he found his feet, he growled out, “I’m going to kill you.” He threw a punch at Brenda.

She ducked his fist and caught him with the frying pan, right to his jaw. This time he hit the floor, out cold.

Lilly appeared between Jackie and Monica, the expression on her face one of abject terror to see Brenda had cold-cocked her husband.

“Don’t look, honey,” Jackie said. “Your boss just got the shit kicked out of him.”

“Husband.”

Monica huffed. “I would not be bragging about that.”

Lilly bent her head in shame. “I know the feeling.”

Jackie lifted Lilly’s chin with a gentle index finger. “You don’t need him, no matter how much you think you do. You’re welcome to come with us.”

“Where?”

“Join our Sisterhood and live in paradise, sweetie, paradise. No more living in fear of a man hurting you, bullying you, or making you feel small. Your choice is this...go with us, and your life will change in ways you cannot imagine, or stay with this shithead and maybe get murdered one of these days. What will it be?”

Lilly stood straight, shoulders back, chin up. “I’ll need a

couple of days to get everything in order."

"Don't let him talk you into staying."

"I won't. I hate that man."

Brenda hugged Lilly, gave her an LZ Foundation card with the address of The Ranch and her phone number. "We'll see you then...in two days."

Chapter Two

Brenda looked out the Mercedes window at the autumn-stripped trees racing by. The sisters were headed back to their home, The Ranch, a massive estate and mansion that Jackie's skin cream business built, one jar at a time. It sat on eastern Long Island, far from the hustle and bustle of the Big Apple, overlooking the Sound and her private beach beyond Inlet Point.

As snow began to fall, Brenda brought up the subject of Lilly. "What do you think the waitress will do?"

Jackie glanced at her. "She'll stay with the jerk."

"How about you, Monica? Is there any hope for her?"

"No."

Jackie huffed. "Maybe we should open a shelter for battered women. It would give more credence to our LZ Foundation."

"Jackie, you have a point, but that'd be like putting a Band-Aid on a jugular vein. Women don't need to be sheltered, they need to be empowered."

"Shit. Look at the snow coming down."

"Go a little slower, Jackie. We're not in a big rush."

"I'm pissed about what Max might do to Lilly in retaliation for you pummeling him, Brenda. You just couldn't let it go, could you?"

"It's not in my nature to turn away from an abused woman."

A ringing cell phone reverberated from somewhere in the car. Brenda looked around. "Whose cell is that?"

"Not mine," Jackie said.

"It must be yours, Monica."

"My stomach is grumbling so loud, I didn't hear it."

"Mine too," Jackie threw in. "We never got a bite to eat, thanks to Brenda."

Monica checked her now silent phone. “Missed call. It was Maria.”

“Call her back. Hopefully this snow didn’t cause Jorge to run off the road.”

Monica speed-dialed Maria. “What do you want?”

“Jorge drove ninety miles an hour with his right hand in his pants, jerking away. Caroline saw him.”

“Put him on.”

“Sure. Jorge,” she shouted. “Monica wants to talk to you.”

Jackie said, “Let me talk to him.”

Monica passed her the phone.

“Hello, Miss Monica.”

“Listen up, Jorge. It’s me. Your boss, Jackie.”

“Yes, ‘m.”

“If you ever play with yourself around Caroline again I will cut your prick off so short you’ll need to sit down to pee. Got that?”

“I’m sorry, ma’am. I can’t stop...not since Brenda and the girls gave me that massage at the pool. Was there something in your skin cream that turned me into a sex fiend?”

“Of course not, Jorge, but we’ve got a pill for that. Ask Chloe for it. Take one and call me in the morning.”

“Yes, ‘m.”

***

The Mercedes arrived at The Ranch thirty minutes later. The snowstorm had turned to a driving rainstorm along the coast. After parking in the garage, the sisters walked into the living room to find the place was as quiet as a tomb. Their sisters were all sound asleep.

Monica whispered, “Goodnight, ladies,” and headed to her room.

On the way to their bedroom, Jackie and Brenda stopped to check on Caroline. They found her sound asleep with Girlie Dog on the bed curled up at her feet. The feeling of love they both felt for Caroline and her sisters came to a screeching halt as they spied an empty wine bottle on the nightstand.

Jackie whispered in Brenda’s ear, “So help me, someone is

going to be grounded for this. Giving a little girl booze. What the hell were they thinking? They must have all been drunk."

"Jackie, I'm sure there's a logical reason for the wine bottle. And they haven't been home long enough to get drunk. Let's just go to bed and ask about it in the morning."

***

A crash of thunder awakened Brenda. The alarm clock read 3am. Lightning flashed beyond the window, followed by more ear-splitting thunder. She got up and stepped to the sash to see how much havoc the storm was raising. Rain beat down on the Crystal Shrine to Loa, which they'd built in Jackie's greenhouse. Another bolt of lightning lit up the crystalline panels and revealed a figure moving about inside.

A burglar? In this weather? At this time of night?

Brenda decided to investigate. Though she only wore a white cotton gown, she grabbed an umbrella and rushed outside. The wind whipped at her gown as she ran toward the shrine door, but even with the umbrella, her gown was soaked by the time she got there. After a quick breath, she quietly entered the sacred shrine.

The rain made a racket on the crystalline panels that made up the walls and ceiling. Outreaching leafy branches of the Sister Tree of Life took up most of the interior, umbrellaing the Pit of Ages and its golden perimeter railing in the center of the floor.

No one lurked about, and nothing seemed out of order. The golden floor tiles were dry and free of footprints. Whatever she'd seen must've been a trick of lightning and shadows.

As she turned to leave, vines slithered up from the pit and quickly looped around Brenda's legs. "Loa?" The vines responded by wrapping around her entire body. She dropped the umbrella and tore at the vines, trying to free herself, but her superior strength was no match for *Loa*'s power on earth.

"Goddess, I pray. Why have you summoned me?"

The vines dragged her toward the pit. Remembering Jenny and how the vines dragged her to her death in the pit, Brenda grabbed the golden rails and hung on with all her might. "Goddess, I pray. What have I done to displease you?" But she wasn't strong enough to stop the vines from pulling her over the rails and down to the floor of the pit where the roots of the Sister Tree of Life joined the vines' deadly embrace.

Fearing the same fate Jenny had suffered for betraying the Goddess *Loa*, Brenda cried out a prayer for the third time since the vines had grabbed her. "Please, Goddess, I pray. Whatever I've done, it was out of ignorance...not out of disrespect. Please Loa, Goddess of All, have pity on me."

Unexpectedly, the vines and roots released her and formed an arch over her head. Brenda, still shaken, peered into the arch, which formed a black tunnel that looked as if it had no end. She picked up a rock and threw it into the blackness. The rock did not echo back an impact against anything solid.

No way am I going in there.

She turned her back to the arch and reached up to take hold of root stubs to climb up to the railing. "Wait, Brenda." The ethereal voice froze her in mid climb. With her heart racing, she dropped down and slowly turned around to look straight into the translucent face of the Goddess, *Loa*, Lord Of All. Her long blond hair floated around her face as if in zero gravity, and her eyes glinted with sparks of starlight. If she was a ghost, she was the most beautiful ghost in the universe.

Thunder crashed.

Brenda staggered backwards until her back pressed against the pit wall. Her body felt suddenly cold, and she began to shiver, a very unusual reaction for a lesbian zombie.

"Fear not." Loa's voice resonated as if the air in the pit had spoken. "I am not here to harm you."

"What do you want of me, my Goddess?"

"You are to do my bidding on earth. I have been waiting for you since the beginning of time. You are my chosen one. You have a pure heart."

"I live to serve you, my Goddess."

"My heart is heavy, Brenda. I have suffered with all the women who have lived and died over the centuries. Men ran the world and women served men. Civilization has progressed some over time, but there are still many places where women are being dominated and slaughtered by men. Subservience to these men must be crushed, once and for all."

"What would you have me do to this end?"

"Very soon you will learn of a very sad tale. A little girl will come to you, right here in my shrine, and she will make a request of you that you will not deny."

"Me? Why me?"

"Men are flawed because they were created in the image of the male gods who had the same flaws. Women do not have these flaws, but because of mistakes made as far back as the Garden of Eden, men took dominance over women who were not perfect until you were reborn."

"Oh dear. I'm far from perfect."

"The male gods are gone, but their evil thoughts still resound off the walls of the universe. These thoughts are sexual and denied to women who are made to cover their bodies that other men may not admire them. This may confuse the emotions of your lesbian sisters. You must use men's impulses to your advantage, be provocative, be strong, but never let your guard down."

Brenda stood before *Loa* in amazement. "My sisters make love to each other, but with men it's only sex for the Sisterhood."

"Unless I deem otherwise, as you will see in a sister you have yet to meet."

"But all my sisters are loyal to you."

"As is Cassandra, the Voodoo High Priestess who brought you to me. She will be on my right hand very soon."

"What are you telling me?"

"You will be summoned to Haiti for a funeral. Now join your sisters, for the sun will rise on a new era of war. I will come to you in your mind when I need you."

Brenda watched spellbound as a radiant light surrounded *Loa* until she could no longer be seen in the brilliance. The light grew smaller and smaller as it flew into the black tunnel of the arch, and then it was gone. The arched vines entwined with the roots on the floor and all settled into a peaceful stillness.

A warm sense of pride replaced the chill of Brenda's first encounter with *Loa* in this new life she'd been given, which now had purpose and meaning.

Somewhere, women will be freed from men's brutal dominance, but it all starts with one little girl.

As she started to climb up the dirt wall, she stepped with her bare foot on what she thought was a rock. Looking down, she realized that she had put her foot on Jenny's skull, its eye sockets staring upward, the jaw cocked open as if emitting an eternal scream. The terror on her face that Black Friday night when the vines had dragged her into the pit was still evident in her bony expression. Such was the price for betraying *Loa*.

The shiver returned.

Brenda climbed the root stubs to the gold-tiled floor of the Crystal Shrine's throne room, retrieved her umbrella, and walked outside. The driving rain was now just a drizzle. Walking toward the house and contemplating all that had just taken place, she looked toward the east and saw in the morning light a physically impossible rainbow of gold and blood-red arches that reached all the way down to the sea. With gladness in her heart she knew that the women of the world had a true ally in *Loa*.

After quietly slipping back into the bedroom, she carefully pulled up the covers as not to wake a constantly amorous Jackie. Still wearing her wet nightgown, she carefully turned on her left side, facing away from her bed partner.

Jackie snorted and sniffed.

Brenda closed her eyes.

Jackie turned over and slipped her hand on Brenda's thigh then immediately pulled back. "You're all wet. Where have you been?"

"The Crystal Shrine."

"In that storm? What for?"

"Loa called me."

"Oh my Goddess. What did she say?"

"A visitor is coming, a little girl who will ask something of me, and I must comply."

"When?"

"She didn't say."

Jackie kissed Brenda's shoulder and pulled at her damp nightgown. "Meanwhile, let me get you out of this."

"You just want to see my naked body."

"And what's wrong with that?"

"You first."

Jackie sat up and slipped her dainty nighty over her head. "Your turn, and hurry up before our sisters wake up and spoil our fun for the night...make that the morning."

Brenda smiled, removed her wet nightgown, tossed it to the floor then ducked under the sheets.

Jackie giggled and joined her.

Soon the two of them were kissing and caressing each other, hot and heavy. Under their sheet-tent, Brenda got on top and ran butterfly kisses around Jackie's full breasts and down her soft tummy.

Jackie let out a loud moan.

"Quietly," Brenda whispered. "You know lesbian zombies have acute hearing. You'll wake the sisters."

"Stop talking," Jackie cooed. "Keep going. Lower. Lower."

The loving desperation in her voice was unmistakable.

Chapter Three

At the Pentagon, Four-Star General Lawrence Taylor was meeting with Donna's old boyfriend, Senator James Hoffman. He'd been known as the tabloid's Playboy of the Senate. A different woman every weekend, a different scandal every month. However, something changed him, and he quickly became a menace to women, a braggart and an exhibitionist. Now even the tabloids considered him bad news.

After going through security, Senator Hoffman was directed into the office of the chairman of the Joint Chiefs of Staff by the General's aide-de-camp, Colonel Wesley Miller.

Wesley saluted the General, closed the door then stood outside the office. Not knowing what the General and Senator were discussing, Miller recalled how the General had changed since the Black Friday party at Jackie's house. *He goes to the party a brave soldier and comes back pussy-whipped.* Maybe they got him drunk on hormone-laced love juice. Wesley didn't know it, but his suspicion was pretty close to the truth.

He pressed his ear to the door.

On the other side, General Taylor sat behind his desk and cut to the chase. "So, what's the matter with you, James? I see all these reports... Look, if you're a pervert of some kind, I can't support your legislation for sensitivity training in the military."

Hoffman stood, more out of desperation than respect. "My life has been crazy, sir, ever since Donna hooked me up with a threesome."

"Why didn't you attend the Black Friday party at Jackie's? A swinger like you would have fit in quite nicely."

"I couldn't go...I was arrested for indecent exposure and lewd acts. I couldn't stop playing with myself in public. I started to feel like I was going gay. At least I thought about my dick all the time."

"That's very disturbing, Senator."

"When I was exposed to HIV...that's an even more disturbing story...the doc put me on this medication that calmed me down. Now I'm back to thinking about women all the time, like before, but I have to take those stupid pills every day."

"Good for you, James, but your reputation is ruined."

"Yeah. And I lost Donna. She's a lesbian now."

"You really have a way with women, don't you?"

"It's Brenda, I'm sure. It's all her fault. She's like some kind of queen bee over the lesbians. She made me into some kind of sex zombie...like...I feel like I'm invincible. We gotta do something about her."

"Don't worry. I'll take care of Brenda."

"And don't give up on my legislation, sir."

"If you behave yourself, I'll consider backing you...for now, anyway."

"Thank you, sir."

Taylor stood. "Now you'll have to excuse me. I have a meeting with the Joint Chiefs of Staff in a little while." It was a ruse, of course.

I have to warn my Queen about Hoffman.

Taylor opened the door, causing Colonel Miller to jump back and stand at attention to salute his boss.

"Wes, show Senator Hoffman out."

When Colonel Miller returned, Taylor said, "Get me a car from the motor pool."

"Where are we going, General?"

"You are not going anywhere. I'll drive myself."

"That's against regulations, sir."

Getting annoyed with his aide and thinking about Brenda, he said, "Wes, I love you like a brother, but I don't give a shit about regulations. I make the god damn rules around here," he tapped the four stars on his collar, "and don't forget it. Are we clear on that?"

Wes smiled. "Whatever you say, General." He grabbed the phone and ordered a car for his boss.

***

Still annoyed at Wes's strict Army protocol, General Taylor drove his acquired car up to the main gate where he stopped and offered his Army ID to a shocked MP. Seeing those four stars on the driver's jacket rattled the soldier. "I-I don't need to see your ID, sir."

"Sure you do, Corporal. What if I'm a Russian spy?"

Looking at Taylor's ID, he said, "It's all in order, sir. Your face matches the picture. Is there anything else I can help you with?"

"Now that you mentioned it, soldier, there is something you can do for me. In case a bird colonel comes down here and asks to see your exit sheet, write my destination as sixteen hundred Pennsylvania Avenue. Got that, son?"

"Yes, sir."

"One more thing. If he wants to see the surveillance video, tell him General Taylor said you're not authorized to show it to him. Do that for me and I'll get you a three-day pass. We got a deal, soldier?"

He saluted with great enthusiasm and a smile. "Yes, sir."

***

Unbeknownst to Brenda that General Taylor was driving in from the Pentagon to pay her a visit at The Ranch, she told her sisters about her encounter with *Loa* and the little girl who would come to the shrine with a sad story and a request they could not deny.

Caroline was now up and eating her Coco Puffs and slipping Girlie Dog nibbles under the table. As usual, she changed the subject to her own little world. "Did Loa say anything about my mommy and daddy?" Her voice sounded matter-of-factly innocent.

The sisters swiveled their eyes to Brenda, each wondering what she would say. Jackie thought it was a loaded question, no win either way, yes or no. *Tell her they are dead and that is all you know.* It was a horrific traffic accident. Caroline was the only survivor.

Brenda decided to tell her, "Yes, Caroline. Your parents are happy living in heaven with Loa, and they are thrilled that you are living with us."

Caroline's eyes got big and bright. "Can I ask Loa to let me see them?"

"You can ask her anything you want, but don't get your hopes up."

"Okay." She spooned cereal from her bowl.

Maria was standing at the window, looking out. "Who the hell is that?"

All the sisters joined her at the window. Caroline got there first and recognized him. "He was that Army guy at our big party."

Jackie frowned. "You all stay here. Brenda and I'll go see what he wants. Let's hope it's not bad news."

Walking out to the portico, they waited for him to get out of the staff car and wondered what had brought General Lawrence Taylor to The Ranch.

As he approached, Brenda read his thoughts: *I hope my Queen can do something about Hoffman.*

"Jackie," Brenda whispered. "He might be a traitor."

Jackie also detected the General's thoughts. "Hoffman's been a problem all along."

Lawrence gave Jackie a hug. "Good to see you."

Brenda spoke first. "What brought you here today?"

"Bad news, I fear. Hoffman's out to get you."

"You must think he's a clear and present danger or you wouldn't be here...so far from the Pentagon."

"Just watch your backsides, ladies. He can create a shitstorm of biblical proportions."

"Won't you come in, Lawrence? Stay a while?"

"I have to get back, but thanks for the invitation."

Jackie gave him another big hug. "By the way, Lawrence, why didn't you just call?"

"My aide, Colonel Wesley Miller has big ears, besides, I can't get a hug over the phone."

Five minutes later, he was back on the road to the Pentagon, five hours away. He was unaware that Colonel Miller had been tracking his journey all the while, thanks to a GPS homing device that had been installed in all military vehicles used by officers. If rental cars had them, why not military vehicles? The General personally had signed off on that directive months ago, but today he had forgotten all about it.

***

Back in the mansion, the sisters were discussing what to do about Senator Hoffman. Maria paced the sitting room. “He’s a traitor and a threat to the Sisterhood *and* our Queen. We should take a vote on whether to kill him or not.”

Chloe stopped filing her toenails. “Sorry, Maria. Only our Queen can authorize a death sentence. But if she does, I’ll be glad to do it.”

“Yeah, Chloe,” Monica said. “You’re the man-hater around here.”

“Donna should do it,” Melinda put in. “She was his fuck-buddy. He treated her like shit.”

Donna shook her head. “I’m not a killer.”

None of them had noticed Brenda standing at the door. “Girls, Hoffman is so full of himself, that he thinks he’s one of us...invincible, that he can talk shit and get away with it. He’s his own worst enemy, and since every dog has his day, there’ll be no more talk of killing him.”

Jackie agreed. “So let’s talk about our Black Friday 2 party. Last time we raked in a bit over a million dollars. Let’s double it this time, girls.”

Chapter Four

As Jackie began to spell out what she expected on Black Friday 2, Brenda's cell phone vibrated. She had been sitting on the bottom stair of the staircase, listening to Jackie. The phone display read: *Cassandra.* "It's Cassandra calling. Hello, Cass—"

"It's Aurora," she said and sobbed.

That's alarming. "What's wrong, Aurora?"

"My mom is dying," she cried.

"That's impossible." The Voodoo High Priestess was Loa's facilitator.

"She asked for you."

"I'll catch the first flight out on American—"

"She doesn't have that much time."

"Then I'll get Alfons to fly me there on his private jet."

"Maybe you can save her," Aurora sobbed out. "The doctors are at a loss—"

"I'll see what I can do."

"Why has the Goddess Loa forsaken her?"

"She loves Cassandra as much as the sun. Something has gone wrong. She wouldn't let her die. Tell Cassandra to rest easy. I'll be there in four hours. Goodbye." She turned to Monica. "Get hold of Alfons and tell him I need his Learjet to fly me to Haiti within the hour. Jackie, book me a helicopter from FSG Airport to JFK."

She walked away with her cell phone to her ear. "Jorge, bring the car around. Pronto."

Monica asked, "What do we do while you are gone?"

Brenda choked back tears. "Pray to *Loa* for Cassandra." She packed a small bag then ran down to the portico.

Jorge was waiting for her with the passenger door opened.

"Where to, ma'am?"

She got in. "The airport."

"Yes, 'm." Jorge closed the door, got in behind the wheel, and took off with the rear tires squealing.

The Sisterhood gathered at the window. There wasn't a dry eye among them.

***

As Alfons' private jet reached its flying altitude of 36,000 feet, Brenda gazed out the window to see the Eastern Seaboard gliding below the speeding aircraft. She downed a Manhattan and prayed to *Loa* to save her friend.

Don't let her die, my Goddess Loa. I beseech you.

She closed her eyes and leaned her head against the window. It felt ice cold. It was then it dawned on her. She had felt the same cold feeling when *Loa* came to her in the pit. But there was no *Loa* here on the plane. She decided the window was cold because the outside air temperature was at least twenty-four degrees below zero.

Carrie, a cute little flight attendant with honey-colored hair and a set of 34DD breasts, brought her another Manhattan.

As Brenda reached for her drink, the jet hit a bump of air and caused her to fumble the exchange.

Carrie jumped back out of the way of the splashing booze. "I'm so sorry, ma'am. That was very clumsy of me."

"It wasn't your fault, Carrie."

"I'll get you another."

"Thank you."

Brenda watched Carrie as she moved her cute little butt down the short aisle. *She would make a wonderful addition to the Sisterhood.*

Brenda suddenly felt as if a hand was placed on her shoulder and returned her attention out the window. Beyond the upturned winglet lay the candy-blue Caribbean Sea. It looked so peaceful to her, so why did she feel so much dread? She muttered, "Loa, you must have heard my prayers. Why have you not answered—

"Brenda."

The tiny hairs on the back of her neck tingled as she

remembered that *Loa* would speak to her mind. "Loa?"

"I'm sorry, my precious one. Your sweet, kind, and loyal Cassandra was welcomed into the realm of eternity four minutes ago."

Sorrow gripped Brenda's chest. "How could you let her die?" she shouted. "You could have saved her life. In fact you could give her back her life right now. Why don't you? You are the Goddess of the universe. You can do anything."

"I could have saved her, but I dared not change what is written in the stars. They have realigned to accept Casandra, and now she is one of them. If I were to change them back, everything would be the same as it was before. You would be once more down-trodden Brenda, homely and fat, standing on the curb, waiting for John Marshall to pick you up. He would not be in agony in hell as he is right now. Instead he would be alive and plotting against you again. Your mother would still die of heart failure over John, and you would blame yourself every day of your life. The Sisterhood *would have never existed, men would rule forever, and women would suffer for all time."*

"I understand. Please be merciful to Aurora. She is also suffering."

Carrie brought the replacement Manhattan. "Are you all right? You're talking to yourself."

"Never mind me." Brenda took the glass. "Just keep these coming."

"Yes, ma'am."

Brenda drowned her grief with three more Manhattans. Truth was, Loa had told her of a funeral in Haiti. But why did it have to be Cassandra? After finishing off the last drink, she buckled her seatbelt for the landing at Toussaint Louverture International Airport, Port au Prince.

After Alfons' jet taxied to a private hangar reserved only for the very rich, Brenda just sat in her seat, listening to the engines wind down to a stop.

Carrie waited for the Captain to tell her it was safe to open the cabin and deplane. She opened the door, which levered down to the tarmac and created steps. Hot, humid air burst in with a bright tropical glare. "Miss Ayler, you can go anytime you want."

"Thank you." She stood, smoothed her dress, grabbed her

small bag from the overhead compartment then strode to the open door where Carrie stood.

"Are you sure you're all right, Miss Ayler?"

"I just learned a good friend has died."

"Is there anything that I can do for you?"

"No you can't...but I wish you could." She started down the steps.

Waiting for her at the foot of the steps were Reinhard and Albert, the two lucky survivors of the Heinrich SS gang in Brooklyn. Looking at them reminded her of how she had planned to kill them too, but decided they could be worth more to her alive. Walking up to them, she had only one question. "Where is Aurora?"

"She's grieving over her mom."

"Where?"

"At his old health clinic. Cassandra's body is there."

"Then that's where you boys are taking me."

***

Getting out of the car, Brenda looked at the old clinic building. It was exactly what she'd expected. The place looked in disrepair: the outside walls had been painted white decades ago, and the peeling flakes of paint revealed a dirty brown undercoat. She walked up the same broken concrete sidewalk where a scant thirteen months ago she'd walked in hopes of a makeover and weight reduction surgery. Her death on the operating table had changed her life in ways she could never have imagined.

At the front door, there was a hand-scrawled note behind the glass that read: *Closed until further notice.* She pulled on the handle but the door failed to budge.

Shit. The front door is still hard to open.

It took both hands to get it to open due to its rusty hinges. The reception office smelled like dirty socks. Ragged stuffed chairs stood about on a dusty wood floor. *Maid's year off?* she mused then heard weeping down the hallway. She followed the sound to an open doorway. It was the same operating room where she'd died, and on that same table lay a sheet-covered body.

Aurora, dressed in a flower-print dress, bent over the corpse of her mother, sobbing. "Kill me, Brenda. Just kill me."

"I'm not here to kill you."

"I wish you would. You took away my manhood, made me into a homely woman with a dick and no balls, and now I have nothing left but my mother's old clothes."

Brenda bent over and hugged her and kissed her on the forehead. "You have me and the Sisterhood, and you have Reinhard and Albert as brothers. You're not alone, and you'll never be alone. Tonight we'll bury Cassandra in the Pit of Ages that gave me life at Loa's decree."

"I wish I could have my old life back...being a man...the doctor at my clinic here, helping fat, ugly people feel better about themselves...having a mother who only practiced voodoo and had nothing to do with lesbian zombies."

She patted her back. "Loa has told me she could bring your mother back to life, but if she did, everything we've done will be undone. I'll go back to being a fat woman who let men walk all over me. That can't happen, Aurora. There's too much at stake for the women of the world. You'll have to suck it up and move forward like the rest of us."

"I wish you'd never come to Port au Prince," she cried.

***

Fifteen hundred miles north to Long Island, the sisters at The Ranch were down in the doldrums. Snow had come to the coast. Monica's cell rang. Her display read: *Brenda.*

After putting the call on speaker, Monica asked, as the Sisterhood gathered around, "How are things going in Haiti?"

"Not so good—"

"Just a minute, Brenda," Monica said. "Caroline," she shouted, "quit playing chase-the-ball with Girlie Dog in the house. Go outside to play."

"We can't. It's too cold out."

"Then go upstairs and play with the dog."

The two scampered off as though everything was right with the world

"Sorry, Brenda, you were saying..?"

"Aurora and I are walking along the shore just like you and I did all of those months ago."

"Tell Aurora we feel very sorry for her loss, and our loss, as well, and tell her we love her. Anything else happening?"

"Yes, and you are not going to be happy."

"What's up?"

"Several months ago Cassandra heard from a friend who had been vacationing in Paris. It seems that Baby Doc had lost his fortune in Europe because of shady business deals, so he came back to Haiti broke. Cassandra felt sorry for him and gave him Jenny's old job running the LZ Foundation's financial department."

"How much do you want to bet that he is bleeding it dry of our money?"

"I think I'd lose the bet."

"I should have killed that bastard when I had the chance." As the rage in Monica built to a boil, the ball came bouncing down the stairs, hit a table leg, and rolled next to her foot. Monica pretended not to notice, instead concentrated on revving up her hatred for Baby Doc.

Girlie Dog came bounding over to get the ball and ran into Monica's foot. She'd put it on the ball, enticing Girlie Dog to try and get it. As Girlie Dog pulled the ball from under her foot, Monica booted her square in the ass. Girlie Dog took off like a shot, ran back up the stairs, and dropped the ball in front of Caroline then sat there shaking.

Caroline picked up the ball and threw it down the stairs at Monica, hitting her cell and knocking it out of her hand. She grabbed it up off the floor and put it to her ear. "Brenda?" The call had disconnected. "Damn." She set the phone on the table, and now a super pissed off Monica ran up the stairs, looking high and low for Caroline and yelling, "When I find you, you are going to get a spanking."

Melinda rushed up the stairs, waving Monica's cell. "It's for you. I think it's a call back."

Monica took the phone. "Brenda?"

"You hung up on me."

"I did not hang up. Caroline is turning into a spoiled brat."

"Focus, Monica. Back to Baby Doc."

"After I decided not to kill him, I told him to stay in Paris, to never come back to Port au Prince. Now you tell me that he is not just back but he is in charge of our money?"

"It gets worse. It turns out that he lied to you about the firing squad executions of the Tomtons Machetes."

"His renegade soldiers raped me...raped and killed my daughter, Maya. Baby Doc said he had executed them in private, at midnight, so the scandal would not get out to the people. He swore on the lives of his grandchildren. That is why I did not kill him."

"The executions never happened. In fact, they were his drinking buddies, and they had a good laugh. Sorry to have to tell you this, but at some point you would have found out anyway."

"I warned him. If I found out he'd lied to me, I'd hunt him down and kill him like a mad dog. But first that lying prick is going to suffer like no man has ever suffered. By the time I'm done with that son of a bitch, even Torquemada of the Spanish Inquisition would be proud of me. Shit. I may even let him watch me kill his two grandkids first."

"No, you won't."

"But he bargained their lives for his own...swore to it."

"This isn't your friend speaking now. This is your Queen. You are not going to harm him or his grandchildren, no matter how big a lying prick he is. You understand?"

Thinking twice that it would be a bad idea to crush her cell in her hand, Monica spoke in a calm voice, "Should I come down to Haiti and kiss his ass for allowing his soldiers to go unpunished for killing Maya, my sweet daughter?"

"I wouldn't give him the pleasure. Just leave him to me and rest assured that piece of shit is living on borrowed time. Meanwhile, I need to find out how much damage he's done to our foundation, and you need to leave Caroline alone. Melinda told me you were upstairs angrily looking for her."

"Are you saying I cannot spank her, discipline her, just let her run rampant in the house?"

"I won't even answer that. You know you love her. You buy her stuff all the time. Remember on her first day at her new elementary school? You didn't just meet her teachers, you read each one of their minds to see if any of them were pedophiles. You said if you had found one you would rip his head off and shove it up his ass."

"I would have, you know."

"She's a lonely little girl and acting out. Give her a break."

"Okay. When are you coming home?"

"In a few days, after I clean up the LZ Foundation mess. While I'm gone, you and Jackie and Melinda come up with a plan for Black Friday."

"I'm going to see Alfons."

"Fine. When you get back then. He should give you a bonus. I hear KOMA LTD's stock went up three percent just last month. His oil company is going gangbusters."

"I know."

"What have our sisters been doing?"

"What they do best, spend most of their time having sex in the pool."

"I should have known."

***

As the rising full moon began to slowly replace the setting sun, Brenda and her extra muscle, Reinhard and Albert, drove up in front of the LZ Foundation's office building. A six-foot-high brick wall surrounded the grounds. Beyond black wrought-iron gates, security guards patrolled the area. Cameras swiveled this way and that, ever vigilant. It was time for Baby Doc to explain the missing money.

A heavily armed stooge stepped out of the guard shack and marched up to the driver's door where he knuckle-knocked on the window. Brenda, sitting in the back seat of the Beamer, operated the switch that rolled down the window. The guard shifted his attention to her. "This private property, lady. You move along now."

Brenda reached out the window, grabbed him by his shirt, and pulled his face to hers. "You tell Baby Doc that his boss is here, and if he doesn't tell you to open this gate, we're busting in. That means you'll be burying him tonight, and then it's the unemployment line for all you guys."

His wrenched black face broke out in a sweat. "Yes. I go. I call him now."

After releasing the terrified guard, Brenda watched him get

on the phone in the shack and start speaking in Haitian creole. He hung up and hit a button on the wall. With a whine, the gates began to open.

"His excellency looks forward to meet you. Please, please go right in."

"Now that wasn't so hard, was it?"

He nodded in rapid fire, his teeth white and eyes bulging.

Brenda rolled up the window. "Drive, Albert."

The beamer accelerated into the LZ Foundation compound.

Reinhard checked his gun clip and rubbed the barrel with his sleeve. The ex-Nazi wannabe's scowl looked like he was itching for a fight.

Albert parked in front of the entrance doors. They all got out. Reinhard stuck his gun behind his belt and covered it with his sport jacket.

As a guard led them up the steps, two more guards fell in close behind them. Too close for Brenda's comfort. Reinhard gave her a sideways glance. She nodded. They had contingency plans for just this sort of welcoming committee.

Reaching the top of the staircase, Brenda shouted, "Now."

Both her men turned around in a flash and disarmed the two guards who immediately put up their hands, only to be knocked down the stairs with the butts of their own rifles.

Brenda saw the lead guard take off running. He ducked through a mahogany door and closed it.

After walking up to the door, Reinhard knocked.

Brenda frowned. "What the hell are you doing?"

"I want him to open the door."

"Back out of the way." Brenda kicked open the heavy door like the hinges were made of papier-mâché. It fell into Baby Doc's office and hit the floor with one hell of a bang.

Brenda strolled into the dusty room like she owned the place. Oh, she did.

The lead guard pulled out a gun and shot her five times.

She looked down at her beautiful dress, it was a present from Jackie, and saw the bullet holes. "You ruined my dress, you idiot."

He dropped the gun and watched in terror as she flexed her muscles and inhaled loudly. The bullets shot out of her body and plinked on the floor.

The guard suddenly realized he'd come face to face with a Haitian zombie. There was no escaping her. He took off the crucifix he was wearing, kissed it, and dropped to his knees before Brenda then closed his eyes and put his hands together and began to pray. "Please, Lord, save my wife, Mary, and my son, Juan Junior, from the vengeance of the zombie, and please tell them I love them, and do not forsake me when I come to the gates of heaven." With that he looked up at Brenda. "I am ready to die."

"What's your name?"

"Juan Senior."

"Get up, Juan Senior."

"You're not going to kill me and eat my brains?"

"You watch too many zombie movies. Where is Baby Doc hiding?"

"He has a secret exit in the john."

Brenda stalked to the bathroom and found a sliding door in the shower that led to a staircase.

The prick is long gone by now.

She stormed back to Juan Senior who was still in the same place with Reinhard and Albert guarding him at gunpoint. "Where's the money...the cash?"

"I do not know."

She gave Reinhard a sideways nod. "Search the office."

While Albert guarded the guard, Reinhard started tearing through drawers and filing cabinets like a tornado on steroids. When he opened the coat closet, US greenbacks spilled out and slid across the floor. "Bingo."

"Ah ha," Brenda said. "There's the money he embezzled. Guess he didn't have time to launder it." She turned to Juan Senior. "You just got promoted to head of security. I'm putting you in charge of finding Baby Doc. There is no way he can get off this island today. Get out there and tell all your friends that the person who finds him and holds him for me gets ten thousand U.S."

"I can do this that you ask." He bowed to her.

"Do you know anyone at a bank?"

"My cousin, Raul, he is the president of El Banco Haiti."

"Count all this money and take it to your cousin's bank where you'll put it in a safety deposit box. Tell Raul that his life depends on keeping every dollar safe. Notify me when you have good news about Baby Doc's capture, and before I forget, tell all those guards outside that they work for you now, and you are loyal to me."

He took a handkerchief from his pocket and patted his sweating forehead. "I will find Baby Doc...and thank you for not killing me."

"Thank them." She pointed to her ex-Nazi musclemen. "Their instructions were to kill you if you moved. Now, if you screw me, they *will* find you, and they *will* kill you. Got it?"

He looked at the bruisers, nodded meekly.

"Come on, boys. I've got some shopping to do."

"Shopping?" Albert asked.

"I can't go home without buying a gift for Caroline."

"Heaven forbid," Reinhard quipped.

***

It was 8:35 pm when Brenda, Albert, and Reinhard got back to the former Haitian Health Clinic that doctor Ernesto Gomez, AKA Aurora, had operated, and the place of death for the old Brenda. She walked down the hall and found Aurora still sitting there holding her mother's dead hand. Brenda put her hands on Aurora's shoulders and whispered, "It's time to go. I'll carry our sweet Cassandra's body and follow you to your truck."

She carefully slid her arms under the corpse and lovingly carried her to the truck bed that was full of flowers and gently laid her down. Meanwhile, Albert and Reinhard were busy pouring gasoline in every room of the clinic. When they were finished, they lit the place ablaze then jumped into the truck bed to make sure the body didn't fall out on their bumpy journey through the jungle to the Forest of Fear.

Arriving at the jungle clearing, Brenda put naked Cassandra in the bottom of the Pit of Ages under the Tree of Life and covered her with the flowers from the truck bed. Roots slithered to the body and wriggled around her in an eternal embrace. Now everyone would wait for the time of transition for the Voodoo High Priestess: midnight with the full moon overhead.

Brenda sat down next to the pit, her chest full of angst and her mind reeling with thoughts of life, death, and eternity. It was such a beautiful night for a funeral, the sky ablaze with stars this far from civilization. Moonlight speckled the jungle clearing with eerie shadows.

Albert and Reinhard stood guard while Aurora came to Brenda with two bottles of Haiti's number one selling beer: Prestige. He handed her a bottle. "Do you think my mom is with Loa?"

"Yes." She took a swig of the warm beer. "I have looked into the eyes of Loa. She loved Cassandra."

"Are you sorry that you died and that Loa and Mom gave you another life?"

"I now have the life I've always wanted. To be important, to have purpose, and being beautiful is a plus."

"But if you had never been reborn you would be with Loa right now."

"Loa is always with me. We'll change the world forever." She took another swig of beer, but this one she spit on the ground. "Cat piss tastes better than this shit."

"How do you know what cat piss tastes like?"

"It's just an old saying."

As the full moon reached its apex, leaves from the Tree of Life fluttered down on Cassandra to make her an earthy blanket under which the roots absorbed every molecule of her body. The tree became a monument to Cassandra that would last until the end of time.

Brenda took Aurora by the hand. "Your mom belongs to the ages now."

"Thank you for this tribute, my Queen."

"Our homage is done here. Let's go. I'll drive."

The ex-Nazis jumped in the truck bed. Aurora rode shotgun. "Where to now?" she asked her.

"The airport." Brenda wrestled the ruts that passed for a road. "Call the flight staff, get them ready to go. They're staying at the Marriott."

***

The flight attendant on Alfons' flight crew, Carrie Carson, was about to put her building orgasm into a holding pattern. Her body was being smushed under Larry Thompson, the copilot who was ramming her all the way home. Just as he let loose with the force of a human jet engine, there came a knock on the door.

He stopped ramming. "Now what?"

"No. Don't stop," she cried breathlessly. "I'm not there yet."

"It can't be good news." He pulled out, rolled off the bed, and got into his shorts.

"You can't just leave me like this."

"Get dressed."

"Finish me, damn it."

"I'm done. Finish yourself."

Trousers on, he rushed to the peep hole and looked out. It was sixty-two year old Captain Zack Parsons. White shirt, captain's hat, he looked ready to fly.

"What's up, Captain?" he asked through the door.

"I got bad news for you, Larry. Brenda wants to leave for Manhattan at three hundred hours. The plane is being refueled right now. I'll wait for you in the lobby."

"Ah, come on, Captain. Me and Carrie are getting it on."

"Oh yeah, Carrie. She's really great in bed. I did her a few times myself. Hurry up now. No time for a shower."

Rushing back to the bed, Larry saw Carrie lying just like he'd left her, legs spread and ready for more. "Get up, will ya?"

"Five minutes, Larry. That's all I ask. You can do it. Make me not regret sleeping with you. Please."

"I said get dressed." He threw her flight skirt at her.

Carrie knew that no amount of pleading would change his mind. He didn't give a crap about her. He'd rather fly a jet than fly united with her. "What's the matter with you, Larry?"

"We're leaving right away for the return trip."

"Shit. I hate working for this private jet service. I'm going to find me a real job with a real airline."

"Are you gonna screw those pilots too?"

"What?"

"You had sex with Captain Parsons? Hell, he's thirty years older than you." Larry cinched up his tie.

"That was before Alfons hired you, ya narcissistic stud."

"You're nothing but a whore. Put your damn clothes on."

She got out of bed, didn't look at him, and slipped into her panties. *Men suck.*

***

Arriving at the hangar, the two pilots and Carrie saw Brenda at the top of the jet's cabin steps, waiting for them in the doorway. As they stepped inside, Brenda moved aside and read their minds. The Captain was thinking about screwing Carrie, the co-pilot was stewing over the fact that the Captain had screwed Carrie, and Carrie was thinking how she hated both of them. Brenda detected her sexual frustration. She had a good orgasm coming but no one to offer her relief from that internal burn.

After the jet got airborne, Brenda sipped on a Margarita and looked down on the lights of Port au Prince and the darkness of the jungle northeast of the city. The full moon was on its downward arc in the western sky. The Milky Way warped around the heavens like a soothing blanket. What a beautiful world... She felt the sting of tears. “Cassandra,” she whispered. “I'll watch over Aurora and keep her safe, my sweet friend.” Pressing her forehead on the window, she sobbed out, “I will love and honor you forever.”

Carrie strode down the short aisle with her blue eyes fixed on Brenda. “You must be tired, Miss Ayler.”

Brenda looked up from her plush seat and read Carrie's mind. *“I'd so love to get it on with you...oh, I can't tell her that.”*

“The plane has a comfy bed in the back...behind the curtains.”

“I *am* kind of tired.”

“Follow me.”

Brenda looked her up and down and gave her a sly grin. “Would you care to join me for a little mile high club action?”

“Oh...” she glanced toward the cockpit, “I can't leave my post unattended.”

Brenda stood. “Don't worry. The pilots are arguing over you. You wouldn't want to interrupt them, now would you?”

Carrie smiled. “Of course not.” She led the way past the galley and pulled the aft curtains apart. “After you, Miss Ayler.”

“Just call me Brenda.” She had to move a little sideways to get by Carrie, and when she did, their breasts rubbed against each other. Brenda could feel the heat of Carrie's lust through their clothing, which would soon be out of the way. She took Carrie's hand and pulled her down on the bed.

As the plane soared at its maximum altitude toward New

York's JFK, Brenda gave Carrie the full lesbian zombie experience, the deep kissing that transferred the virus, the licking of her private nub that rocketed fireworks off the ground, and the bursting orgasm that would change her life forever. Breathless, she slid down Brenda's body to return the favor.

As passions waned, Carrie looked up from her position between Brenda's thighs. "I've never wanted to do this to a woman before. Have I been living a lie...about my sexuality?"

"No, sweet Carrie. You've just been made aware of a better alternative to men and their idea of good sex."

"I like it." She smiled, her lips glistening.

"Welcome to the Sisterhood, Carrie."

Chapter Five

Thirteen hundred miles to the northwest, in Arlington, Virginia, Colonel Wesley Miller was awake and lying in bed with his wife Lynne in his arms, but they weren't making love, they were talking.

"There is something going on with Lawrence, and I can't put my finger on it. He has never been secretive with me before. Why didn't he just tell me that he was going to Long Island to see Jackie O'Neal?"

"Maybe he was horny and didn't want you to know."

He rolled on his side to face Lynne. "Jackie is a tycoon, made billions with her skin care treatment, *Jackie's Soft Skin Restoration Cream.*"

"I have some on my vanity," she put in. "It's all right, I guess."

"She has a corner on the market, worldwide. A bunch of hot women live with her in her mansion, they call it The Ranch, a real nest of lesbians...I heard Senator Hoffman say so himself, so why would Lawrence go there for sex?"

"You're right. Getting laid can't be the reason."

"He was only there for five minutes."

"A long drive for nothing. So...how do you know about these lesbians? Were you spying on the Senator?"

"I overheard them talking in the General's office. Jackie and those girls are up to something nefarious, I'm sure, and they're way too close to the top brass at the Pentagon for my comfort."

"You'll figure it out...tomorrow." Lynne rolled over. "Now go back to sleep."

***

A travel-weary Brenda was glad to be back home before the dawn. As she approached the front door, she heard *Loa* call her to the Crystal Shrine. She strode around the mansion to the greenhouse, and after going inside, she set down her small travel bag, got on her knees by the pit, and reached up to take hold of the gold railing. "Loa. I am here as you instructed."

Bowing her head, she heard Cassandra's voice in her mind:

"Brenda, I am with Loa."

Tears trickled down Brenda's cheeks. The sorrow of losing Cassandra mixed with the joy of hearing her voice.

"Brenda, do not cry. Look hard and you will see me."

She looked into the pit and saw lightning bolts crisscrossing the void but without crackle or thunder. Looking up, she saw Cassandra's face in one of the crystalline wall panels, smiling. "Look around, my Queen."

And there, in other crystal panels, faces appeared, the faces of women who had died for the crime of rebelling against men.

Brenda was awestruck as each one echoed a name, which soon became a crescendo of forlorn voices.

A crystalline panel on her right lit up, revealing a woman dressed in armor, sword in hand, and riding a white horse. *"I am Joan of Arc. I was burned at the stake in 1431 for heresy, for breaking the law of crossdressing. My crime was that I was a woman in man's military clothing. I should have been a heroine of France but died a martyr."* The panel went dark.

Another panel glowed around the face of an old woman with wild dark hair and wearing a peasant dress. *"My name is Martha Corey. I was a pious member of Salem Village Church and denounced the witch trials. In response, the powerful men of Salem accused me of witchcraft. After a sham trial, I was hanged in September of 1692. My only crime was speaking out in defense of innocent women. As the rope was snugged up around my neck, I looked at the men around the scaffold yelling,* "hang the witch,*" and felt only pity for them."* The trapdoor clanked, the rope creaked, and the panel went dark.

Brenda, now gripping the rail with both hands, heard another woman on her left. *"Brenda..."* A crystal panel lit up to show a girl wearing a hijab that only revealed her dark Persian eyes. *"My name is Jasmine. I was only twelve and just past Baligh when my parents told me of my arranged marriage to Ahmed al-Hakim, a man who was sixty and already possessed five wives. He was nice to me, and he was rich, and he offered me money and fine jewels, so I agreed to marry him. That first night he found my virginity difficult so I said no, please wait, but he forced himself in me, hurt me, and because I cried he beat me, then to teach me a lesson, he invited his two brothers to join in. Hasan and Saul performed vile sex acts on me, felacio and sodomy. When they had their fill, my husband Ahmed felt sickened and accused me of being a whore, unholy before Allah. The village Imam, Mohammed Abdullah Abadi, sentenced me to death. One year ago today, I was stoned in the dirt of the road by my husband who cursed me, and his two brothers. One rock hit me in my open mouth as I screamed, and it lodged in my throat. Loa was kind to let me choke to death before my bones were broken and the rocks cracked my skull. The last thing I remember was seeing my mother crying from her knees and waving her hands in the air in grief. I beseech the* Sisterhood *to hunt down the Iman, my husband, and the two brothers, but kill my husband first."*

Tears streamed down Brenda's face. "I'm sorry for you, Jasmine. The Sisterhood will do as you ask. Your husband and his brothers will die, and the Imam. Where do I find them?"

"The village of Baddish in Pakistan on the shore of the Arabian Sea." Jasmine waved goodbye. Her crystal panel faded to black.

Brenda stood, wiped her cheeks, and turned around slowly in a circle, listening to the departed women who'd paid the ultimate price in their battle to get out from under the thumbs of cruel men. Faces appeared and faded in the crystal panels, a kaleidoscope of sadness and strife. A crescendo rose: *"Kill the evil men. Let them burn in the fires of hell forever. Kill the evil men and let us watch their damnation."*

Brenda bent over and pressed her hands over her ears to quiet the voices, but to no avail. She closed her eyes and cried out to the Goddess *Loa*, "I've heard enough."

Then there was only silence in Brenda's battered mind. Looking around, she saw that all the crystal panels were dark once more. The door burst open, and in rushed Caroline followed by Girlie Dog whose tail was wagging at breakneck speed.

"Why are you awake so early?" Brenda hugged her. "The sun's not even up."

"I couldn't sleep waiting for you. Did you bring me something?"

"Yes, honey."

Reaching into the travel bag, she fished around and pulled out a doll dressed in a Haitian gown with a headdress of ferns and feathers, a gift she had purchased in Port au Prince.

"For me?"

"Of course." As she handed it to Caroline, Girlie Dog grabbed it out of her hand and took off like a shot with Caroline in hot pursuit. Brenda smiled and watched the Caroline-Girlie Dog fiasco in amusement. *It's good to be home again.*

On her way to the house, she slipped in the back gate to the pool deck and spotted a half a bottle of white wine on a table. "Nice." She grabbed the wine, sat on a deck chair, and thought about poor little Jasmine. *How can the Sisterhood protect women in countries where the laws seem stacked against them?*

Drinking straight from the bottle, she leaned back and enjoyed the cool breeze coming in from Long Island Sound. Her thoughts turned to the Senator from New York, James Hoffman. *What to do, what to do?* At least she knew now that General Taylor was truly loyal to the Sisterhood. Of course, his affection for Jackie O'Neal could have had a lot to do with his loyalty.

I'm going to call him and ask for a huge favor for Jasmine.

She swigged wine. The sun wouldn't be coming up for another hour. She was starting to miss Jackie and how sexy she looked while asleep.

Girlie Dog barked from somewhere behind her.

Here comes Caroline and Girlie Dog. It looks like she got her doll back.

"Brenda, look. Girlie Dog got slobber all over my new doll. She is a bad, bad dog."

"We can wash it good as new."

"She's still a bad dog."

"Do you want me to take her to the dog pound?"

"No. I love my Girlie Dog."

"I was just testing you, honey. I would never get rid of Girlie Dog, anyway. She's part of our family."

"I know."

"I'm going to bed. You can't be out here by yourself."

"Girlie Dog is with me. I'm not by myself."

"Don't sass me. Up to bed with you and Girlie Dog and don't wake any of your sisters. But first, how about a group hug, you and Girlie Dog." She opened her arms.

Girlie Dog jumped up and Caroline threw her arms around Brenda. As they hugged, Girlie Dog licked their faces.

"Okay. Off with you two."

Caroline and Girlie Dog ran inside.

Picturing Jackie stark-naked and sleeping on her side with one knee drawn up to her chest and the other leg slightly uncovered made Brenda walk faster to the bedroom.

She slipped under the covers and savored the heat radiating from her lover's body. She brushed her lips along the scented skin of Jackie's arm, and felt her own heat build inside. Kissing her neck, she inhaled the freshly shampooed aroma of her strawberry blond hair.

Jackie moaned. She thought she was having an erotic dream of her husband, when she was young, but the lips lavishing her now were soft and gentle, not forceful like his were back in her heterosexual days. Like a dream, his hard body lay on top of her, and she inhaled the gasoline smell he always brought home from his job at the Quick Mart. However, as dreams did, they confused the mind and senses, and in a blur, the body with her now was soft and lithe and smooth, and the air seemed alive with the fragrance of perfume, honeysuckle and rose.

Gasping, she opened her eyes and realized that it was Brenda's lips teasing her libido, and Brenda's perfume that delighted her senses. Jackie pretended to be asleep and let the sweet sensations build, let Brenda do the things she loved to do to her, until her moaning spoiled the ruse. "Oh, Brenda," she breathed. "I see you're back. You must've missed me something awful."

She gathered Jackie into her longing embrace. "It's good to be home."

"How did it go in Port au Prince?"

"Cassandra's funeral was beautiful, under a starry sky. She's with Loa now."

"And the LZ Foundation?"

"Baby Doc is on the lam, but he'll be caught, and then we'll have to decide what to do with him. Whatever we decide, it won't sit well with Monica unless it involves killing him."

"So let her kill him. No skin off our noses."

"She wants to kill his grandkids, too. It was on their lives Baby Doc swore the Tomton Machetes were executed and the sole reason Monica spared his life."

"We can't be killing kids, Brenda."

"You know it. I know it. But Monica is a different story. Her temper is homicidal."

Jackie shivered, wrapped her legs around Brenda's thighs, and drew her in tight, woman to woman. "Let's talk about something a little more pleasant, shall we?"

"Shut up and kiss me."

Chapter Six

The sisters were up and eating breakfast and jabbering about nonsensical this-and-that. Brenda and Jackie had slept in after their lovemaking. Both were famished. The only ones missing were Caroline and Girlie Dog.

"Where are our little troublemakers?" Jackie asked the sisters.

"Still sawing logs." Monica poured orange juice into a glass for Brenda. "They were up all night." Her black hair was pinned up on top of her head, and her ebony body looked absolutely perfect in her white bra and panties.

Not bad for an eighty-year-old woman.

Brenda recalled the night they met, when Monica became Brenda's first lesbian zombie sister. From crippled and old to drop-dead gorgeous young, Monica had to be the most beautiful black woman on the planet.

The other girls around the table were similarly undressed. A little less clothing and The Ranch could be a bonified nudist camp. If not for Caroline's presence, nudism would run rampant with these girls.

Wearing jeans, a pullover, and sneakers, Brenda felt overdressed. She joined them at the noisy table, picked up the glass of orange juice, and tapped the side with a spoon. "Listen up, girls."

The clinking got everyone's attention, and silence quickly pervaded the kitchen.

"We have a busy day ahead. First, wc havc to plan Black Friday Party number two. Then I have another problem to discuss with the Sisterhood. Jackie will now go over our guest list."

"We'll invite the guests we initiated during the original Black Friday party, and a few new ones." Jackie poured a cup of coffee and sat next to Monica at the table. "First of all, Four-Star General Lawrence Taylor. He's Chairman of the Joint Chiefs of Staff, the highest ranked officer in the military. So far he's shown undying loyalty to our Queen."

Donna looked up from her bowl of Coco Puffs. "How much money can a General have to donate?"

Jackie sipped coffee. "Not all assets are monetary. He has connections not open to most people, and he can get things done for us. It's good to have a General in our corner. Brenda, you'll be happy to know General Taylor has invited Admiral Roy Kincade to tag along. He's the commander of US Naval operations in the Mediterranean."

Chloe brought up a good point. "I don't recall him being initiated. He wasn't at the party last year."

Jackie agreed. "We'll get to that later. I've also invited Charles Mantella, CEO of the World News Network, and Monica is inviting Alfons Duda. We all know he's got more money than God."

"He is a tightwad," Monica put in. "But I have a way to get into his wallet." She shimmied her shoulders to wiggle her boobs.

Brenda set down her empty glass of orange juice. "I hear he has a new yacht."

"Yeah. It cost him a boatload of bucks. It is his baby."

"Tell him the Sisterhood needs to use it in a few weeks."

"Where?"

"Athens. I'll tell the captain where to sail from there. Jackie, who else is on the list?"

"We have Matt Simmons, the rich Wall Street banker, and very good looking, six-foot-two, eyes of blue...you know the type. My guess is you girls will be fighting over him before the night is through."

"I'll do him," Maria chimed in.

"Then there's Stuart Jackson, the internet tycoon."

"Shit," Donna spluttered. "That guy's built like a bowling ball."

Chloe jumped in with, "And he's a damn pervert. He grew up watching porn on the internet and munching on pork rinds all day."

Jackie waved off their concerns. "He's rich now. That's all that matters. You girls better show him some respect...and a good time...and you know what I mean."

"Ick," Chloe said.

"Now, what about Senator James Hoffman? He's on the list, but he can't be trusted."

Monica added. "He has been censured for posting pictures of his dong on the web. I doubt he will be a senator much longer."

Chloe jumped in. "I still think we should kill him."

They all looked to Brenda.

"His senate seat is important. Invite him anyway. Who else do you have?"

"There's New York District Attorney Larry Evans. He's a handsome black veteran and a legal whiz. Can't be much over forty, has a chiseled body you girls might be interested in."

Chloe said, "Ick."

"Tom Caldone, the Hollywood movie mogul. Remember his blockbuster *Cave Women of Venus*? He turned a B movie into forty million dollars. I think he's handsome with his black-rimmed glasses."

Maria preened her hair. "Do you think he's looking for his next movie star?"

"The last tycoon on our list is Doctor Peyton Moore, head of the CDC. He's a stupid-rich black-brother with a finger in pharmaceuticals. Brenda?"

"Barring any new prospects, these are the guys we have to work with. Show them a good time at the party."

"And double the donations," Jackie reminded them. "They're not tax deductible, so give our guests something fun they can remember for their well-spent money. What else did you have to talk about, Brenda?"

Brenda told her sisters what had transpired just hours before in the Crystal Shrine while everyone was sleeping, the twelve-year-old girl married to a bully, the repeated rapes, and her stoning in Baddish, Pakistan. "Poor sweet Jasmine wants revenge, and Loa has instructed us to comply."

"When are we going?"

"Soon, Jackie. I need you to coordinate an operational strategy with General Taylor."

"How do we get there? Pakistan is halfway around the world."

"I have some logistical problems to work out. Alfons' yacht will come in handy."

Monica stated flatly, "He will never allow it."

"Don't tell him it's going to Pakistan."

"What else, Brenda?"

"We'll need satellite photos of the village and the topography of the surrounding area. Get General Taylor working on this. We'll also need some firepower to back us up. General Taylor will come in handy there, as well."

"What about someone to handle logistics, communications, and surveillance?"

"Jackie, Robert owes me, and he's an honorable man. He's promised me, if I needed anything, he'd be there for me."

"And he said yes?"

"I haven't told him yet, but I've come up with a cover story for the mission to Baddish."

"What is it?"

"It's a doozy."

Chloe asked, "How many of us get to go on the mission?"

"The more the merrier."

"Count me in."

All of a sudden, Girlie Dog started barking and ran to the front door.

"Monica," Brenda shouted. "See what the hell she's barking at?"

Looking through the door glass, she reported back, "There's a cab under the portico." A woman got out, paid the cabbie, and walked up to the door. "Well, I'll be goddess dammed. It's Lilly the waitress. I guess she's here to join the Sisterhood."

Brenda frowned. "I wonder why she didn't call first."

The doorbell rang.

Chapter Seven

Meanwhile, at the Pentagon in General Taylor's office, Colonel Wesley Miller was going through the General's papers and correspondence, looking for any connection between Jackie O'Neal, Brenda, and the lesbians. He had gotten in to work early, knowing the General wouldn't be in until ten. He had found nothing out of the ordinary until he noticed the General's secure trashcan had not been emptied as regulations required.

He keyed in the code and opened the container where he found pieces of torn paper. He took them to his desk and put them together as if they were a small jigsaw puzzle. Now Wesley could read the words on the 3x5 paper: *Fox Trot Zero.*

"What the hell is Fox Trot Zero?"

He'd never heard of a Fox Trot Zero anything. Glancing at the clock and seeing it was 9:45, he returned the paper scraps to the trashcan, and then secured the General's office.

A while later, at the water fountain in the hallway, Wes ran into a Major who worked in Intelligence. "Have you ever heard of an operational code named Fox Trot Zero?"

"We wouldn't use a codename like that nowadays. Sounds like something the CIA may have used back in the sixties during counter intelligence operations against the Soviet Union. What's this all about?"

The Russians? A cold blade of dread stabbed the Colonel's chest. "I don't know yet."

"Good luck with that."

Wesley walked back toward his office, concentrating so hard on the meaning of Fox Trot Zero that he failed to notice and salute a general walking toward him.

"Hold it, Colonel. Did I miss the memo that you no longer

need to salute a superior officer?"

"I apologize, sir." Wes saluted and held it while he thought fast. "I was preoccupied with a codename that General Taylor might be using for a military operation. It won't happen again, sir."

The General returned the salute. "Maybe I can help you."

"I better beg off, sir. You know how General Taylor wants things kept close to the vest."

"Very well. You'd better salute next time."

***

Back at the Sisterhood's home, they were all gathered in the sitting room, listening to Lilly's tale of woe about Max. To take a drink of water, she put the glass up to her lips, but shaking so hard, she spilled some on her dress. "He's mad as hell because he has no one to wait on the customers."

"That's his problem. You're safe now."

"But he knows I'm here."

"How does he know where we live?"

"He saw your LZ Foundation card."

"You showed it to him?"

Lilly's chin trembled. "It was proof I had friends who would help me get away from him."

Maria glared bullets at her. "Are you just plain stupid?"

"Lay off, Maria." Brenda stood and walked around like she was really thinking hard, then: "Ladies, there are two things we have to do right away. First, because Max is a really big guy, we have to put in a rush order for a lot more mason jars and an equal amount of dogfood labels." Brenda got Lilly to her feet and led her to the center of the room. "Second, we have to initiate Lilly into the lesbian zombie Sisterhood."

Lilly pulled back. "Lesbian zombie? Initiate? What are you talking about?"

Monica closed the sitting room door. The sisters gathered around Lilly, shed their clothes, and tossed them in every direction. Brenda, too. "You're going to love this, Lilly. Take off your clothes."

"You have to be kidding. My body is a good reason to wear clothes."

"That is all going to change," Monica said, now naked as the other lesbian zombies, beautifully black among white and brown flesh. "I'm eighty years old."

Lilly's expression was wide-eyed shock. "No way."

"Jackie and I are in our sixties," Melinda said. "I was on my death bed. Brenda's kiss saved me. She's the Queen of the lesbian zombies. You can trust her."

Lilly placed her hands over her breasts. "I've never kissed a woman before."

"When we're through with you," Chloe said breathlessly. "That's all you're gonna want, Lilly. Lesbian love."

She looked really scared. "But zombie? What's that all about?"

"We're all zombies." Brenda stepped up to Lilly and removed her hands from her breasts. "Haitian zombies. Beautiful, smart, and tougher than any man."

"Okay." Lilly let her hands hang at her sides. "I'm in."

Brenda unbuttoned Lilly's dress, coaxed the straps over her shoulders and down her arms, allowing the dress to flutter to the floor. Monica stepped behind her and released the bra straps, which joined the dress and revealed droopy boobs with stretch marks and areola so dark they looked like bruises. Chloe slipped Lilly's panties down thighs pocked with cellulite and road-mapped with varicose veins. She had a pooched belly and a flabby ass.

She hung her head. "I told you so."

"Don't be ashamed, Lilly. We didn't have perfect bodies before we became lesbian zombies, either."

Brenda embraced Lilly and pulled her in tight. "This is the second best part." She pressed her lips to Lilly's mouth and used her tongue to deliver a hot wet kiss swarming with the virus that would forever make men disgust her and women excite her. She felt Lilly's body relax and guided her to the floor where the naked sisters closed in to kiss and caress every inch of her body while Brenda went to work on a place that could only be called the stairway to heaven. An orgasm was required to make the transformation complete.

The sisters took turns kissing her lips, her neck, and teasing her erect nipples.

Her legs trembled, her back arched, and she cried out in

orgasmic bliss.

Right before everyone's eyes, as she shuddered with pleasure, her breasts became firm and perky and tipped in pink, her belly flattened, and her legs became supple and smooth. Her entire body glowed with new youth and vitality.

"I want to do her," Chloe said. "She's gorgeous."

"Easy there, girl. Let her recover."

Meanwhile, Maria and Donna were getting it on, Monica was kissing Melinda, and Jackie was spread-eagle in a chair, taking care of her own business.

Brenda knew this could go on all night. Chloe joined Monica and Melinda. Brenda considered joining Jackie in the chair, all this smooching and gasping and moaning was turning her on.

It was then that Caroline started banging on the locked door. "Brenda, Jackie, everybody, Girlie Dog needs help."

Panic tore through Brenda like a bulldozer. "Just a minute, honey," she shouted at the door. "Quick, girls. Get dressed."

Lilly's clothes were all in one pile, but the sisters had cast off their clothes like they were on fire, which scattered them everywhere. So they were running around the room like crazy women trying to sort everything out.

"Brenda, hurry," Caroline cried. "Girlie Dog is biting some big fat guy."

Brenda got into her jeans and pullover but left her sneakers for later and opened the door a crack. "What fat guy?"

"He came in the yard and grabbed me, but Girlie Dog got hold of his leg and made him let me go. Now Girlie Dog won't let go of his leg. There's blood everywhere."

"Jesus." She turned back to the room. Everyone was dressed haphazardly but enough to be decent. "Let's go, ladies."

Caroline led them to the front yard. "See?"

Girlie Dog had bitten a chunk out of the man's leg and was chewing on it like an old toy. The man wasn't moving.

"Is he deaded?" Caroline asked.

"The word is dead, Caroline, not deaded." With her hands on her hips, Brenda walked to the man and recognize mad Max.

He groaned.

"No, Caroline, but the way he's bleeding out, he's not long for this world." She knelt next to him. "You should've stuck with your pan-fried trout, Max. You're no match for lesbian zombies."

"You bitches."

The sisters stood in silence as Lilly stormed up to Max. He looked up and raised his bloody right hand as if begging for help.

"Such a big man to be taken down by a little dog." She kicked him in the ribs. "He didn't deserve to be loved by any woman." Lilly walked toward the house, now feeling like a true lesbian zombie sister.

This was followed by high-fives all around.

"You shouldn't have touched me," Caroline shouted at Max. "Now Girlie Dog needs a bath."

His eyes became a blank stare. It was obvious that Max the maximizer was all maxed out.

Brenda stood. "Jackie, get the girls to drag his fat ass to the garage and tell Jorge to bring the car around. I need him to take me to Robert and Maggie's house."

"Yes, my Queen."

Chapter Eight

Brenda was now headed to see Robert and Maggie and little Zoey in New London. She was sitting next to Jorge instead of in the back of the limo. "Are you feeling better, Jorge?"

"Thank you for asking, my Queen. The pill Chloe gave me took away my constant sex drive, but I'm still much stronger than normal."

"The pill counteracted your overactive libido, but nothing can change you back to an ordinary man."

He smiled. "Superman or not, I'll always be loyal to you."

"That's good to know, Jorge."

Pulling up in front of Robert and Maggie's place, she found them, and little Zoey, in the front yard. Zoey was swinging in a windup baby swing, fast asleep.

Robert rushed to the limo and opened the door for Brenda. "It's great to see you again."

Baby Zoey woke up and immediately began to kick and cry. Maggie unbuttoned her blouse, exposed her left breast, and then began to nurse Zoey. "She's a hungry little girl."

Brenda sat with her and Zoey in a porch swing. Robert sat facing them in a patio chair, holding a beer bottle. "What brings you here, Brenda?"

"I've got a mission for you, Robert."

"Mission?"

Brenda recounted everything that had transpired between Jasmine, her husband and his brothers, and the revenge that she wanted from beyond the grave. "Loa insists we do this for Jasmine."

"You want them killed?"

"And the evil Imam in the village. He'd ordered her to be

stoned to death. Him too."

Leaning back in his chair, he took a drink of beer then set the bottle on the floor. "You want me to start a war for the lesbian zombies?"

Maggie jumped in. "She wants to put you in harm's way. Robert, I can't go through another ordeal like the last time you were wounded in battle. This time you might not be so lucky."

Brenda held out the palm of her hand. "No, Maggie. I want Robert to work with General Taylor, the Joint Chiefs, and the Secretary of Defense, under the order of the President, to take out an Imam terrorist in Pakistan. That's the official story and we're sticking to it. Top Secret. He needs a command center set up at Fort Huachuca in Arizona. Robert, I want you to be in charge of the operation there, not to participate in the incursion. General Taylor will get you anything you need, just use the requisition code Fox Trot Zero."

"How many troops will I get?"

"Taylor will take care of that. I hope you can get some soldiers from your old unit to help you in Arizona. Will you do this for me?"

"Yes, but—"

"But nothing, Robert. You owe me."

"All right, but it's going to be hard to keep an operation this big under wraps."

"The General has security handled. Our cover story will be a World Health Organization mission to vaccinate the villagers against a deadly plague that's coming. The Imam will be notified when to expect us. We'll pose as nurses, go in, and take him out, as well as the al-Hakim brothers, hopefully without anyone else getting killed. Maggie, your duty to the Sisterhood is calling. We need your husband. Are you with us?"

Maggie had finished nursing Zoey and sat there with a solemn look on her face. "Robert won't leave the states, is that guaranteed?"

"He'll be in Arizona, directing the operation from a chair in front of several monitors. Perfectly safe."

"Then I'm okay with it." She passed Zoey to Brenda.

Brenda cradled the baby, smiled at Robert and then Maggie. "What do you say, Robert?"

"When do we start?"

"General Taylor will let you know." Brenda kissed Zoey's forehead, handed her to Mom, and strode back to the limo.

Watching her leave, Robert picked up his beer bottle and chugged it dry. "Damn."

***

Back at the Pentagon, Wes was glad to see General Taylor head off for his meeting with the Joint Chiefs of Staff. It gave Wes time to snoop through the General's office. He found nothing at first, but then he got lucky. General Taylor had left his cell phone in the bathroom. Holding the cell in his hand, he thought, his password has always been C25 in honor of his first Army command. Wes typed it, and bingo, he was in. Scrolling down the list of incoming calls, he came to a message from Fleet Admiral Roy Kincade of the US Navy's Central Mediterranean Command on the island of Rhodes.

He clicked on it and received a voice command instructing him to enter a code. "Shit." Then it dawned on him to type in *Fox Trot Zero*. The recorded message started:

"Lawrence, tell Jackie O'Neal I will attend the party. I hope she sets me up with the redhead. She's the one everybody calls the Queen, right? Just let me know which Friday it is."

Mumbling, "Shit," Wes thought, Kincade is going to fly all the way back to the states for a party with a redhead? It must be a sex party...and what is this queen shit all about?

Something fishy was going on, and he wasn't thinking of tuna. *What is Lawrence keeping from me? So help me God, I'm going to find out if my CO is mixed up in some kind of lesbian sex club or deep state Russian spy ring. This is a matter of national security.*

***

Back at The Ranch, Jorge opened the limo door, and Brenda got out and headed to the pool deck where heavy-metal blared from the sound system, and the sisters were frolicking naked like nymphs in the Garden of Eden. All that flesh and sunshine was a turn-on, and the forty-degree air temp didn't faze the lesbian zombies one bit.

She strolled to the pool and saw Lilly lying on a floaty mattress with her legs spread over the sides and her feet dangling in the water. Between her thighs, Chloe was showing her well-deserved appreciation while Maria was enjoying Lilly's perky nipples. Jackie was rubbing Maria's back with one hand and working herself up with the other. On the deck lay the entangled bodies of Melinda and Donna. Brenda figured Caroline was up in her room, playing with Girlie Dog or watching her kid shows on TV, but Monica was nowhere to be seen.

She's probably on her way to tell Alfons the Sisterhood *has need of his yacht.*

Brenda was happy to see the sisters were getting to know everything about Lilly. I should join them, she thought, but her mother-hen instinct told her to check on Caroline instead. She strolled inside and bounded up stairs to Caroline's room. Girlie Dog was sleeping on her bed, but no Caroline. *She must be around here somewhere.* Brenda strolled the grounds beyond the walled-in pool area, peered over the sand berm to see a vacant beach, then decided to check in the Crystal Shrine.

As soon as she opened the door she heard, "Boo."

Caroline jumped out from behind the trunk of the Sister Tree of Life.

The relief of finding her did battle with a sudden burst of anger. "What are you doing in here, young lady? This isn't a playground. I've been looking all over for you."

"I heard a voice calling me. It was Loa." She twirled in a circle. "She let me see my mommy and daddy."

Brenda dropped to her knees in front of Caroline and gazed into her innocent loving eyes. "Sweetie, remember I told you to never tell a fib?"

Caroline smiled. "I really saw them. They were in a beautiful place filled with stars and were happy to see me. I even saw you talking to Robert and Maggie, and you were holding Zoey."

Brenda thought *Loa* wouldn't summon Caroline out of the blue. Caroline must've asked to see her dead parents... "What did they say? Did they have a message for you?"

Caroline clasped her hands. "No."

"Okay, honey. Shall we go now?"

"Can we get ice cream?"

"Sure. Why not?"

"Can my sisters come too?"

The scene at the pool came to mind. "They're a little busy right now."

***

In Manhattan, on the twenty-fifth floor of the Empire State Building where Alfons Duda lived in a five-million-dollar apartment adjoining the offices of his company, KOMA LTD, Monica was showing him who was boss. "Take your pants off, and do it slowly, big boy."

This was a game they played quite often, and Alfons was happy to obey. Monica could tell how happy he was by the size of the bulge in his shorts. "Drop 'em, buster. This is going to hurt."

***

While Alfons and Monica were playing Dom and Sub and would soon be screwing on the floor, over at the Pentagon, Colonel Wesley Miller felt like he was being screwed too. General Lawrence Taylor, sitting behind his desk with his feet propped up, had pushed the intercom buzzer, summoning Wes to his office.

"Yes, sir?"

"Have you seen my cell phone?"

Wes's heart gave him a jolt. He did a phony visual sweep of the desk then suggested, "Maybe it's in the bathroom, sir. I'll check."

Sure enough, the cell was just where he'd left it after breaking the code and learning of the sex party. He returned to the office and handed the phone to Lawrence. "How did the JCS meeting go, sir?"

"The usual bullshit."

Wes decided to go fishing. "I guess that means we won't be bombing Russia anytime soon?"

"About that golf tournament coming up..."

"Yes, sir." *Lawrence changed the conversation from Russia too quickly, like it might be a touchy subject. But why?*

"Do you have the logistics in place for me to tee off?"

"It's still a couple of months down the road, sir." Wes wondered when Lawrence would request logistics for the sex party. Or was it Top Secret? It had to be a front for some kind of counter espionage for the Russians. *Yeah, keeping me out of the loop makes me think you're a traitor, General. Fox Trot Zero, my ass. The Army would never give a sex party a code name, so he has to be conspiring with the Russians.*

"Wes, what's the matter with you? It's like you're off in la-la land."

"Sorry, sir. Just tired I guess."

"You have been working too hard lately. I want you to take some leave. The Army owes you three weeks."

Now he's trying to get rid of me. "I would get bored as hell, General."

"That's an order, Wes, and besides, I'm taking some time off myself."

Now Wes was sure his CO would be screwing Jackie O'Neal, and Putin will be watching.

***

Back at KOMA LTD, Monica, sitting up on her knees, reached over and slapped Alfons' bare butt. "Now that you got your jollies, I need a favor."

"Anything for you, my sweets."

"The Sisterhood needs to use your yacht."

He grabbed his shorts. "You mean for a day cruise?"

"No. We will need to board it in Athens—"

"Grcccc? Out of thc question." He pulled up his shorts. "I'm not running my yacht all the way to the Mediterranean."

"Tell that to Brenda. She won't be happy, and you know what happens when she gets pissed off, and we can't have that now, can we?" She made a scissors with her fingers. "Snip. Snip."

"Okay." He grabbed himself protectively. "I'll ship it to Athens, but you better bring it back in one piece, or else." He drew an index finger across his throat.

***

Back at The Ranch, Brenda was issuing orders that each sister was to contact the men on the list and personally invite them to Black Friday 2. “I’m sorry to say Senator James Hoffman has been removed from the list. As you know, General Taylor has warned us that Hoffman is a threat to the Sisterhood. He’s already spewing fake news about lesbian zombies running around loose.”

Donna said, “Good. I’m glad I won’t have to call the prick, so who do I call now?”

“Admiral Roy Kincade.”

Donna frowned. “I don’t recall him being initiated.”

“Not yet, but I have a plan for just that. I want you to fly to the island of Rhodes in the Aegean Sea. The US Navy has a big anchorage there where Admiral Kincade is in charge. Drop in on him, tell him you’re a friend of Jackie O’Neal. He’ll be delighted to see you.”

“Won’t he think it’s suspicious that a friend of Jackie’s would show up on Rhodes of all places?”

“Tell him you’re there to find a flower, White Myrtle, a new ingredient Jackie wants for her skin cream. Then comes the fun part. Get him to kiss you. Kiss him back good and hard to give him the virus. Nature will take its course from there."

“When do I leave?”

“Tomorrow afternoon at 3:00. JAL Flight 2410 flies direct to Athens, then it continues on to Rhodes. Jorge will drive you to JFK airport.”

Chapter Nine

Two days came and went with all the captains of commerce, finance, government, internet, and the military having sent their RSVPs for Black Friday 2. Their work done for the time being, the sisters goofed off, drinking and flipping cable channels. It was Monica, just back from her screw-a-thon with Alfons, who suggested they watch the Doctor Bill Show.

Bill walked out on stage to a roaring applause. "On today's show we have former senator James Hoffman. He claims lesbian zombies are taking over the world. However, we have to interrupt this show for some breaking news."

JAL FLIGHT 2410 FROM ATHENS AND BOUND FOR RHODES HAS CRASHED IN THE AEGEAN SEA. IT'S FEARED THERE ARE NO SURVIVORS.

Maria spoke up first. "T-this is terrible...those poor people."

Monica swallowed sudden terror burning in her throat, got off the leather couch, and ran out the door, yelling, "Brenda." She found her and Caroline playing go *get the ball* with Girlie Dog. "Brenda, please tell me that Donna was not on JAL 2410 to Athens."

Brenda threw the slobbery ball. "Yeah. What's the matter?"

"The plane crashed." Unable to hold back tears, Monica managed to add, "They do not believe there are any survivors."

Caroline tugged at Brenda's dress. "She can't be dead. We don't ever get killed. Monica told me that's why the car crash didn't kill me."

They took off running to the house, and all the way, Brenda and Monica kept praying to *Loa*, "Save our sweet Donna. Please, please don't let her be dead." Entering the house, they found the Sisterhood in a state of despair, crying and hugging each other.

Caroline repeated what she'd said only seconds before, only this time stomping her right foot. "You all shut up. Loa will not let her be dead."

Brenda knew that was not the case. Cassandra had died. "Loa decides who lives or dies, Caroline."

Not believing Brenda's words, Caroline ran up the stairs, sobbing, with Girlie Dog right behind her. The pup sensed something was wrong, whimpered, and tucked her tail between her legs.

Melinda spoke up. "I told her she was stupid once...and now she's gone. I wish I'd been nicer to her."

Chloe banged her fist on the coffee table. "If I had never gone over to Hoffman's apartment all of those months ago, she would still be alive today, but no. I had to kiss her. I had to turn her into one of us...to rescue her from that lecher Hoffman. What I really wanted was to have her all to myself. It's my fault she's dead." That outburst ended in tears. She pressed her head down on a couch pillow and cried.

***

When Donna came to, she was floating facedown, surrounded by drifting dead bodies and feasting sharks. She spit water and coughed. *What the hell happened?* Debris of all kinds: luggage, pillows, clothing, bobbed in the waves. Her body was coated with slimy jet fuel, it floated on the water in disfigured rainbows, and the air tasted like it could ignite at any second. The aft section of a plane, terribly broken, teetered and dipped. J-A-L was painted on the tail.

Reality struck her. "The damn plane crashed?" she shouted. "What kind of shit is this?" Fighting panic, she looked around, hoping to see other survivors nearby. "Hello. Anyone there?"

The dead did not answer.

As the sun set, she treaded water to wait out the coming night. The water was cold enough for hypothermia to set in, if she were a normal person. A normal human. But no. She was a lesbian zombie. In some ways she was already dead, but in others, she had more life in her than all of civilization.

How the hell am I going to get out of this mess?

Sometime before dawn, she was lying on her back, drifting along with the tides when her head hit a chunk of debris floating by. Reaching up to a torn flap of aluminum, she tried to pull herself up on the flat surface, but the slime of jet fuel in her dress and on the smooth surface caused her to slip back into the sea. She reached up again, only to meet with the same results. Clinging to the stubborn life-raft, she waited for daylight in hopes of finding a way to climb onboard.

As dawn broke and the stars winked out, she worked her way around the floating wreckage and realized it was part of a wing. And the sun revealed another thing she wouldn't have expected in a million years. A dead woman was lying face up on the wing, completely naked, a blonde woman with perfect breasts, perfect curves, but no hint of bloating. She had to be sleeping.

"Hey," Donna shouted, hoping to wake the woman. "Are you dead?"

Nothing.

"Hey. You. On the wing. Help me." She splashed water on the naked body and got a twitch in response. "Help me up."

The head turned to her, then her eyes popped open wide. "Oh, my god. Another survivor."

"I can't get up...keep slipping down."

The naked lady crawled to the edge of the wing. "Take off your dress."

"Huh?"

"It's soaked in jet fuel. That's why you keep slipping."

"Okay." She wriggled out of her dress, and it actually floated on the surface. "I see what you mean."

"Come on." The woman offered her a hand up, and a second later, they both lay naked together on the surface of the wing.

"I'm Donna," she said breathlessly. "Donna Pearson."

"Carrie Carson. I was a flight attendant. "I don't know why I'm still alive."

"I remember now. You brought me a Manhattan. I didn't recognize you with your clothes off."

"Yeah. My first flight on JAL. I worked on a private jet before this...for KOMA LTD. Funny story, that is, and long."

"I'm not going anywhere."

They both laughed.

"There was this gorgeous redhead client, my god, just thinking of her takes my breath away, she was my first lesbian experience on a long flight from Haiti to New York."

Donna looked into Carrie's eyes. *Brenda?*

"I've never been the same since."

Now Donna knew. "You made love to Brenda Ayler?"

"You know her?"

"You could say that. Why did you quit KOMA?"

Carrie looked away. "I couldn't stomach the captain and co-pilot groping me anymore. Now don't get me wrong. I ate up the attention, even did both of them, but after Brenda, ick. Not interested anymore."

Donna laughed out loud.

"What's so funny."

"You and me, Carrie. We are sisters."

"Nah."

"You're a lesbian zombie just like me."

Carrie felt her breasts. "I'm a zombie?"

"That's why you survived the crash. Brenda made you a member of the Sisterhood, gave you the virus, gave you an orgasm. Loa must've meant for us to meet on this flight."

"Loa?"

"The Lesbian Goddess of the Universe."

Carrie looked around as the wing bobbed in a watery desert and more sharks cruised in to feed on the dead. "This Loa of yours has a morbid way of introducing people."

"She's your Loa now, too. I think it's going to be a while before we're rescued. How about we take the time to get to know each other better?"

"I thought you'd never ask."

Donna gathered her naked new sister into her arms. "Have a nice flight." Lips met and oily bodies wriggled together under the Aegean sun, a flight on a wing and a prayer they would never forget.

***

Back on Long Island, the Sisterhood sat up all night, watching the news and praying to *Loa*. Caroline finally conked out about two in the morning. She was lying on her side with her head on Chloe's lap. Girlie Dog was there, too, woofing in her sleep as if chasing a squirl in dreamland.

The others sat in silence as a news ribbon that ran nonstop across the bottom of the screen kept repeating the same newsflash: *US Navy destroyer deployed to the crash area 140 miles southeast of Greece and 130 miles northwest of Rhodes in the Aegean Sea. Two Navy helicopters spearheading search and rescue mission to scout for possible survivors. There were 472 souls onboard the 380 Airbus, which had - until now - a flawless record.*

This was no consolation to the Sisterhood.

At 4:35am, Caroline got up to pee and saw her sisters had dozed off. The voice in her head could not have come from one of them. *Crystal Shrine. Crystal Shrine.* She snuck outside and took Girlie Dog with her. When she got to the doors they opened as if by some magician's hand. She held tightly to Girlie Dog's collar, and they stepped inside together. As the sun wouldn't rise for another hour, the throne room was pitch black, and the gold tiles beneath her bare feet were cold.

"Look at me, Caroline."

She turned toward the voice and saw *Loa* in a single crystalline wall panel, and the room became bright as day.

"Caroline, honey, I want you to tell Brenda these numbers. 37 point 08333 and 26 point 01667. Can you remember them, honey?"

"Yes."

"Now run and tell her right now."

With excitement blooming in her chest, she ran inside. "Brenda. Brenda."

Monica stirred on the couch. "What is all the racket about?"

"I have to find Brenda."

"She is out on the pool deck."

Caroline found her dozing in a glider rocker and woke her up. "Brenda," she said breathlessly. "*Loa* told me to give you these numbers. 37 point 08333 and 26 point 01667. What does it mean?"

Brenda sat up straight. "Coordinates, honey. Loa's telling us where we can find Donna. Wake up your sisters."

Running into the house, Caroline yelled, "Wake up, everybody. Sister Donna is not dead."

Girlie Dog started barking and followed Caroline around.

Brenda rushed in and took over. “Jackie, call Admiral Kincade. Give him these coordinates. 37 point 08333 by 26 point 01667. They came straight from our Goddess *Loa*.”

Monica got to her feet. “Does that mean she is alive?”

“I don’t know, but we can hope.”

***

Meanwhile, Donna and Carrie were trying to make the best of a bad situation. The sun and the oily jet fuel were giving them gorgeous tans, but the balmy weather was about to turn stormy. Dark clouds were creeping in from the west. Lightning bolts struck the water. Naked on an airplane wing was no place to be during a storm.

Carrie clung to Donna’s arm. “Can lesbian zombies drown?”

“I’m more worried about those sharks.” Triangular fins cruised circles around their precarious platform.

To complicate matters, the sea was getting choppy, tipping and teetering the wing to angles that made holding on difficult, and as the wind rose, sea spray soaked their bodies. Worse, air bubbles gurgled up from under the wing, and the water was closing in around them.

“We’re sinking.”

The wing bobbed. Donna clung to the winglet and Carrie clung to her. “At least we’ll go down together.” Carrie kissed Donna’s salty lips.

A shark charged up the wing, splashing water and gnashing teeth at the girls. Donna ripped out its left eye. The shark flopped back in the water, and because it was now bleeding from the empty eye socket, the other sharks attacked it.

All the commotion caused the wing to sink deeper. Donna and Carrie had all they could do to keep their entire bodies out of the water. As they clung on for dear life, the air-thumping sound of rotor blades in the sky made them look up. A helicopter slewed in. *US Navy.*

“We’re going to be rescued,” Carrie shouted over all the noise and the downwash of air.

A machine gun laid down a spray of bullets that created a row of geysers, scattering the sharks. One shark took a direct hit, blowing it to bloody pieces. The other sharks were no longer interested in their prey on the wing and went after the easy meal.

A loud speaker announced, "Hold tight, ladies. We'll get you safely to our ship. You are now under the protection of the United States Navy."

Overjoyed, Donna stood up on the bucking wing and waved but promptly slipped and fell into the water. As waves slapped her in the face, a sailor in full scuba gear jumped from the copter and landed a few feet from her.

He swam up behind her and slipped his arms around her midsection then pulled her tightly to his smooth wetsuit. "I got you." He grabbed the cable hook and safety strap the helicopter had lowered and secured her to the rigging. "All set."

As the cable lifted her out of the water and up toward the helicopter, he saw that she too was as naked as the woman on the wing. *My God...these poor women. They've been through hell...but I don't see a scratch on them.*

Donna yelled down to him, "Thank you."

Now the sailor turned his attention to the lone woman on the wing. He tried to climb up, but the wing was too slippery.

"You have to take off your clothes," the woman said.

He thought about how that would look to his crewmates in the helicopter and decided to hang on to the wing flap and hope the gunner above could keep the sharks at bay.

"I'm AIRRs First Class Frank Leatherwood, ma'am."

"Flight attendant Carrie Carson. Sorry I lost my uniform."

"We'll have you out of here in a minute."

He looked up at naked Carrie, and she looked down at him, and reading his mind, she knew he was genuinely concerned about her safety and not the least bit lustful over her nakedness. A true gentleman. "What's an AIRR, sailor Frank?"

"Aviation Rescue swimmer, ma'am. My dream is to sign up for submarine school in New London, Connecticut."

"You must love the Navy."

"It's my whole life, ma'am."

"Just call me Carrie." She wiped salt from her lips. Her rescuer was a man's man, for sure, but his presence so close to her nakedness didn't garner the response from her libido she'd expected. No wonder...after being naked with Donna and learning they were both lesbian zombies, men didn't have the same appeal.

The helicopter cable came back down.

"Okay, slide into the water. I'll catch you."

Moments later, she was strapped to his body and they were hoisted up together. The wrecked wing below bobbed up and down and got smaller and smaller, and the downdraft from the rotors intensified. Her oily, fuel soaked hair slapped her in the face. Seconds passed like hours, and she soon set bare feet down on the floor of the helicopter.

Donna was sitting on a bench seat with a mustard-striped Navy wool blanket wrapped around her. "We're going to be okay," she shouted.

"I know."

The men unstrapped her, draped a similar blanket around her, and she sat next to Donna. As the helicopter banked away, she saw the wing section sink below the choppy surface of the Aegean Sea.

***

Back at the Sisterhood's mansion, the joyous occasion was just getting started. The sisters were already planning a big welcome home party for Donna.

Television newscasters were talking about the miracle of JAL Flight 2410. The sisters gathered around to hear the good news.

"We have a live feed coming in now."

The scene switched to the deck of a Navy ship and a man wearing a poncho, slick with rain. Wind whipped his hair around. "This is Thad Harper reporting for WNN aboard the Destroyer *USS Carmick* in a stormy Aegean Sea where the rescue helicopter has just recovered two survivors from the plane crash."

The camera swung to the aft helicopter pad where Donna and another woman stepped from the cabin. Both were wrapped in Navy blankets. Their hairdos were oily and matted, and from here, looked like dreadlocks. Sailors led them away.

A loud cheer went up from the Sisterhood.

"It's a miracle."

Caroline, feeling she was the one who saved Donna, had to rub it in. "See? Told you so. Sister Donna doesn't look dead to me."

A joyous Brenda picked her up and spun her around. "You were absolutely, positively right, little one. She's okay."

Monica said, "The other woman looked vaguely familiar."

Brenda put Caroline down. "She was the flight attendant on Alfons' private jet."

"Oh, yeah...but how did she survive?"

"She and I had a quicky on the flight home from Port au Prince. The pilots had been treating her like a slut. We'll be welcoming her to the Sisterhood very soon."

Caroline danced around with Girlie Dog. "Oh boy. We get a new sister."

Jackie's phone rang. "It's Admiral Kincade."

"Put it on speaker."

"Hello, Admiral."

"Jackie. I've ordered a Navy chopper to fly Donna and Carrie from the USS Carmick to Athens. From there, Delta Airlines will fly them to JFK courtesy of General Taylor."

"Thank you, Admiral. We were so worried."

"See you at the party."

The call disconnected.

Just when it seemed things could not get any better, Brenda's phone rang. She looked at the display. "It's Robert."

"Brenda, Maggie and I are so glad Donna is all right."

"It was touch and go there for a while."

"Thanks to Goddess Loa," Maggie shouted in the background.

"What's going on with Fox Trot Zero?"

"I'm waiting for a call from the General."

"Keep me informed." She hung up and all the sisters joined Caroline and Girlie Dog in their joyous dance.

***

Eleven hours later, Donna and Carrie strolled into Terminal 4 at JFK and were immediately surrounded by reporters and cameras from all the major networks.

A World News Network reporter aimed a microphone at Carrie and asked, "What was going through your mind when you realized the plane was going to crash?"

"I'm not a good swimmer."

"What went wrong up there?"

"I'll leave that answer for the crash investigators. I just serve beverages and snacks."

"How did you survive?"

"Turns out I'm a better swimmer than I thought."

"You look great, no cuts and bruises—"

A man's voice jumped in. "That's because she's a lesbian zombie."

Everyone turned to see disgraced Senator James Hoffman holding a sign that read: *The End Is Near!*

Reporters swiveled their microphones to him.

"Lesbian zombies turned me into a sex maniac and caused me to lose my seat in the Senate. All you news hounds better listen. They want to take over the world and turn everyone into sex-crazed zombies."

Two police officers stepped in to escort him out of the area, but he kept raving on. "It's Brenda, the redhead, I tell you. She's the queen bee of the lesbian hive. We are doomed. We are doomed." His voice echoed off in the distance.

Cameras swung to the only redhead there. And microphones too. Brenda showed them a poker-face. "Obviously he's mentally ill."

Carrie said, "I'm glad we're back in the good-old US of A."

The WNN reporter returned to the main story and pointed his microphone to Donna. "What was going through your mind as you clung to life all night in shark-infested waters?"

"I hoped they weren't hungry."

That got a chuckle from the crowd.

"No, seriously," the reporter said.

Knowing that millions of people were watching WNN, and that she had to distance herself from Hoffman's rants, she said, "I prayed to the blessed lord Jesus to save the souls of all those poor passengers and to forgive me of my sins and let my parents know that I love them."

***

Meanwhile, the NYPD muscled James Hoffman to the garage where he had left his car. As the maniac was no longer a threat, the police officers turned their backs on him and headed back to the terminal. James was still screaming, "Doomed, I tell ya. We're all doomed."

One of the cops yelled back, "You better shut up or you'll wake up in Bellevue's nut ward."

"Forgive them, Father, for they know not what they do." He got to his car, fumbled the key fob and accidentally kicked it under the car. "Damn it." He set the sign on the ground, got on his knees, and felt around for the fob. Nothing. "Damn it." He got his face down low and looked under the car. There it was, an arm's reach away. He turned his head to reach for it and saw red high-heeled shoes walk up to him. Looking up, he saw Brenda.

Panic shot through him like a hot bullet. He got to his feet. "What do you want, bitch? You can't kill me. I've got the virus too. And I'm gonna put an end to your quest for world domination."

She smiled at him. "Relax, James. I'm here to give you a message from Donna. She's had a rough time out there at sea, had a lot to think about. She wants you to know that she loves you."

He threw her a narrow-eyed glare. "She does?"

"Yes. I'd like you to go on the *Ladies' Point of View* show and tell your story about how you met and fell in love. Tell everyone you've changed your womanizing ways and want to marry her. You might even get your Senate seat back."

"Bullshit. Put me on that show and I'll tell the world about you and your lesbian zombie virus, how Donna and Chloe gave it to me. Some fun that was, two on one, and I end up saying 'take me to your Queen.' You women are dangerous, and so am I, and I'll prove it to everyone on national TV."

While James was thinking it over, Brenda was thinking too. *If you think I've screwed you over before, well, shithead, you ain't seen nothin' yet.*

"Okay. I like your angle about lesbian zombies. The topic should draw a large audience...mainly women, but you need to sound believable. I'll get you on the show as quickly as I can. Donna will be so pleased."

"I want to hear how she loves me from her own mouth."

"She'll tell you on the set, on live TV. How's that?"

Leaning his back on the driver's side door, he studied her face, looking for anything that could give her lie away, but got nothing. "You surprise me, Brenda. Maybe I was wrong about you. I *will* invite you to our wedding. I know that Donna would like that."

"James, I'd like that too, and I'm so glad we've had this conversation. I'll have someone contact you about the time slot on the show. Here. Let me give you a hug before I leave."

James felt her breasts pushing against his chest. *I just might bang you after the show. Then I'll double-bang all her girlfriends, Donna twice.*

Brenda got a kick out of that thought. *Dream on, fool.* He'd always be a misogynist. With a luscious red-lipped smile, she handed him his key fob then turned and walked away, her beautiful butt moving from side to side. She knew he was watching, looked back, and blew the sucker a kiss.

Chapter Ten

As the limo pulled up to The Ranch, Caroline jumped out and ran to boxes that were stacked up by the door. She tried to open one but couldn't. Monica looked at them and turned to the sisters. "These are the mason jars and labels we ordered."

Carrie looked puzzled. "What are they for?"

"Dogfood." Lilly told her the sordid story about Max. "Don't worry. You won't have to help grind him up. I want to do it all by myself."

"Do what?"

"It's a lot like canning peaches."

"Girls. Come on," Brenda rallied the sisters. They sat out on the lawn, drinking and listening to Carrie and Donna tell the story of their ordeal on the Aegean Sea.

"Brenda, you should have seen the hunk who rescued us," Carrie said. "AIRRs First Class Frank Leatherwood from the USS Carmick. His dream is to go to Navy submarine school in New London." She hugged herself. "I hope I'll see him again someday...to thank him properly."

Brenda patted her shoulder. "If Loa is willing, you will."

Caroline and Girlie Dog ran around playing with the ball. Even from the yard, the sisters could hear the growl of the meat grinder as Lilly ground up Max to fill the mason jars.

After about three hours, a blood-soaked Lilly came out and announced, "Max fit into one hundred and twelve jars. There are seventy-five jars left over."

"We can get a refund for the jars we didn't use."

"Let's keep them," Brenda said. "I doubt Max will be the last canning job we'll have to do. Another wife-beater will come along eventually and those jars will be put to good use then. Now, go take a shower, but first, wash off with the garden hose. Don't want you dripping blood through the house, and hurry up. You smell awful."

"I could just go down to the beach and wash off in the surf."

"What? Are you crazy? You'd attract every shark within a hundred miles."

Lilly raised a bloody finger on her right hand. "Good point."

An hour later, a thoroughly clean and smelling wonderful Lilly, thanks to Jackie's *Roja Parfums*, walked by Brenda.

"Come on, Lilly. That's Jackie's favorite perfume you have on. She's going to be pissed."

"So what? I'm a lesbian zombie now. If she gets pissed, she can follow me to my room and punish me good."

Brenda had just dialed Charles Mantella, CEO of the World News Network and, while listening for the phone to ring on his end, yelled at Lilly, "It's your ass."

"I hope so."

The phone connected. "Brenda?"

"Hello, Charlie. I want you to do something for me."

"Name it, my Queen."

"I want you to use your influence to book someone on your *Ladies' Point of View Show* in two days."

"Let me guess. It's your two sisters who survived the plane crash. Am I right?"

"You are two-thirds right. Along with my sisters, I want that nutjob former Senator James Hoffman to be a special guest on the show. Can you swing it?"

"Of course. If the hosts have to reschedule some of their guests for another day, I'm sure that's okay."

"Between you and me, Charlie, it'll be the highest rated episode of *Ladies' Point of View* of all time."

"Consider it done."

"Thanks. I'll see you at Black Friday 2, right?"

"Wild horses couldn't keep me away." An elated Charles Mantella, thinking of all those beautiful women at the party, felt a throb in his trousers.

***

Dawn rose for Robert, Maggie, and baby Zoey. While Maggie sat up in bed, nursing Zoey, Robert walked up and kissed both of them on their foreheads. The kiss was so gentle, Maggie detected a sad message in his lips. He was dressed in his desert combat fatigues. "Where are you going?"

"Arizona."

Maggie switched Zoey over to nurse on her other breast. "The General called? I didn't hear the phone."

"It's all set. I'm going to an old base that was used mainly in World War Two. It's still on the Army's property inventory list but has been abandoned. We're using it to stage and monitor the mission to Pakistan."

"How long will you be gone?"

"Two weeks." He kissed her and left on his mission for Brenda.

***

Back at the home of the Sisterhood, Melinda was serving breakfast when Jackie got a text message on her phone. *"We got him. Baby Doc was trying to leave Port au Prince on a private sea plane. No money stolen."*

"How about that? Juan Senior says they caught Baby Doc."

Monica immediately went on a rant. She paced the kitchen like a prowling hyena. "I cannot wait to see his ugly face and watch him cry and beg for mercy while I kill him very slowly."

"No you won't," Jackie said. "We recovered all the money he embezzled."

"I don't give a goddess damn about the money. I just remember what happened to my precious daughter. Baby Doc is going to die. Hell. Brenda crushed the skull of a two-timing prick for a lot less than that."

Brenda put her foot down. "Monica, stop—"

"You may be my Queen, but that was my daughter. I will die before I let that murderer continue to walk on the earth, enjoying his grandchildren while my Maya lies in a cold grave."

"Why do you have to be such a hothead? He didn't rape and murder your daughter. His father's soldiers did."

"He said he had them executed, but he lied to me to save his own neck from the guillotine. Guilty as charged."

As the exchange between Brenda and Monica went back and forth, Caroline sat at the breakfast table, eating Coco Puffs from the box. She would look at Monica bitching to Brenda and then at Brenda replying to Monica's bitching. In an effort to restore peace, she shouted. "Both of you shut up. Ask Loa what she thinks Monica should do."

Brenda and Monica looked at Caroline and then smiled. "That's a good idea. Now come give us a hug."

Now that the dark cloud of sister-against-sister had subsided, everyone, except Caroline and Girlie Dog, decided to take advantage of the nice weather and go for a walk on the beach. The sand was cool on their bare feet, and the breeze was brisk, perfect for the gulls to soar and swoop above the waves rolling in.

Standing by a beached rowboat chained to cinder blocks in the sand, the sisters were discussing the upcoming Black Friday 2 Party when Jackie's cell vibrated. The interesting thing was that she had shoved her cell down in her thong since her bikini had no pockets. Now the vibrating cell sent tingles through her body, stimulating her libido to the extent that she was sorry she had to answer the call.

It was General Taylor.

"Would you call me right back? It might take me a minute to answer...unfinished business, you know, so keep it ringing." She hung up and promptly stuck the phone back in her thong.

Her sisters just stood there looking at her like *what the hell is she doing?*

The phone vibrated again. Jackie's eyes rolled back and she shivered in ecstasy.

"Are you going to answer that?" Chloe asked.

"In a minute." Her breaths came short and fast.

"What are you doing?"

"Hold on." Her phone vibrated. Her heat rose. And just like that she went over the edge with a shuddering moan. "Oh, yeah."

Chloe slapped a hand on her forehead. "Oh my goddess. You just invented a new way to have an orgasm."

"You...think so, Chloe," Jackie muttered, breathless.

All the sisters shoved their cell phones into their own panties.

"I hope I get a call," Maria said. "Even if it's a wrong

number."

Pretending she didn't notice everyone in the Sisterhood was hoping for a cellular orgasm, Jackie finally answered her call. "Hi, Lawrence. What's up? Your office? Fine. See you then." She hung up.

"What was that about?"

"He wants me at the Pentagon to go over some details about the Pakistan mission."

Chloe groaned. "No he doesn't. He wants sex."

"You're probably right, Chloe. But I'm just bowing to Brenda's wishes. Just because he calls her *queen* doesn't mean he doesn't care about good old guy-on-girl sex anymore."

***

Later on, the Sisterhood, now in the sitting room, was more intrigued with the idea of a new lesbian zombie sex game and couldn't care less if Jackie would have sex with General Taylor. Even Monica was ready for a break from the usual talk of taking over control of the world from men.

Lilly came up with the idea as to how the game she called *Sorry wrong number* would be played. "Now, sisters, with everyone's cell phones in their panties, one sister will stand with her back to the rest of you while I dial one of your numbers randomly. Does everyone have their cells set on vibrate?"

They all cooed and giggled.

"If your cell starts to vibrate, do your best to not show any reaction, no moaning or body movement. I'll keep calling the number on constant redial while the designated sister turns around to look at each one of you. You'll keep your cell held tightly between your legs. The one I'm calling will be trying to hold back her orgasm. If the designated sister thinks she knows who I'm calling, she'll walk up to her and kiss her. If she's right, kiss her back and let your orgasm loose. If she's wrong and you're not having an orgasm, say, "Sorry wrong number." We'll rotate designated sisters, and I'll rotate phone numbers, so let's get started. Chloe, would you like to lead off?"

A Power-ball winner was never so elated.

***

By the time each sister had multiple orgasms and moved the party to the pool deck, Jackie had arrived at General Taylor's office in the Pentagon. She knocked on the door and Lawrence opened it.

"Jackie, come in." He closed the door and joined Jackie in front of his desk. "I have a problem."

"About the Pakistan mission?"

"No. It's Colonel Miller. He's been nosing around in my office, hell bent on finding out what I'm keeping from him. I tell you, he could blow the lid off Fox Trot Zero before we even get it off the ground."

"Have you told Brenda?"

"I'm hoping you can break it to her. This is a real problem. I have served with Wes for twenty years. He's not a prick like Senator Hoffman."

Jackie took the liberty to sit in the General's chair. "You can forget Hoffman. He'll be dead before long."

"I don't want to know anything about that." Lawrence leaned on the desk. "I never liked Hoffman. He wanted sensitivity training in the military. Sensitivity training, my ass. What I don't get...how come I didn't turn into a sex-crazed maniac like him?"

She tilted back in the plush leather chair. "The virus affects different men in different ways. You're a one-woman man, General. Hoffman would screw a woodpile if he thought there was a snake in it. The lesbian zombie virus simply brings out the inner man. What kind of man is Colonel Miller?"

"He's a good soldier. Happily married. He's my friend. I don't want him involved with Brenda and Loa and all her sisters. I'm hoping there's a way to let him in on what we're doing but keep him out of the loop on the real reason for the operation."

"Put him right in the middle of it. He won't be able to see the forest for the trees." She stood, swiveled Lawrence around, and set him in the chair. "Now let's discuss something else."

"Like what?"

"How about one of my famous blowjobs?" She got on her knees and unzipped his pants. "This will take your mind off Wes for tonight."

Chapter Eleven

Back at the Sisterhood's lair, Caroline ran into the sitting room with her phone. "I made a new friend on Facebook Chat."

"That's nice." Brenda didn't even look up from her book.

"His name is Danny, and he has two daughters the same age as me."

Now Brenda looked up. "Two daughters?"

"He posted their pictures, and I think I could have a happy time playing with them."

The sisters exchanged doubtful looks.

Melinda spoke up first. "Why don't you show us, honey?"

Caroline proudly held up her phone. "See how nice they look. He said that he could give me a ride to his house and that it would be our little secret."

"He said that, huh?"

"Yeah. I don't know what it means but I really want to play with his daughters, Mindy and Suzie."

"Maybe we should meet Danny first...and his daughters. Does that sound okay?"

"Can I go with you?"

"No, honey. We'll call him in the morning."

"I don't know his phone number."

"Don't worry. We'll get it from the phone company."

"You promise? In the morning?"

"Sure do, honey."

The sisters, knowing it was a come-on to find little girls, kept their suspicions to themselves so as not to upset Caroline.

Melinda thought, if he is a disgusting pedophile then he's soon going to discover that the Sisterhood will teach him a new version of *Sorry Wrong Number*, the deadly version.

Later that night, Brenda couldn't sleep, thinking about the pedophile. As it turned out, none of the sisters were sleeping. They were all on the same page as Brenda.

Monica crept into Caroline's room and opened her Facebook page. Finding nothing to incriminate the pedophile there, she checked the chat room. She hit the jackpot. There were twelve messages from *Dannylovespuppies* where he talked about his twin daughters, Mindy and Suzie. Four chats were supposedly from the daughters with pics attached of them having a great time at Sea World and saying how they couldn't wait to meet Caroline.

Well, the pedophile is going to get his wish.

When she saw that Caroline had given him the address of The Ranch, she got a chill then sent him a message from Caroline: *Hi, Danny. I'm all alone in the house tonight because my parents are out of town for the next three days, and my babysitter is spending the night with her boyfriend. Could you bring Mindy and Suzie over so we can have a slumber party?*

He replied: *We're on our way. Meet us outside.*

She had to think fast then typed: *I'll wait in the lawn chair out front. Bye.*

From there it was a mad rush to rally the sisters, make a plan, and take up strategic positions outside, all without waking Caroline. The lawn chair was set up, pillows, a blanket. The only thing left to do was wait.

After about thirty minutes, an old Toyota Corolla drove slowly past the house, came back around, and drove by again. On the next pass, the car stopped.

Danny, *Dannylovespuppies* to his innocent victims, got out of the car and cautiously looked around. He was a short fat man in his thirties, scruffy enough to never have been on a real date. Slowly he walked up to the lawn chair and pulled the blanket off what he must've thought was Caroline sleeping. When he realized there were two pillows lying there, he whispered, "Oh, shit."

As he turned around to make a hasty retreat, he found himself surrounded by beautiful women with nasty snarls on their lips.

"You must be Danny," Brenda said.

"No. I-I am lost and I think I'm at the wrong house."

"It's the right house, you prick." Brenda glared at him and asked her sisters, "What should we do to the damn pedophile?"

The sisters responded in one voice. “Kill him.”

The man tried to run, but ran into Monica’s closed fist. His dentures flew out and landed in a pile of Girlie Dog shit.

Chloe came around and kicked him in the ass.

He went down on his hands and knees, his face over the excrement. “Please. I didn’t do anything.”

Girlie Dog pranced up and pissed on his leg.

Brenda stood above him, arms crossed. “Pick up your teeth and put them back in your mouth.”

“But there’s dog shit on them,” he spluttered toothlessly.

“Do as I say or die. What’s your pleasure?”

Chloe stepped up. “Let’s just kill him and get it over with so I can go back to bed. I need my beauty rest.”

He rolled over on his back. “Are you all nuts?”

“Sic him, Girlie Dog.”

With a Doberman growl, she lunged at Dan-the-dead-man’s crotch, tore into his pants, and chomped on his balls.

Danny Boy screamed bloody murder.

Growling, her teeth clamped solidly on his balls, she shook her head fiercely, like she’d nabbed a squirrel, and ripped Danny’s jewels from his body, scrotum and all.

Brenda feared his screams and curses would wake up Caroline. “Maria, put a pillow over his face.”

Danny cried out, “No. No. Don’t. I’m sorry.”

She got a pillow from the lawn chair, and Donna helped press it down on the pedophile’s mouth to muffle his pleas as he flailed on the ground and tried to kick Girlie Dog away. However, the she-wolf was relentless, charged in for a second mouthful of man meat, and came away with the molester’s tool of disgrace. His muffled screams would do him no good.

While Girlie Dog chowed down, the sisters jumped on Danny’s arms and legs to hold him still while he bled out. Finally the fight reduced him to a sniveling mess.

“Monica, Lilly,” Brenda said. “Get rid of this piece of shit.”

“How?”

“Feed him to the fishes. Donna, Maria. Drive his car to the Cedar Point trailhead. Leave it unlocked, keys on the floor...a make sure you don’t leave any fingerprints.”

“Why not just set it on fire?”

"A fire will attract attention. The parked car will look like Danny-the-molester went for a hike and mysteriously disappeared."

Lilly didn't say a word as she pulled the pedophile up by his arms and Monica took hold of his feet, and they carried him down to the boat on the beach. He begged for mercy as they swung him back and forth and threw him into the boat.

Maria drove off in the Toyota, and Donna followed in the Mercedes. The remaining sisters watched Lilly and Monica throw the cinder blocks and chains into the boat then carry it to the surf. The feat required the strength of a Navy Seal team, but for lesbian zombies, it was easy. They climbed in and started rowing through the breakers until they were a half-mile out where the water was at least one hundred feet deep. There they got busy chaining two cinder blocks around Danny's waist, and then they grabbed him once more by his arms and legs and sent him into the deep six. His pleas for mercy were quickly drowned. The sharks and bottom feeders would soon devour Girlie Dog's leftovers.

***

The next morning, Caroline bounded down the steps with Girlie Dog close behind. The sisters were at the kitchen table drinking coffee. They looked like they'd been up all night, their hairdos frazzled, no makeup, and still in their nightclothes. Caroline dance up to Melinda. "You're going to call Danny this morning. Can we do it now?"

Everyone looked glum. "Sorry, Caroline, but your new friend was caught last night, attempting to molest a little girl. He's been put away for a long time."

She glanced around the table at all the sad faces. "But what about Mindy and Suzie. They must need a new place to live."

Monica set down her coffee cup. "Honey, there never were any twin girls for you to play with."

"No. You're lying. I saw their pictures."

"Dannylovespuppies was lying to you. It's a dangerous world out there, Caroline. You have to be careful who you talk to on the internet."

"No. No. No. They were supposed to be my new friends."

Crying, she ran up the stairs, back to her room, and slammed the door.

The sisters felt great sadness for Caroline.

Monica clenched her fists. "Poor little thing. She was really hoping she had found new friends."

Brenda looked over the Sisterhood, full grown women, beautiful and sexy, then realized Caroline's problem. "Sisters, we need to find her some kids her own age to play with."

Monica stood. "I know just the thing." She left the table, rushed upstairs, and knocked on Caroline's door.

"Go away."

"Caroline." She opened the door and walked to the bed where a very distraught Caroline was bawling. "I'm sorry this happened to you." Pushing her bangs away from her face, she added, "Let's go to your school and invite all the little girls in your class to a happy party here at the house."

She sniffled. "Really?"

"What do you say?"

"Friends to play with? That's nice, but they have their own homes and families. I want a sister my own age."

"That won't be easy, honey." *Where am I going to find an unwanted little girl? Maybe a mom and daughter seeking shelter from an abusive man. Convert both of them. Whatever I do, I'll have to run it by Brenda.*

Caroline sat up and hugged Monica. "I love you. You're my new mommy."

"That is really sweet, honey. Now let's go down to breakfast. We have a party to plan."

"Can it be a sleepover?"

"We'll see."

Chapter Twelve

In the unseasonable heat of Arizona, Captain Robert Johnson once more wore his Army fatigues. The only difference was that his uniform did not have anything showing his old rank. No captain's bars here. He just wanted to pass for anyone wearing olive drab camo fatigues.

After renting a car, he drove through the town of Sierra Vista to Fort Huachuca. Driving up to the front gate, he was surprised to see a military policeman on guard. He was Sergeant First Class Mack Guiles from his old Ranger company.

"Mack, how the hell did you hear about this place?"

"We all received direct orders, sir, to report here no later than yesterday at 1400 hours."

"How many of us are here?"

"Counting you, there are seven of us from our old squad. If you don't mind me asking, why aren't you wearing your captain's bars?"

"Because this place and all the personnel here were supposed to be secret. Does Fox Trot Zero mean anything to you?"

"No, sir."

"At least something is still a secret."

"Sir, every man in Charlie 2-5 was told you were a quadriplegic after our last mission, but you're not paralyzed. I guess that was just Army scuttlebutt, I'm happy to say."

"Mack, go round up the rest of *A-Squad* and tell them we'll meet in the mess hall at 1500 hours."

"But, Captain, there won't be anyone here to man the gate."

"Don't worry about it, Mack. I don't think we'll be overrun by the Taliban here."

***

Twenty-four hundred miles east of Arizona, Wes Miller was also busy, but he was thinking about lesbians. With his wife Lynne, he drove to the Pentagon, even though he was on a forced three week leave and had no business in the building. Unaware that General Taylor would be advised of his arrival, he showed his ID to the Military Police then parked his car in his assigned spot.

"Okay, Lynne. Wait here."

He got out and trekked to the entrance doors and through security then proceeded down the long hall to General Taylor's office. Once inside, he started going through a new stack of files and documents in his in-box, hoping to find anything related to Fox Trot Zero. Halfway through the first folder, he heard General Taylor talking to someone right outside the door. *Damn. He's not supposed to be here. What happened to him taking time off too?*

He was trapped.

The door opened. Taylor wasn't surprised to see him. "What are you doing here, Wes?"

He stood at attention. "Ah...um...just looking for a file I left around here somewhere."

"You just couldn't stay away, could you? I should have you arrested for disobeying a direct order."

"Sir, but sir..." panic laced his words, "please. My wife, you know Lynne, she's in the car waiting for me. I can't leave her in the parking lot. Please don't have me arrested."

The General couldn't do that to his good friend. "Go home, Wes. I'll call you when I need you. You're dismissed."

Wes felt like he'd just dodged a howitzer shell. "Thank you, sir." He ran all the way back to the car. Breathless, he got in and banged his forehead on the steering wheel. "Damn. Damn. Damn."

Lynne set a gentle hand on his arm. "I gather you didn't find what you were looking for."

"Nothing on Fox Trot Zero. Lawrence is up to something. He walked in like he was expecting me."

"Trust him, Wes. He's a good man. Deep in your heart you know that. He won't do anything to harm this country."

Wes took a long breath, held it, then exhaled in total relief of not being arrested.

"Now let's go home."

He started the car and vowed to find out what was going on.

***

The next morning, Monica took Caroline to school. Her plan was to see Caroline's teacher and come up with a party idea for the girls in her class. The thirty-seven-year-old, Miss Jill Anderson, had never married and never missed a day teaching class.

Getting there forty-five minutes before class started, Monica held Caroline's hand as they walked in through the massive front doors. A woman was standing with her back to the entrance, oblivious to their presence and talking on her cell phone.

Caroline said, "That's my teacher."

Monica put her finger to her lips to shush Caroline, and then listened in on Jill's conversation. "I know Betsy has autism," came from the phone, "but it's hard for her to learn when the other children are making fun of her."

Jill's desperate voice was heartbreaking. "But Betsy is trying her best."

"She's way behind the other students. They're reading at a fourth-grade level and she's reading at a second-grade level."

"I don't think it's her fault, it's the other children in the classroom—"

"They try to be nice but she just yells at them."

"She's frustrated is all. Give her another chance. Please."

"I'm sorry, but I'm going to recommend that she be homeschooled. She's too disruptive to the other students."

Jill hung up, but as hard as she tried, she couldn't stop tears from welling in her eyes. *But Betsy tries so hard.*

"Excuse me, Miss Anderson," Monica said.

She turned to see Monica and Caroline then quickly wiped her teary cheek. "C-can I help you?"

Monica looked at Jill as if she could see right through her. "I think the question is can I help you and Betsy."

"Who are you?"

"I'm Monica Abelard."

"How do you know my daughter's name is Betsy?"

"This is my daughter, Caroline. She told me."

Caroline glared up at Monica and blurted out, "No I didn't."

Monica flinched at Caroline's childish honesty. "Maybe it was when we came in to enroll Caroline a while ago. I think I overhead a counselor mention your name and that you have a daughter named Betsy who's autistic."

"Yeah, well, as you can see from my tears, it hasn't been easy."

"There is a new experimental drug just out that works wonders on children with autism. I am sure that your pediatrician has never heard of it. Would you like to come over to our house and bring Betsy along with you?"

"Where do you live?"

"We live with Jackie O'Neal."

"You mean the rich skin cream lady?"

"Yes. She actually discovered one of the main ingredients in the capsules that reverses autism."

With that news, the five-foot-eight-inch tall brunette with brown eyes hugged Monica. "Please tell me it's the truth."

"It is the truth, so help me goddess."

With a puzzled look on her face, Jill asked, "Goddess?"

"Maybe you'll get to know her someday."

"When did you want us to come over?"

"Tonight would work for us. If six would work, Jackie will send her driver over to pick you two up."

"Six will be fine." Jill shook hands with Monica and gave Caroline a hug. "See you in class, Caroline, and I love your dress."

"I can't wait to meet Betsy."

***

Back in Arizona, Robert was not happy. Sitting in a mess hall that served no food and had seen better days 75 years ago, he looked at stacked cases of C-Rations on the table and warm cases of beer the boys had brought with them. There were six Rangers sitting with him, those who had made the trip from various posts where they were stationed, the same men he had served with in Afghanistan.

Passing around warm bottles of beer, he said, "Okay, boys, listen up." He stood. "This is a top secret mission to take out a terrorist in Pakistan, an Imam named Mohammed Abdullah Abadi."

"Never heard of him," Gee said.

"The INS has compiled intelligence that suggests he's a local Taliban leader."

"Yeah? The same intelligence that said there were weapons of mass destruction in Iraq?" He laughed.

Then they all laughed.

Robert shrugged. "Our job is to provide logistical support from this old base for a company of Rangers who will provide cover fire, if necessary, for those who will carry out the actual assassination mission in a village in Pakistan."

It was Second Lieutenant Edward Richardson who asked the obvious question. "What unit will take out the terrorist?"

With his arms folded and a stern look on his face and walking back and forth, Robert answered, "Ed, that is a really good question. I'm going to tell you, but remember, as of now, this information is secured under the laws of military justice and the code words Fox Trot Zero. It's a unit you've never heard about. Mention it to anyone outside this room, and you'll spend the rest of your life in Leavenworth military prison."

"Jesus H. Christ, Captain. What kind of unit is it that we've never seen or heard of before?"

Platoon Sergeant Jerry Madonna said what everyone was thinking. "What are we talking about? Platoon size, company size? I assume maybe a rifle company?"

Robert told them in two words. "Eight women."

They looked shell-shocked.

"And I can only tell you they're not like any women you've ever met."

The room fell mute.

It was Sergeant-Major Tennyson Henry who broke the silence. "What are they going to do?"

"They're going in as World Health Organization nurses to vaccinate the villagers against a plague outbreak that's coming. They will take out the terrorist. In case his Taliban buddies show up and start a fight, we'll be here with the electronic gear, surveilling the action and monitoring communications."

A noisy deuce-and-a-half pulled up outside.

"That's our equipment. For the next four hours, consider yourselves grunts and get everything unloaded, set up, and running."

"Are we ever going to meet these badass women?" someone shouted from the ranks.

"You never will. Consider yourselves lucky."

***

Brenda and her sisters were waiting on the front lawn at The Ranch for Jill and daughter Betsy to show up. They didn't have long to wait. Jorge drove the Mercedes up the driveway and got out and opened the door for Jill and Betsy. Although he had a smile on his face, he thought, Goddesses damn it. That kid yelled constantly the whole damn way. Shit. I don't know what Jackie wants with them, but I sure hope I don't have to put up with driving that kid anywhere again.

Monica, wearing her bright blue pant suit, met Jill and Betsy at the car door. Running toward the car were Caroline and Girlie Dog. Before Jill or Monica could say anything, smiling Caroline ran up to Betsy. "You wanna play?"

Sweet little blue-eyed Betsy with her strawberry blond hair set in a pony tail clung to her mother's leg. "I don't want to, Mommy."

"Go ahead and play, sweety. It's good to make a new friend."

"No. No. No." She stomped her feet, dropped to her butt, and started pulling grass up by the roots.

Caroline jumped in. "Betsy, do you want to race? I won't run too fast."

Betsy wiped her snotty nose with her hand. "I guess so." She looked up at her mom. "Can I?"

"Surc, honcy, but don't run too fast."

Betsy did her best to keep up, but Caroline was leaving her in the dust. Girlie Dog sensed what was happening, started barking and running next to Betsy. Caroline turned around and ran back and took Betsy by the hand and ran slowly to the house.

In the meantime, Monica was busy introducing Jill to the sisters. As each sister hugged her, Jill was thinking about Betsy. *Oh dear God please, please don't let her have another temper tantrum.*

Brenda, reading her mind as she made eye contact with Jill, thought, Jill won't believe the transformation that will have taken place when she sees Betsy again. "Welcome to The Ranch."

Up in Caroline's bedroom, Caroline and Betsy were coloring in a large coloring book that Brenda had brought home from Haiti. Caroline was coloring inside the black lines, whereas Betsy was coloring everywhere except inside the lines. Frustration drove her to tear out the page and rip it up. "I can't do it. I can't do it." She broke a crayon in two and threw a piece of it across the room.

About that time, Lilly brought each of them a glass of Kool-Aid.

Taking a timeout from coloring, the two of them, using straws, blew bubbles they drank. When Betsy's glass was empty, she picked up the broken crayon and started coloring another picture. This time though, she colored in the lines and wrote her name at the bottom of the sheet using a dark blue crayon. "Look. I did it."

This was the first time she'd seen Betsy smile.

Girlie Dog, who had been lying on her back, looking at the girls bottom-side up, turned upright and pranced to Betsy and licked her face while his tail showed his approval of Caroline's new friend.

"She wants to go outside and play with the ball."

While the two ran down the stairs, an excited Girlie Dog caused Betsy to tumble down the staircase. Jill, panic stricken, ran to the stairs, praying to god that Betsy was okay. She knelt beside her daughter. "Honey, are you hurt?"

Betsy got up as if nothing had happened. "Look, Mommy, I colored the picture and stayed in the lines and even wrote my name."

Jill took the picture and saw that it was perfectly colored inside the lines. Stranger still, Betsy had never been able to write her own name. Before she could reply, Betsy and Caroline were off and running outside to play *catch the ball* with Girlie Dog. As she stood up and watched her daughter run, she remembered how Betsy had been afraid of stairs at the school and would only go down them if her mother held her hand.

It was then that she realized none of the sisters had come over to see if Betsy was okay. She slowly turned around and saw the Sisterhood staring at her.

Brenda broke the silence. "You want to know how this is

possible, don't you? One minute you have a beautiful little daughter that was suffering from a severe case of Autism, and the next minute she is a perfectly normal little nine-year-old girl."

The look on Jill's face was stupefied terror. "Monica, you said there was something Jackie put in capsules that could cure Autism. Did you drug my daughter...in the Kool-Aid?"

Monica looked at Brenda. "Do you want me to tell her."

"No, I'll do it. Jill, we put a virus in the Kool-Aid."

"What?"

"Now I know what you're thinking. We poisoned her. Put that thought out of your mind. You're also worried about the pap smear you had taken two weeks ago. It came back positive for uterine cancer. Your biggest fear is who will take care of Betsy if the worst happens. You also tell people that you were married and that your husband died. It was really a date that had gone violent, leaving you pregnant."

Jill's face turned red with rage. "How dare you people invade my privacy. I'm going to get my daughter and leave. If you try to stop me, I'll call the police."

"Nobody's going to stop you, but before you go, ask yourself how it is that Betsy can now color pictures like any other little girl?"

Jill tore up the picture. "I think Caroline did this. It's a vicious joke...she should be severely punished."

"How do you explain her falling down twelve steps and not having suffered a single bump or bruise?"

"Sometimes it takes a little while for bruises to show." Jill stormed to the front doorway. "Betsy. Come on, honey. We're going home now."

At the door, Brenda bent down and gave Betsy a hug.

"Can I come back tomorrow and play with Caroline again?"

"Honey, after your mommy sees all the things that you can do, I'm sure she'll bring you back tomorrow." Looking up at Jill, Brenda added, "We are having pizza tomorrow for dinner, and I know your mommy loves New London Pizza without onions. Isn't that right, Jill?"

Jill stared at Brenda in disbelief.

"One other thing, Jill. Take Betsy to your fourth grade class tomorrow. You'll be pleasantly surprised at how well she does."

“Impossible.” Taking hold of Betsy’s hand, she rushed to the Mercedes where a waiting Jorge opened the door. Betsy got in the back seat, and Jorge buckled her up.

Jill, furious over what had taken place, sat up front with Jorge and questioned him all the way back home, but she didn’t get any information about Brenda and the other women. “You need to live with them to understand them.” Jorge parked in front of her house. It was then she realized Betsy had not said a word the entire ride, but had colored a picture that Jill knew was blank when she had gotten in the car, and it was colored inside the lines. Astounded, she asked Jorge, “What has happened to my daughter?”

“She drank the Kool-Aid.” He handed her his calling card. “I’m available twenty-four-seven.”

Chapter Thirteen

At 6:00am on the last day of his life, former Senator James Hoffman got up, took a nice long shower, and as the water beat down on him, he went over the plan he'd concocted for when he would be on the WNN show *Ladies' Point of View*. He took his time shaving then used a spray deodorant that had a red rose smell to it.

He slipped on a short-sleeved shirt, buckled his belt, then shoved the cold barrel of his .32 caliber revolver in his waistband. A sport coat would cover it nicely. He looked into the mirror, not knowing it would be the last time, and liked the way the sleeves made his biceps look like he was a workout king. Invincible. Women on the show were all in their mid-forties and were not what he called raving beauties, however, he reasoned his time on camera would make him look good and get them to fantasize about him.

At 8:15am sharp, Joseph drove up in Alfons Duda's new Cadillac Escalade. James was waiting outside his apartment building where six months earlier, from the Waldorf Astoria across the street, Brenda had thrown a bottle of champagne from a fifteenth-floor window to his fifteenth-floor balcony and almost hit him in the head. Now he knew how that was possible. *She's a damn lesbian zombie.*

Getting into the car, he saw Brenda dressed in a beautiful blood-red dress. She was leaning against the opposite door with her legs spread in a manner that suggested an open invitation for James to partake of her gifts.

She thought, I don't want the idiot think I'm going to let him do me right now. "Oh, James, I really want you, but we'll have to wait until the interview is over and you have made history by saving the world from us mean lesbian zombies. Right after the show, just as soon as we get back in the car, I want you to jump on me and do your thing, but for now, just stick your hand between my legs to tide me over until then."

Looking at Brenda, he decided to play along, so he scooted closer to her, touched her softness, and ran through his mind what he would do to her later. She stared at him coyly, as if she too were having the same thoughts. However, he could do no more than cop a feel before Joseph pulled up in front of the WNN building.

Inside, as James was taken to makeup, the host of the show, Dippy Gelderbloom, got Brenda alone in her dressing room. "What's with this guy?"

She reached out and put her hand on Dippy's shoulder. "The short answer is that he's crazy. I know my friend Jackie O'Neal is one of your largest sponsors, and between you and me, she has a close relationship with your boss Charlie Mantella, if you get my meaning."

"Oh, I get it, all right. Charlie has a close relationship with half the dumb blondes in Manhattan."

"Well, we need you to expose Hoffman for the fraud that he is."

"He's some kind of zombie, I hear? What's that all about?"

"That's what he told me, and he said he's going to prove it right on your show."

Pushing her dreadlocks aside, Dippy asked, "How?"

"Your guess is as good as mine. Just be prepared for anything."

Within a few minutes, James was out of makeup and ready to shock the world. As he walked on stage to take his seat of honor, he saw Brenda sitting in the middle seat of the first row beyond the stage lights. He and Dippy were the only ones present on stage so far. While Dippy went over her notes, James surveyed the crowd of women who had tickets to this one and only event.

His eyes darted around as he looked for women he would like to bed. *That one sitting next to Brenda would be real good...nice big tits,* great body, *light brown hair, maybe 5' 8" tall. She looks like she would really enjoy a good man on top of her, but Brenda will get it first...in less than an hour.*

It was then that the other ladies came out from behind a

curtain. They waved at their adoring crowd. Taking her seat next to James on the right was Mary Cottonwood. She was a stout woman in her late forties with light gray hair, and she was a devout Christian. He knew she hated him already. Shaking her hand, he thought, I wouldn't touch you, bitch, if you were the last woman on Earth. Then things looked up for James.

In came Betty Bigalow. Reaching past Mary, he shook her hand, and before he let go, he rubbed her knuckles with his thumb. She pulled her hand away.

Yeah, baby. With your black hair and slim body and nice tits and still being in your twenties, I would lay you right here on the floor.

As the fourth lady took her seat next to Dippy, James looked past her and saw, to his astonishment, Donna and Carrie watching from back stage. *What the hell are they doing here?*

Paying no interest in Diane Dawson, the last woman to strut in, at nineteen with blond hair down to her shoulders and huge tits, he figured she was one of Charles Mantella's girlfriends.

Dippy had just introduced James to the audience. The applause was cut short when he stood. "You two come on out." He pointed to Donna and Carrie. "This is a setup. Those two were on the plane. Nobody could have survived that crash unless they were zombies. That's right. I said it. They are lesbian zombies, and they're going to take over the world."

The audience gasped...then started laughing.

Not wanting the show to get out of hand, Dippy stood and put her hand on his shoulder. "James, if you can't be civil we'll have to terminate your appearance on my show."

"Don't you get it? The lesbian zombies made me into a sex-crazed maniac zombie."

"You're a zombie?" Dippy asked in her professional interviewer tone.

"Damn right I am. When zombies take over the world, nobody ever dies. Brenda is their Queen, and the worst part is they believe that God is a woman. Don't believe them, folks. They are Satan's spawn."

Dippy shouted, "Turn off the cameras."

James pulled out his revolver. "You turn off the cameras and I'll shoot miss dreadlocks in the head."

The audience gasped. Nobody was laughing now.

"Sit down, you ugly bitch. I'm not through talking yet. There's a virus in their saliva that converts normal God-fearing women into lesbian zombies. Don't let their good looks fool you. You never want them to touch you. I let them touch me, and now I can't stop thinking about sex."

"Really? You're the Playboy of the Senate. A womanizer. You're still you, Mister Hoffman. A pervert."

Security arrived with NYPD backup, guns drawn and aimed at Hoffman. "Drop the gun now."

"You can't kill me. I'm a zombie too. I'll show you." He put the gun barrel to his chest.

Brenda jumped up. "No don't." To make her concerned act look genuine, she ran up on stage, but not fast enough.

He pulled the trigger and died instantly at 10:12am.

***

Back at The Ranch, the sisters were watching the *Ladies' Point of View Show*. At first, they thought James' shouting and shooting were part of the interview. After all, the show had been known to host outlandishly weird guests. But not this time. When James shot himself, it caused his body to land on the large table *The Five* sat around, spattering it and everyone sitting there with blood. His body didn't stay there very long. Only the part of his torso above his waist lay on the table. The majority of his lower body weight made him slide back and fall to the floor, out of range of the cameras that were still running.

It was Lilly who spoke up first. "Ladies, now that's what I call a dramatic exit from this Earth."

"What an idiot," Monica said. "He was never a zombie."

***

The word got around in a hurry. Back in Arizona, the Rangers saw the feed from WNN while they were finishing the setup of their electronic gear.

Barry Gee had been watching the news feed first-hand. "Man, get a load of those three women. God damn they're gorgeous."

Sergeant-Major Henry, staring at the screen, pumped his hips like a dog on a bitch. “I’d like to take a shot at the redhead.”

Robert shook his head. “You might die trying.” Just then his cell rang. He had a pretty good idea who it was. Putting his cell to his ear, the first sound he heard was Zoey crying followed by Maggie’s voice. “Are you watching this?”

“Yeah. It’s really something, isn’t it?”

“Do you think Hoffman managed to convince anyone about my sisters?”

“Not a chance. Hey, why is Zoey crying?”

“She has gas. I put a warm towel on her tummy, so she’ll feel better soon.”

“I have to get back at it. In three weeks or so we’ll have everything wrapped up.”

“You said two weeks.”

“Yeah, well, you know the Army.”

“We miss you.” Rocking Zoey in her arms, Maggie added, “Thank goddess she’s finally asleep.”

“I love you. Gotta go.”

***

Jill was walking out of her classroom when she heard the news about former Senator James Hoffman’s suicide on live TV. She had no idea who he was. *Just another crackpot in the city.* She rushed to the teachers’ lounge, anyway, to see it for herself, caught the replay on the flatscreen. *Oh my god. It’s them. Three of the women I met last night, and that one is Brenda. Should I tell the authorities they must be the lesbian zombies Hoffman was talking about? No. They’ll think I’m crazy like the guy who shot himself.*

She had to consider the facts and what was good for Betsy. Number 1. Whatever was in that Kool-Aid completely cured Betsy. Number 2. If they’re zombies, they sure aren’t like the ones in the movies. They’re the nicest women I’ve ever met. Number 3. Jorge said I’d have to live with them to understand them. That would be nice. I’m barely getting by on my teacher’s salary. Number 4. Betsy would be so happy because she would have a friend her age. She couldn’t stop talking about Caroline all morning.

When I pick up Betsy from her special-ed school, I’ll tell her we're going to see Caroline. I'll call Jorge for a ride and tell him to call Brenda and tell her to order those pizzas. Maybe this meeting was ordained by God, or as they say, Goddess.

By the time Jill had picked up Betsy from her last day of school, nobody could believe what a perfect angel she was, told the principal that Betsy would not be coming back, and got home, Jorge was waiting for them. While on the road to Jackie's ranch, Jill asked Jorge about Caroline. "Which one of those girls are Caroline's mother?"

Glancing at Jill every now and then he told her the whole story. "Monica is the closest sister to her. Her real parents were killed in a horrific head-on car crash with a wrong-way motorhome. Caroline came out of the mangled car without a scratch."

"A miracle?"

"Before that, Caroline was a very sick girl, not long for this world, when Monica saved her, kinda like she did Betsy. Jackie O'Neal's high-powered lawyer, along with Caroline's wishes, convinced Illinois to give Monica custody of the orphan."

"Betsy sure does like Caroline."

"I think they'll be good for each other."

For the rest of the drive, Jill mulled over what all this meant. *It's hard to believe that an eight-year old could survive such a horrible accident. One thing is certain, though. Caroline is Betsy's only hope for a normal life.*

The Mercedes turned up the curved drive to the portico of The Ranch. It was time for her to turn on a happy face.

Once more, the sisters came out en masse to welcome Jill and Betsy. There were smiles galore, and Caroline and Betsy and Girlie Dog were soon headed to Caroline's room to watch Frozen on television.

As the sisters headed for the front door, the pizza delivery guy from Long Island Pizza pulled in with their order. Once inside, they rushed to the kitchen with their piping-hot bounty.

"So, Jill," Jackie said. "Another benefit of hanging around here is the fastest pizza delivery service in the country."

"Why is that?"

"Because I own all the Long Island Pizza stores in the eastern United States."

"Well, I must say, Jackie, that is impressive."

Caroline and Betsy smelled the pizza and came running down the stairs. They grabbed four slices and two sodas and, without so much as a thanks, ran back upstairs with Girlie Dog in close pursuit.

Jill watched the trio go. *Look at how happy they are.*

Melinda came in pushing a cart that contained beer, wine, sodas, and bottled water. *No Kool-Aid?*

As they ate their pizza and downed beverages, Carrie said, "So Jill, tell us about yourself. We already know you have a sweet little girl, but what would make Jill's life perfect?"

"Now that Betsy is a perfectly normal nine-year-old girl, all I have to worry about is uterine cancer."

Brenda said, "Join our Sisterhood and that problem will go away."

Jill examined her Coke and wondered what was in it? Then: "I don't understand Sisterhood. Does it have anything to do with the lesbian zombies that Hoffman guy was talking about?"

Brenda stood. "Sisters, I'm going to show Jill the Crystal Shrine, and while we're gone, do what you all do best. Get naked and jump in the hot tub."

The girls giggled and squealed as they stripped to the buff and headed out to the pool deck where the hot tub was set among a forest of potted ferns.

"Well," Jill breathed. "That is certainly interesting."

"Come with me," Brenda said. "We can join them later."

Walking out to the Crystal Shrine, thoughts ran through Jill's mind. *I guess they're all lesbians but they seem like normal women. Not zombies.*

"We're like all other women except in one way."

"You're lesbians?"

"No, Jill, that's not it. All women have lesbian tendencies, more emotional than physical. The late Senator Hoffman was right, though. We are zombies."

"Come on. You don't look like zombies."

"Fact and fiction are two different things, Jill. I'm the original Haitian lesbian zombie."

"Are you going to take over the world...like that crazy man said?"

"We have several goals. But first, there are advantages to being a lesbian zombie. For example, you harbor dark thoughts about Betsy's father, but you can't bring yourself to kill him. Still, you'd like to see him hanged, or gutted, or set on fire."

Jill stopped walking. Her expression was wide-eyed terror. "Brenda, how can you possibly know that?"

Brenda turned back to face her. "I can read your mind. It's one of the advantages I mentioned earlier. So I know you may be a mild-mannered school teacher, but deep down in your soul, you have homicidal thoughts."

"Please don't tell the other girls."

"Honey, some of the sisters have killed a man who'd done them wrong, but we never kill women. So you could be right at home here. Besides, from seeing your memories, Jerry Henderson has it coming. He got you pregnant, abandoned you, and wouldn't pay his child support."

"He made me feel like the scum of the earth."

"Honey, men have shit on women since time immemorial. Even cavemen are depicted dragging women by the hair, club in hand. Don't you think it's about time we turn the tables on them?"

"How many men have you killed?"

"Doesn't matter, but the number is going to climb."

After giving Jill a tour of the Crystal Shrine and telling her about Goddess *Loa,* Brenda popped the question. "Jill, it's time for the moment of truth. Are you with us, or do you want Jorge to take you and Betsy back home? If you choose to leave, however, Betsy will revert back to her autistic self and you will die of cancer. Now you wouldn't want that to happen, right?"

Jill shuddered. "What do I have to do...you know, to become a l-lesbian zombie?"

"It starts with a kiss, then you have to give yourself completely to the Sisterhood. Preferably in the hot tub."

"Will it hurt?"

"It's a lot of fun, really."

"Then kiss me."

Brenda embraced Jill and gave her a full-on, open-mouthed kiss with a lot of tongue and passion then, with one final lick to her upper lip, released her.

Jill gasped. "That's the best anyone has ever kissed me." The thought of all those naked women in the hot tub not only interested her now, joining them became a sudden need that welled up deep inside where her hottest fantasies had lain in wait to be awakened. She took Brenda's hand. "Let's go. I want to meet my new sisters right away."

They ran to the hot tub, stripped off their clothes, and jumped into the bubbly waters of paradise. The inhabitants were thrilled and frolicked around Jill with welcoming affection.

Monica said, "Jill, look at this." She picked up the remote and pointed it at the flatscreen mounted on the wall under the eave. The image showed Caroline and Betsy asleep on Caroline's bed with Girlie Dog cuddled between them.

"That's so cute." The scene made Jill cry.

It was then that the sisters embraced her and began her transition into the Sisterhood. Chloe dipped under the bubbling surface, and the girls leaned Jill against the edge and spread her legs. Jill felt the tenderness that only a woman's mouth and tongue could apply to her lips down there. It didn't take long for the starry heavens above to blur in a wave of carnal delight. At that moment, something changed inside her body, a freshening, a tightening, a strengthening of her limbs and core. She now knew she was a lesbian zombie.

Chloe surfaced, and as water ran down her face, she kissed a thoroughly satisfied Jill. "And that's how we play submarine."

Chapter Fourteen

Over at KOMA LTD., Alfons was still pissed off at the thought of Brenda and the Sisterhood commandeering his yacht, even temporarily.

Monica came by to check on his progress. He was on the phone, so she waited in the doorway behind him.

"Oceanwide Shipping? All right. I want to ship my yacht to Athens, and it better not get a single scratch."

Monica knew Alfons really loved that boat.

"Yes, it can be sailed there, but I don't want to put all those hours on my engines."

She listened to the one-sided conversation and stifled a laugh.

"That's right. Do you know how much those engines cost? I'd rather you wear out your engines....I didn't ask you what it'll cost because I don't give a shit. Besides, if you try to screw me, I'll buy your whole damn company and fire everybody's asses, starting with yours."

Monica stepped up. "Alfons, give me the phone."

"What? Why?"

"Because you sound like a jackass. Now give it to me."

With a groan, he gave her the phone. "His name is Tomas. Maybe you'll have better luck with the idiot."

She pushed the phone's mouthpiece against her hip so Tomas couldn't hear what she said to Alfons. "Be a good boy and I will reward you when I am through here."

"It better be a damn good reward."

Talking to Tomas, she said, "Send KOMA the invoice. He will pay it, no problem."

Tomas got off track. "Are you from Haiti?"

"Yes. Why?"

"You have a beautiful accent."

"Thank you, Tomas. I will e-mail you the information."

"It was nice talking to you."

"Yes, it was nice talking to you too. Have a great day." She hung up the phone. "Alfons, if you just be nice you can get whatever you want a lot quicker than being a dick. Besides, nobody is going to wreck your precious boat."

"It's a yacht...not a boat."

"Calm down, I get it."

"I hope so. Now come here and bend over the desk."

Monica did as she was told, it was that game again, and now minus her Blooms Midi Skirt, her panties came off next.

"Hey, what's your cell phone doing in here?"

"It is a long story."

After he set it on the desk with her panties, he put the meat to his favorite black woman. She wasn't thinking about his grunting with each thrust. She was thinking about how to break the news to him about Brenda's other demand, an all-girl crew to pilot the boat from Greece.

I better call it a yacht so he does not get mad again.

While Alfons humped away, Monica's cell began to vibrate from her panties, an arm's reach away. It was Brenda's ringtone. She reached for the phone, but it was hard to grab because her whole body was bumping around. Finally, on her elbows, she put the cell up to her ear. "I am kinda busy right now."

"So how's everything going with the boat?"

Monica gasped. "Now is...not a good time."

"What's all that bumping and grunting I hear on my end? Are you breathing hard?"

"Alfons is getting his reward for letting us use his boat."

"Yacht, dammit," he yelled through gritted teeth.

"I know what you two are doing." Brenda laughed. "Tell him to hurry up."

"Brenda says for you to hurry up, Alfons."

His grunts of lust became groans of frustration. "Damn it. I can't screw while she's listening." After one last thrust, he gave up in disgust. *Why the hell couldn't she have waited thirty more seconds before calling?*

"I will call you back." Monica hung up, held her position

over the desk, and wiggled her ass. "You could have pretended it was a threesome."

"You know I don't...prefer white girls." Breathing hard and sweating, he stood up straight and put his tool away. "What did your Queen want this time?"

"She wants an all-girl crew to pilot your yacht."

"I'm surprised she doesn't want to fly my balls from the masthead." He spanked her bare butt. "But I know just the crew she's looking for. I've used them before. Tell Brenda I have no problem with her request. Now get dressed."

Monica felt empathetic for Alfons and remained bent over the desk.

"What are you doing?"

"You didn't finish so I thought you might want to give it another try."

"Not now. We'll do it again...maybe at Black Friday number 2. Now scat. I have a yacht to prepare for shipping."

***

Back at The Ranch, Brenda was looking around for Chloe to fill her in on what Jackie had in mind for Black Friday 2. She couldn't find her. Jackie was sitting next to the pool with Melinda, who was manicuring Jill's fingernails.

"Has anyone seen Chloe?"

"She and Donna went to Hoffman's funeral. I told Jorge to drive them."

A perturbed Brenda looked at Jackie. "I would have gone with them but they never asked."

"Brenda, Donna was probably afraid that you would have asked his parents to pay for the cost of the bullet."

This brought a laugh from Melinda and Jill.

About that time, Brenda got splashed with water as Caroline, Betsy, and Girlie Dog jumped into the pool. "Girls, we don't mind if you play in the pool, but be considerate of others, and for goddess's sake, get Girlie Dog out of there."

Girlie Dog climbed out on her own and made a beeline for what was left of Jill's ham sandwich, devouring it in two bites then shook the water off her body, splattering dog water all over

Brenda. "Come on, girls. You see what happens when you let the dog in the pool?"

In unison, Betsy and Caroline laughingly said, "We're sorry."

***

Over at New York City's Marble Cemetery, the service for the late Senator James Hoffman was just breaking up. The pond-side gravesite under a shady oak was too good a resting place for him. Donna, who felt some sorrow for James' demise, stood by the coffin still resting on a bier. After the mourners had left, she placed a red rose on the coffin and whispered, "You dumb bastard." As she and Chloe turned to leave, they were confronted by three men dressed in black suits.

"Too bad, isn't it, ladies? Poor James. Got suckered into killing himself by a lesbian zombie. You two bitches, or should I say lesbian zombies, are coming with us."

"They're not going anywhere with you yay-hoos." That came from Jorge standing behind them. He brandished an Army Colt .45, the business end pointed straight at the men in black. "Which one of you jerks wants to die first? Let's see a show of hands."

Donna stepped back to stand beside Jorge. "Just let them go. We don't want any trouble."

"I don't know, Donna. I was looking forward to killing them right here and now. Plus it would save on their burial costs since they're already at the cemetery."

One of the three, a big bruiser, six-foot-four and 245 pounds, puffed out his chest. "You ain't got the guts to shoot anyone. You're just a lousy chauffeur." He charged Jorge, who promptly shot him in both knees. The fight instantly bled from the bad guy. He was now busy rolling in the grass and screaming in pain.

The other two goons reached under their coats for their guns.

"Uh, uh." Jorge had the drop on them. "Take your guns out with your left hands and toss them on the ground."

After they'd finished doing as ordered, one of them got cocky. "You're gonna regret this, mister."

"I'm shakin' all over, now walk backwards until you get to the coffin."

They did as instructed, hands up, but both looked like they

might leap for their guns at any moment.

"Good boys. Turn around. Face the coffin. Do it now."

The bad guys exchanged conspiratorial glances but decided to comply.

"See how easy it was to live another minute?" Jorge glanced at Mister Kneecap, still moaning and hugging his knees in a fetal position. His black pants were a red-bloody mess. "If you boys move, you're never gonna see your mommas again."

They didn't move.

Jorge stalked to the bleeder, got to him just as he pulled his gun, and stomped on his right arm, forcing him to drop the weapon. "You don't learn too good, buddy." He kicked him in the left knee, which solicited another painful scream, and then Jorge picked up the dropped gun, threw it into the pond and did the same with the other two guns.

Glancing back at Donna and Chloe, he said, "Go back to the car, girls."

"Don't shoot them," Donna said. "Brenda won't like that."

"These butt-wipes got it coming, but unfortunately I have better use for them alive, well, at least one of them."

The girls sprinted toward the limo parked in the lane.

"Now you boneheads listen up. First one to give me the name of your boss lives."

All three remained silent.

"Smart move." Jorge stuffed his gun behind his belt. "Tell your boss to leave the lesbian zombies alone or he'll wind up like this piece of shit wallowing on the grass. Oh yeah. Better call him an ambulance before he bleeds to death. Now, before I go, you boys owe me a thank you."

"Are you nuts?" Kneecap shouted. "You shot me."

"Get one thing straight. I saved your lives today. Those two girls would've torn off your arms and beat you to death with them. Fools." Jorge turned his back on them and trounced back to the limo.

On the road back to The Ranch, Chloe and Donna hugged each other in the rear seat. Both were in a state of shock. Donna said, "How did they know who we were?"

"I don't know, girls."

Chloe moved to the forward cabin seat and patted Jorge on

the shoulder. "Thank you."

"No problem. Just doing my job. However, if I hadn't been there, Goddess only knows what would have happened to those guys. The Sisterhood would've had a hard time explaining the bloodbath to law enforcement."

"What can we do to repay you?" Donna cooed.

"A blowjob would be nice, you two taking turns would be nicer. Oh, and naked. You gotta be naked."

"We'll take care of you tonight, won't we, Chloe?"

Chloe scowled. "ick."

"Just kidding, girls. Somebody better call Brenda."

***

Brenda had just gotten showered and dressed when her cell rang and Donna relayed all that had happened at the cemetery. To say Brenda was upset would have been putting it mildly. She stormed downstairs and called the sisters together. "There'll be a war council meeting when Donna and Chloe get back." With that said, she rushed out to commune with *Loa* in the Crystal Shrine, leaving the sisters dumbfounded.

Sitting in her throne formed in the branches of the Sister Tree of Life, Brenda closed her eyes. "Loa, this is an emergency." No ethereal voice came into her mind. There was a traitor in their midst, someone who had ratted out the Sisterhood and sent goons to do their bidding. She picked at her fingernails and prayed that none of her sisters had committed such an offense.

Just then, Betsy and Caroline came running in with Girlie Dog, all playing a game of tag, running around the tree and the pit and scuffing up the gold and red floor tiles. Girlie Dog won every game. Brenda waited and waited but no Loa. She was about to tell the kids to leave, thinking they were the reason Loa hadn't spoken to her, when she heard Loa's voice: *"Let them play. I will only tell you this, my sweet Brenda. There are no traitors in the Sisterhood. No infiltrators either, so put these suspicions out of your mind. Jorge will take care of the problem."*

"How?"

Loa didn't answer.

Walking back into the house, she found Donna and Chloe and

the rest of the sisters in the sitting room, waiting in silence for her to start the meeting.

Brenda stood where she could see all the sisters. “I think you all know three strangers attempted to kidnap two of us. Loa has said to me that the Sisterhood is innocent and have nothing to fear.”

“Who would do such a thing?” Jackie asked.

“I don’t know and Loa didn’t say, only that Jorge would take care of the problem.”

“Okay. Let’s talk about the Black Friday Party.”

Jill raised her hand. “What can I do to help?”

“You’ll wander around the party and entertain the men as you see fit.”

“What about Betsy and Caroline?”

“They’ll be on a sleepover with Maggie and Zoey.”

The sisters sat around for three hours, drinking and trying to figure out who knew about them and came up with one possibility: the threat had something to do with the late James Hoffman.

Jackie saw an opening. “Sisters, it’s now 8:15. I’ve made reservations at a new seafood restaurant in Montauk. Jorge will drive us in the limo. He’s on his way here as I speak.”

The door bell rang.

“Melinda, would you get the door?”

“We’ll get it, Betsy sang. “Come on, Caroline.” They took off running like a shot.

“Don’t those two ever walk anywhere?”

“No. They don’t,” Lilly put in. “Their energy is boundless.”

The words were hardly out of her mouth when the girls walked back in, looking white and visibly upset like they were about to cry. “Jackie, a policeman is at the door. Something happened to Jorge.”

Jackie’s heart jolted as she stood. “I’ll get it. He probably got stopped for some minor infraction. I’m friends with the Chief of Police. I’ll clear it up in no time.”

In unison the girls said, “No. We read his mind. Something bad happened.”

Jackie walked into the room with Police Chief Dan Baker. “Girls, go upstairs and play...and take Girlie Dog with you.”

“Ah...we never get to hear nothing.”

"No lip," Monica said.

They walked slowly up the stairs with Girlie Dog behind them, her tail bent down and not wagging, as if she too knew something was wrong.

Jackie said, "Chief, you have the floor," and then stood next to Brenda to hold her hand. She remembered a party before she was a lesbian zombie. She had gotten a little tipsy, and since Dan Baker was the last one there, she did him right on the floor. In this moment, she was still admiring his six-foot physique and bulging muscles, the deepest eyes she'd ever seen, and she was reading his mind.

God I would love to bang her again. I wish I didn't have bad news for her now.

"Dan, we're all adults here. Give us the bad news."

He cleared his throat. "One of our highway patrol officers found a limo in a rest area. Your limo. Skid marks indicate it had been run off the road."

"Oh no," Brenda said.

"The car had bullet holes in the doors and fenders, and the windshield had been shot up. There was blood on the driver's seat. Shell casings from a .45 caliber military-grade sidearm littered the front seat. About twenty feet away, we found a lot more blood, a location where we believe one of the shooters stood. The bullet trajectories traced from the car to that blood pool and from two other directions, indicating three shooters. Also we found a blood trail indicating someone had dragged the wounded shooter to a getaway car, where the trail ended. The ground was littered with M-16 cartridges."

"What about Jorge?" Jackie shouted. "I don't care if some criminal took several rounds from Jorge's gun. I hope the guy is dead. Get to the point about Jorge."

"Jackie, he's missing. We don't know if he's alive or dead, but we're sure he's injured."

Caroline had been listening from the top of the stairs. "He's not dead," she yelled. "Loa would have told me."

"Caroline," Monica said firmly. "Go to your room now, and stay there...and close the door."

"Who is *Loa*?" the Chief asked.

Brenda jumped in. "Some wonder-woman type she saw on

the Kids Movie Network, no doubt."

As the Chief began to speak again, his voice was interrupted by the thud of Caroline's door being slammed.

"I can't blame the little girl," Dan said. "She's obviously very fond of Jorge. Jackie, do you know if he had any enemies who would want to do him harm?"

"No. There was an incident after the Senator's funeral, but we don't know who was responsible for accosting two of our girls."

"This looks like a hit job, but we don't think it's gang related. Banger punks don't go around with M-16s. Plus the shooters had set up a military-style crossfire."

As the Chief went on about military tactics, Jackie was thinking about General Taylor's aide-de-camp Colonel Wesley Miller. Shit. The General had warned the Sisterhood that both Wes and James were a threat. *Maybe he had something to do with the attack on Jorge.*

When the Chief was through telling the sisters everything he knew as of right now, he said, "I assure you I'll keep you updated if anything new comes into my office. The FBI has been called on to help with the investigation. I'll show myself out." Then he left.

"Sisters..." Jackie said. "I've known Jorge since he came to the US five years ago from Colombia. He'd been a hitman for the cartel, one tough son of a bitch, until he had a change of heart after he shot a mother and baby. They lived, and as he'd promised God, he fled that life of violence. He worked hard to earn his US citizenship. I love him like a son. We'll get him back alive, and goddess damn it, if we can't, somebody is going to pay in blood. Make that a lot of blood."

Brenda stood. "Let's hope we get a ransom call in the next two days. That way we'll know who to kill."

Chapter Fifteen

Eleven hours later, Wes drove his rental car to the main gate to Fort Huachuca. The guard shack looked like a broken-down outhouse. There were no MPs around so he drove right through. At ten miles an hour, he checked out the buildings on either side of the road, dilapidated barracks mostly, and a leaning water tower that read *HUACH...* to overlook the blight left by the Army's neglect.

This can't possibly be where those six Rangers were headed.

As he drove through the ruins, he came to an array of buildings that didn't look in such decay, administration, mess hall, latrines...but equally abandoned.

He turned in and parked in a vacant lot choked with tumbleweeds then stalked into the largest building, which turned out to be a mistake.

Four heavily armed soldiers surrounded him in the lobby. Their fatigues showed no indication of unit or rank. A knot gripped his throat. "Easy, boys. I'm Colonel Wesley Miller from headquarters. What's going on here?"

The soldiers remained mute. Another unidentifiable man walked in, and the soldiers made way as he approached the Colonel and saluted. "Captain Robert Johnson, sir. I'm afraid you'll have to leave the area immediately."

The Colonel thrust back his shoulders. "You see these eagles? I outrank all of you, so I give the orders. What's going on at this installation?"

"I'm not at liberty to say, sir. My men will show you out."

"I am *not* going anywhere until you tell me what's going on. Or would you rather I call in the Military Police and order your asses arrested?"

"Colonel, with all due respect, you don't have the need to know, and you don't have the necessary security clearance to any information. I'd tell you the same thing if you were wearing four stars on your shoulders. You can't order me to break the law of Article 47 of the UCMJ, the Uniform Code of Military Justice."

"God damn it. You will fess up, Captain."

"Negative, sir. If you don't leave, I'll report your conduct to General Lawrence Taylor at headquarters. Maybe you know him. Perhaps I should get the General on the line and report you right now."

That suggestion tightened a knot in the Colonel's throat, like a noose, only tighter. "No. that's not necessary, Captain."

"Sergeant-Major Henry, show the Colonel back to his car and make sure he gets safely off the base."

"It will be my pleasure, sir." He set his hand on his holstered sidearm. "You first, Colonel."

Minutes later, and driving away from Ft. Huachuca at a high rate of speed, Wes realized he'd made a mistake coming here. If word of this trip got back to Lawrence...*I'd be screwed.*

Damn it to hell. Maybe all I'd done was step in a pile of shit. The gall of that Captain to quote the UCMJ. He knew how to stomp on the balls of authority.

He decided to go back to D.C. with his tail tucked between his legs. Lynne would be happy. He'd tell her his hunch amounted to nothing and she'd say *I told you so, Wes,* followed by a condescending kiss.

Shit, shit, shit. I still don't know what Fox Trot Zero is all about.

***

In a motel room, somewhere far enough from the city center where traffic noise was minimal, Jorge regained consciousness.

His left leg burned from a superficial gunshot wound and his face felt like it had been used for a punching bag. He remembered two tough-guys taking turns with their fists. *Where the hell am I?* He looked around a dilapidated motel room, upturned mattress, frayed curtains closed, the chair he was tied to, and the goon standing guard. He remembered being run off the road, glass shattering in a hail of bullets. He'd pulled his Colt and drilled one of the shooters he saw standing in a headlight beam. *That guy must be dead. At least I'm alive, but these guys won't be around for long. They have no idea what and who will be coming after them.*

"Good," a goon said with a Mexican accent. "You are back. Maybe you talk now?"

"Fuck you." Jorge groaned. It hurt to talk.

"Then you are going to suffer more." The man was in his early thirties, bald, tattooed around the neck, pointy chin beard, and enough muscle to qualify as a professional WWE wrestler. "You know why you are still alive?"

"You love me?"

"You are not my type, hombre. Tell me what you know about lesbian zombies."

"Shouldn't you be home licking your boyfriend's popsicle?"

"You got a big mouth for a guy that will soon be dead."

"Do yourself a favor, Mack—"

"Louis." He leaned to Jorge's face. "My name is Louis. Look good at the last Louis you will see on this earth."

"Cut me loose, Louis, and my friends may forget your foolishness."

Louis slammed a fist into Jorge's jaw.

He spit blood, saw stars. "I'm going to kill you for that."

"Some high-up people want to talk to you. They will be here soon. I suggest you tell me what I want to know. They will not be so gentle with you."

"I'm shaking all over, can't you tell?"

"I go now, take a piss. I will be back. Don't run off."

"I'll be right here waiting for your friends."

Watching Louis go into the bathroom, Jorge knew he could escape at any time, however, he was interested in Louis's friends. Probably the same goons at the funeral. He heard piddling in the toilet. "You want to know about zombies..." He worked loose the rope on his arms. "You're going to meet the real ones very soon."

Louis returned, zipping his zipper. "While I was taking a leak, I thought how impatient I am for information about your zombie friends. My friends are late in coming, so I will not be so nice no more." He took out wire cutters with jaws big enough to cut through cable. "Maybe a few missing fingers will convince you to talk."

Jorge cringed. "Let's just wait for your friends."

"I don't think so." He grinned a toothy grin. "I think that I will start with your trigger finger, the one you used to kill a really good Christian friend of mine last night. We buried him out back to keep away the smell."

Jorge smiled. "Hey, that's good news."

Louis approached with the cutters, snapping the jaws.

In a split second, Jorge ripped his arms from the ropes and grabbed Louis by the throat. "Surprise." He squeezed tighter and tighter. As Louis struggled for breath, Jorge lectured him. "I have the strength of ten men, you fool, but I'm not nearly as powerful as the lesbian zombies you're so interested in."

Louis kicked his feet, dropped the cutters, and with his hands, tried to pull Jorge's death grip from his throat. His lips were turning blue and his bulging eyes leaked blood.

"I'll just hang out here and wait for your friends."

Louis quit kicking. Jorge let go and he fell in a heap to the shag carpet.

Out front, car doors opened and closed. Jorge frisked the dead goon and came up with his gun, a nifty Glock, probably stollen. The doorknob rattled. He ducked behind the door. When it opened he let three men walk in before he grabbed the last guy, a goon with dreadlocks, and now with a gun to his head.

Jorge kicked the door closed. "Hello, gentlemen."

They turned around. One wore a three-piece suit and a felt hat. The other wore a wife-beater T and jeans. They all looked Mexican and shocked to high heaven.

"It's time we had us a little talk." Jorge wagged the gun at them. "If you've got one of these, drop it on the floor. No funny stuff or this guy goes back to Mexico in a pine box."

"Cuba," Felt Hat said. "You don't know who you are messing with."

Guns hit the carpet then wife-beater noticed his dead buddy on the floor. "Louis...you killed Louis?"

"And I'll dish out the same to you guys if you don't tell me who you are and why you're interested in my girls."

Felt Hat did the talking. "Your girls, hell? They are lesbian zombies."

"What's your beef with them?"

"They killed our golden goose in Congress."

"Hoffman?"

Felt Hat nodded. "Si. We had him in our pocket."

Jorge shoved Dreadlocks across the small room to stand with his friends. "Who's we?"

"The Cuban Mafia. We bribed him, bought him off, now he is dead and of no more use to us, thanks to your lesbian zombies."

"He shot himself."

"Hoffman warned us about them."

"He warned everybody that would listen, and trust me, he was right, but you boys don't want to tangle with those girls. Go get yourself another congressman. You'll live longer."

The Cuban gangsters shared nervous glances between themselves and dead Louis.

"Now get outta here." Jorge opened the door.

Wife Beater shouldered Louis and stepped outside.

Felt Hat remained defiant. "This is not over, gringo."

"It better be, for your sake."

The mafia thugs filed out.

Jorge collected their dropped guns and spotted a flyer on the floor...from a very familiar church. "Son of a bitch."

He exited through the back door.

***

Back at the Sisterhood's headquarters, the sisters were in a state of mourning over Jorge. They were certain that he was no longer among the living. With his zombie strength, he would have freed himself a long time ago, if he could.

As the grandfather clock in the hallway rang out the hour nine times, there was a hard knock at the front door. No one wanted to answer it, so Betsy and Caroline did the now-dreaded honor. The other sisters sat around mute, the only sound coming from the wooden chair that Donna was rocking.

A sudden and gleeful cry came from the girls. They ran into the living room, jumping and skipping. "He's here."

In walked a very tired looking Jorge. Each member of the Sisterhood rushed to him, all hugging and kissing and laughing with joy.

Brenda greeted him last. “What the hell happened?”

“It’s a long story.”

“How did you get away?”

“Another long story. They weren’t very smart.”

“Who?”

“The Cuban Mafia.”

Jackie gasped. “Oh, my Goddess. Why did they target us?”

“Looking for payback...on account of their dealings with Hoffman.” He sent Brenda a glum expression. “But their influence in America goes deeper than that.”

She frowned. “The White House?”

After taking a folded paper from his pocket, he handed it to Brenda. “Worse.”

When she examined it, her eyes narrowed. “I’ll be damned.”

Chloe asked, “What is it?”

“A flyer...from...The Church of the Risen Jesus.”

“No shit.”

Jorge sat in a chair. “I found it on the floor of the motel room. Could be the Cubans are using the church as a home base.”

Jackie looked over Brenda’s shoulder. “Or maybe they simply went to church there. Cubans are very religious.”

Brenda sighed. “It seems the Reverends LeRoy and Janice Parker may have abandoned our network, and to think that I cut them some slack. Maybe I’ll give them a chance to redeem themselves, then again, maybe not.”

Maria had a better idea. “I vote to kill ‘em.”

“So do I,” Donna chimed in. “Maria and I were the ones who had to have a foursome with those two pigs. Plus, Brenda, they kidnapped Jorge. For crying out loud, what do you want to do, pin a medal on them?”

“We have to find out what may have turned them against us, but don’t forget, Janice is our sister, and we don’t kill women for any reason. LeRoy on the other hand, he’s fair game. Now let’s hit the sack. This has been one tiring day.”

Caroline tromped around, all proud with her nose in the air. “I told you Jorge wasn’t dead.”

A joyous Brenda lifted her up and swung her around. “Yes you did, little girl, just like you said about Donna.”

Jill picked up Betsy, and both girls were swung around. They giggled and yelled with delight, and all the noise brought a revived and happy Girlie Dog downstairs.

All was back to normal at The Ranch.

***

At the Church of the Risen Jesus, among the Bibles and hymnals scattered about, Reverends Leroy and Janice were going at it hot and heavy in the pews. Thanks to the lesbian zombies, he was a sex-crazed maniac, and it was up to Janice to keep him satisfied, even though she was now a lesbian and rather disgusted by his amorous adventures between her legs.

The phone in the church office was ringing off the hook, but he wouldn't let anything interrupt them. This left the caller, Alejandro Diaz, AKA Felt Hat, no choice but to leave a message. *"I have lost two men, and one wounded with no knees. The lesbians have a worthy protector. After much deliberation, we have decided to go back to Cuba where it is much safer to conduct our mafia businesses. We thank you for the sanctuary you have provided during our visit to your country. Holy Mary Mother of God, may the lesbian zombies have mercy on the world."*

Chapter Sixteen

The sisters were all up and finishing brunch when Brenda and Jackie came down the stairs. Jill was in the library with Caroline and Betsy, homeschooling them temporarily. Jorge was up in a spare room, sleeping. Jackie had bandaged his leg wound and told him to stay off his feet for a couple of days.

The doorbell rang.

Monica looked out the window and saw a police cruiser in the drive. "Jackie, that cop is back. Do you want me to let him in?"

"I'll talk to him." At the door, she turned back to her sisters. "Everybody make yourselves scarce." She opened the door to Chief Baker. "Good morning, Dan. Come in. Care for a cup of coffee?"

He stepped into the foyer, holding his hat. "No coffee for me, thanks." He took a long breath then: "I'm sorry to report, we haven't found a trace of Jorge. We've got ten officers, two detectives, and an FBI agent on the case, but unfortunately—"

"Dan, I should have called you...Jorge is upstairs resting right now."

"What?" Dan scowled.

"He escaped from his captors last night."

Dan looked toward the staircase. "I need to speak with him."

"Sorry, Dan. He was wounded. I patched him up and don't want him on his feet just yet."

He looked at his hat. "Tomorrow then?" His eyes rose to Jackie's face. "I'm certainly happy that he's okay, but I've got a job to do. Can you bring him to my office, say 10am? I'll have the DA there."

"Fine. Then I'll bring my attorney."

His brows furrowed, puzzled. "Jorge won't need an attorney.

He was the injured party. We only need to know what happened. What are you afraid of?"

"Two men are dead, Dan."

"Two? We don't have any bodies."

"You may find them eventually. Look. I don't want some hotshot detective charging Jorge with murder, making it look like it was all his fault. The DA might want a feather in his cap with another conviction. Jorge killed them in self defense. Wouldn't want you guys to forget he's the innocent party."

"Jackie...I assure you—"

"It wasn't the Saint Valentine's Day Massacre. He barely escaped with his life. If the DA even smells like he might press charges...I'll...I'll get him busted back down to past-due parking tickets. I'll—"

"Okay. Okay, Jackie. Relax. Bring your lawyer."

"He's not just any two-bit lawyer, either. We're talking Shelton Abernathy, the retired judge of the United States Supreme Court. He'll smoke your DA."

Dan was speechless, his cheeks puffed out like he might pop.

She glared at him. "Don't take this personally, Dan. I'll always cherish the time we spent on the rug, but we're talking about Jorge, here. He's kin to me."

"I get it, Jackie. See you tomorrow." He mashed his hat back on, turned a military about-face, and fled.

She watched through the window as a thoroughly pissed off Chief Baker got into his squad car and backed up at a fast clip, nearly running over a mother duck and her five ducklings crossing the road.

Brenda strode up behind her. "Jackie, are you okay?"

"No, damn it. I'm pissed. The meeting tomorrow won't last more than fifteen minutes. It's a waste of time."

"Then this Jorge debacle will die out, thanks to you."

She turned from the window. "I need coffee."

***

Back at the Church of the Risen Jesus, under the arched ceiling and stained glass windows, Leroy and Janice were exhausted. LeRoy's lollipop was black and blue, and Janice walked with a limp to the church office. Johnson and Johnson didn't make a bandage big enough to mend her wounded bun.

The recorded message Alejandro Diaz left made them forget about their aches and pains. She glared at her oversexed husband. "How did the Cuban Mafia know about the lesbian zombies?"

"Hoffman told them," LeRoy replied, still holding himself gingerly through the front of his pants.

"But why are his men dead and wounded? There must've been a confrontation, probably with Jorge, the way it sounds." She glared at LeRoy accusingly. "What did you do?"

He limped to his desk. "I may have told them about Donna and Maria..." He plopped his fat butt down in his chair. "That they'd probably be at the funeral."

"You ratted out my sisters to the mob? How stupid can you be?"

"Look what they did to me. Those bitches made my dick the most important thing in my life. I can't sleep. I can't eat. All I want to do is fornicate and masturbate. The Cubans wanted the same thing as me, a little vengeance, so I helped them out. What's wrong with that?"

"Vengeance is mine, sayeth the Lord. You fool. If Brenda puts two and two together, we're in big trouble."

LeRoy grumped. "You may have been suckered into the Sisterhood, but I never bought into their Goddess Loa, Lord Of All, crap. And I'm sick of throwing our money at their LZ Foundation. What's in it for us? Not a damn thing. It's all Brenda's money now."

"She's our Queen, LeRoy."

"Your queen, Janice. Not mine."

"Damn. Don't you see? She's not going to be happy with us."

LeRoy huffed. "How can she find out we tipped off the mafia?"

"You tipped them off, LeRoy. Not me."

"There's nothing to tie us to them. We've got nothing to worry about. Now come over here and sit on my Snickers." He had it out, wagging it around.

"Screw you, LeRoy."

"Yeah. That's the spirit."

"I'm a lesbian. I like being a lesbian. It's a big improvement over having a fat slug like you on top of me."

"Get over here, anyway. I didn't say you had to enjoy it."

What a prick. She should pay Brenda a visit and tell her the truth. *I have to start thinking of self-preservation. She could get rid of LeRoy then I can be with any woman I want,* which was much more pleasurable then being prostrate with a smelly man who loves his dick more than life itself. But still, she did enjoy the money and lifestyle he afforded her.

"Well?" LeRoy bellowed. "Are you coming or do I have to do it myself?"

I should take him with me to The Ranch and put a bullet in his head right in front of the Sisterhood...prove my loyalty...but then there's the money and lifestyle. Ah, hell with it. "I'm coming, LeRoy."

***

While things had turned back to happy times at The Ranch, the same couldn't be said for Robert, General Taylor, or Colonel Wes Miller, or for that matter, Alfons Duda. From the harbor tower, he was watching his yacht being loaded on a ship transporter. *They better not scratch it. I'll sail it back to my dock and to hell with the Sisterhood.*

Shit. Who am I kidding? I'm not going to cross Monica. I can replace a yacht but not my head if she decided to rip it off for disobedience. Goddammit.

The transport ballasts were filled with water, sinking the deck below the surface, and his yacht, *Three Sheets to the Wind*, was floated in place above the deck. Giant cradles cradled the hull, and with a blast of noise and bubbles, the deck rose with the yacht now securely in place.

Good. Now I can go back to work.

***

As Robert was busy setting up the satellite tracking so he and his team could watch the action on the ground in Baddish, he got a call on the hotline from General Taylor.

"Captain Johnson, we have to solve the Colonel Miller problem before he figures out what we're doing for the Sisterhood.

If I let him in on Fox Trot Zero and deploy him with our boys when they hit the sand, will you take him into your confidence?"

Robert considered the complexities of a rogue Colonel sniffing around. The incursion team would be far from the Sisterhood in the village, providing security against Taliban insurgents and cover-fire for the operation, if needed... "If we can keep him on a need-to-know basis, the secrecy of our mission could be maintained. He could spearhead any battle that may arise along the perimeter, however, if he enters Baddish, I'll have to kill him, make it look like he was killed in action."

"He's not to die, Robert. No matter what. That's an order. Hell. He saved my life twice, even took a bullet meant for me."

"Understood, sir, but I'm sure the Taliban won't be so sympathetic. Promote him to Brigadier General so he can direct security operations from behind the lines."

"I wish I could say that would work. Wesley Miller is a fighter. He'll never send his troops into battle without him leading the charge."

"I figured he was a hardnose that way."

Leaning back in his chair with the U.S. Army logo embossed in the leather, he made a final demand. "Keep him, safe, Robert. Watch his back with those satellites up there. I don't want him dying for Brenda's mission of revenge."

"Fox Trot Zero is not a babysitting service, sir."

"Do the best you can." The hotline went dead.

***

At 10am sharp, Jorge, Shelton Abernathy, and Jackie entered Chief Baker's office where Ben Baylor, the District Attorney of Long Island greeted them. Dan and Jackie exchanged challenging glances.

After everyone was seated at a conference table, Baker began. "Jackie, you were right. We discovered two bodies at a motel down by the tracks, both buried in shallow graves out back." He turned to Jorge. "You had a busy night, my friend."

Jorge grimaced. "They made the wrong choices in life, sir."

The DA spoke next. "The Chief tells me the event preceding the deaths appears to be a carjacking gone bad for the carjackers.

The question is, under the law, did your client have the right to kill them to protect his property, namely a limo from being stolen?"

Retired judge Shelton Abernathy tapped his pen on the table. "It wasn't a property crime. From what Jorge has told me, they attacked him, kidnapped him, and they were going to kill him. As his lawyer, I suggest self defense is viable in this case, under the law."

Baylor shifted some papers on the table. "I must say what an honor it is to be sitting in the same room with a great Supreme Court Justice." He singled out a document, held his index finger on it. "However, my office is ready to turn this case over to a Grand Jury for possible prosecution. Murder Two times Two." He slid the warrant toward the defense lawyer.

Abernathy ticked his tongue. "Ben, Ben, Ben. We can dispense with this case in five minutes, but first I need to remind you that I'm on the selection committee to find a replacement for Judge Greg Simpson who died suddenly of a massive heart attack."

"It was a terrible blow to the state of New York."

Abernathy grumped. "He was a prick. I never liked him, but I think you would be the right man to replace him."

The DA gasped. "I'm flabbergasted, sir, but—"

"I'd be happy to submit your name for recommendation, but first we have to put this sham of a case behind us."

A smiling Ben ran his hand through his red hair and looked the old lawyer in the eyes. "What case?" He withdrew the document and tore it in half. "I don't see a case in front of us."

Chief Baker rose from his chair. "That wraps things up here. Thanks for coming in, Jackie." He nodded to Jorge. "Stay out of trouble."

On the way back to The Ranch, a joyous Jorge felt relieved and happy at the same time, and he enjoyed driving the new replacement stretch limo that Jackie bought to replace the one that got the hell shot out of it. He was smiling and talking to himself. "This one is even better than the last one."

Jackie, from the plush back seat and surrounded by LED lighting and gold-embossed mirrors, called Brenda. The call went directly to voicemail, so she left a one-word message. "Done."

***

Colonel Wesley Miller was sitting at the dinner table, holding a bowl of mashed potatoes when the phone rang.

"Do you want me to get the phone, dear?"

"No, Lynne. I'll get it." He set the potatoes down and answered the phone. It was the General, which kicked up his heartbeat. "General?"

"Wes, I got a call from Captain Johnson in Arizona. He said you dropped by his base of operations. I guess you pissed him off."

"General, let me explain—"

"Wes, he wants you to join the mission."

"Mission, sir?"

"Fox Trot Zero."

Wes didn't know whether to jump for joy or shoot himself in the foot and get a medical deferment. Finally, the General was going to come clean. "What's it all about? Captain Johnson wouldn't tell me even though I outranked him."

"He was right not to brief you. I deliberately left you out of the loop, but now I need you to be in charge of the security forces that will provide cover for our medical people going into the village of Baddish in Pakistan. I want you to get on a flight back to Arizona. This time Captain Johnson will be expecting you. Don't be too hard on him, Wes. Remember, you were a lowly captain once yourself."

"Excuse me, General. Lynne looks worried. I need to tell her there's nothing to worry about." He muted the phone. "Honey, everything is fine. I'm getting a new assignment so I have to finish this call." He stood and moved to the living room.

A perturbed Lynne returned to her meal. How many times had she eaten alone because the Army interfered?

After about ten minutes, he returned and sat down and took hold of his fork. "Sorry about the interruption."

"Honey, you better tell me what's going on."

"It's nothing, really."

"Don't lie to me, Wes."

He set down his fork. "All right. I found out what Fox Trot Zero is all about."

"Is General Taylor in cahoots with the Russians or not?"

"Actually, no...not even close. Turns out there's a plague in Southern Pakistan that could destroy the entire population on Earth if it's not stopped. The World Health Organization is sending doctors in to vaccinate the people in a village there. I'll be in command of a unit of US forces supplying security for the operation."

She dropped her fork. "You're being deployed to a warzone again...a warzone with a deadly plague? I thought the General was your friend."

"He's making it worth my while. He sent in the paperwork to the Secretary of the Army promoting me to Brigadier General, and I won't be going anywhere near the plague. I've been ordered to Fort Huachuca for a complete briefing."

"What? You're going back to Arizona again?"

"In two hours. Military flight this time. So let's hurry up and finish dinner. I've got some serious packing to do."

***

The next day at Fort Huachuca, preparations were going pretty well, and then, as the door to Robert's control room opened, in walked Colonel Miller like he owned the place. Robert and his men were at work wiring up some communication surveillance electronics and didn't notice the full bird fly in, however, sentry First Lieutenant Gee did.

"Attention all ranks, officer in the building."

Robert's men turned around, dumfounded.

"What's he doing back here?" Sergeant-Major Henry asked. "How many times do we have to throw him out?"

"Relax, Tennyson." Robert approached the Colonel and saluted. "Boys, a-ten-hut."

Robert's men snapped to attention.

This show of respect made the Colonel's day. "Captain, let's get off on the right foot this time."

"Excellent idea, sir. It's good to have you aboard. And congratulations on your promotion."

"I'm not a general yet, Captain. How did you know?"

"Army scuttlebutt travels at the speed of light."

Miller sneered. "You didn't answer my question, Captain."

"The news came from headquarters in the Pentagon. General Taylor himself, sir."

"Captain, I'm not going to dress you down this time, but in the future, report any breach of security to me immediately."

"Yes, sir. Shall I remind the General, as well, sir?"

"Yeah. You do that." His military glare could have cut steel. "As you were, men. I want a complete briefing on the status of your operational readiness in one hour." He looked around the makeshift control center: boxes on boxes, crates on crates, dust on dust. "And somebody better clean up this shithole." Colonel Miller left the building.

Everyone looked pissed as a cat in a bag. First Lieutenant Barry Gee summed up what everyone was thinking. "What is that prick doing here, Captain?"

"Security measure. General's orders. We're stuck with him for the foreseeable future, boys, so we better get used to it."

***

Back at The Ranch, Brenda was holding court on the pool deck where the Sisterhood sat together in a semicircle. "Okay, sisters, Jackie and I have decided we'll have Black Friday 2 after we come back from Pakistan. I want Jill to know that Betsy and Caroline will be spending Friday night with Maggie and baby Zoey. As some of you may know, her husband, retired Army Captain Robert Johnson is in Arizona with men from his old unit, working on the Pakistan mission."

"What's the mission about, Brenda?" Carrie asked from her cross-legged position in the semicircle.

"We'll be going to Baddish to bring justice for sweet twelve-year-old Jasmine. She was raped by her husband and his brothers then murdered by the order of Mohammed Abdullah Abadi. He's the local Imam who calls the faithful to prayer five times a day, between stonings and beheadings. We're going to clear his schedule for him."

Chloe stood, thrust her fist in the air. "Let me kill the prick."

"Sorry, Chloe. Monica already has dibs on that honor."

Monica folded her arms and scowled. "He will suffer greatly. I promise you."

"Why her?" Carrie questioned the choice. "She seems too nice to kill anyone."

Maria laughed, chugged from a beer bottle, and pointed it at Monica. "We have no doubts, right, Brenda?"

"Right, Maria. I hadn't known her five minutes before she blew a would-be rapist's head off with a shotgun."

Monica chuckled. "I was a cranky old black woman back then."

Jill raised her hand. "Can I say something?"

"Of course. You have the floor, Jill."

She stood and looked over the sisters sitting on either side of her. "My mind has been grappling with...well, listening to the homicidal comments of my sisters, I'm worried that I'll let you all down by not being able to kill some guy, even if he has it coming."

Lilly handled the same worry with alcohol. She was a little more than tipsy when she stood, and she staggered toward Jill to give her a kiss, tripped over a squeaky toy Girlie Dog had left lying around.

Jill caught Lilly on the way down so she wouldn't crack her skull open, and then laid her gently on the pool deck. "You're sloshed."

"And you're a lesbian zombie now. In a heartbeat, without hesitation, you'll kill to protect the ones you love. That's what Jackie said." Lilly reached up, ran her fingers up Jill's leg and up under her dress. "Your ass feels really good. Let's get this meeting over... I want to do you."

Jill bent over and smiled at Lilly. "You can do me when you sober up."

Lilly didn't hear what Jill had said. She'd passed out on the deck. Girlie Dog pranced up, put her head under Lilly's dress, sniffed around then came out with her squeaky toy. That's when Jorge stepped through the back door with Betsy and Caroline, all back from the ice cream shop. Girlie Dog lost interest in the toy and ran to the trio, wagging her tail and begging for a treat.

Betsy set an open cup of vanilla ice cream down, as usual, and Girlie Dog went nuts, licking her treat so excitedly that the cup kept moving across the floor and she kept following it. Betsy and Caroline couldn't stop laughing.

As she watched her daughter's joy, Jill thought, thank you Goddess *Loa*. I'm content here with my sisters, and Betsy was so unhappy, now look at her. Drunk Lilly was right. *I'll kill to protect that little girl.*

***

Jerry Henderson, Betsy's biological father and deadbeat dad, had been desperately searching for his daughter since the special ed school told him she was no longer enrolled. She was no longer autistic. She was a normal little girl.

It was some kind of miracle that baffled them.

He'd kept tabs on Jill and Betsy, but always stayed far enough away that he'd never be caught for the cheapskate he was. Child support was not his responsibility. Jill was the dumb bitch who got pregnant. She's the one who created an autistic baby. It was her fault. Let her pay.

Now, some say he'd gotten religion, others thought his conscience had gotten the best of him, but he knew the real reason for his quest to find his daughter. She was no longer autistic. No longer a problem child. He could walk with her, run with her, color with her, sing with her; he could be a normal dad to a normal little girl.

But that goddamned Jill had moved. Took off to places unknown. Vanished, but now all that had changed. His search was about to come to an end.

It was the strangest thing, as if God himself had a hand in his quest. He'd gotten a sudden urge for ice cream and headed for Dairy Queen. That's where he saw Betsy, standing with, running with, and laughing with another little girl, normal as could be. His brain had a hard time understanding the transformation. He would have approached her then, snatched her up, and driven off, but there was an adult with them, a brick of a man who drove them away in a limo, so Jerry followed them to this remote estate overlooking the Sound.

He parked in a view area, backed in his gray Honda so it faced the estate, not like other cars parked facing the beach. From a good quarter mile away, he scanned the manicured grounds with binoculars, the ritzy two-story mansion, curved drive, fancy portico, and an elaborate greenhouse. *What is she doing in a place like this? Had a rich family adopted Betsy? Had Jill married into money?* He spotted the girls and a happy dog playing in the front yard. A gorgeous redhead and Jill joined them. He drew in a quick breath. *She looks better than ever.* But something smelled bad about this place, all these pretty women but no men since the limo had driven away. So now he would wait, and watch, and bide his time to be reunited with his daughter.

Betsy, daddy's back.

***

Since all lesbian zombies possessed strong premonition instincts, Jill, standing at the window overlooking the Sound, wondered why a cold chill crawled down her back. For some reason, Jerry's face flashed through her mind. She remembered how he'd scowled at her before he left, that anger in his eyes, the disgust on his curled upper lip. The memory was so vivid it caused her heart to lurch. It felt as if that same face was glaring at her now, lurking nearby, staring, plotting...

He'd said he couldn't stand being around Betsy anymore. She was too embarrassing. Then he said the cruelest words of all. *"It's your fault she's a worthless autistic child. You did this to her."*

The memory of his words made her want to vomit. Still, she wondered, *If I'm no longer the mousey young woman who'd taken hold of this arm and begged him to stay as tears ran down my cheeks, then why am I so terrified by my own thoughts?*

Brenda stepped up behind her and slipped her arms around her waist. Her flowery scent and gentle touch wasn't enough to quell Jill's near-crippling anxiety. "I'm sorry, Brenda. I must look a frightful mess."

"What's troubling you, honey?"

"It's him."

"Who?"

"That no good son of a bitch...Betsy's father. For some reason I can't get him out of my mind. He's had a grip on my heart for the last hour."

"It's all over now. Forget him."

"Betsy and I are so thankful for the Sisterhood, and Betsy loves Caroline and Girlie Dog." Fresh tears burned Jill's eyes.

"We're thankful Goddess *Loa* let us find you and Betsy." Brenda held Jill a little tighter.

"We're so happy, but I'm so afraid something will screw it up for us...like...what if he comes back?"

"He wouldn't dare."

"What if you get killed in Pakistan?"

"We'll be fine."

Jill sniffled. "What do we do while all of you are gone?"

"How about a trip to Disney World?"

"You're kidding, right?"

"Jorge can take you and the girls. It'll be fun. See all the sights, ride all the rides. Check out Epcot and Universal."

"Are you saying he'll drive us all the way to Florida?"

"Of course not. Monica's boss, Alfons Duda, can provide his Learjet to take you. Jorge and Joseph, Alfons' driver, can be your security guards. You'll be perfectly safe at all times."

Jill turned in Brenda's embrace and came face to face with more beauty than a sunrise. "Being a lesbian zombie certainly has its advantages, but should we impose on Mister Duda?"

"He doesn't mind, trust me. He'll do anything for Monica. The man is smitten."

"But she's a lesbian—"

"I know. I know, but you have to understand Monica. She was eighty years old when I met her, a crippled black woman with a hair-trigger temper. Couldn't blame her, though, her best carnal days were decades behind her, and now she has a new lease on life, so anything goes. She loves loving and being loved, and she loves being beautiful, but she's deadly as a black mamba."

"Brenda, thank you. Let's go tell the girls about the trip."

"Sure, honey."

With that, they strolled outside to see what the girls and the sisters were doing, found them playing chase-the-ball with Girlie Dog in the front yard. By a stroke of luck or Loa's hand, Brenda caught a glint of sunlight flash off a lens in the beach view area a quarter mile away. Her zombie vision revealed a man seated in a Honda parked backwards, binoculars to his eyes and pointed at the estate.

She stared back. A litany of threats raced through her mind: *Cuban Mafia. Church of the Risen Jesus. Colonel Wesley Miller. A Hoffman brother. The police. FBI.* With her heart banging on her ribs, she turned to the festivities. "Girls, everybody, get in the house."

They looked at her as if she'd grown a second nose.

"Go. Go."

The sisters were like herding squirrels to the front door. Once safe inside, Jackie asked, "What is it, Brenda?"

"We have a stalker."

Chapter Seventeen

Over in the Aegean sea on the island of Rhodes, the *USS Carmick* was pulling into the US Navy anchorage. Frank Leatherwood watched sailors tie the ship to the pier, but he wasn't thinking about the precision teamwork involved. As the bowline was being secured, his thoughts went back to the rescue of Donna and Carrie. *God I'd love to meet Carrie again.*

He remembered looking at her naked body on that wing as the cable hoisted her friend up to the chopper. His memory of Carrie's beauty would stay with him forever, probably the best memory he'd take from his tour of duty as a rescue swimmer.

God, if you let me find her, see her, be with her, make love to her, I'll hang up my flippers for good.

He sighed. I may as well lose that fantasy. She's probably got a civilian boyfriend anyway.

***

Back at the Pentagon, Colonel Wesley Miller strode down the hall to General Taylor's office, chin up, chest puffed out as if he were already a Brigadier General.

Entering the office, he saw a black Major stand so quickly his chair flew back and hit the wall as he snapped to attention and saluted.

"Major, what are you doing at my desk?"

The African American stood proud. "Major Glen Feldman, sir. I'm General Taylor's new aide-de-camp."

The Colonel frowned. "I've been replaced so soon?"

"It's true, sir. The General is awaiting your arrival."

Wes removed his cap. "I feel like a damn pinball around here...*go to Arizona...get back to headquarters*. What the hell is going on?"

"Not for me to say, sir. I've been instructed to show you in and as soon as you arrive."

"This better be important." Wes stormed through the door. "General—"

"Ah, Wesley." He didn't even look up from his desk. "I see you met my new aide-de-camp. He's got to be less of a pain in my ass than my last one."

Wes remained stone-faced. "You wanted to see me, sir?"

He looked up and smiled. "Your promotion to Brigadier General has been approved by the Secretary of the Army." Taylor stood and reached out his hand. "Congratulations, General."

With a big smile on his face, Wes accepted the handshake with the enthusiasm of a politician. He couldn't wait to tell Lynne. "Thank you, sir."

"Now take off those eagles, General, so I can pin on your stars."

Pride swelled inside Miller's chest as he removed his eagles. *I'm a general. The Army has finally recognized my worth. I can't wait to get my own aide-de-camp grunt. I'm a general, dammit, a general.*

Taylor pinned the stars on Wesley Miller's shoulders, stood back, and saluted him. "General, the troops you will command are from Bravo Company, 3rd Ranger Battalion. They are the best of the best in this business."

Wes craned his neck and strained his eyes to see the new shine on his shoulder loops. "I'm only assigned one company, sir?"

"I realize that a Brigadier commands a regiment, not just a company, but you got this job because no one knows how to defend a fixed position better than you. That's why I've chosen you to lead this mission to Baddish. The World Health Organization's nurses are not equipped to quarantine the village. That's your job."

"When will we deploy?"

"The Rangers are on standby, any day now. You'll have a twenty-four-hour window to get to your destination. Are you ready for an airdrop?"

"I can handle it. When will my troops arrive in Arizona for training?"

"They're not. Transporting that many men could draw attention to our mission. You're going to Fort Leonard Wood."

"Hell, Lawrence. In Missouri? We hated that base."

"Just get there, prepare your men, and wait for your marching orders, but please, Wes, don't exhaust your boys before they get to Pakistan."

"How long do I have to get ready?"

"Wes, you know the Army drill. Hurry up and wait."

***

The call came and Jackie got the message. Alfons' yacht was in the port of Athens, Greece, with its all-girl crew. Now the Sisterhood had to fly to Athens.

After Jorge dropped them off at JFK's Terminal 4 for their Delta flight, he drove Joseph, the girls, and Jill and Lilly to Alfons' private jet hangar.

Jerry Henderson had followed the limo at a distance. His tenacity was beyond anything any one could have expected. He checked with the flight desk and learned the Learjet captain had filed a flight plan to Orlando. Turned out the clerk knew Captain Zack Parsons very well, biblically he figured, and informed him the passengers were destined to Disney World. She even knew the hotel they would stay at because she was going to meet Parsons there later that night.

The girls were the first ones on Alfons' jet. They ran up the steps with Girlie Dog right behind them. Looking around as everyone claimed seats, Caroline remembered how she had been on this plane before. It was the time Monica had picked her up in Illinois, the day after her mommy and daddy were killed in a head-on collision. Memories came back, how a policeman found her in the wreckage, how the firemen got her out with the jaws of life. The policeman was nice to her, let her sit in his police car, gave her a bottle of water and a little Teddy Bear. She never saw her mommy and daddy again, until Loa showed her how happy they were with her.

So Caroline sat in the same seat she'd taken on that flight with Monica to her new home and new sisters.

Betsy danced up to her. "You wanna draw some pictures with

me?" She held up paper in one hand and crayons in the other.

Caroline's train of thought was broken, so she gladly joined Betsy on the floor where they started drawing. Betsy drew a picture of a dog and a horse playing in a field, but Caroline drew a picture of policemen and firemen and smoke and flames. The more she drew, the angrier she got at the old people who'd killed her parents. She grabbed the black crayon and made big Xs all over the picture then drew another picture of two old people then angrily marked them out, too.

Jill looked at Caroline's two pictures. "Who are these old people, Caroline?"

"They are the bad people who killed my mommy and daddy. I hate them, I hate them, I hate them."

Jill sat on the floor and hugged Caroline as she cried and kept repeating, "I hate them."

Girlie Dog, sensing something was wrong with Caroline, sat next to her and put her ears down and set a paw on Caroline's leg.

Betsy's expression was one of concern. "What's the matter with Caroline, Mommy?"

"She's just upset by a memory. Tell her you love her."

"I love you," Betsy said, then went back to her picture.

The flight attendant brought them milk and cookies and a bone for Girlie Dog. "Now everyone get seated for takeoff."

Jerry Henderson got himself on a Delta flight bound for Orlando. Sitting back in the seat, he too was remembering the past, the horrors of fathering a less-than-perfect child, the hatred he felt for Jill for bringing such a monster into the world. However, he had to wonder how Betsy got over her autism to become such a beautiful and happy child. And from what he'd seen through the binoculars, Jill was looking younger than ever.

He huffed. *Good for both of them, but shit is going to hit the fan in Disney World.*

***

In Athens, the sisters departed a bus that dropped them off at the Port. They saw Alfons' yacht moored at a pier, three hundred feet down the concrete walkway, and then another hundred feet down the pier. The yacht, *Three Sheets to the Wind*, was a good

175 feet long with four decks glistening white and gold in the morning sun.

"Monica."

"Yes, Jackie?"

"Let's rename the ship to *Girls' Night Out*. Get the crew to paint over the name on the stern."

"Alfons will go ballistic. This boat...I mean yacht, is his baby. I don't think that's a good idea."

"Monica, dear, you worry too much. I'm sure you can do something for him that will make him okay with it. Let's get aboard. We can discuss Alfons later."

As the sisters strolled up the gangway, the first one to meet them was a five-foot-seven platinum blonde wearing a tight white skirt and a matching blouse that showed off her D-cup cleavage. Her green eyes glistened as she smiled and offered Brenda a hand aboard. "Welcome, Miss Ayler. I'm Kathy Lansford, your Captain for this voyage."

Accepting her hand, Brenda felt a pleasant twitch down below. "It's going to be a long trip, Captain, so I guess there'll be plenty of time to get to know you better." She wanted to say *plenty of time to strip you down in my cabin and introduce you to sister love.*

Glancing at Brenda's cleavage, she smiled. "I certainly hope so."

The glance didn't go unnoticed. *Kathy is looking at my breasts and doing her best to act as if she isn't. I'll let her get up-close-and-personal with them once we're out to sea.*

Kathy welcomed all the sisters with the same interest in their femininity. "Now that you're all here I'll ready the ship to cast off."

"Easy, Captain. Before we sail, I want to check out the weapons you have on board."

"Weapons? Why would we have any weapons? Flares in case of an emergency. Why do you ask?"

Brenda filled her in on the facts. "We'll be sailing through the Gulf of Aden with Yemen on our port and Somalia on our starboard. These are the most dangerous waters in the region, well within striking range of Somali pirates."

Kathy took a step back. "Pirates? Mister Duda didn't say

anything about pirates or sailing through the Gulf of Aden. All we've ever done is cruise up and down the east coast and around the Caribbean. We thought we'd just be cruising the Mediterranean on this voyage. I need to call him and tell him this trip you want cannot be done."

"Don't worry about it." Brenda hugged the Captain's shoulders. "You'll just have to make a little detour to Rhodes, the home port of the US Navy's Mediterranean Command."

Kathy pulled away. "You really think the Navy will give you weapons?"

"Hell yes. Admiral Roy Kincade is the commanding officer. He'll give us whatever we need to defend Duda's ship against pirates."

"Even if I knew how to fire a gun, I don't think I could actually shoot somebody."

"What's your alternative? Do you let some unwashed, smelly, and ignorant pirate with camel-shit breath rip your clothes off and rape you while his buddies watch and wait their turn, or do you fight to defend your honor and your ship?"

"Well, fight, of course, but—"

Brenda laughed, and her sisters joined in. "Relax. I'm just busting your chops. You and your crew won't have to fight any pirates. We'll do the killing if any problems arise."

"You?" She looked over her beautiful passengers, pictured them in the hot tub, naked, sunbathing on the top deck, naked, drinking and dancing the night away, naked. Not a killer among them. "We need an armed escort ship to go where you ask."

"Nah. We've got it covered. Don't worry."

Captain Kathy reached for a deck phone. "Sanderson, report to the main deck. Pronto."

Not a moment later, up strolled a gorgeous creature with beautiful dark brown hair and the most perfect body and tits that Brenda had ever seen on a natural woman. "Do tell," Brenda breathed. "Who is this beauty?"

"She's our Second Mate Tammy Sanderson. She's also our Chef, twenty-one years old, and for what it's worth, she's also a lesbian."

Brenda didn't comment but thought, I don't have a problem with that. Absolutely no problem with that. Captain Kathy doesn't know I can read miss Second Mate's mind and she thinks I'm pretty hot too. Before we leave port we'll have to stock up on sex toys and hard rubber dildos and maybe some lesbian porn videos.

"Second Mate Sanderson," Captain Kathy said. "Set course for Rhodes."

"Aye, Aye, Captain." She headed for the bulkhead staircase and all eyes admired her magnificent form.

Melinda broke ranks. "Well then..." she fanned her face with her hand, "who's going to show me to my cabin?"

Twenty-five-year-old Electrical Engineer Jane King led her down the passageway toward her quarters. Melinda was enjoying the view as five-foot-six Jane swayed her cute ass to a cabin door right next to one with Brenda and Jackie's names on the placard.

Shit. Brenda and Jackie's cabin is right next to mine. Hopefully she wouldn't have to hear...*Don't stop it feels so good. Oh, that was great. Now it's my turn...*all night.

Meanwhile, topside, Monica, Carrie, and Donna were being treated to Margaritas fixed by former New York City bartenders, Deck Hand LeeAnn Roach and First Mate Joan Turner. They'd quit working at *The Manhattan Bar and Grill*, dumping their boss who couldn't keep his hands to himself. This was their third voyage on Alfons' yacht.

Both girls wore matching bikinis and had mixed strong-enough Margaritas in two large pitchers to get the crew of the *USS Carmick* drunk. In fact, these bubbly bartenders were already half blitzed.

At a round deck table, LeeAnn sat between Carrie and Donna and Joan sat between Donna and Monica. It was five-foot-seven LeeAnn, sitting in the semicircle of hot bodies who spoke up. "Would one of you ladies help me get this top off? It's such a hot day, don't ya think?" Her blue eyes darted about in anticipation of who would take her up on her offer.

It was Carrie who untied the strings of LeeAnn's top, and as she turned sideways, the sisters could not help notice what a beautiful tan she had. Her perky C-cup breasts were hidden under her long blond hair with only her pink nipples peeking out.

Joan stood. "Lady Godiva isn't the only one who has something to show off." She and LeeAnn were the same height, but Joan's smaller breasts had bigger nipples that slightly pointed upward. Before she could reveal more by taking off her flower-print bikini bottoms, cat calls rose from workmen on the pier.

It was then that Monica read both girls' minds:

Joan thought, *Too bad, boys, Mister* Duda laid me already.

LeeAnn was thinking, *Bet you guys want a blowjob like I gave Mister Duda.*

Joan waved to the men.

LeeAnn's next thought was, *You guys don't want her, besides Mister Duda liked my tits better than Joan's small bumps.*

Monica interrupted their musings. "Did you two have an orgy with Alfons Duda?"

Joan and LeeAnn giggled. "Why? Do you know him?"

"I'm his girlfriend."

LeeAnn glanced at Joan. "Oh, oh. She's the black woman he said would kill him if she knew what we were doing."

Monica stared them down. "When did you girls have this Alfons swap party?"

"The night before we flew to Athens to get on this yacht."

Monica beat down the heat of jealousy, gulped her Margarita then set off to find the deck hands. *Jackie wants this yacht renamed, then so be it.* She found Sue Smith and her shipmate Jean Stantan. "Get out your paintbrushes, girls. I want you to white out the yacht's name on the stern and paint *Girls' Night Out* over it."

Sue looked aghast. "We can't do that. Mister Duda will have a fit."

"Sure you can, and who cares, the three-timing bastard has it coming."

While the deck hands painted, Monica went for a dip in the pool, alone, trying to cool her overheated temper. When they finished, Monica sent Alfons a couple of pictures.

Alfons didn't get the pictures until he got to his office the next day. "What the hell?" *I can't believe this?* Monica sent him a picture of herself leaning over the stern rail above the new name painted on his yacht, *Girls' Night Out*, and another one of her flipping him the bird from each hand. Shit. There was only one thing that could have pissed her off that much. No, two things.

Those bimbos must have told on me. I should've never hired that crew of sex-crazed women.

While he sat in his easy-chair and moaned to himself over the name change, he looked out his big picture window at the New York City Skyline. He didn't know that his yacht, *Girls' Night Out,* was dogging the Greek archipelago at a top cruising speed of fifty knots, en route to Rhodes and the US Navy anchorage.

Chapter Eighteen

Things were going great for the girls and Jill and Lilly. They had ridden practically every ride at Disney World, all while under the watchful eyes of Jorge and Joseph. There was only time left for one last ride, The Haunted Mansion. Jill could tell the girls were tired but not ready to go back to their fabulous room at the Disney Resort.

As they strolled toward the mansion ride, Jill and Lilly discussed how wonderful it was being lesbian zombies. Little did they know they were being followed...by Jerry Henderson.

They stopped at Cinderella's Royal Table for a late lunch and to meet Cinderella in person. Pictures were taken, autographs signed, and the girls were thrilled to dress up as princesses while they waited for a table.

After eating, when Jill and Lilly got up for a potty break, they thought nothing of leaving the girls at the table. They would be safe because of their two bodyguards sitting nearby. Jorge wouldn't allow anyone to try anything with the girls.

Jerry, standing by the blue draperies, waited until Jill and her friend were well out of sight then nonchalantly walked up to the girls' table. "Wow. You're both beautiful little princesses, just like the real Cinderella."

With big smiles they said in unison, "Thank you, mister."

Jerry kept a keen eye out for Jill, and shot glances about, looking to see if he'd drawn any unwanted attention. "I see you've been on a lot of rides this morning."

"We're going to the Haunted Mansion next," Caroline said.

"We're not scared," Betsy told him.

He couldn't believe how hard his heart was beating. Betsy's arm was so close, he could just reach out, grab it, and run, but he saw Jill and her friend returning. Damn. He had to scram. “You princesses have a nice day.” He hightailed back to his watching spot by the curtains. He’d been so busy planning his next move that he failed to notice the two men watching him.

I’ll strike in the darkest part of the mansion, snatch Betsy off the slow-moving ride, and shoulder her out the back emergency door. With all the loud growls, shrieks, and screams in the mansion, no one will be alerted if Betsy screams. Once I get her outside, I’ll tell her I’m her dad and that she’s safe with me. Then we can walk out of Disney World, hand in hand, the way dads and daughters do.

Lilly and Jill got back to the girls, and they were off to the Haunted Mansion. Jerry slipped away behind the curtains, determined to get on the ride before them...and without drawing attention from the crowd.

After waiting in a long line, it was finally time for the girls to get on the ride, a train of high dome-backed chairs, each seating two. Jill and Lilly got in the nearest chair, Jorge and Betsy the next, and Joseph and Caroline behind them. No one knew that Jerry had managed to commandeer a seat by himself, ten chairs in front of them.

Haunting voices greeted them as the ride began.

Jerry was wrong about one thing. Instead of echoing screams and shrieks from the riders, there were mostly *oohs* and *aahs* and *“look at that”* and “*how cool*.” And the ride wasn’t all that dark...candelabra-lit halls, a library, and creepy dancers in a ballroom...until the train of chairs came to a dark room, a lighted ethereal bride, and ghostly forms rising to a starry ceiling. Jerry jumped out of his chair and slipped into the darkness.

The girls were mostly silent as the ride went on, their eyes wide with amazement. Jorge thought it wasn’t all that scary...until a hand reached out of the darkness and yanked Betsy out of the seat beside him.

Her sudden scream was quickly muffled.

Panic cannonballed through his chest. He leaped out, looked left and right, but she and her captor had melted into the dark recesses of the ride.

“Betsy,” he shouted as he ran through a maze of cables and platforms. His acute hearing picked up a muffled squeal, so he sprinted in that direction, dodged spooky automatons, a man walking his hound dog, a knight in shining armor, and he ducked between fake walls and zigzagged across cluttered floors backstage. A wedge of light split the darkness as a back door opened then quickly shut. "Betsy."

He burst outside and squinted into the bright Florida sunshine, looked left, looked right. No Betsy. No phantom. Woods. Trees and more trees.

"Betsy."

The squeal came again, this time to his left, somewhere in the trees. He jumped the rail and ploughed through the underbrush. "Betsy. Where are you?"

"Stay away from us," a man's voice shouted.

"You're not my daddy," Betsy shrieked.

"I'm coming, Betsy." Jorge pushed toward the voices until he encountered water, an oily swamp of sorts, or a channel to one, and he damn near fell in.

"We'll be happy," came the voice from his right.

"Let me go."

Jorge pressed through the trees, the bugs, the heat, and a few yards farther, he stumbled upon a man on his knees in front of Betsy. "Stop being a brat."

"Let her go," Jorge said flatly.

The man stood. "She's my daughter," he shouted to Jorge. "Stay out of this."

But Jorge wasn't there to argue. He delivered a right hook to the would-be kidnapper's jaw, knocking him backward into the swampy water. He flailed like a goose in the jaws of a crock. "I can't swim." He went under.

Jorge took Betsy's hand. "Let's go. We're missing the ride."

They got to the ride's exit as Jill and Lilly strolled out, oblivious to the near-disaster that had occurred behind them on the chair-train. Their expressions showed total confusion as Jorge and Betsy walked up, hand in hand.

Jill's complexion turned ghostly white. "How did you get out here before us?"

Joseph came out with Caroline, and she ran to Betsy. "That ride wasn't very scary."

"It was scary for me." Betsy hugged Caroline and trembled.

"What the hell happened?" Jill demanded. "How did Betsy get all dirty?"

"She met her father."

Jill clutched Betsy protectively. "He was here?"

"Must've followed us. I'd seen him talking to the girls earlier, just thought he was being friendly, so no problem, but this time he grabbed Betsy off the ride, and I ended the reunion, permanently."

"You killed him?"

"Turns out he can't swim. Not my fault."

Shock widened her eyes. "He's dead?"

"Last time I saw him, his swimming lesson wasn't going very well." He turned to the girls. "Anyone for ice cream?"

***

Back on *Girls' Night Out*, the sisters were resting up and enjoying the beauty of Nisyros Island, it's volcanic cone and rocky coastline, fifty-five miles from Rhodes.

Carrie, topless and enjoying the sun from a deck chair, checked her satellite phone where she found a picture of Caroline and Betsy in princess dresses and holding sticks of cotton candy.

"Donna, look at this, how cute they are, having so much fun."

She joined Carrie in the chair, tan bodies together, two peas in a pod but much more delicious. "Cute? They've got cotton candy everywhere, in their hair, on their dresses. Jill and Lilly will have a tough time cleaning them up."

"But they're so happy. Brenda, take a look at this."

Brenda took the phone and it buzzed. She checked the display. "Jorge?" She answered.

"Brenda, I thought I'd better let you know what happened here. Betsy's deadbeat dad tried to kidnap her."

"What did you do to him?"

"I solved the problem, but a floater might show up in the swamp...if the gators don't get to it first."

"How's Jill taking it?"

"She said Betsy had no use for a fair-weather father."

"Give her our condolences." She disconnected the call.

Second Mate Tammy Sanderson rolled in, pushing a cart of lunch sandwiches and drinks. "Who died?"

"Nobody important." With the wind playing in her crimson hair, Brenda looked around. "It's so beautiful here. How about we anchor for lunch and ask Captain Kathy to join us? Better yet, invite the whole crew."

"Great idea." She sashayed to the staircase that would take her up to the bridge.

Brenda looked over her sisters. "We're going to layover here for lunch."

Chloe popped the top on a beer. "It's party time."

The growl of the engines subsided, the yacht slowed to a stop, and the sisters heard the grumbling rattle of the chain as the anchor was released into the water. They ran to the gunwale to watch it make a splash.

Just then, Brenda got a call from Admiral Roy Kincade. "Brenda, General Taylor called me about your request. I have sent the information to Captain Marquez on the USS Carmick. He'll meet you at the anchorage, give you whatever weaponry you need, and a couple of his men will train you. Is there anything else I can do for you?"

"I understand Frank Leatherwood is on the Carmick."

"Yes. A swimmer."

"He rescued two of my girls from the plane crash. Could you see to it that he's assigned to train us?"

"Consider it done. Anything else?"

"No, that's it. I'm looking forward to seeing you at our Black Friday 2 Party."

"I'm raring to go, as is General Taylor."

"I promise you guys a great time. See you then." She closed the satellite call and looked for Carrie among all the cute butts along the gunwale. "Oh, Carrie. Come here, please."

She bounced over, all happy and sexy. "What's up?"

"That sailor who rescued you—"

"Yeah. Frank...ah...Leatherwood."

"His ship is going to be at the Naval base when we arrive. When you see him, make sure he knows how lucky he is to see you."

Carrie threw her arms around Brenda. "Aye, aye, my Queen." She ran back to the girls to watch the anchor chain tighten. The yacht was secured in forty feet of water.

Now it was time for the sexiest lunch party ever.

Holding fast in the calm waters of the Aegean Sea, *Girls' Night Out* was alive with music and laughter. The crew had secured their stations and joined the Sisterhood in joyous mischief on the Promenade Deck.

Brenda and Jackie had hooked up in the hot tub, as usual, and Donna and Chloe got naked in the pool. Monica hung with Joan at the open bar where they cheered Melinda and Maria and Sue as they bikini-wrestled in the volleyball sand pit. The sweaty trio had already lost their tops.

The resident lesbian, Tammy, dressed in a teeny weeny leather bikini and over-the-knee snakeskin boots was taming Jane with a leather flog to her bare ass. Captain Kathy and Jean joined the girls in the pool, and a game of submarine ensued.

Carrie, nervous and excited about seeing her rescuer again, sat with LeeAnn by the fountain and discussed her conflicting sexual preferences. Frank was a hunk, a handsome hunk, a heroic hunk, but Carrie would rather play with LeeAnn's soft supple body than Frank's frankfurter, thanks to Brenda's mile-high club initiation on Alfons' Learjet. "I'm not attracted to men like I used to be."

"Do him anyway." LeeAnn took hold of Carrie's hand. "But do me first." They headed to the Lido deck game room for some private games of their own.

Yes. Love was in the air. Whisky and wine flowed freely, and the frolicking nymphs aboard *Girls' Night Out* didn't have a care in the world.

***

The next morning, *Girls' Night Out* was again underway toward Rhodes on this sunny morning in the Aegean Sea. The constant drone of the diesels and the occasional bump from the chop made for an exhilarating ride. On the breezy Promenade, Brenda was lying on a deckchair, wearing a pink and white bikini and a pair of Cartier sunglasses, when Jackie strode up, naked as the day was long, and claimed the deckchair next to her.

Turning her head and pushing her sunglasses up, she squinted at Jackie. "I thought the party was over and yet you're still naked."

"I can't help myself. We're out here in the middle of the ocean, a million miles from prying eyes, the wind, the sun, the sea spray, clothes are such a bother. Besides, I may go back to the pool for seconds on the submarine ride."

"So what are you doing up here?"

She sat up in the chair and turned to face Brenda. "Have you given any thought to exactly what we're going to do when we get to Baddish? I mean, we've got the four vials laced with strychnine ready. There's a red dot on the labels, and another one hundred placebos with plain white labels. But we can't just walk into the village and start inoculating everyone. Besides, how are we going to find Ahmed al-Hakim and his brothers?"

"The Imam has a list of everyone to be vaccinated. When the brothers sign in at our phony WHO table, we'll give them the red dots. The Imam will get his last."

"What do you think Loa will have to say about this?"

"I have to assume she knows. The ghost of Jasmine appearing in the Crystal Shrine the way she did is proof enough that Loa approves of Jasmine's vendetta. She certainly doesn't think we're out here on vacation."

"I'm sure she thinks the husband and his brothers have it coming, and even the village's vicious Imam, Mohammed Abdullah Abadi, but shouldn't we turn all the women into sisters, you know, lace their placebos with the virus?"

"What for? Their lives are hard, yes, but it's the only life they know, and with the Imam terrorist out of the way, their lives will improve. They don't need the complications of the Sisterhood."

Jackie lay back down in the chair. "Do you think the men who followed the Imam will stand by and do nothing when they see him croak after he gets the shot?"

"It'll take fifteen to twenty minutes for the first muscle spasms to set in. We'll tell the people they got the shot too late, that the plague got them, pretend to save them, but alas, it was Allah's will that they died."

"Brenda, I like the way you think."

She set her ten-thousand-dollar sunglasses back in place and let the drone of the engines and the churn of the chop soothe her troubled mind.

Revenge is a dirty business.

Chapter Nineteen

Later that morning, *Girls' Night Out* rumbled into the anchorage and moored next to the *USS Carmick*, whose sailors were told the yacht carried volunteers from the World Health Organization. Bikini-clad women lined up along the gunwale and waved to the sailors ogling them from the deck cables of their ship. The battle-gray juggernaut displayed the number 33 in bold white letters on the bow.

They all shared the same thoughts. Party time.

It was AIRRs First Class Frank Leatherwood who spotted Carrie in a white bikini. His heart started jumping around in his ribcage. To see her again was like the heavens had opened and shot sunbeams down all around him. He waved and jumped up and down. "Carrie, over here. Carrie."

From her position on *Girls' Night Out*, Carrie looked at the Navy ship: its twin fore and aft cannons, double smoke stacks, and the flag-bearing masthead that towered over the superstructure. She waved at the white-uniformed sailors lined up on the deck from stern to bow...where she suddenly spotted Frank going nuts. *Oh My Goddess.* "That's him."

Brenda slapped Carrie's fanny. "Go get him, sister."

She rushed for the gangplank.

Naturally, every sailor on the Carmick thought she was waving at them, but only one was right. Frank sprinted to Captain Marquez who was watching the yacht's crew of women tie her up. "She's here, sir, the woman I rescued from the plane crash. Permission to go ashore?"

"Permission granted."

Frank ran down the gangplank to the cheers and whistles of his shipmates then sprinted toward Carrie who was running toward him, barefooted and breasts bouncing. They met in the middle of the pier and threw their arms around each other.

"I thought I'd never see you again," he whispered in her ear.

"You're taller than I remember."

Her sisters started chanting from above. "Kiss him. Kiss him." And the sailors joined in. "Kiss her. Kiss her."

She looked into his brown eyes that seemed to be melting at the sight of her. "You heard them. Kiss me, sailor."

And he did, but little did he know, he was getting a hot dose of a virus that would change his life forever. Then again, little would he care.

LeeAnn nuzzled up to Brenda. "She had me worried last night, but it looks like she pulled it off. It doesn't even look like she's faking it."

"She's not." Brenda felt a warm sense of melancholy seeing the two lovers kissing on the pier. Could have been a World War Two poster, sailor in white, woman in white, her knee bent and foot raised behind her as she kissed her man welcome home. "Her feelings are real. Time will tell if his feelings for her are worthy."

Then Frank and Carrie walked hand-in-hand toward town, down narrow streets Marc Anthony and Cleopatra had walked 2100 years earlier, now flanked by the ancient stone walls of a medieval fortress. At a corner, he stopped her, looked her up and down. Stunning as she looked in her bikini, the memory of her naked on that wrecked wing dogged him. He wanted more. He wanted it all.

"What's the matter, Frank? Never seen a girl in a bikini before?"

"There must've been something in your kiss. I can't take my eyes off you."

"Yeah? Watcha gonna do about it, sailor?"

"All I've thought about from the last moment I saw you was God I hope we meet again. And here we are. God answered my prayer."

"Maybe it was Goddess Loa."

"Whatever divinity it was, I'm eternally grateful. So what do you say we find a room?"

"Patience, Frank. Let's eat first, then you can have anything you want for dessert, and I mean anything. After all, a damsel in distress must reward her savior fittingly."

He gazed into her eyes. "You don't owe me anything and I don't expect anything, but something inside me is on fire for you, something I've never felt before."

Carrie had that same burning glow and felt Loa was guiding her actions and emotions, for whatever reason, she didn't know. She hooked her arm in his. "Then let's eat fast."

As they walked into town at a faster pace, Frank had one thing on his mind. *I gotta find the nearest hotel.*

After a lunch of glazed sea bass, wedge potatoes, and Cannonau Red Wine in the rose garden at 4 Pomegranates, they walked the tree-lined corridors of Old Town and inhaled the scents of Greece wafting from various shops along the way: grilled meats, flowers galore, Greek coffees, olives, and frankincense. A romance novel could not have been more romantic. One might have thought these two lovers had stepped right off the pages. When they came upon the Colossus of Rhodes Hotel, these lovebirds were ready to get off their feet and enjoy some dessert. After checking in as Mr. and Mrs. Smith they collapsed on the bed and into each other's arms.

"What a wonderful afternoon," she said.

"I feel as if I've known you my whole life."

"Whatcha want for dessert, sailor?"

He tweaked a brow. "Let's see...I want to start with—"

Someone knocked on the door.

Frank growled, "Go away," then softened. "Now where were we?"

"Carrie? Are you in there?"

She sat up. "Brenda? What the hell?"

"I hope she's not your mother."

"Get the door. Hurry."

The good sailor obeyed, and there stood two gorgeous women, the likes of which he'd never seen before, a truly stunning redhead, and an equally desirable strawberry blonde bombshell, both wearing short summer dresses and lip-smacking smiles. The fire inside him exploded in thoughts of threesomes and foursomes, tits and ass as far as he could imagine, then poof, the fantasies faded when he noticed what the redhead was holding: folded dress blues.

"Huh?"

The brunette held a hanger with a very small dress in one hand and a pair of shoes in the other. "We thought you two might need some clothes."

Carrie flew off the bed. "Brenda, Jackie, come in."

Brenda looked Frank over. "Not bad." She stepped inside.

Frank frowned. "Ladies, right now clothes are the last thing we need."

"It's okay, Frank." Carrie took the clothes and set them neatly on the bed, for now. "It's very thoughtful of them."

"How did you get hold of my uniform?"

Jackie jumped on that question. "I asked your Captain."

"You know Captain Marquez?"

"Yes. He was very nice, and Admiral Kincade had told him to get us anything we need, including this three-day pass." She handed it to him. "Lucky man."

Frank stood in astonishment. "I don't know what to say."

"Try thank you," Brenda put in. "Works every time. And while you're thanking us, you can add one more thing. We've taken care of all costs you incur at this hotel."

Carrie took hold of Frank's arm. "Three days in paradise."

He looked at the three-day pass and almost sobbed out, "Thank you."

Brenda winked at Carrie. "We'll leave you two alone now."

Frank showed them out, and when he closed the door he looked again at the pass. There it was, the signature of Captain Marquez, real as rain. "I can't believe this. It's like a dream come true." He then turned to look at Carrie. She was standing by the bed, naked as the day they met. His breath hitched. "My god." That fire flared up big time.

Smiling she said softly, "Your dessert is ready."

***

Back at the Church of the Risen Jesus, there wasn't a single car in the parking lot. Reverend Janice Parker was pissed. She didn't believe LeRoy's line of bullshit about *The Jesus Is Coming Seminary* being so successful that it ran over another day. He wouldn't be home until this afternoon. *How many whores did he sleep with at the seminary*?

Inside, the halls and sanctuary of the church were as quiet as a tomb. On Sunday, she couldn't hear herself think, it was that noisy with the congregation singing, praying, clapping, and conversing. All of those dumb bastards loaded up the offering plates and listened to her shithead husband telling them that their hard-earned cash was going to do Jesus' holy work.

Bullshit.

When she got to the church office, she was surprised to see the door ajar. She stepped inside and screamed. The place had been ransacked, file drawers spilled, desk drawers pulled out, books scattered, and furniture upended. Worse, the door to the safe lay wide open. Shit. Where two and a half million in hard cash was stacked, the shelves were now bare, except for a piece of paper. She unfolded it and read:

Janice, I know Brenda will never forgive me for ratting her girls out to the Cubans. Yes. I took the money so that I can go into hiding. I need it for Shirley and me to live on. I know you think she's a bimbo, but she loves me, and better yet, she's not a lesbian. I hope you will forgive me. Goodbye forever. LeRoy.

She wadded up the note and made a three-point shot into the trashcan. Son of a bitch. *I will never forgive you. Brenda will hunt you down, and when she finds you, you will die while I watch. And I hope she puts Shirley in the oral division of a Chinese whorehouse for the rest of her life.*

Janice righted the overturned desk chair and sat where LeRoy had formerly set his fat ass. Tomorrow she'd call Brenda and tell her what happened to the money that was destined to the LZ Foundation's coffers. She would also assure her Queen that she'd be loyal to her and the Sisterhood forever.

***

At Fort Leonard Wood, Wesley Miller, the first one-star General to only have a single company under his command, was going to wake up his cadre of Rangers. It was time to show them the mission objective, using the layout of Baddish that Captain Johnson had sent him.

Wes looked at the rolled-out map and thought the Captain did one hell of a job on the details. Baddish would be easy to defend.

I can position 1st platoon on the north side and 2nd platoon east and 3rd platoon on the south side. The moored Navy destroyer, USS Carmick in the Gulf of Oman can cover our rear.

One thing bothered him though. There must be one hell of a plague in that village for the nurses from the World Health Organization to go in to stop it from spreading.

My orders are to secure the village perimeter and protect those nurses, and my Rangers will do just that.

***

While Frank and Carrie were eating fine foods, playing in the Aegean Sea, enjoying the nightlife of Rhodes, and making love for the past three days, the sisters were busy equipping the yacht with provisions for the long sea journey ahead. Sailors from the Carmick trained the girls on firearms, rifles, and fifty caliber machine guns. The Navy even threw in a few anti-personnel hand grenades. *Girls' Night Out* was soon ready to set sail into dangerous waters.

Carrie kissed Frank goodbye at the gangplank to his ship, and full of life and spirit she bounded back onto the yacht where her sisters besieged her with questions.

"What did you do?"

"Where did you go?"

"Was he good in bed?"

"Tell us all the sordid details."

The *USS Carmick* steamed away, the yacht soon afterwards. Brenda and the Sisterhood didn't know the Carmick had been ordered to shadow the yacht across the Mediterranean, through the Suez Canal, along the banks of the Red Sea to the Gulf of Aden, and finally into the Arabian sea.

Brenda felt confident that, back in Arizona, Robert was keeping track of them, keeping close watch from government satellites high in orbit. So the ladies' days were spent lounging in the sun, frolicking in the pool, and drinking and dancing well into the night.

To the casual observer, the yacht was just a bunch of rich

women showing off their boobs, but to the Somali pirates, it was a floating gold mine.

***

One hour out of the Bab al-Mandab Strait, the sisters' party-cruise was suddenly interrupted by gunfire. Brenda and Jackie ran to the Promenade Deck to get a full three-sixty degree view around the yacht. Starboard and aft, open-hull powerboats that looked like they could have come from the Stone Age flew over the yacht's wakes and crashed back down in a spray of seawater. Skinny black men fired assault weapons in the air, and the lead boat's helmsman shouted into a megaphone in broken English, "You...in yacht. Stop. You..not be harmed." More gunfire followed.

Bullets pinged off the upper radar dome above Brenda's head. "Yeah, and I'm Santa Claus." She leaned over the upper rail. "Girls to the armory. Lock and load." One of the Navy guys had told her to say that.

Second Mate Sanderson was already on the marine radio. "Mayday, mayday, mayday. *Girl's Night Out* is under attack by pirates."

The *USS Carmick* received the transmission. "Full speed ahead," Captain Marquez ordered down to the engine room.

The girls were not waiting for help. Now fully armed, Brenda and Jackie opened up on the nearest pirate boat from their high perch. Two fifty-caliber machine guns the Navy had mounted on bow and stern let loose a barrage of firepower, both guns in the hands of bikini clad beauties, Sue Smith and LeeAnn Roach. A line of geysers shot up and tracked across the mid-beam of a starboard boat. Black bodies fell overboard, and the boat began running in circles on a pilotless rudder.

On the other side of the yacht, Monica and Maria concentrated M-16 auto-fire on a boat that had buzzed up close to the yacht's port beam. The bow-pirate was twirling a grappling hook rope like a lasso. He took a bullet to the brain. His buddy got one in the chest. Two others returned fire, but both paid the ultimate price for missing their targets. For the sisters, it was like shooting fish in a barrel.

Several pirate boats sped ahead of the yacht and cut zigzag

wakes across her bow, which stirred up the water and created turbulent chop. The yacht pitched and yawed, throwing off the aim of its defenders. The sisters might well have been jumping on a bed and trying to shoot mice scurrying about on the floor. Kill-shots were at zero, and more pirate boats swarmed in for the attack.

Back on the Carmick, Frank was locked and loaded as he jumped aboard the chopper with two gunners and the winchman. His guts were tight with worry over Carrie and the other women. "God keep them safe...and you too Goddess Loa." He'd take all the divine help he could get.

The chopper lifted off the helipad and roared out ahead of the much-slower ship. Frank gripped his M-16 and itched to kill the pirate bastards who dared to murder and pillage in international waters. As the chopper neared the yacht, he could see rounds coming hot and heavy from both sides. The girls were putting up one hell of a fight.

From the bridge, Captain Kathy started evasive maneuvers of her own, spinning the helms-wheel right then left, ramming boats that got too close. To starboard, another grapple hook swinger raced up, and Joan lobbed a hand grenade to greet them. Black men jumped out just as the explosion tore the boat out from under them.

One dumbass pirate had the nerve to stand up and drop trou, knowing the women would see his shlong. Chloe saw it, all right, tracked him in her sight scope and waited for the yacht's rock to settle before its reverse roll. "Come on, big boy. Show me what you got just a second longer." Up came the target. She squeezed the trigger. Instantly the bullet turned him into a girl. Just then, a missile struck the boat and blew it to smithereens. She looked up and saw a Navy chopper slew into the battle and scatter the pirates like flees from a tick-collar.

The fight was over in less than ten minutes. Three pirate boats were on fire and sinking. As Captain Kathy steadied the yacht and slowed to a stop, Brenda called all her sisters together. "Everyone all right?"

The girls looked around, nodded, and realized one was missing. Carrie.

As the chopper hovered overhead, the girls set out to find their lost sister. Some rushed forward, some rushed aft, but it was

Sue Smith, from her station at the aft fifty-cal, who found her sprawled on the swim deck. "Over here," she shouted.

The sisters gathered around her, saw a bullet hole in her chest. Blood splotched the front of her one-piece white bathing suit. "Oh, no." Brenda kneeled next to her and kissed her lips. "Come on, honey. You can make it." The wound healed over and Carrie opened her eyes.

Everyone released sighs of relief.

Carrie reached up and grabbed Brenda's arm. "I saw Loa." Carrie gasped. "She told me I'm going to have a baby."

"No way," Monica said. "Lesbian zombies can't get pregnant."

Brenda glanced around at all her sisters. "If it's Loa's will, then it will be done."

As the downwash from the chopper slewed in overhead, Carrie sat up. "I'm going to be a mother...oh my Goddess...Frank must be the father."

"Congratulations," Brenda said, her hair all a-fly in the downdraft. "Now let's get you on your feet."

Hovering above, Frank harnessed up to drop to the yacht's swim deck, the safest clear area for him to set down. Leaning out, he saw bikini clad women help Carrie to her feet. *What the hell happened to her?* Cinching his helmet he yelled. "Let's go."

The winchman lowered him on the cable. On the way down, he spotted sharks feeding on pirates, dead ones and live ones. One headless body slammed into the side of the yacht, followed by a mouthful of gnashing triangular teeth that bit the body in half. A feeding frenzy was in full swing. Dinner of the week. The water churned red with blood.

As his feet touched down on the deck, Frank unclipped the cable hook and headed straight to the women surrounding Carrie. He pushed his way through and got the shock of his life. Blood. Blood on her swimsuit...but she seemed fine. "What the hell?"

"She's fine," Brenda said. "Just a bloody nose."

Frantically, he looked her over and had to agree, but still, that was a lot of blood for a bloody nose. "We need to take her to the infirmary on the Carmick. Let the docs check her out." He radioed up to the chopper. "Send down a harness."

"Yes, sir."

He glared at Brenda, anger cutting into his chest like a sharp blade. "Who the hell are you people? You have more pull than the Secretary of the Navy, and it looks like you went looking for a fight and found one."

Brenda touched his arm and he yanked it away. "And where did those machine guns come from. Come on, fifty-calibers on a pleasure yacht? I didn't see those when you pulled into Rhodes. The Navy must've outfitted you to go Rambo, but you're all just a bunch of beautiful women."

Brenda sighed. "Looks can be deceiving, Frank. Nobody is going to mess with us."

"Oh, yeah? Those pirates could've killed the woman I love."

Now a wide-eyed Carrie stepped in and grabbed his arm. "You love me?"

"Ah...yes, ma'am. Sorry to have to break it to you this way, but I'm pissed. I refuse to let these women or the goddamned Navy put you in danger."

"Frank," Brenda said as soothingly as possible. "Let me tell you something that'll make you very happy."

"Nice try, Brenda." The harness swung down and he grabbed it. "She's coming with me."

Brenda watched him hook Carrie up, then: "When you get her back on the Carmick and you're satisfied she's all right, I'll see to it that you accompany her to our home in New York."

"You don't have that kind of pull."

"You wanna bet? Got you that three-day pass, didn't I?"

Frank's brain nearly exploded. He remembered telling God that if he could be with Carrie, he'd hang up his flippers for good. This wasn't a game of truth or dare. He'd meant it, and even now, standing in the downdraft of the job he loved, the Navy could easily slip into his past, all for the love of Carrie. That fire inside, the burn he'd felt when he'd first kissed her, was there for a reason. She was his destiny.

"I know you believe me, Frank. She is your destiny."

He levered open the face-shield on his helmet and gazed into Carrie's eyes. "I need to know that I'm *your* destiny."

"You are, Frank. You are."

Without taking his eyes of hers, he clipped her harness to his. "Take us up." As the cable tightened and swung them clear of

Girls' Night Out, he had to say, "Here we are again, going up to the helicopter together."

She smiled. "Ain't love grand?"

Below, the yacht's engines roared to full throttle, and the bow wash once again cut through the gulf waters toward Pakistan.

Chapter Twenty

Back in New York, Alfons was eating his breakfast in the first floor restaurant of the Empire State Building, like he had done for the last six years. Bacon, eggs, and more bacon, he was about to get indigestion. The breaking news trailer was running across the bottom of the many flatscreens around the restaurant. Videos from the US Navy chopper on the scene showed bullet holes in his yacht. "Son of a bitch."

Every customer in the restaurant heard his expletive rant that went on and on, so someone called the cops. They showed up and took him outside. Two of Manhattan's finest put him in their patrol car to question him. Cop number one asked the obvious question, "What's your problem?"

Alfons' face glowed angry red. "What's my problem? The yacht that got into a shootout with pirates off the coast of shit-land is my yacht, as is the restaurant I just got thrown out of."

The cop was doing his best to stifle a laugh. "Man, you're really having a bad day...and it's only morning."

"It's not time for breakfast in the Gulf of Aden. There's a time difference between my yacht and Manhattan. If you guys had ever been farther away from home than Brooklyn, you would have known that."

Cop number two chimed in, "Hey, pal, we served three tours in Iraq, so don't lecture us. We're sorry about your boat—"

"Yacht."

"Okay, boat, but as far as your restaurant goes, we should arrest you for serving the most overpriced food in Manhattan. It's good food, but we can't afford it on our cop salaries. Now you're free to go. But no more rants. You're disturbing the peace of everyone around you."

"It's a yacht, not a boat." He got out of the car.

"We hope the rest of the day goes better for you."

After storming back into his restaurant, he ordered a new breakfast sent up to his office.

Now calmed down, he called Monica.

Monica looked at the incoming number and hesitated to answer, but she knew that he would just keep calling back. She connected the call. "What do you want?"

"Monica, how could you do that to me?"

"We didn't do anything. It was the pirates that shot up your boat...I mean your yacht."

"You sailed it in harm's way. What happened to the Mediterranean cruise? I didn't authorize—"

"Jackie wants to talk to you." She handed off the phone.

"Alfons. It's so good of you to call. Now, before you say anything you'll regret, I want you to know that I'll pay for all repairs to your yacht as soon as we get back. How does that sound?"

"I have good insurance. You pay the deductible."

"Agreed. See you at Black Friday 2. Monica said she would show you a much better time than those two bimbos."

Alfons gulped. "Good. I'll hold her to that. I hope the rest of your trip is safe, bye."

***

At Fort Leonard Wood, no sooner had Wes given his Rangers the next twenty-four hours off, he got a call from General Taylor. "Hello, General."

"Robert tells me our most recent satellite recon shows Taliban militants gathering outside Karachi. Time to muster your troops, Wes. A C-5M Super Galaxy Transport will arrive at Fort Leonard Wood tomorrow at 1200 hours. Be ready."

"We will."

"Good hunting."

Wes hung up and called Lynne. "Sorry, sugar. We deploy tomorrow...but..."

"What is it, Wes?"

"This mission may be more difficult and dangerous than I

first expected. I only have one hundred and fifty Rangers and ten officers when I really need two companies, just to be on the safe side."

"That's why they put you in charge, dear. They need the best in the business. You'll be fine."

"See you when I get back."

"Love you." She hung up.

Before he called his second in command to cancel the twenty-four hour pass and call everyone in, he took a moment to engrain in his memory Lynne's last words, the sound of her voice, and he could only hope he would hear it again.

***

Forty eight hours later, the Rangers, under the command of General Wesley Miller, made the jump from 2,000 feet, one mile from Baddish, and quickly set up their defensive positions around the outskirts of the village. Dawn would break within the hour, but the encampment was under blackout orders and totally dark. Above, the Milky Way touched the desert sands and the rugged mountains in the distance.

Now anchored offshore, activity on the yacht was silent but swift as the sisters got ready to go ashore. The seven lesbian zombies wore white nurse-dresses with the red letters W-H-O embroidered on the back. Their white tennis shoes made squeaking noises on the steps as they shuffled medical bags and a folding table down to the swim deck. There was no giggling and flirting. The sisters were dead serious.

Thc *USS Carmick* had dropped anchor four hundred yards behind *Girls' Night Out.* Launch doors in the hull were opened, platforms lowered, and under a crimson glow, heavily armed sailors launched two landing rafts and motored toward the yacht's swim deck. There, the unarmed and fragile-looking girls crawled over the rubber inflated side tubes and took positions on the plank seating. The sailors loaded the gear and made the sisters don lifejackets.

By the time they were underway, sunlight glowed on the horizon in anticipation of daybreak. A desert breeze blew its hot breath across the waves as the landing rafts rode the curling swells to shore, a stretch of sand between rocky outcrops, cluttered with moored and beached fishing boats.

The girls jumped out, tossed their lifejackets, gathered together the medical bags and folding table then watched the rafts back out, motor around, and accelerate to top speed to fly over the waves, crash down and race back toward the Carmick.

The beach was void of swimmers this early, but signs of life included wooden lean-tos and sun-shields without walls, one with a sign that read *Scuba Club* in English and Arabic. A sandy road led away from the beach and curved into a village of mostly flat-roofed dwellings and sheds set helter-skelter, and more sand. There wasn't a tree as far as the eye could see.

Before the sun broke over the horizon, a man's chanting voice wailed hauntingly across the village, a song of sorts from the Imam calling his people to morning prayers. Women wearing full-body burkas and men in baggy pants and long sleeves appeared in the road with their prayer rugs and trudged toward the sound, their sandaled feet kicking dust into the breeze.

"Come on, sisters," Brenda said. "Follow them."

Three hundred feet up the road, they came to a square, of sorts, a flat area of sand edged by brick hovels that shared the space with a transmission tower. The people laid out their rugs, men to the front—women to the rear, removed their shoes, and stood facing toward Mecca to begin.

The Imam, wearing a black robe and white pakol hat, strode to the front, turned to face Mecca, and began reciting the morning prayer in Arabic.

The sisters had the same thoughts about this murderer of children. *He's going to die a brutal and painful death.*

Brenda read his mind and was surprised to learn the Imam actually believed in his righteousness. Allah demanded a high price for his reverence, a price he was willing to pay with the blood of his brethren.

The sisters set up the table and arranged the phony vaccine bottles and genuine syringes in a professional manner. There were cotton balls and rubbing alcohol to keep the ruse authentic.

The Imam turned back to his flock. "Salam a Alaykum. May peace be upon you," ending the morning prayers just as the sun broke over the horizon.

Everyone stood and gathered up their prayer rugs.

It was then Jackie noticed how the sand glistened in the rising sunlight, like there was something special about it. She scooped up a handful, let it sift through her fingers, and savored its softness, perfect for her new line of facial scrub products.

Brenda batted the sand from Jackie's hand. "Stop fooling around. Focus."

The Imam spoke to his faithful followers. "Today we have nurses from the World Health Organization to immunize us against a terrible plague that is coming." He shuffled to the table, and from inside his robe, he produced a list, which he handed to Brenda. "Everyone line up over here. Men first, women last. I have been assured the vaccine is safe though some of us may experience side-effects, but I assure you they are very mild."

The sisters took their positions at the table, armed themselves with fresh syringes and cotton balls. The four red-dot vials were easily at hand.

Brenda checked the list of names, found the three al-Hakim brothers present, and started checking off names of the other men as they got the placebo.

"Name, sir?"

"Sada ala-Badir."

She checked off his name. He moved to Chloe's station where she applied a good scrubbing of alcohol, then on to Melinda who delivered the harmless injection. The line moved swiftly.

"Name, sir?"

"Ahmed al-Hakim." He had the skin of pig and the beady eyes of a desert rat. "And these..." He turned to the two men behind him. "are my brothers, Hasan and Saul."

Restraining the urge to rip out their hearts, Brenda calmly checked off their names and directed them to Maria who cleaned the arms, then to Monica who administered death to the rapist brothers. "May peace be upon you." They'd be long down the road before the seizures struck.

There was one red-dot remaining.

Mohammed Abdullah Abadi, the Imam himself, stepped in front of the women in line and pulled up the sleeve of his black robe. "Allah Akbar."

Monica doubled up the dosage from the red-dot vial and

stabbed the needle into the arm of Jasmine's killer. He didn't even wince.

She emptied the syringe. "May peace be upon you."

He stepped back and stared at Monica. "You are the most beautiful woman I have ever seen, like a black angel sent from Satan himself." His eyes went crossed. A tremor racked his arms, then his shoulders, then his head started flailing on his neck. His knees buckled, he fell to the ground, and his entire body went into spasms, legs kicking, back arched. Gagging noïses came from his throat as bubbling phlegm gurgled from his lips.

The women stood back in shock, their wide eyes visible through the slits in their burkas.

Brenda jumped into action. "Go, everyone. It's the plague. The vaccine came too late for him." She grabbed a needle loaded with the placebo, rushed to the stricken Iman, and gave him a useless shot in the ass, right through the robe. Sweat leaked from his pores as if his body were squeezing out every drop of water. His breaths came fast and shallow and his face turned blue. Within seconds, his jerking and gagging ceased. Brenda looked up to the women standing back in fear. "It was Allah's will."

The desert breeze chilled and Brenda saw the ghost of Jasmine hovering over the dead man. "I am here to take your soul to hell." A thump of air, then a blast of heat, and then she was gone.

Brenda stood. "Pack it up, girls. Our work here is done."

***

General Wesley Miller and his company of Rangers hadn't seen so much as a snake move across the desert they were guarding. The ground temperature had already risen to a hundred degrees, and the swirling winds were like a blast furnace to his face.

What's taking those women so long?

His satellite phone buzzed. It was General Taylor.

"Heads up, Wes. Robert reports a caravan of Taliban trucks out of Karachi are racing to your position."

"How the hell did they know we're here?"

"Communications picked up an alert about the USS Carmick

anchored offshore. That's got them all in a tizzy."

"Hell." He hung up and grabbed his two-way. "Attention all squad leaders. Lock and load. We've got company."

He'd no sooner said the words when the first mortar shells whistled in, blasting geysers of sand in the air all along their line of defense. Gunfire rolled across the desert. The enemy had the high ground, and they could pick off his men like they were ducks in a shooting gallery.

"Medic. Medic," men cried.

"Fall back," he screamed into the two-way then switched to the Trans-star com-link. "Carmick, this is Sand Toad. We need a little help out here."

As Wes and his men retreated toward the beach at a full run, cannons boomed in the distance, again and again, as the *USS Carmick* unleashed the mighty power of a US Navy destroyer. Gigantic fireballs mushroomed over the desert, followed by thunderous concussions that slugged Wes in the back and made the sand jump all around his running feet. Crossing the road, he saw three local men on the ground, flopping around like fish out of water. *What the hell is wrong with those guys?* A barrage of concussions made them quickly forgotten.

In spite of the overwhelming firepower being hurled at them, the Taliban fought back with the sizzling spew of an RPG. The rocket propelled grenade streaked over the village and flew harmlessly out to sea, or so he thought until a horrendous explosion echoed back. By the time he got to the water's edge, a yacht anchored offshore was ablaze, and multi-million-dollar parts were raining down and splashing into the water. "Holy shit."

Again, the Carmick's cannons blew smoke and fire. It was 400 yards farther out to sea and beyond the range of an RPG. Sonic booms cracked across a clear blue sky. Hell rained down on the Taliban.

In all the chaos, Wes couldn't help but notice the beautiful W-H-O nurses, all leggy in their white dresses, running down the beach. They jumped into waiting rubber landing rafts. It suddenly occurred to him how defenseless the nurses were, how fragile, how much they needed his protection. "Hold this position, boys."

The Rangers dug in and picked off Taliban charging from the village. Turbans and blood flew through the air.

"Second squad. Hold our left flank." A bullet blew the radio out of his right hand. Shocked at first, he didn't feel the burn, but when he looked at his palm and saw the spurting blood, the pain hit him like a two-ton truck. The bullet had gone clean through. "Medic."

Bent over, he clung to his wrist with his good hand, hoping he wouldn't bleed to death on foreign soil. His vision blurred and he felt dizzy. Out of the haze, a redhead in white appeared before him, her visage surrounded by a halo of light, absolutely stunning in every way. She looked at his hand. "Oh boy."

"Is it bad?"

"If you ever want to wipe your ass with it, then yes, it's bad." She tore a strip off the hem of her dress as easily as if it were made of paper. "I can see shattered bones and severed ligaments. It may have to be amputated."

"Lose my hand? No, oh no." His head got really fuzzy, as if he might pass out or puke. Maybe shock was setting in.

She spit on the wound and wrapped up his hand. "That'll have to do for now." She seemed to fly to a waiting raft and dove in with two other angels.

Dumbfounded, he watched the raft speed her away. "Who was that angel of the battlefield?" He tried to work his fingers, but that was a bad move. The pain was crippling.

Fireballs blossomed along the only dirt road leading to the village, cutting off Taliban support and reinforcements. It was now a battle of attrition, the winner determined by whose men could hold out the longest.

Wes pulled out his sidearm and got to work.

***

Monica threw herself into the bottom of the Navy raft. Bullets zinged overhead. Jackie, Melinda, and Chloe were with her as the pilot pulled a U-ie and motored full speed into the oncoming waves. The raft shot up into the air and crashed back down. During that moment of zero Gs, she hung in midair and glimpsed more rafts speeding toward shore, *the Navy to the rescue,* and then she slammed back into the bottom of the raft. Once the ride smoothed out, she sat up on the plank seat and witnessed the bloodbath on the beach. Then morality hit her like a board to the chest. *How many good men had to die for Jasmine's revenge?*

A second raft fell into formation alongside her. Brenda, Maria, and Donna were safely aboard, their hair streaming behind shocked faces. *What are they looking at?*

She turned her gaze out to sea and saw a most horrific sight. *Girl's Night Out*, what was left of her burning hull, made a desperate bob in the water, as if reaching up to gasp its last breath, then slipped below the surface of the Arabian Sea.

"What happened to our boat...er...yacht?" she asked the raft pilot.

"Taliban RPG, ma'am. Direct hit. It was spectacular."

"Spectacular? What about the crew?"

"They're fine. All abandoned ship. We picked 'em up. They're on the Carmick right now."

She put a hand on her chest. "Thank Goddess." Then another problem formed a pit in her stomach. "How are we getting home?"

"You'll be shuttled to a base in Bahrain and flown back to the states."

She felt suddenly sick, like the adrenaline that belted her system was as poisonous as the strychnine vaccine.

Alfons is going to kill me.

***

Wes wasn't the only causality of the battle. Many men were wounded, but no KIAs. He and all his Rangers were soon shuttled off the beach to the *USS Carmick*.

Being a Brigadier General, Wes was treated to plush officers' quarters with a view of the ocean. He wasn't there five minutes when someone knocked on the door. Opening it, he found himself face to face with Captain Marquez. "Welcome aboard, sir. It's a pleasure to have an Army General with us." He saluted.

Wes returned the salute.

"I see your hand is bandaged. What happened?"

"I took one for the team."

"You should see the medic."

Wes flexed his fingers. "Odd. It doesn't hurt a bit." He balled a fist, effortlessly. *How the hell is this possible?*

Marquez opened the door and shouted to the duty officer, "Get me a corpsman in here on the double."

"Yes, sir."

Moments later, a corpsman entered the plush cabin and saluted. "What seems to be the problem?"

Perplexed, Wes sat on a bed fit for a luxury suite at the Hilton. "I don't understand..."

"Let me take a look." The corpsman unwrapped the white makeshift bandage, saw it stained red, then looked at the General's palm. "Huh?" He turned the hand over, looking for any kind of wound, but found nothing. "Sir, as you can see, there's nothing wrong with you."

Shock blurred his vision as he stared at his hand, perfectly healed. Events tumbled through his mind, the impact of the bullet, the spurting blood, the angelic nurse, the torn strip from her dress, the spit... *Why did she spit on it*? There was something angelic about that nurse. If he voiced his suspicions now, these guys would think he was suffering from PTSD. "Doc, you're right. In the heat of battle, weird things can happen."

The corpsman left, not knowing what to think.

Marquez said, "Let's go to the Mess Deck. Great victories always make me hungry."

Chapter Twenty-One

Word spread fast all over the world about the American women who risked life and limb to vaccinate the people of Baddish, Pakistan, against a deadly virus that took the life of their Imam and three brothers of the village. Seeing that the people of the world could not get enough news about the Saviors of Baddish, as they became known, politicians jumped into the limelight.

Senator Wayne Morgan, along with the other ninety-nine members of the Senate, recommended the heroines for the Medal of Freedom. With the evil Imam eliminated, the Islamic hammer above the heads of the faithful women of Baddish had been removed. Most had traded their burkas for salwar kameezzes and simple hijabs. However, there were men in the Taliban who despised these American women and desired retaliation in the name of Allah. Because of this possible threat to the homeland, the President resisted the Congressional recommendation, but under extreme political pressure that, if he didn't agree, he might lose the next election, he finally signed the executive order, live on the nightly news, and invited the women to the White House to receive their awards.

General Wesley Miller and the Rangers under his command, along with the sailors of the *USS Carmick*, made appearances on news broadcasts and nightly talk shows. Fox News, CNN, MSNBC, they all wanted to get in on the ratings war, but the great military battle and victory outrated the Saviors of Baddish. WNN made the biggest score on the Bill Barker show when he offered high-drama romance to his viewers.

Looking into the Camera, Barker said, "On tonight's show we have two very special guests. Frank Leatherwood and his lovely bride Carrie." They were sitting on the couch, like love doves on a wire, next to Bill's desk. "Frank, I'll start with you. I heard you met Carrie on the wing of the plane that crashed in the Aegean Sea."

"Yeah, Bill. Carrie was one of only two survivors. As I was lowered from the chopper, I thought even then that she was the most beautiful girl that I had ever seen."

"I heard she was naked."

"Yeah, well, that too, but I never dreamed I would make her my wife, which came to be true quicker than I ever imagined."

"Carrie, what was your first impression of Frank?"

"I thought he was really cute and very polite."

Barker, with a big smile, chuckled. "You're standing on the wing of a plane, naked, and the first thing you thought was that he was cute? Weren't you worried that a storm was coming?"

The camera zoomed in on Carrie's face. "No. Not with a big strong sailor standing next to me."

The audience applauded.

Barker said, "We'll be right back."

Meanwhile, at The Ranch, the sisters were gathered around the screen. Jackie said, "Knock off the talking. They're going to run my new commercial."

"Do you suffer from wrinkled aging skin? Then we have just the thing for you. Here's the president of Jackie's Skin Care Products, Jackie O' Neal. 'Ladies, when we were in Baddish, helping the people, I was impressed at how soft the sand was, and that got me to thinking. This sand would be perfect as an ingredient in my new Soft as Silk Facial Scrub. The sand that we are now importing from Baddish has helped the village's economy and, as you know, made the women there more independent.' Look for Jackie's Soft as Silk Facial Scrub in a store near you."

Bill Barker returned. "While we were away at commercial break, Carrie told me she has some wonderful news to announce to the American people. Go ahead, Carrie."

"Frank and I are going to have a baby."

The Sisterhood all screamed in unison.

Monica gasped. "Brenda, this cannot be true. She is a lesbian zombie, and like all of us, she cannot get pregnant."

"This is the wish of our Goddess, Loa, so all miracles are possible. Carrie is our sister and will forever be our sister. Okay, girls. The show's over. Everyone in the pool."

***

Robert had just finished closing down Fort Huachuca and, at the Phoenix airport, drank a couple of beers with his Rangers from Charlie 2-5, and then he said goodbye before heading down Concourse B to his gate.

First Lieutenant Barry Gee yelled at him, "Pleasure serving with you again, Captain."

"Robert yelled back, "Until next time."

"Hey, Captain."

He turned around to see his men flipping him the bird.

They all laughed.

Robert saluted them with a bird-finger to the brow. As he got on the plane, he thought how great it felt going home to his family and getting back to his civilian job at the company he owned.

***

Over at The Ranch, the sisters had been eagerly awaiting Caroline, Betsy, and Lilly and Jill to return from Disney World. Jorge drove up in the new limo, and the Florida-tanned tourists jumped out and ran to their sisters, screaming and giggling and hugging. After Jorge unloaded the trunk, the girls grabbed their stuff and ran into the house to show off the souvenirs they'd bought for everyone. Girlie Dog tail-wagged to each sister and jumped up on them. Brenda sat in the LazyGirl chair to watch the happy reunions.

Betsy rushed over and jumped up on Brenda's lap. She made an *oof* sound, but recovered quickly. "Did you two have a good time?"

"Yep. It was the best time ever. I missed you, sister Brenda."

Hugging Betsy, Brenda said, "And we all missed you."

Caroline, not wanting to be left out, ran over and joined in. As the girls blabbered on and on about what was the most fun, Brenda just smiled and thought about what comes next.

We have nine days until Black Friday 2. Before then we have to meet with the President to get our Medals of Freedom, Monica has to face Alfons about his destroyed yacht, make sure the Girls'

Night Out crew is invited to the party, get Carrie and Frank a nice house in New London, and get Kincade to assign him to the submarine school there.

Brenda and Jackie had a full plate and would need to depend more on all the sisters.

At 3:00am, Brenda went downstairs and made a call to Admiral Kincade on his private cell. “Roy, I need you to do me one more favor.”

“For you, Brenda, anything.” He was hoping to get hooked up with her at the party.

“I would greatly appreciate it if you would have AIRRs First Class Frank Leatherwood relieved of his duty on the Carmick and station him on the Navel Base at New London, Connecticut, for submarine school.”

“I’ll take care of it right now, Brenda. See you at the party.”

Five hours after Brenda had talked to Admiral Kincade, there was a knock on the door of room 218 at the Travelodge in New London, Connecticut. Frank put on a pair of shorts to answer it. Carrie just pulled the covers up over her bare breasts. Frank opened the door. Standing there were two Shore Patrol sailors. “Are you AIRRs First Class Frank Leatherwood?”

“Affirmative.”

“We have orders for you.” They handed him a brown 9x12 envelope, and written on it were the words *Orders for Frank Leatherwood from the Department of the Navy*. When he looked up, the sailors were already walking down the stairs.

Frank sat on Carrie’s side of the bed.

She pulled the covers down and looked at him. “What is it?”

“Orders from the Navy.”

“What does it say?”

“I’m about to find out.” He opened the envelope.

“To: AIRRs First Class Frank Leatherwood. You will report to Headquarters Company Submarine School USN Base, New London, Connecticut, in three weeks from today at 900 hours.”

“Frank, that’s great.”

“Yeah. My life’s dream.” He got up and looked in the mirror as if trying to imagine himself in a Submariner’s uniform.

“So why don’t you look happy?”

“Brenda has a lot more pull with the Navy than I ever

imagined. I can't help but think this assignment comes with strings attached."

"You worry too much, Frank."

The room phone rang. Carrie answered it. "Hello?"

"Carrie?"

"Yes?"

"You don't know me. My name is Maggie Johnson, and I'm one of your sisters, though I don't live at The Ranch. Brenda wanted us to meet, so I'm calling to invite you and Frank to our house here in New London for dinner tonight. Then we can show you your new house across the street from ours."

Carrie gasped. "New house?"

Frank shot her a sideways glance.

"Jackie bought it for you."

"Really? Jackie bought it?"

"Jorge will pick you up at 4:00pm. Okay?"

She glanced at the phone as if it weren't real then looked at Frank, saw the dread in his eyes. "We'll be ready. See you then."

She hung up the phone then motioned to Frank. "Come here, honey. You can't make me any more pregnant than I am now."

"Jackie bought us a house?"

"Isn't that wonderful?"

Frank sat on the bed in deep thought, then: "Do you realize that less than six weeks ago we didn't know each other existed? The only thing on my mind was submarine training in New London. Now look what has taken place since I pulled you off a broken wing floating in the sea. I spent the best three days ever with the most beautiful girl in the world, picked you off a yacht in a helicopter, flew back to Manhattan with you. Somewhere along the way I got you pregnant, had a Navy Chaplain marry us, got into a cream puff Navy school, and now a new house. There's got to be something to that *Loa*, Goddess of the Universe you've been telling me about."

"I knew you'd come around, dear."

***

In front of the Empire State building, a monolith to the tycoons of industry, Joseph parked Alfons' stretched limo in the loading zone. Monica stepped out to face the music for Alfons' bullet-riddled yacht lying at the bottom of the Arabian Sea.

And he was worried about a few scratches.

He'd summoned her to his office and even supplied Joseph and his limo to make sure she complied. "Wait right here, Joseph."

"Yes, ma'am."

On the elevator ride up to the twenty-fifth floor, she wasn't worried about his anger, *make that rage*, because she had a surprise for him. However, getting to the surprise would require negotiating a minefield of reprimands and cusswords.

Stepping out of the elevator, she braced herself for the storm and entered the massive KOMA LTD offices. The staff threw her dagger-glares as she walked past them. Alfons' rage had everyone on edge and blaming her. She walked into his office.

Alfons was sitting in the dark, his back to the door. "I told you I don't want to be bothered until Monica gets here."

"Alfons, it's me."

He spun his chair around. "Monica." He stood. "You promised to bring my yacht back in one piece."

"Alfons—"

Walking toward her, he yelled, "My insurance won't cover the loss because it was due to an act of war."

"But Alfons—"

"Why was my yacht in a damn war zone?"

"It was for a good cause, Alfons."

Now he was shouting in her face. "I ought to throw your ass out this window."

"Nah." She placed a beautifully manicured black hand on his chest. "You would not harm the best black woman you have ever had."

He held his breath, let it out with a groan, then stormed back to his desk and plopped down in his chair. "Yeah. You're right, but I've had my fill of Brenda. Tell her I'm done. Finished. Finito."

"Come on, Alfons. Take a ride with me. Joseph is waiting downstairs."

"Why can't you let me suffer in peace?"

"Get up. Let's go. I have something to show you."

"Damn." He couldn't deny her anything, and he knew she knew it. He followed her past his staff, much like a whipped dog with an invisible leash.

Alfons didn't say a word as Joseph drove to the Brooklyn docks, just pouted the entire way.

Joseph parked in a passenger loading zone.

Monica nudged Alfons. "Are you ready?"

"No. I'm mad."

"Come on."

They got out and walked to the docks where the richest of the rich moored their expensive toys. The yacht tied up in front of him, water lapping at its hull, stopped him cold. The name on the stern read: *Three Sheets to the Wind.*

"What the hell?"

"Brenda thought you'd like this one just as well as *Girls' Night Out*, so Jackie bought it." Monica took his hand and walked him up the gangway to a royally carpeted atrium with glass elevators and crystal chandeliers.

"My God. What did this cost her?"

"Don't ask. You like it?"

"I love it."

"Then let's try out the master suite."

On the way up in the glass elevator, she clung to his arm as he gazed around with his mouth agape. "Forget what I said about Brenda."

After a three hour screw-a-thon with Alfons, Monica was glad to be on her way back to The Ranch. *Thank goddess all is well with Alfons now that he has his new yacht. It's a much bigger yacht so his all-girl crew will have to hire more women crew members. I am sure he will not mind.*

Now back home, she watched Caroline and Betsy on the lawn, driving Girlie Dog crazy with a bubble-blowing machine. Brenda came out and walked Monica back to the house. "Tomorrow we have to be at LaGuardia at 6:00am. Alfons' plane will take us to DC."

"No rest for the heroines."

"Monica, we have to implore our sisters to behave. They'll be meeting the President of the United States. We can't have any of their stupid girl shenanigans like trying to kiss him, goddess damn it."

At 5:00am, Brenda made the sisters line up for inspection.

She walked down the line like a drill sergeant, but stopped at Chloe. "You don't wear a miniskirt to the White House. It's not a pickup bar. Another thing. If the President asks you why you went to Pakistan, stick to the phony reason we were there. Don't say we really went over there to kill a child murderer for Jasmine, and on the way we shot the hell out of some pirates. Lastly, if you get the chance, compliment the First Lady on what she's wearing. Say she looks beautiful."

Maria asked, "What if I don't like her dress?"

"Keep it to yourself, or the President will berate you on TV and online. Okay, sisters, any other stupid questions?"

Finally, after hugging and saying goodbye to the girls and Lilly and Jill, the Sisterhood was ready to make its mark on Washington.

They were about to pull away in the limo when they heard, "Wait, wait." It was Chloe. She had changed to a more suitable dress...only halfway up her thighs.

Jackie counted noses this time. Seven. "Okay, let's go."

At the White House, in the East Room, the seven sisters sat in a semi-circle of chairs in front of a raised podium. Members of the press corps were photographing them from every direction, and as girls would be girls, they were hamming it up for the cameras.

Someone announced, "Please rise for The president of the United States."

The sisters stood, as did everyone in the room.

The President stepped directly to the podium. He wore an expensive suit and red tie. "Thank you very much. Thank you. Be seated. Today I have the pleasure to award each of these beautiful American women the Presidential Medal of Freedom. Before I get to that, I want to acknowledge the presence of two great men who are here with us today. First is General Wesley Miller who was in command of the Rangers who provided perimeter security."

Wes stood and nodded ceremoniously to the applauding onlookers on his left and on his right.

Wearing a big grin, the President added, "I think the Taliban will think twice before taking on the US Army Rangers again. If they do, they'll want to make sure their life insurance is paid up."

Everyone laughed and continued the applause.

After Wes sat back down, Lynne patted his thigh. "I'm so

proud of you."

The President cleared his throat. "The next man I want to acknowledge is Admiral Roy Kincade who was previously in command of all US Navy operations in the Mediterranean." Looking at Roy, he added, "Don't look so shocked, Roy. I'm not firing you. As of today you are now a member of the Joint Chiefs of Staff. Take a bow, Roy."

Roy saluted the President and then sat down. The folks around him gave him attaboy slaps on his shoulders.

"Roy's part of the mission was to secure safe passage for our Saviors of Baddish as they passed through pirate-infested waters. He tasked the *USS Carmick* with that job, and those sailors showed great courage fighting off the pirates. Their commander couldn't be here today, but let me tell you, Captain Marquez did an outstanding job blasting the Taliban with cannon fire."

The applause was deafening.

"It's time to present your medals, ladies. Please come up."

The sisters lined up beside the podium to raucous applause. As the President placed the blue and white ribbons around each sister's neck, Brenda felt pride in her girls, but something felt off about this whole affair.

"Congratulations." He stepped back. "Thank you, ladies." He turned and left without taking questions from reporters.

Chapter Twenty-Two

In New London, Maggie and Robert led Frank and Carrie across the street to show them their new home. Robert gave Frank the key. Frank was spellbound as he opened the door.

The house had everything, vaulted ceilings, high windows, carpet, ceramic tile, furniture and appliances, all new.

Carrie said, "It even has a nursery...crib...changing table...animal mobile and matching wallpaper."

Maggie smiled. "So you like it?"

"I love it."

"Good. I decorated it."

"Sister, thank you, thank you. Can I hold Zoey again. I need to start getting in some baby practice."

Carrie and Maggie sat in the nursery while Frank and Robert sat out on the back porch, drinking beer.

It was Frank who brought up the subject that had been on his mind since the three-day lovefest in Rhodes. "You know, Robert, it has been my experience that nobody does something for nothing. Now I really appreciate what Jackie and Brenda have done for me. Hell, if it weren't for them I'd still be on the Carmick, brokenhearted over missing Carrie." He swigged beer. "But I fear they want something from me in return."

Taking a slug of his own beer, Robert looked at Frank and thought he was a good man who just needed to lighten up. "I'll tell you this. They won't ask you to kill anybody."

"After seeing what they did to those pirates, I figure they can handle any threat that comes along."

Robert agreed. "The Sisterhood has been good to me."

"So how did you get involved?"

Robert's expression turned thoughtful. "I met Maggie in a

coffee shop."

"That's romantic...I guess."

"My dad went there every morning, met her first. He thought I might be good for her...and vise versa, but I never met her until after he died. I inherited his company. You may have heard of it. Galaxy International Inc."

"Wait a minute. You own Galaxy International? Hell, they made the electronics updates on the Carmick. Your company has got to be one of the biggest corporations in the country."

"Actually, it's number twenty-seven. Brenda had nothing to do with that, but I'll tell you what Brenda did do for me. On my last patrol in Afghanistan, I suffered a bullet wound to my neck...made me a quadriplegic."

"Really? You're fine now."

"I thought I was doomed, told Maggie to forget me and make a new life for herself and our baby."

"What a downer, man." Frank swigged beer.

"Maggie called Brenda for her help."

"Is she some kind of neurological specialist?"

"I don't know. She gave me, for lack of a better word, a virus, according to her, some kind of protein molecule that's been in development in Israel for years." That was a lie, of course. He couldn't tell Frank he'd married into a sisterhood of lesbian zombies. "So here I am, good as new. To this day I owe her my life."

"That's the most incredible story I've ever heard."

"If she needs anything, all she has to do is ask."

"That's the way I feel about Carrie...ever since our first kiss." Frank looked at his beer bottle as if staring right through it. "But Brenda? I don't know. I feel as though I have to agree with her wishes. She has some powerful friends, I'll give her that. Her connections got me off the Carmick, a transfer I would've fought tooth and nail if not for the submarine school she offered in its place."

"The Naval base is only two miles up the Thames River from here. An easy commute. And the sisters live on Long Island, right across the Sound. Have you been to The Ranch?"

"Not yet." Frank finished his beer. "But I'm sure I'll see it soon enough." He tipped his empty bottle. "Care for another?"

"I better get Maggie and Zoey home. We'll have plenty of chances to get together in the future, *neighbor*." He stood and offered Frank an official welcome to the neighborhood handshake. After the manly man-to-man, they lumbered back inside.

Maggie and Carrie came out of the nursery. "Did you boys solve every military problem in the world?"

"Maggie, let's leave these lovebirds to their new nest."

Goodbyes were exchanged and they were out the door.

Frank asked Carrie, "What do you think?"

"I'll tell you later...if you're a good boy tonight." Grabbing his hand, she led him up the stairs to break in their new bedroom.

***

Across Long Island Sound, in the early morning, Brenda, Monica, and Jackie were sitting outside in lawn chairs, discussing the Medal of Freedom ceremony at the White House. Brenda looked peeved. "Did you notice what really happened in the East Room?"

"The girls did not get us in trouble."

"The President, did you hear him, what he said?"

Monica and Jackie shrugged.

"Yeah, I thought not. That son of a bitch, all he did was talk about General Miller and Admiral Kinkade, what great jobs they did, and Captain Marquez. They could have landed on the moon. Not one word was said about how great a job we did. The ceremony was all about the Army, all about the Navy, and we were chopped liver...like women don't count in the scheme of things."

Jackie scowled. "You're right, hang a medal on us but praise the men. They took the limelight, and we were the sideshow."

Monica spat. "He is a son of a bitch, all right."

Brenda stood. "That shit's gotta stop."

"What do you suggest?" Jackie asked.

Brenda pulled her out of her chair and threw a best-buds arm around her shoulders. "How would you like to be my vice-president?"

Monica gasped.

Jackie could've been a feather in the wind. "You gotta be shitting us, Brenda. You're going to run for President?"

"Damn right we are."

***

Across the street from Robert, Maggie, and crying Zoey, Frank and Carrie were lying in bed, looking at patterns on the ceiling made by sunrays beaming in through tree branches swaying in the wind. With her head resting on Frank's left bicep, Carrie wondered what she could say about the Sisterhood without mentioning the fact they were lesbian zombies.

Readjusting the position on his arm, she thought she wouldn't say anything unless he brought it up. Then she'd play dumb as if she didn't know what he was talking about. *One thing for sure, he loves me dearly. I could probably explain my sisters, and he wouldn't leave me, but why risk it?*

"I had a very interesting conversation with Robert last night."

Yup. He had to go and bring it up. "What did you two talk about?"

"Did you know Robert served in Afghanistan?"

"No."

"He came back a quadriplegic. Bullet through his neck."

Carrie rose up a little. "No way. He's fine."

"That's what I said, then he handed me some cock-n-bull story about Brenda saving him with some protein molecule-slash-virus developed in Israel."

"I don't know. I guess so." She was playing dumb.

"Tell me what you two ladies talked about."

"Mainly baby stuff and how she had a long labor with Zoey."

"It's a shame Brenda didn't have any of that so-called virus that she gave Robert when he was in the hospital."

"Do you think it works on child birth? I'd take some." *Dumb. Dumb. Dumb.*

Frank huffed. "Tell me what the virus is. I'll get you some."

"I don't know."

"What *do* you know, Carrie?"

"I know that we met. We fell in love and I'm now carrying our baby. I know we have a beautiful home. We have wonderful friends. Powerful friends who would do anything for us. Friends that got you off of the Carmick. If they hadn't, you wouldn't be lying next to me right now."

"And don't forget submarine school."

"Frank, I don't like playing twenty questions with you. It feels like an interrogation. I really don't know what to tell you. If the way things are going for us right now isn't good enough, just tell me. Brenda will pick up the phone and have you transferred back to the Carmick by tomorrow morning. Or you can drop all the questions and be grateful for the blessings we have right now. What's it going to be?"

"Carrie, I'm sorry, but weird is weird."

She flew off the bed. "I'm going to take a shower and go see Maggie. Maybe she'll let me hold Zoey again."

"Okay. I'll drop the subject."

"Great idea." She stepped into the master bath.

"I love you, Carrie, with all my heart. Don't let Brenda send me away."

"You've got questions, I get it." She turned on the shower. "Maybe you can get answers from Brenda tonight at Alfons Duda's yacht party."

"I thought his yacht sank. In fact I know it did."

"His new one is bigger and better. Jackie bought it for him. We're going to christen it. Big shebang. You gonna come?"

"Of course," he said to the steam rolling out of the bathroom. "Honey, please, let's not argue about your friends."

"Sisters."

"All right. Sisters. I was out of order."

"Okay. Wear your dress blues. I want my man to look his best. After all, Admiral Roy Kincade and General Lawrence Taylor will be there, so you better be a good sailor." She stepped out through the steam like a goddess from the mist, towel wrapped around her body. "Now come and kiss me." She dropped the towel.

After Carrie left to see Maggie and Zoey, Frank lay on the bed with his fingers interlocked behind his head and watched the patterns sway on the ceiling. *What's the matter with me? I've got the perfect life. Hell, Brenda and Jackie are no different than anyone else...except they're rich and powerful. I should be grateful and learn to shut my big mouth.*

Frank heard the front door open.

"Hey, Frank," a familiar voice shouted. "You in here?"

“Yeah. Upstairs.” Frank put on his Navy regulation shorts and a tee shirt. “Give me a sec, I’ll be right down.” He stabbed his feet into his shoes and headed downstairs. “What’s up?”

“I came over to fill you in on the Sisterhood.”

“Was Carrie complaining to Maggie about me?”

“She said you have questions she can’t answer.”

“Okay.” He directed Robert to sit at the table. “Let’s start with Brenda.”

“Look, when I was strung up in that spine contraption at Walter Reed, praying that I would die, Brenda came to my rescue. I don’t know how she did it, but within a couple of minutes I could move my arms and then my legs. About five minutes later I was sitting up and then I got up and walked. I was back at a hundred percent and out of the hospital the next day. I don’t care how she did it, Frank. That’s the truth. Just as you shouldn’t care how she’s helped you and Carrie.”

“But at what price?”

“Come on, Frank. Lighten up. Some things in life are free. Friendship. Love. Dignity. All you’ve got to do is want it, believe it. Have a little faith. Speaking of which, the Sisterhood believes in *Loa,* the Goddess of the Universe.”

“Carrie told me about Loa. God isn’t God. Doesn’t that bother you?”

“People believe in different deities. Jesus, Mary, Buddha, Allah, King Kong. Nobody’s wrong. Nobody’s right. So, no. It doesn’t bother me, and it shouldn’t bother you.”

“Then what about her relationships with the higher-ups like Kincade and Taylor? She must have something on those guys.”

“Respect, Frank. Mutual respect. Whatever their bonds are made of, it’s working in our favor, so my advice to you is to accept it.”

“Yeah.” Frank sighed. “Thanks, man. You made me feel a lot better.”

“Great.” Robert slapped the table. “I got an idea. I’m sure you two have been invited to Alfons’ yacht party tonight.”

“Yes. Carrie made it clear she’s going. I’m a tagalong.”

“How about riding with us? Make it a double date, well, double and a half if you count Zoey.”

“Sounds good to me.”

"Come over at 1600 hours. And be ready to party."

***

Later, Robert drove his Land Rover, and Frank rode shotgun. Carrie and Maggie were gabbing in the back. Zoey started getting mad again because, like all babies, she constantly wanted more breast milk. As she suckled, Carrie reached over and pulled down part of Maggie's blouse so she could watch. "That is so cute. I can't wait until I'm doing the same with our baby."

Robert pulled into the Brooklyn Docks and found a place to park. It wasn't easy. There were a lot of cars on account of Duda's party. Heavy Metal music blasted from the upper deck.

Walking up the dock to the yacht, Frank let go of Carrie's hand when he saw Admiral Kincade talking to General Taylor at the foot of the gangway. They were having a hardy laugh over something and didn't notice Frank and Carrie until they were ten feet from them. Frank stopped and saluted. "Good evening, Admiral Kincade, and you too, General Taylor." They returned the salute then Admiral Kincade took Carrie's hand, kissed it and looked at Frank. "No wonder Brenda asked to have you relieved from duty on the Carmick. You wanted to get back to drydock and make this lovely young lady your wife."

"Affirmative, sir."

"Frank," the General put in. "I'm sorry the Army didn't get you first."

"Actually, General, I've got sea salt in my blood."

"How about the way those girls handled the pirates?"

"Admiral, only a fool would take on the Sisterhood and the United States Navy. It's a one-way ticket to Davy Jones' Locker."

"Now I know why Brenda holds you in high regard. You're a good man to have in a fight, if she needs one."

"Maybe, General, but I'm still in the Navy. I'll leave the fighting to you Army guys."

"If you ever change your mind, Brenda could get you out in thirty minutes. Hell, I think Brenda could get the devil out of hell in thirty minutes."

They had a good laugh, but Frank wasn't so sure it was a laughing matter. Walking up the gangway, Carrie asked him, "Do you still think there's something sinister about my sisters?"

"No. You have me convinced, honey."

Just as soon as they got on deck, Carrie made a beeline to join her sisters at the bar where they were getting looped. They had brought Betsy and Caroline, now in the care of Joseph and Jorge. The all-girl crew of the sunken *Girls' Night Out* was getting wild with six new lesbian crew members. They'd all be naked by midnight.

As the evening wore on, Frank was flying solo. The sisters were smashed, and Robert had emersed the General and Admiral in war stories. Jorge and Joseph took Betsy to the galley for ice cream and left Frank to entertain Caroline, who was equally as bored. She liked Frank right away, so she told him everything about what had happened to her.

"After my mommy and daddy were killed in the car wreck, Monica came and got me. Now I'm in the Sisterhood. And I have a doggie."

"What's the dog's name?"

"Girlie Dog."

"Is she a friendly dog?"

"Sometimes, but not all the time. There was a time when Lilly's husband came over to our house, and he grabbed me, but Girlie Dog bit him in the leg. Blood squirted everywhere and I watched him die. He was a bad man."

Shock raced up Frank's spine. "Oh my god. Sorry you had to see that. Did Brenda call the police?"

"I don't know. I'm just a kid."

Chalking the fantastical story up to Caroline's imagination, Frank asked, "Who are your best friends?"

"My best friend is Goddess *Loa*. She told me some numbers to tell to Brenda, and they led to my sisters in the plane crash where they were alive."

"Yes. I was on the rescue mission."

She patted his arm. "You're the good guy. My other best friend is Betsy. Before her, I didn't have any friends and that made me sad. So sister Monica went to the school and talked to sister Jill, and she said Betsy was autistic, and the kids made her cry. So sister Monica gave her some Kool-Aid, and now she's smart like me."

"Kool-Aid?" *There must've been something in it...like a virus?* "You said your parents died in a car crash. How did that happen?"

"A motorhome with some old people in it hit our car. I was the only survivor. The jaws of life got me out. My mommy and daddy are happy with Loa now. They watch over me every day."

The music stopped. People started moving toward the exit, some stumbling, some holding each other up.

"It looks like the party is over." Frank saw a woman he recognized from the yacht after the pirate battle. "Who's that black woman waving at you?"

"She's my new mommy, Monica." Caroline took off running and caught up with Jill and Betsy, waved goodbye to Monica, and then the three of them disappeared as they ran down the gangway to catch up with her other sisters and Robert and Maggie and Zoey.

Frank leaned on the gunwale and thought about his friends on the Carmick in the Arabian Sea, and then he thought about all that Caroline had said. She had a very active imagination. Maybe she saw some horror movie or had a nightmare. *I've got to quit questioning every little thing.*

Just then, he felt Carrie's hand on his back. "Time to go. Everybody's leaving except Monica and Alfons. Joseph will take them home later."

All the way back to New London, Frank mulled over the strange events that had happened. *What the hell have I gotten myself into?*

Chapter Twenty-Three

The sisters staggered downstairs for breakfast. Memories of the yacht party were still prevalent in their hungover minds. Just then, Alfons' Limo pulled up and Monica got out.

Brenda looked at Jackie. "Looks like she pulled an all-nighter."

"I'm surprised as you are. Maybe he offered her something special."

"You mean like a yacht full of women."

"The all-girl crew? Could be."

It was then, out the corner of her eye, a shadow in the Crystal Shrine moved, and she heard Loa's call like a whisper in the wind. "I'll be right back."

At the greenhouse, she opened the door, and Caroline and Betsy ran up out of nowhere and tried to go in with her. "Sorry, girls. I have to speak with *Loa,* alone."

"Ah shoot."

"*Loa* will talk to you some other time."

Brenda went inside and shut the door on the grumbling girls. Though she loved *Loa* with all her heart, she still felt fear in the presence of the Goddess of all that existed. She slowly turned from locking the deadbolt and saw the Goddess *Loa* sitting in Brenda's throne chair, her long white dress, golden hair, and beauty beyond compare. In her mind, Brenda heard *Loa*'s voice. *Come here, my sweet and loyal Brenda, and get down in front of me on your knees.*

Brenda knelt and saw through Loa as if she were a ghost, but she knew it wasn't a ghost who spoke to her now:

"It was after the male gods brought forth all the stars of the universe, stars that breathed life into my ethereal spirt and beautiful form. But my beauty only brought me pain, as the male gods made me their sex slave to mock my solar mother's wishes for equality. Before she sacrificed her own being that I might live free, she endowed me with the power of lust, by which I plied the gods with lasciviousness and wine I'd made from crushed elderberries, an ocean of wine greater than all the seas on Earth, from which they drank non-stop for a million years until that sea turned dry. Then they slept, and that's when I implanted Telomeres in their cells, the same biomechanism that makes human cells grow old. Their otherworldly bodies aged and slowly turned to sand. They begged for mercy, but sand they became and sand they remained. Then one day, I scattered the sand into the winds of Jupiter where it will spin around and around forever. However, there was a wave of sand that blew back toward the earth. I could not catch it so I blessed it in the name of all women to be. Over the eons I lost thought of it, until it appeared in the windblown sands of Baddish, a parting seed from the male gods who had deprived women that which they had given so freely to men. Dominance. Now that blessed sand will ascend women to dominance by Jackie O'Neal's hand."

Brenda had gotten the message. The sands of Baddish were in Jackie's *Soft as Silk Facial Scrub.*

Loa added, "Women around the country will be beautified and empowered and grateful to Jackie, and women's equality will soon be written in the stars, however, you must win the White House first." Loa's ethereal form faded into the Sister Tree of Life.

Go now, Brenda, and do my bidding.

***

When Brenda got back inside, Caroline and Betsy were sleeping. Jackie and Monica decided to finish off a full bottle of Chateau Petrus, all 2,500 dollars' worth. Brenda poured a glass for herself and joined her sisters in the sitting room. She raised her glass to them. "Here's to our campaign for the Presidency." They toasted. "Monica, I want you to be in charge."

"I do not know anything about politics."

"Contact the election commission. They'll tell you what you need to do. We'll announce our run for the White House at the

Black Friday 2 party. Jackie, write the announcement. Melinda, you're on catered food service. Prime rib, steak, lobster. Spare no expense. Jill, I want you and Maria on optics, banners and flags and ribbons and bows. Donna, presentation, from music to china and linen. Lilly will help you. Chloe, whisky, wine, and beer. You and Lilly can bartend. Wear something like Hugh Hefner's playgirls. Jorge will handle security, and—"

"Brenda..." Jackie set her glass on the end table. "You're all fired up. What did Loa tell you out there in the Crystal Shrine?"

Brenda sat in the LazyGirl. "She—"

The door bell rang.

Jackie glanced at her diamond Hermès wristwatch. "Who the hell could be calling at this time of night?"

The bell rang again. Brenda set down her wine glass as Monica got up from the couch. "I will get it."

Moments later, with Monica leading the way, Janice Parker staggered into the room, drunk as a skunk. She stumbled to Brenda and fell to her knees. "If you want to kill me, get it over with." Tears streamed down her face.

Brenda sat there regally, arms crossed under her breasts. "Oh, sister, my poor sister, I would never think to kill you, but if I ever find that slob husband of yours, I'll cut off his balls with a really dull pair of scissors. We'll see what kind of a macho stud Reverend LeRoy is then."

"Janice..." Jackie said, "remember our code? We would never harm a woman or a child, but abusive men are fair game, and there are plenty of them to be dispatched to hell."

"But the Church of the Risen Jesus is broke," Janice cried. "LeRoy stole all the money. I'm useless to the Sisterhood. What are you going to do with me?"

"I always thought you were good with figures, the money kind, whereas LeRoy only handled women's figures. So here's what I want you to do. Go to Port au Prince and take charge of our LZ Foundation's treasury. You might like Port au Prince. The beaches are disgusting and it rains a lot, but you'll have two brutes to provide muscle in case you need it. Juan Senior is safekeeping some of our recovered cash, but keep an eye on a guy named Baby Doc. He's Monica's boyfriend."

Monica put her face up to Janice's, and spit her words as she spoke. "I hate that lying prick, and Brenda knows it. She is just trying to get my goat."

Wiping spittle off of her face, Janice said, "It looks like she did a good job."

Monica sat on the couch and chugged the expensive wine as if it were lowly beer.

"Get off your knees, Janice. Have a seat." Brenda indicated the nearby Bashir armchair. "Monica, get her a glass of wine."

Jackie said, "Now where were we? Oh. What did Loa say?"

"Jackie, just keep making your *Soft as Silk Facial Scrub* with that sand from Baddish. I think you're on to something big."

"It's selling like tacos on Taco Tuesday."

Monica strode to the bar and poured a nice glass of wine for Janice, and with her temper out of control like this, she spit into it, just because she could be a real bitch. When she returned, Brenda was talking about the Black Friday 2 party.

"In two days, there'll be many rich and powerful men here. Janice, I'll put you in charge of collecting contributions to our LZF campaign. Record and report every penny. Then you'll do like your sisters, entertain the guests in whatever way you like."

"I can handle that."

Monica handed the spiked glass of wine to Janice. "Enjoy."

She drank it down like a sailor on shore leave. Within moments, she wobbled in the chair, her eyeballs crossed, then she sat up straight, sober as a judge. "I feel kinda horny."

Monica laughed. "That is because I spit my virus in it."

"But I'm already a sister in the Sisterhood."

Monica got up, sashayed to Janice, and gave her a passionate kiss. "You just got a booster."

***

Black Friday 2 was only fifteen hours away when Brenda called General Taylor. "Lawrence, I'm not happy that General Miller and Roy Kincade stole the limelight at the Medal of Freedom awards ceremony."

"Yeah. Sorry I missed it."

"Neither of them spoke up for us, for my sisters, or acknowledged our role in their success. We were humiliated, so I want to humiliate Wes in a bigger way, something that'll be like a punch below the belt."

"Brenda, I've done everything you've asked me to do, but I don't want you girls to do anything to Wes. He's my friend."

"Lawrence, relax. I'm not interested in doing anything to Wes. I'm more interested in Lynne."

"Lynne?"

"What do you know about her?"

"She's loyal to Wes, as he is to her, a hard-core Catholic, never misses a mass, and she loves Pinochle, plays once a week with the officers' wives."

"What does she know about the Sisterhood and The Ranch?"

"How should I know? I'm not privy to their pillow talk, but he knows I'd gone there to see Jackie, and he thinks The Ranch is a nest of lesbians."

"Hey. He wasn't too far off, now was he? Tell me about these Pinochle games."

"It's a pretty exclusive club."

"Inform Wes that one of Jackie's friends, namely me, wants in, and have him tell Lynne that I love to play Pinochle."

"Do you know how to play?"

"I'm a fast learner."

"So then what?"

"I'm going to get to know her then give her the full lesbian zombie initiation. After I'm done with her, she won't want anything to do with her husband anymore, and Wes will be humiliated that his wife left him for another woman."

"I don't know, Brenda. Their bond is pretty tight. She worships him. He can do no wrong. And he never does anything without keeping her in the loop."

"We'll see about that, General."

"What about Kincade?"

She scoffed. "I've got him right where I want him."

"Okay, Brenda. I'll work out something while you read up on Pinochle. See you at the Black Friday 2 party."

"Bring your checkbook."

***

As the sun went down in the west, Jorge returned from Maggie's after taking Betsy and Caroline there for a sleepover. He stood at the door to greet the arriving guests to Black Friday 2. The front yard bristled with political signs in red white and blue: *VOTE for WOMEN'S EQUALITY, #MeToo FOREVER, THE LZF PARTY ROCKS, VOTE LZF*. The stars and stripes hung from the portico: flags, pennants, buntings: folded and fanned. *Born this Way* by Lady Gaga rocked from the sound system.

Brenda and Jackie watched from the window as a military four-door sedan pulled up the drive and stopped under the columned portico. An Army Sergeant First Class and a Navy Chief Petty quickly jumped out and opened the two back doors of the car. They stood at attention as General Lawrence Taylor and Admiral Roy Kincade got out. Jorge escorted them into the foyer where Jackie and Brenda waited, two beauties side-by side.

"Hello, General." Jackie embraced him. "Good to see you."

"You're looking marvelously young." He kissed her cheek.

Brenda greeted Kinkade with a hot wet kiss on his lips. "Admiral—"

His hard military expression softened. "Please call me Roy."

"Roy, I can't thank you enough for coming."

"You're welcome." He glanced around. "What's with all the political swag?"

"We have a very important announcement to make tonight."

"Will I see you later?"

She smiled, showing off her perfect teeth. "Yes you will, Roy." She gave him an anything-you-want wink.

Jackie led both men into the sitting room where Chloe and Lilly, dressed in Playboy bunny ties and tails, escorted them to the open bar. Brenda's kiss was already stroking Kincade's libido. "You girls are breathtaking." Lilly handed him a whisky sour. "Your favorite, right?"

Now thoroughly enamored, he tipped his glass to Lilly while Chloe offered General Taylor a 7&7. Both men began conversing about the political atmosphere around them, all the flags and banners on the wall and hanging from the ceiling. "What the hell's going on around here, General?"

As *Revolution* by the Beatles rocked the foyer, Jackie returned to Brenda. "Good Goddess those guys are horny as hell."

"Pay before play," Brenda said.

Jorge introduced their next arriving guest. "Ladies, Mister Charles Mantella of WNN."

The balding man with bulldog jowls and a prominent paunch stepped up to Brenda and took her hand. "Thanks for inviting me. What's the big occasion?"

"You'll know soon enough. Did you bring your checkbook?"

"American Express all right?"

Brenda smiled slyly. "Of course. Jackie will show you in."

She led him to the sitting room where blonde bombshell Chloe was seated at the bar, legs crossed at the knees and luscious thighs that led all the way to heaven. "May I fix you a drink, sir?"

"Man o man o man Manhattan." His eyes damn near bounced on the floor. "I was hoping I'd see you here tonight."

She stood and wiggled her bunny tail. "I live here. Manhattan, coming right up." She mixed the vermouth, whiskey, and bitters.

He inhaled a quick breath, leaned on the bar, watched her add ice and stir the drink. "Chloe, right? I never forget a blue-eyed blonde."

"Funny. I forget your name."

"Charles Mantella. I'm CEO of World News Network, highest rated in news coverage of all the channels. You can call me Charlie."

"Of course...Charlie." She strained the drink into a frosted glass. "I remember you now, from last year's Black Friday. You're an animal."

"What-a-ya-say we go upstairs, young filly?" He was no John Wayne but he tried.

"Can't you see I'm working here?" She skewered a cherry to garnish the drink then set it in front of him. "Enjoy."

"Maybe later?"

"Maybe never."

Lilly slid up next to her. "Chloe, I need a highball for Larry Evans."

She glanced at the handsome black man Jackie was introducing to the General and Admiral. "Not my type."

"He's a New York District Attorney."

"Big deal. When are the girls from the yacht getting here?"

"Patience, my lovely lesbian."

"Lesbian?" Mantella frowned and stepped back from the bar.

"Yes, Charlie," Chloe cooed. "When those hotties get here, you'll be glad I turned you down."

Jackie rejoined Brenda in the foyer just as Jorge announced their next guest. "Ladies, Mike Simmons, president of the New York Stock Exchange."

"I'd do him," Jackie whispered to Brenda. She had to agree. The man was an Adonis.

Mike presented himself to the women, tall, dark, and handsome. "Ma'am." He had to bend down to kiss Jackie's hand then Brenda next. "I didn't realize this would be a political gig."

"We'll tell you all about it later." Jackie led him to the sitting room to join the tycoons of industry and the great leaders of the military.

Lilly rushed to him as if he were her most favorite customer at Max's Diner. "Mr. Simmons, may I get you a drink...or anything else you might like?" She struck a pose that would bowl over most men.

He looked her up and down, well, mostly down, as he towered over everyone. "Rye whiskey on the rocks will be fine."

"Ooh, nice." She sauntered off toward the bar, her bunny tail hopping.

Brenda showed Stuart Jackson, the bowling-ball-shaped internet tycoon and purported pervert, the way to the sitting room, along with Dr. Peyton Moore, a wealthy black man, head of the CDC, and an outspoken opioid crisis warrior. Maria and Donna welcomed them with flutes of champagne and come-hither smiles.

Moments later, Jackie escorted movie mogul Tom Caldone into the fray of bubbly conversation and rising testosterone. Melinda greeted him with a silver tray of hors d'oeuvres balanced on the tips of her fingers. "For your pleasure, Mister Caldone." As he munched on a Ritz garnished with caviar, she set a soft hand on his arm. "So, Tom. What would it take for me to get a role in your next cave women movie?"

He swallowed fish eggs. "Can you act?"

"No," she swooned, "but wouldn't I look tempting in that skimpy fur outfit and bones in my hair?"

He framed her face in a square he made with his fingers and

thumbs, like directors did, then backed up for a wide-angle view of her body. "By Jove, I think you're right."

Just then, the room exploded with shrieks and giggles as the all-girl crew of *Three Sheets to the Wind* blew in like a summer storm. There were tall women and short women and bouncy boobs and bodies built like marble Madonnas. Not a one of them wore a stitch of unnecessary clothing.

LeeAnn and Chloe rushed to each other and hugged and kissed like long lost lovers. Tammy bounded in with a babe under each arm: Sue and Jane, all bouncing like cheerleaders hopped up on catnip. Maria and Donna joined them in a fleshy group hug.

Captain Kathy, wearing all-white: a short-sleeved shirt with the tails tied above her navel, short-shorts that revealed tiny crescents of tush, and high heels that gave her the shapely legs of a Victoria Secret model, was more reserved, maybe due to the four gold stripes on her shoulder loops. The military men were attracted to her like sharks to blood in the water.

Joan cut off Jean on her way to corral Dr. Moore, leaving her to dodge the perverted leers of Stuart Jackson and Charles, Charlie, Mantella of WNN. As the hoopla escalated to jubilee, Jill and Janice swooped in, flinging red white and blue confetti and streamers of silver and gold as they danced around the roomful of astounded men.

With Alfons Duda on her arm, Monica pranced into the mayhem like a Haitian beauty among chickens and swine. *American Woman* rocked the sitting room while wine, whiskey, and caviar primed the men's libidos for the carnal entertainment they hoped would come later.

And as all good times must end, Brenda entered the sitting room and rang a gold dinner bell. The quieted crowd looked to the doorway. "Dinner is served."

Everyone funneled into the mansion's seldom-used dining room, expansive in its width and breadth with dual chandeliers above a long table set with the finest crystal, china, and silverware ever created. Brenda joined Jackie at the head of the table as the girls and their guests filed in. Admiral Kinkade sat cattycorner to Brenda, as did General Taylor to Jackie. Some pairing had taken place in the sitting room, and those couples found high-back chairs next to each other: Donna drew the short straw with Charles,

Charlie, Mantella of WNN, Monica and Alfons Duda, of course, Chloe hooked up with Larry Evans, the New York District Attorney. If she had to entertain a man, let it be a black handsome veteran. Jill got dibs on Mike Simmons; muscles and money were attractive to her. Melinda got her paws on Tom Caldone, still hoping for a role in *Cave Women from Venus Part II*, and Dr. Moore pulled out a chair for Maria. The others pretty much sat boy-girl and girl-girl, depending upon their inclinations.

Brenda rang the bell again to get everyone's attention. "Welcome to The Ranch. Before T&A Catering begins serving dinner, we..." she tipped her head to Jackie, "have an announcement to make."

A murmur rose from the guests and girls.

"Drum roll, please." The sound system complied, and a giant red white and blue banner unfurled behind her.

BRENDA AYLER and JACKIE O'NEAL for the WHITE HOUSE.

"We are kicking off our campaign for the Presidency."

Hail to the Chief trumpeted from the loudspeakers. The room erupted in applause. Brenda and Jackie hugged each other while the mayhem reached a crescendo.

Brenda rang the bell. "Most of you know Janice Parker."

She entered the room carrying a calculator and satchel. Her strapless corset teddy revealed sumptuous bumps and curves wrapped in sparkling gold. "Business before pleasure, boys."

Brenda thrust her fist in the air. "Get out your checkbooks and donate to our campaign like your lives depend on it."

As Janice collected generous contributions, Admiral Kincade leaned to Brenda's ear. "Why in the world do you want to be President? You know it's a man's job."

"Roy, darling. That is exactly why we are going to win the White House. The male chauvinism in this country must end. And you are to blame."

"Me?"

"At the awards ceremony, you could have spoken up for us, but no, you and your Captain Marquez and General Miller accepted all the credit for a mission well done. You men got the citations from the President and we got the booby prizes."

He stared at her in wide-eyed shock, as if the truth were as powerful as a lightning bolt.

"When we're through, you boys are going to be working for us girls. How's that grab you?"

"By the balls, Brenda. By the balls." He pulled out his checkbook. "How much do you need?"

So Black Friday 2 would go down in history as the most successful fundraiser ever. The best part was the pleasure that followed the business. T&A Catering served the most lavish dinner in the most lavish fashion, and afterwards, the entertainment could only be likened to the grandest of Roman orgies. Women and dance and booze and nakedness thrust The Ranch into the realms of fantasy. In the hot tub, the pool, the backyard, on the beach, and in the bushes, by way of fornication and fellatio, the lesbian zombies recruited the loyalties of those Brenda had need of in her bid for the White House. As for the women of the nation whose votes were essential, Jackie's *Soft as Silk Facial Scrub* would soon turn them to compatriots of the LZF Party.

With the wheels of the lesbian zombie political machine in motion, there was one last ritual of the Black Friday tradition to complete. At twenty past twelve, when the moon rose to its apex, Brenda called the partygoers into the Crystal Shrine. It was time to pay homage to Loa, Goddess of the Universe.

God fearing men and women would be repulsed by the paganistic temple before them: the majestic Sister Tree of Life with its throne of branches on which Brenda regally sat, the golden tiles that led to a pit, The Pit of Ages, where vines and roots intertwined, all surrounded by a golden railing, and all encased in crystalline wall and ceiling panels through which moonbeams shown down on the attendees within. Most of the men were drunk on booze and sex as they took in the scene with bleary eyes and exhausted souls.

"Loa welcomes you," Brenda said in a voice befitting a choir of angels. "For those of you who don't believe in our Goddess, she will speak to each of you, not in her voice, but in the voices of your loved ones who have departed this earth. I give you the Goddess Loa, Lord of All."

They listened intently to the voices in their heads, voices of mothers and grandmothers, sisters, wives, and daughters, their bodies lost to time, but their memories everlasting.

Stuart Jackson dropped to his knees and tears rolled from his eyes. He heard the voice of his daughter, dead eleven years ago after suffering heart failure from a birth defect. *"Daddy, I'm sorry I left you so young, but I'm healthy and warm in Loa's embrace."* He raised his arms to Brenda on her throne. "I believe. I believe. Loa is my Goddess and you are my Queen."

Not everyone's response was as dramatic as bowling-ball Stuart's. Most looked up to the moonbeams with reverent eyes.

Monica reacted the harshest when she heard her murdered daughter's voice. *"Mamma, I know you tried to avenge my death, but you were deceived by the son of the man who allowed my rape and murder. Forgiveness goes a long way here in heaven. Forgive Baby Doc for lying to you and go in peace, Mamma."*

Monica prayed, *Loa, please tell Brenda to send me to Port au Prince where I will slaughter Baby Doc. You must know how I have suffered over the loss of my Maya. You know he lied to save his neck from the guillotine.*

Loa's voice came to her. *"I hear your sorrow, Monica. However, the name Baby Doc is still written in the stars, as are all living humans, a sign that reveals mercy in your heart."*

Monica looked up at Brenda with tears in her eyes. "For Baby Doc there is no mercy."

Brenda gazed down on her most favorite black woman in the world. "Against your daughter's wishes you will do murder?"

"It is my decision, not Maya's, and Loa has read the stars wrong."

Brenda beseeched her. "The sins of the father are not the sins of the son."

"He lied. That's sin enough for me."

Larry Evans, having heard his sweet grandmother's voice, was next to bow to Brenda in allegiance. "The New York Department of Justice is at your service, my Queen." Mike Simmons pledged the support of the Stock Exchange; Tom Caldone, Hollywood access to the film industry; and Dr. Peyton Moore gave his nod to Big Pharma's financial assets. Charles, Charlie, Mantella of WNN knelt to Brenda and pledged national television coverage of her campaign.

Brenda stood. "Go then, back to the party and celebrate a new destiny for women in this country."

Chapter Twenty-Four

While the country was in the throes of its new beginning, Lynne Miller was about to face hers. At forty-eight years old, her periods had stopped, not a drop in two months, so she'd made an appointment at Walter Reed for a check up on her female parts. Menopause came to all women during their lives, so she was sure her time had come to be barren, not that it mattered. She'd not ever known childbirth anyway.

The doctor entered the examination room where Lynne, wearing a paper gown, was sitting on the paper-lined table. His mood seemed solemn, his expression serious. "Missus Miller, I have some bad news for you."

Lynne shuddered...like the earth had moved, tilted as if it would pitch her off into the darkness. "What's wrong?"

"You're pregnant."

She gasped. "Pregnant?"

"About eight weeks along."

Confusion crumpled her brain like paper into a wad. "Why is that bad news?"

"You'll need an abortion, of course. You're too old to have a baby."

"Abortion? Oh my God. My husband and I should decide... We've always wanted a child but...couldn't." She let it go at that.

"Okay." The killer of babies adjusted his stethoscope. "It's risky but your decision."

"Can I see the baby with one of those ultrasound machines?"

"At twenty weeks, yes. Best we can do now is a vaginal ultrasound to detect the heartbeat. I can order one for you."

"Now?"

"Sure. Why not? I'll be right back." He left her alone in the exam room.

Lynne knew her heartbeat could be detected from space. Wes was going to be shocked...happy... Oh dear...suspicious. It was his fault she'd never gotten pregnant...not enough swimmers.

He's bound to think I've been with another man. And he's not one to believe in miracles.

An orderly wheeled in a cart. The machine it carried looked like a small laptop with...with a probe on a cord. The screen read: *VScan.*

How hard can this be?

The doctor returned. "Back in the stirrups with you, Missus Miller."

She knew the drill. Knees spread, it was a bit drafty down there. He rolled a stool between her legs, and with no foreplay or warning, worked the slippery cold probe into a place she should have enjoyed. The laptop reported gushing and gurgling and sloshing between heartbeats. "It's so loud."

"That's your heartbeat," he said.

"I never knew it was so noisy down there."

"I can filter a lot of that out...ah...here we go." He lifted the laptop so she could see the screen. "The yellow line, looks like an EKG but without all the spikes and oscillations. Just one, and faint at that."

Excitement swelled in her chest as she saw the yellow line, well, one of the yellow lines. "Just one?"

"Just one."

"Then why do I see two lines?"

"Two? He turned the laptop so he could see the screen. "My God. You're right. Two. You're going to have twins."

"That's wonderful," she sobbed out.

"Twice the risk for a woman your age. You could die."

"So be it. Nobody is killing these babies."

He smiled. "Congratulations. You're going to be a mom."

If my husband doesn't kill me first.

***

Next stop for Lynne, the Pentagon, and the office of Brigadier General Wesley Miller, father to be...of twins. She barged right past his aide-de-camp and headed straight for Wes's door.

"You can't go in there, ma'am."

"I'm his wife, and I go where I please."

Pushing through the doorway, she found herself in the middle of a meeting. Wesley, two Captains, and a Major glared at her with incredulity. She'd brought the meeting to a quick halt.

"Gentlemen..." Wes said, "this lovely lady who just burst into our meeting is my wife, Lynne. We'll have to continue this meeting at another time. You're dismissed."

Filing out, the Major said, "All of us are married, sir, and we completely understand. Even a General doesn't outrank his wife."

They all laughed, including Wesley. When they were alone, "What is it, honey, that brought you all the way to the Pentagon in the middle of the day?"

"What I have to say can't wait 'til you get home."

"That's stating the obvious. Let me guess. You won at Pinochle? What? A hundred bucks?"

"I just came from my doctor."

"Which one. You must have ten—"

"My gynecologist."

"Oh. That sounds serious."

"I'm pregnant..."

He stood there wobbling like he might fall over.

"With twins."

Now he leaned against the desk so he wouldn't hit the floor. "Twins? Holy shit."

"We're finally going to be parents."

He frowned. "Now wait a minute. Something is rotten in Denmark. I don't have enough swimmers to impregnate a cricket."

She scowled. "No. Don't even go there, Wes. You know me better than that. This is a miracle, that plain and simple."

He looked at his hand, the one shattered by an AK-47 bullet, now completely healed. That was a miracle...so why not this? He pulled her into his arms. "It's wonderful news, Lynne. I love you to pieces."

The phone rang. "Damn." He pushed the intercom button. "Not now, Major. Hold all my calls."

"It's General Taylor, sir."

"All right. Put him through. He guided pregnant Lynne to his chair behind the desk as if she were some fragile china doll and made the mother-to-be nice and comfy.

"Yes, General."

"I'm told Lynne just arrived in your office."

"Yes. She's here...with good news."

"I'll be right there." He hung up.

"What's that all about, Wes?"

"I don't know. He's coming over."

Seconds later, his aide-de-camp announced General Taylor's arrival.

"Show him in."

The General entered. "So what's this good news?"

"Lynne's pregnant...with twins."

He looked at her sitting in the high-back behind the desk. "Really?"

She nodded. "And I don't want to hear anything about my age."

"Never occurred to me, ma'am. You're having twins, huh? Congratulations."

Wes and the General shook hands. "You needed to see me about something?"

"Lynne, actually." He turned back to her. "Will you still be playing Pinochle?"

"I'm pregnant, not braindead, Lawrence."

"Good. I'd like for you to do a close friend of mine a favor. She has a friend who'd like to join you and the girls for a game or two. Can you arrange it?"

"Consider it done. Next Wednesday at my house. Tell your friend to tell her friend, 2pm, and don't be late. We can use some fresh money in the game."

***

Back at The Ranch, Brenda and Jackie were assessing the damages from last night's Black Friday party. Confetti and political swag were scattered everywhere, not to mention beer bottles, wine bottles, and every imaginable piece of torn clothing. "Donna and Jill better get this place cleaned up."

"They're sleeping in."

"Monica too?"

"Her bed wasn't even slept in."

Brenda figured she'd slipped off with Alfons, probably to the yacht for some privacy.

They toured the pool deck where potted ferns had been knocked over, sopping towels and bikini parts lay here and there, and deck furniture was upended every which way. "Slobs."

Jackie sighed. "We'll have to drain the pool and hot tub. Goddess only knows what's floating in that water."

They found Janice on the floor in the Crystal Shrine with her satchel open and her fingers going clickity-click on the calculator keys. Checks and cash and credit card slips lay around her in some kind of order that only she understood.

"How'd we do?" Brenda asked.

"We killed it. I don't have enough zeroes on my calculator to add it all up."

"You're kidding."

"Yes, but still, I'm up to 147 million dollars, and I've yet to count the pledges. Duda threw in a hundred million because he didn't have to buy a new yacht."

"We have to get this money to our bank account in Haiti."

Janice collected her stacks and put them in the satchel. "I'm ready to go anytime."

"But first..." Brenda said, "you have to close out the books on the Church of the Risen Jesus."

"There's no money left." Janice buckled the satchel.

"We can't have the books lying around for anyone to find."

"Right."

"Janice, you and I and Jackie are going to church."

Jackie called Jorge on her cell. "How soon can you get here?"

"Twenty minutes fast enough?"

"We'll be waiting."

In the back of the limo, all the way to the church, Janice hugged the satchel in her lap. She felt proud that the Sisterhood trusted her with this much dough.

Brenda's cell vibrated. It was Maria. "Monica called, said for me to tell you that she'd be back in three days."

"What's she doing, another lovefest with Alfons?"

"She didn't say. I thought you would know."

"Shit." She hung up.

That got Jackie's attention. "What's up?"

"Monica's gone."

"Where."

"Where do you think?"

"Port au Prince?"

"Exactly," Brenda hissed. "She just has to kill Baby Doc. In some ways I don't blame her, but I wish she'd told me she was leaving."

"Brenda, she has to settle this in her own way, in her own time. It's a damn shame that beautiful woman can't control her temper."

"It's going to be the death of Baby Doc, that's for sure. We should call ahead and warn Aurora. Maybe she can talk some sense into Monica."

"Yeah. When pigs fly."

Jorge turned the limo into the parking lot of the shuttered church. A lone car was there, LeRoy's Lincoln sedan.

"It's that son of a bitch," Janice said.

Jorge parked next to the son of a bitch's car. The sisters got out and stalked up to the driver's door. LeRoy was slumped behind the wheel, drunk or dead they didn't know which. Cash was strewn across the front and back seats, hundred dollar bills, maybe a million's worth of clutter. The doors were locked.

Brenda pulled Janice aside. "Go get the books. We'll deal with LeRoy."

"I want to watch you kill him."

"No you don't. It won't be pretty."

Janice skulked off toward the church, mumbling something about *vengeance is mine sayeth the Lord. Bullshit.*

Brenda said, "Jorge, break a window and grab him before he has a chance to start the car and skedaddle."

From the trunk of the limo, he pulled out a baseball bat and strode to LeRoy's door like he was stepping into the batter's box. "Better back off, ladies." Like his boyhood hero Barry Bonds at Yankee Stadium, he gave his Louisville Slugger a couple of practice swings then swung at the window, which instantly exploded on impact. "Homerun," he quipped.

LeRoy jumped. "What the hell?" Blasted from whatever he

was dreaming, he saw Brenda and realized he'd awakened to a nightmare.

"Drag his sorry ass out of the car, Jorge."

He popped the lock, opened the driver's door, grabbed LeRoy by the throat, and onehandedly yanked him out.

LeRoy hit the pavement like the sack of shit he was, kicking and screaming, "Don't kill me. Don't kill me." Begging suited him, but when it looked like Jorge was going to slug him, he resorted to lying in his own defense. "It's Janice's fault. She's a whore, always bad-mouthing you. Put all this money in my car. I was counting it when I fell asleep...I was going to put it back in the safe."

"No you weren't, you lying prick." Janice had returned with a stack of ledgers in the crook of her arm. "You stole the money and ran off with some bitch named Shirley. Where is she, anyway?"

"She left me for another woman. I can't catch a break from all you lesbian bitches. So go ahead and kill me. My life ain't worth shit anyway. Jesus will welcome me into heaven for preaching his name all these years."

Brenda looked down at the pathetic excuse for a man, lying on the asphalt and wallowing in self-pity. To kill him now, when he had nothing to lose, seemed a useless punishment. Besides, there was still the matter of the missing money he'd stolen. "Jorge, get him up off the ground."

Jorge grabbed him by the shirt and yanked him to his feet.

Brenda, poking him in the chest with her index finger, backed him up against the Lincoln where he cowered like a fool. "So LeRoy, here's the deal. You're going to reopen the Church of the Risen Jesus and give us every-other dollar you collect until the stolen money is repaid. That's two point four million bucks, you hear? The cash you have in your car, keep it, buy whatever you want with it, live it up, enjoy your life."

He stood a little straighter. "What's the catch?"

"I never want you to bother Janice again, because if you do, on that day you will surely die."

***

As United flight 305 began its descent to Port au Prince,

Monica recalled the voice of her sweet daughter in the Crystal Shrine.

"Mamma, forgiveness goes a long way here in heaven. Forgive Baby Doc for lying to you and go in peace, Mamma."

She looked out the window and saw the ghost of her daughter, Maya, dancing on the wing. She wore her favorite flower-print dress, which, along with her long black hair, fluttered wildly in the wind. Monica put her hand on the window, wishing she could reach out and touch her. She was so close yet so far away, somewhere in time and space to the end of eternity. Hot tears bloomed in Monica's eyes. "I miss you, my sweet Maya."

The jet landed with a bump and a roar. Maya waved and was gone. Monica clutched her hands and remembered Brenda's words. The sins of the father are not the sins of the son.

I have a lot of soul searching to do.

After getting off the plane, Monica decided to commune with Maya at her grave, which was located not far from the airport. Using only the moon and stars for light, she walked the dirt road to the Cimetiere des Drouillard, and entered the path into a maze of tombs and markers, ancient as the island's history. Sixty plus years of rain and sun had all but erased the name on Maya's cross of stone.

Tears welled in Monica's eyes as she knelt before the cross, bare knees in the dirt, and shuddered under the onslaught of memories of the horrific events that had brought her to this place so many decades ago. "I have heard you, Maya, my precious daughter, your plea for forgiveness and peace in my life."

The ghost on the wing appeared on the weathered cross, the little black girl's dress, pretty as the day it was sewn.

"The hate in my heart for Papa Doc and his son Baby Doc is ever-present. They ruled our island. His soldiers raped and pillaged the townsfolk, and you fell victim to their violence and murderous ways. I hear you, Maya, and I remember Loa's vision of Baby Doc's star still aglow in the heavens because mercy also resides in my soul, so I will honor your wishes and leave here with a lighter heart and peace of mind."

The ghostly girl's smile shined bright, white teeth and skin black as night, and then she was gone. Monica's tears streamed down as she recalled Maya's nickname, Cookie, because she loved

Oreo cookies. Such a little memory that seemed so big right now, Oreos were rare back then, a luxury on this poor island. *As was my daughter*.

When the moon had risen to its apex, Monica wiped tears from her cheeks and stood. “Goodbye, my sweet Oreo.”

Back at the airport, she walked straight to the counter. “I want a one-way ticket to JFK.” She offered up her passport and credit card.

The agent, a full-figured Haitian beauty all of five-foot-two said, “Didn’t you just come in on flight 305?”

“Yes. Now I want to go back to New York.”

“You look like you’ve been crying. Is anything wrong?”

“I am fine. How about that ticket?”

“I’m sorry you didn’t have a chance to see our beautiful country.”

“I have seen enough.”

“I’ll transfer your suitcase from 305 to 307, which leaves in an hour. Maybe you can come back sometime soon?”

“I am sure I will. I was born here, but sadly, this place does not seem as beautiful to me as it once did when I was small. The government was corrupt then, as it is now, and that will never change. Men of power rape and murder the lesser of us and get away with it.”

The agent, pleasant as could be, handed her the new ticket. “Have a nice flight.”

Chapter Twenty-Five

Over at Wes's house, Lynne was in the process of beating him in a game of Pinochle, all the while talking about their twins who were still seven and a half months from birth.

Laying down his cards that showed he lost again, he said, "Lynne, thanks for letting General Taylor's friend play cards with you."

"Is she any good?"

"I don't know, but she loves the game and wants to learn to play better."

"What's her name?"

"Brenda Ayler."

"I hope she's not living in sin like Jackie O'Neal. All those lesbians around. Gives me the willies. What faith is she?"

"I don't know, but she's very devout in her beliefs. Get me a beer, will you?"

She got up from the table and got him a cool brew from the fridge, happy as always to serve her man.

***

In a NO WAITING ZONE outside the terminal at JFK's Passenger Pick up, Jorge parked the limo and left the engine running. Jackie and Brenda sat in the plush cabin, talking about the campaign and Monica's shortened trip to Haiti while waiting for her to come through the exit doors. And sure as shit a cop showed up, knocked on Jorge's window.

He rolled it down. "Yes, officer?"

"You can't wait here. Move along."

Jackie opened a back window. "Officer, we're waiting for a VIP passenger to be rolled out in a wheelchair. Two minutes.

Please don't make us move the car for that small amount of time."

A redhead, more beautiful than a full moon rising, came to the window. "It'll take twenty minutes for us to drive back around."

Tapping his ticket pad, he really didn't want to inconvenience these pretty women. "Okay, ladies. It'll take me three minutes to complete my beat, so I don't want to see you when I come back around."

"Thank you, officer," the women cooed.

As he walked away, he knew he'd been played.

When Monica rushed out the sliding doors, Jorge took her suitcase to the trunk while Jackie let her into the back seat. Their boisterous reunion was as noisy as a gaggle of hens.

Brenda sat elbow to elbow with Monica. "What happened in Haiti?"

Jackie poured whisky from the car-bar. "Did you kill him?"

"You know..." she looked down at her hands folded in her lap, "I have been so angry...temperamental...so aggressive sexually. Poor Alfons...because of the hate I have carried in my heart like a footlocker. My daughter made me take a good, hard look at myself...and I remembered Oreo cookies."

Jackie and Brenda shared confused glances.

"Dunking an Oreo in milk, it is satisfying to change it to melt-in-your-mouth goodness, but it is still an Oreo cookie. Murder is the same way. It may be satisfying to murder a lowlife like Baby Doc, but it is still murder. And revenge for his lie does not undo the terrible actions of his father that cannot be undone. Maya is gone, as is all that her life would have brought into this world. No amount of revenge will change that which only forgiveness and peace can deliver."

Brenda patted Monica's bare thigh. "I think Loa was testing you...and me too."

"You?"

"LeRoy came back and I let him live."

"What about our money?"

"He's working on it." Kissing Monica on her cheek, Brenda added, "We love you and we're glad you're back. This day is turning out really good. Take us home, Jorge."

He accelerated the limo toward the airport exit.

***

At The Ranch, the only sisters sleeping were Caroline and Betsy. The rest of the Sisterhood sat around on the pool deck and downed three bottles of Chenin Blanc wine. Chloe looked at Janice, then the freshly cleaned pool, and then back to Janice. Their eyes met and Chloe popped the question. “How about a game of submarine, Janice?”

A little shiver tingled the back of her neck. “I’ve missed you so much.”

Monica strode to the pool’s edge, dropped her thong, then: “You don’t have to ask me twice.” She dove in with barely a splash.

“Come on, Brenda,” Chloe shouted and jumped in cannonball style.

Brenda, already tipsy and now dripping water, shed her bikini. “Sure. Why not?” As queens do, she chose the regal way to enter the pool...using the steps and handrail.

Janice stood and disrobed while all her sisters watched. Being a lesbian zombie, she had no doubts about her body, how perfect it was in every way: small perky tits with aroused nipples, sensuous curves a Ferrari couldn’t handle, and since LeRoy had left, she’d shaved down there to present smooth softness for her sisters to enjoy.

“Come on, Janice,” Maria implored. “Race you.” She and Melinda took the dive. Of all the sisters giggling and splashing about, only one had her eyes on Janice’s presentation. For that attention, Janice gave her a little fashion show, sans-clothes, a long-legged stride to the pool, a turn to the left, a sly smile over her shoulder, a turn to the right and a bump with her hips. The girls grabbed her ankles and dragged her into the pool. Chloe got to Janice’s presentation first. This game of submarine was going to come with torpedo speed and carnal explosions.

***

Sitting on top of a fiery mountain on Polaris, the North Star, Loa watched the winds of Jupiter blow around and around the sandy remains of the male gods. She remembered how she dispatched them so long ago, how the winds blew sand back on the earth, and now that blessed sand would help deliver a fatal blow to man's dominance over women. Now, and at the same time, she looked down on her faithful, Brenda and her Sisterhood, as they frolicked in the pool like oversexed nymphs on a tropical island. It took even a goddess's imagination to picture these same women in charge of the home of the brave and the land of the free.

With star fire hissing and whooshing around her, she thought of the unborn twins of Lynne and Wesley Miller. One male. One female. *I feel better since there is one of each.* And they would be born for a reason. Lynne's sudden fertility had nothing to do with her husband's swimmers, or lack thereof, *but more due to my will on earth.*

She thought about Wes and the jolt of virus he'd received when Brenda spit on his wound. *Maybe there was not enough virus to mean anything more than healing his shattered hand. I will watch him and see if he changes physically and mentally, that he might be a zombie... No. He is flesh-and-bone human, but will he be a Judas to Brenda or a believer? A liability or an asset? His stars have yet to align either way. One thing is for sure. When this war is over, men will never rule over women again.*

Satisfied her plan for womanhood was sound, she began to sing in the enchanting voice of the Sirens of the Sea:

♪ *A year of nights, a year of days. Moonshine turning into rays. There never was, but there could be, a place in heaven, for a goddess like me. I start my journey when the stars expand, and lay my legacy in a woman's hand.* ♪

***

Brenda and Jackie were the last of the sisters to hit the sac. As they lay there naked, arm-in-arm with only a sheet covering them, it was Jackie who broke the silence.

"Tomorrow, we need to get the LZNN off the ground. Charles Mantella can help us."

"I like that, Jackie. LZNN, Lesbian Zombie News Network, but why would Mantella agree to help us, in a sense, his new competition? He's already agreed to promote our LZF Party on his airways across the country. We don't need our own television network."

"I just thought it would be nice to own—"

"A new gown would be nice to own, Jackie. You must spend your money wisely."

"You're right, Brenda. That new yacht for Alfons put a dent in my billions."

"Besides, Charles Mantella has already arranged our first presidential interview on his network."

Jackie turned on her side to face Brenda. "What if they ask for the meaning behind our LZF Party. You can't tell the world it's the Lesbian Zombie Foundation Party."

"Almost zero percent of the public will think LZ stands for Lady Zaharias, an obscure leader of the women's movement for equal rights back in the 1680s. I'll either explain it or tell them it just sounds cool. LZ. LZ. LZ. Kinda rolls off the tongue."

Jackie laughed and reached around Brenda's head to draw her in for a quick kiss. "Brenda, darling, our average American woman doesn't know crap about women's history. All they care about is that they can vote, they can drive, they can wear bikinis in public, hell, they don't care who suffered to get them these freedoms. They didn't call it women's suffrage for nothing. I love our sisters, but none of them know about Susan B. Anthony, Alice Paul, or Ida Wells. I think all our girls have is a Ph.D. in sex."

"You have a point. Nobody is going to care what LZ means."

"Oh, General Taylor called. You're all set to play Pinochle with Lynne Miller. Next Wednesday at 2pm. He'll text me the address in Arlington Virginia."

"We'll need Alfons' jet to fly me there."

"No problem." Jackie turned over to face the bay window and look out at the Sound. "Let's get some sleep. Okay?"

"I have one more question, Jackie. How are sales of your *Soft as Silk Facial Scrub* going?"

"Off the charts." She yawned. "The sand I added from Baddish is loved by women around the world. It works wonders on their complexions... almost like magic."

"It's something much better, Jackie."

That perked her up. "What? The lesbian zombie virus?"

"Eons ago, Loa blessed the sand. It doesn't change women into lesbian zombies. It beautifies women, and their gratitude pays off in loyalty to you, your product, and your message. Our message, Jackie, and when election time comes they'll show that gratitude and loyalty in their votes for the LZF Party. Loa has told me this."

Jackie had to laugh. "What a way to rig an election."

"Not at all. You're a rock-star among women. Elvis, the Beatles, and the Rolling Stones all wrapped into one beautiful package. Your fans will support you to the ends of the Earth. Besides, it's all for women's equality."

"I'll sleep well knowing that. Goodnight."

"I love you, Jackie."

"I love you too, my Queen."

Jackie was soon sound asleep but Brenda wasn't. She was thinking about the upcoming interview on Charles Mantella's *Political Hour* on WNN.

She'd talk about their women's independent political party, the LZF Party, a party that will showcase women candidates running for state legislatures and the US House and Senate, and encourage women to vote LZF. She'd have to remember to say, *Both parties will think we're a joke and laugh, but they won't be laughing on election night.*

She was giggling over that thought when a tune came to mind, a melody she'd never heard before, words she didn't know but somehow knew:

♪ *A year of nights, a year of days. Moonshine turning into rays. There never was, but there could be, a place in heaven, for a goddess like me. I start my journey when the stars expand, and lay my legacy in a woman's hand.* ♪

Then a thought sent a chill down her back and opened her eyes wide. *Woman's hand? What woman? Me?* It was the voice of the Goddess Loa in her head. She was dreaming or singing the song...and somehow Brenda had tuned in.

Now she couldn't get that tune out of her head.

***

Later that morning, Joseph drove up in Alfons' limo to take Janice Parker to the airport, where she'd fly to Haiti on Alfons' private jet. She carried her satchel full of political contributions, all of which were reported to the proper agencies. Her job was to handle the LZ Foundation and the LZF Party's finances from Port au Prince and send weekly reports to New York. Her only regret: she'd miss her sisters something fierce, especially the pool parties. Her years of preaching God's word with LeRoy seemed as long ago as the dinosaurs.

Next limo to pull up under the portico was Jackie's new ride with Jorge behind the wheel. Today he'd play babysitter to Betsy, Caroline, and Girlie Dog; they'd go to Central Park while Brenda was being interviewed at WNN. He got out and took his position at the rear door to await his passengers.

The sisters watched out the window as the girls and Girlie Dog ran to the car. "Kids never walk anywhere," Chloe said.

Brenda joined them, Jorge closed the door, and they were off and running.

As they rode down to Manhattan, Brenda, with an arm around each little sister, thought how Goddess Loa had made her life complete in ways that she could never have imagined. Just two years ago, she had no self esteem. She hated the way she looked, and no matter what she tried, she could never lose weight. Now she was slim and trim and beautiful and running for President of the United States. Only a Goddess could orchestrate such a chain of events. *Thank you, Loa.*

Jorge pulled up and stopped in front of the WNN studios. Professional as he was, he got out and opened the rear door for Brenda. "Good luck, my Queen."

She stepped out, elegant as any movie starlet on Oscar night. "Come back in one hour." She waved to the girls. "Have fun at the park."

Girlie Dog barked.

Once inside, she was hustled through makeup, which required little effort, then she waited offstage with Charles for her introduction.

He whispered in her ear, "Don't let these Pre-Madonnas get to you. Each one is going to try and outdo the other two with tough questions for you."

"Thanks for the advice."

"Ladies and gentlemen, WNN welcomes Presidential candidate Brenda Ayler."

She strode out on stage to bright lights and halfhearted applause. Cameras followed her to three women standing in line to greet her. The first interviewer she met was Arlene Simpson, a gray-eyed, gray-haired white woman she'd seen on television before, maybe in her fifties and well fed. Holding out a dainty hand, she quickly learned Brenda's handshake stirred her in ways men seldom did.

"Arlene, I am so happy to meet you."

Next in line was Adela ala-Omani from Saudi Arabia. She was decked out in western clothing: tan pant-suit, white blouse, and red blazer, and she wore the traditional hijab, light blue. A very colorful woman of Islam.

Brenda reached out to shake her hand but was rebuffed. In hopes of breaking the ice, Brenda smiled and spoke softly, "So nice to meet you."

Last came Marylin Dixon, a vivacious young woman in her early twenties who looked sexy as hell, which seemed to be a requirement for reporters nowadays. Her macho handshake told Brenda she was a man-hating lesbian. Good for the campaign, bad for lesbian zombie material. She'd probably vomit at the sight of a naked man.

"Marylin, it's so nice to meet you."

"Shall we get started?" The three women took chairs arranged in front of a blue podium adorned with the seal of the United States. The nameplate read: Brenda Ayler for President.

Arlene Simpson started off with, "Tell us about your running mate, Jackie O'Neal. Why is she on your ticket?"

Brenda adjusted the microphone. "She's been a leader in women's skin care all over the world, a brilliant businesswoman and marketing guru. Name recognition is paramount in a campaign. Her *Soft as Silk Facial Scrub* has made her a household name and a heroine among women who love their soft and smooth complexions. She's a trusted advisor, and she'll make a great vice-president."

Adela got the next question. "What makes you think your LZF party can compete with the top two?"

"Our platform is women's equality. The other guys are all about corporate greed and systemic welfare."

"A women's party? Do we really need another party on the

ballot?"

"Men are welcome too, as long as they are pro-women's equality. I'm not talking about women's rights. We've already fought for and attained the same rights as any man. I'm talking about equal pay for equal work, equal opportunity in business and education, equal advancement in the military."

"All sounds fine and dandy," Omani put in. "But I grew up under Sharia Law. Women are highly regarded, protected, and, of course, punished for our indiscretions. Such is the price for our safety and security in a world run by men. Would you have those protections taken away from us?"

"If you like your protections, you can keep your protections, however, modern, forward-thinking women deserve a fair playing field. You take from that what you will."

A murmur rose from the audience.

The program director cut in. "Ladies, can we have a question from Marylin now?"

Marylin asked, "Miss Ayler, this LZF Party of yours...your opponents have translated it to mean the Lesbian Fornication Party, mostly because the F word isn't allowed on the airways."

"My opponents are misogynistic bullies."

"Can you clear that up for us here? What does LZF stand for?"

"We stand for women's equality."

"The letters, Miss Ayler. I'm sure you know what I mean."

"What does it matter? I could tell you about Lady Zaharias, a rather obscure women's libber from the 1680s, or I could say we just like the feel of the sound as it rolls off our tongues. We're not here about letters, ma'am. We're here about changing the system in this country."

At that, Arlene Simpson cut in. "What do you say to the late Senator James Hoffman's accusations that you are some kind of queen bee in a lesbian hive that's out to take over the world?"

Brenda gripped the edges of the podium as if it were the ledge of a tall building. "If women's equality is good for this country, why can't it be good for the entire world? We're sick of being tromped under the heels of men. Me and my girls took out a terrorist, faced capture, imprisonment, and death, and who got the credit? The President, the Army, and the Navy. We were the fourth ring in a three-ring circus. The chauvinism in this country must come to an end. The LZF Party is a means to that end, and I call for all women to join us in the final battle of the sexes."

"I like men opening my doors and holding my chairs."

"I suppose you like the catcalls and whistles as you walk by, too?"

"I'm not a whore."

"Show some respect for yourself."

The director intervened. "Ladies, settle down."

"You settle down," Brenda shouted back. "You're not running this show anymore."

"Oh yeah?" The director cut to a commercial. *"Try Jackie O'Neal's new beauty product, Soft as Silk Facial Scrub..."*

The catfight didn't stop there.

"Not all women want to emasculate men."

"Yeah. We women like being pampered."

The director shouted, "Show's over."

Two security officers rushed up and cleared everyone off the stage.

Charles Mantella was waiting in the wings. Brenda walked up to him, cool as a summer salad. "How'd I do?"

"Knocked 'em dead, girl. Knocked 'em dead."

Chapter Twenty-Six

Back at The Ranch, the sisters were glued to the tube, waiting for the show to proceed and concerned about the long commercial break. "I wonder what's going on," Maria said.

Monica answered, "Maybe they had to cut away because Brenda slapped the shit out of someone."

Donna stood and smiled at her sisters. "I hope she did. That crack about Hoffman was totally unnecessary."

BREAKING NEWS flashed across the flatscreen, and heavy intro music led to an announcement. *"We're breaking away from the studio to our roving reporter in Central Park. Thad? You there? What do you have for us?"*

A reporter appeared on the screen. "This is Thad Harper reporting for WNN. What you're about to see are the bravest little girls in the city." A video clip ran, trees and grass slewed to an old woman on a park bench, feeding pigeons. "Watch closely, as a thief is about to meet his match. The lowlife in the hoodie runs up and steals this old woman's purse and then runs toward two little girls and their dog playing on the grass. Instead of bowling them over, he's kicked in the leg by one of the little girls. Down he goes. See that? His leg is bent backwards, compound fracture, I'd say. Now watch him grab a knife from his belt. The other little girl stomps on his arm and kicks the dropped knife halfway across the soccer field. Their little dog launches into the fight. Look at that. The dog has just savagely bitten the thief in his unmentionables. As he writhes on the ground, watch what our little heroines do next. They take the purse from him and run it back to the shaken senior citizen. In the background you can see the NYPD slapping cuffs on the bad guy. This was all caught on a passerby's cell phone, folks."

A cheer went up at The Ranch, and the proud sisters gave each other high-fives. Jackie proclaimed, "Sisters, you know what this means. Pizza and ice cream for dinner tonight."

***

Robert looked out the front window to Frank and Carrie's house, hoping to see Maggie returning from a visit with her sister. He held Zoey in the crook of his arm. She was hungry and screaming up a storm. Frank, standing behind him, said. "Is she coming yet?"

Seeing no movement across the street, Robert decided to take Zoey to her mother. "Come on."

Maggie must've noticed them crossing the street, as she ran out to take Zoey. "Carrie has morning sickness, Frank. Let her sleep. She'll be okay soon." Maggie and Robert left him standing there.

Relieved they'd gone inside and Zoey had stopped crying, he sat on his front porch swing and thought about Robert. *Man, that's going to be me in a few months. I'm glad submarine school will be done by then, and I'll be out at sea.*

His respite didn't last long as a recovered Carrie came out and joined him in the swing.

"Did you see the news?"

"No. What did I miss?"

"Caroline and Betsy stopped a mugger today in Central Park."

"Come on. How can two little girls—"

"It's all on video. Those little girls are pretty damn tough. Betsy broke the thug's leg, Caroline broke his arm, and Girlie Dog bit him in the balls."

"Doesn't that seem odd to you?"

"There's nothing odd about my sisters, Frank."

"Maybe they're some new kind of super females, and if they are, then they're starting their crime fighting pretty damn young. Makes me wonder what kind of damage Brenda could do." He glanced at her sideways. "Or you, for that matter. You survived an un-survivable plane crash without a scratch."

"I'm not like them."

"Still, I wouldn't want to piss you off. I might wind up in the hospital or the morgue."

"That's silly." She elbowed him in the ribs. "What are you doing out here all by yourself?"

"Just thinking about being a dad."

"Yeah. About that...Maggie and I were talking—"

"Oh crap."

"The Navy is going to take you away from your new family, Frank, to who knows where in the world...in a submarine, no less. I don't want you to go."

"Comes with the job, honey."

"Maggie says she can get Robert to hire you at his company. Just think. A civilian job with nine-to-five hours. You won't have to leave us."

He looked at her sideways. "Really. I can't believe you just said that."

She crawled up in his lap and threw her arms around his neck. "Brenda can make a call to Admiral Kincade, get you a hardship discharge so you can stay with us."

"Jesus Christ, Carrie. You can't be serious."

"If you're out to sea, what's a girl to do?" She planted butterfly kisses on his cheek and down his neck. "I might have to work one of the Sisterhood's Black Friday Parties, give the men who attend whatever they want. It's a very good way to raise money."

"You want me to believe your sisters are a bunch of whores?"

"We do what we have to...for the Sisterhood. Now if you were here, I wouldn't be called on to fundraise for the LZ Foundation or the campaign."

"You'd sell your body for the Sisterhood?"

"Whatever Brenda wants." She got off his lap. "Your choice, Frank, a civilian job or the Navy. My virtue hangs in the balance."

"This is total bullshit, you know."

"Try me."

She sauntered back into the house.

***

Back at the Johnson's house, while Maggie nursed Zoey,

Robert went out and got the mail. Back inside, he fanned through the envelopes and came up with one for Maggie, addressed by hand. "Hey, you must have a secret admirer."

Juggling Zoey, Maggie tore open the envelope. "I'm about to find out." She read it, and hand shaking, she put the letter down on the table and began to cry.

Robert read the letter written in block letters:

> Maggie, Maggie, Maggie, I'm the man who popped your cherry. Remember me? You were a nice tight whore, but you thought you were too good for me, so I took what I paid for by force. Yes, I was one of Big Bad Brooklyn Daddy's customers. I raped your mother, too. She was a whore with a taste for crystal meth, right? I think it's my public duty to tell everyone what a whore you are. I will spread your filth all over social media. Everyone will know you're a whore mother of a whore child. But seeing as how I'm a little short on cash, you get me $500,000 and I will forget all about your nasty little ass. In three days, you will get another letter telling you where to leave the money. Good luck with your baby Zoey.

Holding Zoey tight, Maggie cried, "Robert, what are we going to do?" She collapsed on the couch.

He sat next to her and pulled her teary face to his shoulder. "I'm going to kill him."

"We don't know who he is or where he lives."

"I'll find out."

Maggie bawled. "I remember the night...I was just sixteen. He was a short fat slob...smelled like a dirty gym sock...his breath was disgusting, almost worse...than the rape itself. He hurt me...made me bleed...made me sick."

"He'll pay. I promise."

"Goddess Loa, please comfort me in my time of need."

The Goddess Loa was listening. Maggie's tears touched her heart. She picked up an asteroid and threw it at the speed of light into the atmosphere of Earth, creating a meteor shower the likes of which the inhabitants have never seen. *Look up, sweet little Maggie, look up and know that I will not forsake you. Remember*

610 Navy donuts. Go for a ride and its meaning will dawn on you.

***

Down in Brooklyn, Maggie's rapist, Billy Bob Foster, lay on the couch, daydreaming about how he was going to spend all that money he would be getting from Robert and Maggie. His dog, a vicious pit-bull named Butch, lay with his head resting on Billy Bob's bare leg. He was kicking and growling in his sleep, not that he was in a fight with another big dog but with a female dog half his size and weight. He woke up with a yelp and started licking his balls.

Billy Bob put the porn movie on pause long enough to kick Butch off the couch then shove his hand in his pants before continuing the show. He moved his feet to the coffee table, careful of the bag of pretzels, but a money shot on the screen caused his foot to slip, and the pretzels spilled on the floor. Butch hustled to the scene and started munching away. Billy Bob decided to let Butch have them and turned his eyes back to the porn video where two women started munching on each other. After working up a sweat playing with himself, he ran the video back to the beginning and watched the whole thing all over again, as if he'd missed the plot.

***

Robert was on a mission. Out of the blue, Maggie wanted to take Zoey for a ride down Navy Street to the donut shop where they first met. "610," Maggie said then went in and bought two double chocolate donuts and a Coke. The check came to $4.99. "Not 610."

On her way out, she saw a fat man sitting with his back to her, eating out of a box of twelve donuts and downing them with a quart-sized bottle of chocolate milk. Confused, she got in the car. "610 and donuts have got to mean something."

"We're on Navy Street. You've got the donuts. 610 should be right here." He put the car in gear, and as he drove past the donut shop's front window, Zoey started crying and waving her arms. Maggie looked back at Zoey in the car seat. "What's wrong with her? Gas maybe? I hope our next baby doesn't have that problem."

He pulled the car into a fire lane. "Better check her diaper." He turned off the engine. "Ah...next baby? Are you...I mean...are you pregnant again?"

"Exact-a-mondo."

His heartrate jumped. "How did that happen?"

Rubbing his hand, she looked into his blue eyes. "It's obvious how it happened, so I'm not going to dignify your stupid question with the answer." Just then a parking officer walked up to the window: yellow vest, badge, and all. "You can't park here. Move it now or get a ticket."

Sometimes events happened just by chance. Another ten seconds one way or the other, and fate would turn life in a different direction. However, nothing happened by chance where the Goddess Loa was involved.

Robert started the engine, looked back to reverse but had to wait for a car to pass. It was then that Zoey started yelling again. Maggie looked up and saw her rapist crossing the street with a donut box in his left hand, and in his right, he held a leash connected to the collar of a big pit-bull. A knot formed in her throat. "It's the rapist." She swallowed hard. "Follow him." Driving at two miles an hour, they followed Billy Bob for three blocks, having to stop when they saw him stop...so butch could take a dump on the sidewalk. He then walked another block to 610 Navy street.

"610. That's it." She could hardly breathe.

He clomped up four steps of broken concrete then ducked into a brownstone one-level house that must have been built in the nineteen thirties.

Robert glanced at Maggie. "He's going to die tonight."

"I want to go with you."

"You're staying home with Zoey. I've killed men in battle over money and power. This time I'll kill to protect my family. So, end of the conversation."

"He raped me," she screamed. "I want to watch him die."

"No you don't."

Their yelling made Zoey start crying and kicking her feet, causing her shoes to fly off and promptly land on the floorboard.

"Maggie, I give in to you on everything, but not this time."

In resignation, Maggie leaned between the seats, picked up

Zoey's shoes, tied the laces together, and hung them on the rearview mirror.

After riding in silence all the way back to New London, Robert thought Maggie didn't seem so upset now. *I guess she thought about it and decided I'm right.*

As soon as Robert pulled in the driveway, Maggie was out of the car like a shot, rushed around and got Zoey out, and ran up to their front door, and holding Zoey in one arm, she unlocked the door, stepped inside, and slammed the door in Robert's face. *Ah, shit! This is ridiculous.* He turned the doorknob...but it was locked.

"Maggie. Let me in."

"You can sleep in the gutter for all I care."

Walking around the outside of the house, he spotted an open window on the second floor. "I'll show her." He got a ladder out of the shed, propped it up on the wall, and moments later, he wormed his way inside. Just as his feet hit the floor, Maggie ran in. He ducked her first swing and threw her over his shoulder.

"Put me down, you big ox." She beat on his back with her fists, all the way down to the basement. "No sex for you for a month."

He set her on her feet but held on to her waist. "I'll tie you up down here until I get back."

"You wouldn't dare."

"Maggie, would you really hold out on me for a month?"

Hugging him and looking up at that adorable face that she dearly loved, she laughed. "I suppose not. You go ahead and kill that son of a bitch...but make him suffer...a lot... and make him beg for mercy."

"And all this time I thought you were of the fairer sex."

***

It was the night of the new moon. Robert turned onto Navy Street and killed the headlights. It was pitch black. He could barley see Girlie Dog's black eyes as she sat next to him, tail thumping on the seat. Brenda was kind enough to let her sleep over with Zoey. "You keep close and keep quiet in case that pit-bull gives us any trouble." The tail-thumping ceased.

Now standing at his open trunk, Robert took out his Army

Colt .45, slapped in a ten-round clip then chambered a round. He jammed the gun in the back of his pants then grabbed his murder kit, a canvas bag with all the tools he'd need to end the rapist's life and burn down his damn house.

Sure, he could've called the cops, dredged up Maggie's past for everyone to condemn, testify in court as to the blackmail, but the statute of limitations would prevent him from paying for his real crime, the rape of a sixteen-year-old girl. Even so, Robert could hear the defense attorney's spiel to the jury now. *"She worked for Big Bad Brooklyn Daddy. She was a whore. What did she expect? It wasn't rape. It was an illegal business transaction. She was the one committing the crime."*

No. Murdering this prick was the only way to protect her from her past. There was no turning back now.

He signaled Girlie Dog to stay and climbed the crumbling steps to the porch where he knocked on the door. The porchlight winked on. A moment later, the door opened with a squeal, and there stood the fat, pimple-faced rapist with a sawed-off shotgun pointed at him.

"Hey. I know you," he grumbled out.

"I brought your money." He lifted the bag in evidence.

The rapist studied the bag and actually drooled tobacco-stained spittle. "Now this is what I call real service."

"May I come in?"

"Just set it on the porch and step away."

"Don't you think we should count it?"

That stumped him for second or two, then: "I guess you're right. Come in real slow like." He held out his left hand to take the bag. "Heavy. That's good."

Now that the rapist's hands were full, Robert reverted to his military training and grabbed the shotgun, a two-handed twisting motion that disarmed the rapist but triggered an attack response from the pit-bull. The growling beast didn't get two lunges before Girlie Dog intercepted him. Teeth and claws went to work, throats growling and jaws throwing slobber. During the distraction, Robert grabbed back his murder kit with his left hand and produced the .45 with his right. With his right boot, he kicked the front door closed.

Girlie Dog made lunchmeat of Butch's balls.

Robert made the rapist pee in his pants.

"Nothing personal," he pleaded.

"Oh, it's personal, all right."

"Call off your dog, man. He's jackin' up Butch something fierce."

"He's a she, you moron. Come, Girlie Dog."

Yelping and yiping, Butch dragged himself into the kitchen, leaving a wide trail of blood.

Girlie Dog ran to Robert, wagging her tail and licking blood off her snout as she sat at his feet.

Robert wagged the gun at the rapist. "Sit." He indicated a nearby wooden chair with the barrel of his .45.

"Hey, man..." the rapist sat as instructed, "you can keep the money. Forget this ever happened."

Robert opened the bag. "Look at that. No money." He took out a bungy cord and strapped him to the chair. "Now that we're both comfortable, what's your name?"

"Billy...they call me Billy Bob."

Robert glanced around, spotted a laptop on the coffee table with a porn movie playing. Crumpled tissues. Vibrators. Dick rings. He didn't dare touch any of it. "Gross." Then he glanced at the walls, the pinned up polaroids: girls tied up by the wrists and ankles, women gagged, eyes filled with terror. On the fireplace mantle: necklaces, earrings, panties and bras, all hung with care. "You've got quite a collection here, Billy Bob."

"A guy's gotta have a hobby, man. Let me go, will ya?"

That's when he spotted a picture of Maggie in a schoolgirl skirt and blouse. She was standing with an older woman, maybe her mother, a big black brick of a black man, probably Big Bad Brooklyn Daddy, and this puke in the chair had his arm around Maggie.

Son of a Bitch.

He yanked the picture off the mantle, pulled the photo out of the frame, and folded the paper to fit in his pocket.

Billy Bob twisted back and forth in the chair. "Let me loose, man. I promise I'll never harm another girl, never rape another woman."

"Too late, Billy Bob." That's when he noticed a tattoo on the side of the rapist's neck. It read: *Maggie* in elegant cursive. Then he noticed the inked sleeves tattooed on his arms were actually the names of his other victims: Pamela, Angela, Doris, Nemo. *Nemo?* Anger built in Robert's chest like a hot grenade. He returned to his murder kit, dropped in the Colt, and pulled out a butane torch, no bigger than a Bic lighter.

"What's that for?" Billy Bob shouted.

"Tattoo remover."

"Hell you say."

Robert flicked an intense blue flame to life. It hissed like a poisonous snake. He stepped up behind Billy Bob, clamped his head in the crook of his arm, and set the flame to his memorial to Maggie's rape. Robert had heard a lot of men scream during his time on the battlefield, but this rapist's scream beat them all. And burning flesh had that pungent smell one never forgets.

"Why'd ya do that, man? Why'd you do that?" He was kicking around like a skunk in a bear trap.

Robert shut off the torch, put it in the bag, and came out with his .45. "Goodbye, Billy Bob." He pulled the trigger and blew out the back of his head. It was the end of the rapist.

Girlie Dog sniffed the spattered cranial debris then sat on her butt and scratched her side as if it were just another day at The Ranch.

At two in the morning, the house went up in flames. Robert sat in the car, took the picture from his pocket, unfolded it then called Maggie.

She answered all in a huff. "Is it done?"

"Sugar Cakes, to steal a line from the Wizard of Oz, he's not only legally dead but regally dead. And I have a souvenir for you." He refolded the photo. "See you in an hour. Bye."

Chapter Twenty-Seven

Back to Jackie and Brenda, they were now on their way to see the office space that could serve as their headquarters for the LZF Party, where an army of volunteers would work the phones in a bid for the Presidency of the United States.

"Brenda, it's going to take a lot of women to help us out."

"You're right, and we'll get them, plus, there'll be a lot of young men trying to kiss up to us, and we'll make good use of them, too."

The limo pulled up to the curb on Maiden Lane. "Jackie, I like the building and location already, and I love all those windows, and WNN is only a stone's throw away. What's the rent?"

"Don't worry about it. I'm a billionaire, remember?"

As they got out of the limo, they were greeted by Jane Gray, the twenty-five-year-old leasing agent. Both Brenda and Jackie thought the same thing as Jane walked up to them with a comely and pleasant smile. *I wouldn't mind a three way with her.*

Jane thought the same thing, as her sexual orientation leaned more toward the girls' side of the gym. The boys' side was always so smelly. "It's nice to meet you. Jackie, I would recognize you anywhere, great facial scrub, by the way, and Brenda, I saw you on WNN. What a slug fest."

Being diplomatic, Brenda answered while trying to keep her gaze from diving into Jane's very nice cleavage. "Women can be brutal, but I can't understand why any woman would want to be a slave to a man."

As the trio of beauties entered the building, Jane thought she would love to be Brenda's sex slave. "Oh, I would never agree to being a man's property. What do you think, Jackie?"

“I absolutely agree. I’ve had to deal with men all my business life. There wasn’t a day gone by that I didn’t hear a condescending or arrogant comment from a man, especially when I first started my skin-care business. Would you like to know what happens now? Men are afraid of me. They know that I’m far richer than they are, and I don’t take shit off any man.”

“So, Brenda, have you ever had a man-problem?”

Thinking she would love to kiss her, Brenda said, “Yes I have, not unlike millions of woman world wide.”

Jane’s thoughts came to Brenda in the same context of kissing but a bit more specific on the location of that kiss. “So what did you do, tell him to take a hike?”

“You don’t want to know, Jane, but rest assured, he was very sorry he ever cheated on me.”

Jane stopped in the hall that led to the spacious offices. “You killed him?”

“Let’s not joke around when it comes to two-timing losers like my ex-fiancé.”

With that said, the three of them laughed as they strode to an office where a *FOR LEASE* sign hung on the double doors. “It’s been vacant for several months.” Jane unlocked the latch and invited them inside.

Inspecting the expansive office area, void of all furnishings and décor, Jackie and Brenda paced the dusty hardwood floor, looked out the smudged windows, investigated an adjoining conference room with built-in wi-fi, cable, and phone jacks, checked the kitchen’s water-spotted sink and dull stainless steel counters, even ran the garbage disposal and peeked into restrooms that needed a heavy dose of Lysol.

After rejoining Jane at the doorway, Jackie said, “Could use a good cleaning, but we’ll take it. History will be made in this room on election night. Let’s call it LZF Central.”

“I like that,” Brenda said.

“Then we have a deal.” Jane delivered handshakes to her new clients, a connection that bore more emotion than business tradition.

As they left a very happy Jane to do the paperwork for their new headquarters, Brenda and Jackie were left to discuss ways to get Jane to join the Sisterhood.

***

As the sun rose the next morning, Brenda was not thrilled about flying to Arlington to play Pinochle but knew she'd have to endure the challenge to get close to Lynne. She stood at the limo's front passenger door and waited for Jorge to open it. When he figured out she didn't want to ride in the plush executive cabin, he closed the back door and complied with her wishes. She slid into the front seat and buckled in.

Jorge, now behind the wheel, glanced at her. "I never took you for someone who wanted to play cards with some old biddies."

"Well, Jorge, that makes two of us."

"Then why are you going to do it?"

"Revenge."

"Why?"

"Remember the Medal of Freedom awards fiasco, my friend?"

"Yes 'm."

"Humiliating, to say the least, and General Wesley Miller didn't give any credit to the Sisterhood. So I need to meet his wife, and when I'm done with her, she'll be a new sister and leave him for another woman."

"Humiliating, indeed." He accelerated the limo out the drive and headed for JFK International Airport.

Unbeknownst to Brenda, she was about to meet one heartbroken Lynne Miller who was terribly ill with cramps and morning sickness, so ill she'd canceled the Pinochle games, but forgot to have Wes inform the General to call Jackie to tell Brenda the bad news.

It was a quick jet trip from JFK to Ronald Reagan Airport, and Alfons had arranged a limo to take her to Lynne and Wesley Miller's house near Fort Myers and Arlington Cemetery. He stopped in front of a blond-brick two-story on Del Ray, got out, and opened the door. She stepped out onto a sidewalk lined with beautiful trees and manicured lawns.

"Right up those steps, ma'am. I'll wait here."

"Thank you." While walking up the few steps toward Lynne and Wes Miller's front door, Brenda started thinking about ice tea, Young Mountain Tea, to be exact, but she had no idea why that thought had come to her.

Standing at the door, she took a deep breath and rang the bell, hoping the women wouldn't laugh at her lack of Pinochle skills. No one came to the door. She checked her watch: 1:59 pm. *I'm not late.* She was sure it was Wednesday. She rang the bell again. The chime was clearly audible through the closed door. As she turned back toward the limo, she heard a click behind her and turned back to see the door ajar. A weak voice said, "Oh, dear, I'm sorry. Pinochle has been cancelled for this week. I'm not feeling well."

Brenda approached the door. "You are Lynne Miller?"

"I wish I were dead."

"What's wrong?"

"Cramps and morning sickness—"

"You're pregnant?"

"Twins. I have to go back to bed, now."

"I'm Brenda Ayler...from New York."

"Oh, Brenda...I'm so sorry..." Lynne toppled to the floor.

Brenda pushed the door open and knelt beside the stricken woman. "Lynne...Lynne."

"I'm so weak I can't move."

"Let me help you." Brenda got Lynne to her feet, an easy task for a lesbian zombie, and helped her to the Lazy Boy recliner where she gently sat her down and raised her feet. "There."

"Oh, thank you. I'm so sorry to be a bother."

"Bother? Where's your husband?"

"Working...as usual."

Her earlier thought of tea suddenly struck her. "Do you have any tea, Young Mountain Tea?"

"My favorite. In the kitchen, left upper cupboard."

"Hang tight." Brenda rushed to the kitchen, found the tea and tall glasses, in which she mixed the tea with cold water, and helped herself to ice cubes from the fridge.

When she returned with the drinks, she handed one to Lynne. "This should make you feel better."

Lynne took a drink. "They say I'm too old to have these babies. I'm so afraid I'll miscarry."

"You'll be fine." Brenda gazed at five-foot-six-inch Lynne Miller, her light brown hair, *obviously only her hair dresser knows for sure*, and her chubby body, and it became quickly apparent that avenging her husband's mistake would not go by way of the Sisterhood. No way would she turn Lynne into a lesbian zombie and risk those innocent babies, safe within her womb.

Brenda held up her tea glass. "Cheers."

"You're so kind." Lynne slowly drank the tea while Brenda sat on the divan across from her. "I may have misjudged you, Brenda. My Wes thinks you're a lesbian. You have sex parties. Is that true?"

"Yes. I'll have to invite you sometime."

"Oh dear. I'm not built for those things."

"I'm also running for President, me and Jackie O'Neal."

"My goodness, that's right. You're so brave."

"So are you, with those twins, and all. I couldn't do it."

She finished her tea, inhaled, exhaled, and smiled. "I'm feeling so much better now."

Yes, Lynne was back to her old self again, all gabby and giggly. For the next hour, they discussed everything about her life with Wes, how hard it was to be a military wife, and with the kids coming, how much harder it would get, but she didn't care. God had blessed her with children, a blessing she accepted with open arms. Brenda let her think that, didn't lay any Goddess Loa truths on her, she was just happy to have gotten to know her, straight as she was.

"It's time I catch my plane back to New York."

Lynne got up, fine as could be, and walked her to the door. "Such a pleasure to meet you, Brenda. I'm so glad you didn't get the memo about the cancelled card game. We might not have ever met."

"The Lord of All works in mysterious ways." She left a kiss on Lynne's cheek and walked down the steps to the waiting limo.

***

Upon arriving back at The Ranch, Brenda couldn't find anyone in the house. "Jackie. Monica." Girlie Dog bounded in from outside, tail wagging a mile a minute.

"Where are the sisters, Girlie?"

Girlie Dog took off running toward the pool, and out on the pool deck, Brenda was soon attacked by two very wet little ones,

Caroline and Betsy, each grabbing Brenda's legs. "Brenda's home. Brenda's home."

"I missed you too. Let me go now, sweeties."

"We're having so much fun." They ran back to the pool, leaving a trail of water on the deck.

Glancing around, Brenda saw that it was lesbian zombie goof-off time, as usual. Her sisters had better enjoy the day because things were going to change very soon, and activities wouldn't include playing submarine like Lilly and Donna were doing right now in the hot tub.

Her observations were interrupted when Melinda threw an arm around Brenda's shoulders. "Are you the Pinochle champion now?"

"I didn't have to play a single hand to get Lynne Miller to go from despising me to loving me."

"Is she one of us now?" Chloe asked. "If so, can I have her first...ah...next?"

"The problem is...she's a little pregnant, so she's off limits." Movement in a deck chair caught Brenda's eye. "Jill, would you be a dear and wake up Monica. The way her hips are going, I think she must be having a wet dream."

Caroline ran up. "What's a wet dream, Brenda?"

"None of your beeswax. Go play in the hot tub...no wait...the pool, yeah, stay close to the pool."

"Ah, Brenda. You never tell us nothing." She stomped to the pool and jumped in.

"You know..." Melinda put in, "the Sisterhood is a wet dream."

Jill strutted back in her almost-nothing bikini. "I woke her up and now she's pissed."

"Her dream was that good, huh?"

"So, our Queen," Melinda said. "While you were out and the Sisterhood was doing what they do best, I was busy making the final arrangements on furnishing our new LZF offices."

"What's it going to cost us?"

"Less than a million bucks."

"Does Jackie know?"

"Yes. Pricey, she'd said, but the optics will prove to be worth it. Now we need to come up with a slogan and a logo."

"I have a slogan idea."

All the sisters turned and looked at Chloe.

Monica, with the sound of frustration in her voice, said, "Pray to tell," and sat at the pool's edge. Her hair was all a-frizz as if she'd been pulling on it during her sexy dream. "What is it, Chloe?"

She steeled herself for criticism. "I was in an antique store a while back where I saw a poster from World War Two of Rosie the Riveter. The heading read *We Can Do It.* All we have to do is put your picture, Brenda, on a poster with the words, *She Can Do It as Your President.* What do you think?"

Brenda pulled her into a big hug. "That's a brilliant idea."

The other girls agreed with, "Hell yeah," and, "I love it." All the sisters joined in to hug and kiss her. Even Donna and Lilly, back from the hot tub, got in on the action. Their submarine must've sunk or gotten blown out of the water.

Monica said, "I'll get to work on Chloe's idea right away. Meanwhile, Melinda, assign three sisters for cleanup detail. You supervise. Jorge can drive you down to LZF Central to clean and mop the place and get it ready for the furniture. Jill, stay here with Betsy and Caroline. Make sure they feed Girlie Dog, and Maria, you're in charge of political swag. We want our offices decorated to the moon."

"I've got lots left over from Black Friday."

"Great."

"And I volunteer for the cleanup crew," she added.

Lilly and Donna volunteered too.

Monica pointed a beautiful index finger at them. "And no goofing off, you hear?"

***

Back in New London, there was a lot of goofing off going on. Robert and Frank were drinking beer on the back porch, and Maggie and Carrie were inside, chitchatting about babies.

It was Frank who had breaking news for Robert. Reaching out with his beer bottle to Robert's, who did the same to Frank's, they gave the bottle necks a manly tap. "I told Carrie I'd take you up on your job offer at Galaxy International if Brenda got me a hardship discharge from the Navy."

"I'll be happy to have you onboard, Frank." He accented that statement with a swig of beer.

"You do realize, of course, the chances of me getting out of the Navy early are slim to none."

"Miracles happen. Look at me."

"You're right about that. An hour ago, I got a call from Admiral Kincade."

"Yeah?"

"He granted my discharge effective immediately."

"All right." Robert raised his bottle. "Welcome to civilian life."

Frank didn't show the same enthusiasm. "You know how much I wanted that job on a submarine? It was my life's dream."

"So? Life is taking you in a new direction."

"Come on, Robert. How the hell did Brenda get that kind of pull with the Admiral? Either she's jumping his bones or she's some kind of Queen of the Universe."

"You might be pretty close there, Frank. I'm going to get another beer. You want one?"

"I can't believe you think this is normal."

Chapter Twenty-Eight

There were big expectations at WNN as Jackie and Brenda took their seats for a joint campaign interview. Both were impeccably dressed in business blazers and skirts. Of course, there was a lot of leg to be seen above their spiked high heels. The stage lights were bright, and the cameras seemed intrusively close.

The director announced: "Welcome to *The Threes* on WNN, coming to you live from New York City. And here are your hosts for today's show, Diane and Laura." He could have been announcing a World Wrestling Federation match, his voice was that exuberant.

Diane and Laura strutted out on stage, waving to the audience they couldn't see behind the bank of bright lights. The hosts wore matching pants and sleeveless blouses, one African American, Diane, plump but pretty with white hair, and her counterpart, Laura, white with privilege and cute as a bunny's fluff.

Brenda and Jackie stood for the traditional handshakes then everyone seated themselves in their respective chairs.

Laura led off with, "We usually interview one guest at a time, thus we call our show *The Threes*, but today we have two guests with us, the LZF Party's candidates for the highest offices in the land. Please welcome Brenda Ayler and Jackie O'Neal."

Joyous applause followed, much more enthusiastically than the previous interview show, which meant they were gaining support from the masses.

Diane threw out the first question. "Jackie, why does this country need another political party?"

"Because the other parties only want women's votes, and then we're supposed to scurry back into our kitchens like quiet little mice until the next election."

Laura followed up. "Why do you want to run for President, Brenda?"

She placed her index finger to her lips, looked up with a thoughtful slant to her brow, then dropped a bomb. "Because the other two candidates are two old white guys. One has a tough time remembering his own name, and the other never met a woman he didn't want to screw."

A bit of a gasp resonated from the audience.

"Brenda, you certainly have a colorful way of making your point."

"There's been too much old-school in the White House. Sex scandals. Secret liaisons. Under-the-table handshakes." Brenda smiled. "Diane, my speech may be colorful, but my luscious red lips speak only the truth. Color it. Spin it. Ignore it. Call it fake news. None of that hype changes the facts. Men are the problem. We need more women in government to keep them in line."

Jackie high-fived Brenda, a show of solidarity. The audience loved it. When they settled down, Laura put out the next question.

"Jackie, tell us one thing you and Brenda would do in the White House to blow away both established parties."

"Laura, to contradict the values of liberals and conservatives alike, we'd push for our *Rent to Buy Act*, which simply says that if someone lives in a place for ten years and pays their rent on time and takes care of the property, they have the right to buy it out from under their landlord at current market value with no down payment...and with approved credit, of course. Middle class home ownership goes up and wealth trickles down from the top, like it always has."

"What if the owner doesn't want to sell their investment property?"

"Too bad. This idea has been in practice for years in Holland. There they take the money from the sale and buy more investment property. It's a win, win, Laura. Money changes hands, capital gains fatten the treasury, the housing market booms, and the middle class benefits, especially women since they make less than men, and everyone gains more assets to show for their hard work."

Diane gave that hypothesis a nod. "I can see why liberals and conservatives would go bananas over that kind of economic backstabbing, but you'll still need to get your idea through

Congress."

"With the support of millions of American women and our Goddess, the LZF party will sweep the majority in both chambers. The obstructionism in Congress will end."

Laura decided to jump on that statement. "So who's this Goddess you mentioned?"

"Loa, the Lesbian Goddess of the Universe."

That crooked her brow. "Lesbian?"

"Yeah. You got something against lesbians?"

"No, but...well...never mind."

Brenda picked up all kinds of sexy brain waves coming from Laura, some of which could never be revealed on television. "I can see by the cross you're wearing around your neck that you are a Christian."

"I am. What is your religion called? It's something new, right? Sounds like paganism. I mean, that's okay. It's a free country to worship as you please, but something just seems off here. You're certainly too young for the hippie culture."

"We don't label our religion, as do Catholics and Protestants, Christians and Jews, Buddhists and Muslims. We believe Loa is the true universal goddess, a female deity, daughter of a star, who destroyed the male gods of literature and lore."

"Right." Now Laura got testy. "To a lot of American voters, that's going to sound a little way out there, if you know what I mean. Could cost you the election."

In her earpiece, Laura got a message from Charles Mantella. "Knock it off, Laura. Get back to politics."

Diane spoke up. "I like the woman goddess idea...but couldn't there be a male god too?"

"There was," Brenda said, "but the Goddess Loa got tired of being groped so she turned the male gods to sand. What do you think is spinning around in the storms on Jupiter?"

"That's blasphemy."

The audience grumbled.

After quickly cutting to a pillow commercial, Charles stormed in and pointed at Laura and Jackie. "Ladies, please stay on topic. This isn't Jerry Springer. I don't want to lose my audience."

He couldn't have been more wrong. WNN's ratings launched out of sight. On a competing network, Eileen was watching and said to her program director, “Oh, I like these two. I mean I really love them. Book them on my show right away.” Not to be outdone, Jim Vanity wanted them on his show too, but not to showcase them. No. He told his producer, “They may be beautiful women, but I’ll make short work of those two lightweights.”

After about twenty more minutes of generic questions, as per the instructions of a rattled Charles Mantella, the show was over, but there would be many more, and Brenda and Jackie knew they would have to be prepared for anything.

As they walked out to the limo, Jackie asked, “So what do you think?”

“It went okay, but we’re going to run into more gotcha questions during these talk-shows, especially the more we embarrass the establishment. Then those guys on the liberal and conservative battleground will jump at the chance to discredit us. The more outlandish we sound, the more press we get.”

“But those networks are never on the same side of an issue. We’ll always get blowback from one or the other.”

“You’re right, but this time someone has come along who can be a threat to the political parties they back. We might cause them to band together and go against us.”

“Yeah. And the squeaky wheel gets the grease. LZF will be a household name quick as wildfire across California.”

Little did anyone know then, but a ground swell of women voters had just risen across the US of A. This expanding rebellion against men and God would soon threaten the entire American political establishment. The good-old-boys would fight back, and the lesbian zombies would be in for one hell of a war.

***

Meanwhile, in New London, Maggie was driving Carrie to her doctor appointment for a prenatal checkup. They were happy to have some girl-to-girl talk time. Maggie decided to tell Carrie the good news. “I’m pregnant with baby number two.” A carload of teenage girls couldn’t have screamed more jubilantly.

Frank was delighted to have some alone time. Robert was busy taking care of Zoey, so he wouldn’t be coming over for another beer bash on the back porch.

Filled with trepidation, Frank sat at his computer and Googled Brenda Ayler. There must've been a million websites, blogs, and articles about the Presidential candidate and women's equality. Overwhelming at best, he couldn't read all this—

An ad popped up for a website that specialized in finding missing persons. Twenty bucks. He figured it was a longshot but it was only twenty bucks, so... *What the hell.*

He signed up and signed in. A page with a form opened, looked easy enough. Name: he typed *Brenda Ayler*. Last known city: *New York*. Last known residence: *I don't know the address.* He typed *The Ranch*. High school: *I don't know that either.* He left it blank. Church: He typed *NONE*. Last known location:

Jesus Christ. I'm getting nowhere fast.

He saw another link on top of the page: *National Missing Persons Registry. She's not missing.* He clicked it anyway. Name: *Brenda Ayler*. He hit the *SEARCH* button. The cursor became a circle going round and round...a page opened. It read *Brenda Ayler* across the top. The photo was of a redhead, all right, but this woman was, to put it bluntly, fat and ugly. Missing from: *Denver, Colorado.* Last known location: *Haiti*. Destination: *Port au Prince.* Note: *No record of her return to the United States.* Reporting party: *Fred Jensen. Uncle.*

"If you see this person contact the Colorado Bureau of Investigation."

He leaned back in his chair. "That's twenty bucks I'll never see again."

Then he spotted another link. Photos: *Additional photos supplied by Fred Jensen.*

He clicked the link and got a real shocker. There was the Brenda Ayler he knew, or damn close to it, in her high school photo, with the same red hair. "Son of a bitch."

A million questions raced through his mind... amnesia... runaway... witness protection... fugitive from justice...

I need to contact Fred Jensen too—

There was a knock on the door downstairs. "Frank?"

As the door opened, Frank took a shot of hot adrenaline to his bloodstream. Shit. He turned off the computer and ran down to greet Robert. "Hey."

He brought Zoey in a carry-all and a six pack of light beer.

"You're not too busy to have a beer with your new boss, are you?"

Frank changed from detective mode to host mode, but his brain was on fire. A fugitive wouldn't run for President. Witness protection wouldn't allow her to run for President. Amnesia? He didn't think so. *She must be a runaway*...but from what?

"Hey." Robert cracked a beer. "Earth to Frank. What are you thinking about?" He handed him the freshly opened bottle that burbled white froth.

"Ah...nothing." He didn't want Robert to know Brenda was in his crosshairs again. *Shit. I gotta get into The Ranch. See what I can find.* He chugged his beer.

Chapter Twenty-Nine

While the campaign was heating up in the states, Janice was having a good time running the LZ Foundation in Port au Prince. Money was pouring in. She would send weekly reports to Brenda. While Jackie kept tabs on Janice, LeRoy was living it up on Jesus' church money, but the Sisterhood's share arrived on time after every Sunday service.

Jackie assured Brenda that Janice was keeping such a perfect set of books, that if they ever got audited, the election commission and the IRS would find nothing out of place that could be detrimental to the future of the Sisterhood.

What nobody knew, though, was that Janice was banging Baby Doc every other day and twice on Sunday. There was definitely a shortage of lesbians on the island.

***

Heading toward home, Brenda gave Jorge some new instructions. "Take us to LZF Central so we can see how hard the sisters are working to get ready for opening day."

Jorge turned right on Joe DiMaggio highway. "Thanks to light traffic, I'll get you there in fifteen minutes." At the same time he thought those girls would be goofing off. *Lazy is their middle names.*

Jackie grumped. "Brenda? You don't think they're actually cleaning up the place, do you?"

Brenda sighed. "One can always hope."

After fifteen minutes, Jorge, true to his word, pulled up in front of their Presidential Election Headquarters, LZF Central. Once inside, their jaws dropped. Lilly and Donna were boxing up cleaning supplies and looked surprised to see Jackie and Brenda standing in the doorway."

The floors shined, the windows gleamed, and the light fixtures glowed. The aroma of floor wax and ammonia spray lingered in the air.

Jackie spoke first. "This place looks great. Hell. We could eat off these floors."

Maria was still holding a mop. "We worked really, really hard so you two would be proud of us."

Melinda walked in from the attached conference room, hurriedly buttoning her blouse. "We're just finishing up."

As each sister got hugs from Jackie and Brenda, four Hispanic men walked out of the conference room. They all wore bib overalls, rubber gloves, and sweaty faces. "Gracias, ladies. Same deal next time. We work for pussy, no money, and bring these two senoritas. I get the redhead."

Jackie looked at Brenda. "See? What did I tell you?"

"Girls, you ought to be ashamed of yourselves."

"You guys get out." Jackie grabbed one guy by the ear. "This was a one-timer." She dragged him to the door. "No pussy and no work because there won't be a next time." She booted him in the ass on the way out. His three compadres scrambled out after him.

Then there was only silence in the place until Donna asked, "So how did the show go?"

It was Sisterhood kiss-up time.

Brenda glared at each sister. "I'll pray to Loa that each of you wakes up tomorrow with a really sore bun."

Lilly raised her hand as if she were a customer at Max's Diner. "I won't. Juan got down on his knees and worked hard on the floor. When he got done, we traded places. He stood up and I got down on my knees. He was a quick-fire...less than five minutes. Done. It was a good bargain and cost the Sisterhood nothing."

"Wow, what a deal, Lilly." Brenda scowled. "But you haven't learned a damn thing about hard work and reward."

"Hey, I know about that. I was a waitress. I busted my ass for tips."

"You're not a waitress anymore. You're a sister, all of you, part of a team. We all work together and don't trade our favors for someone else to do the work for us."

"All right," Maria said. "But we had more fun doing it this way."

"Come on, girls. Let's go home. And maybe you can start acting like ladies for a change. That would be refreshing."

***

As the limo got within a block of The Ranch, Jorge braked for two New York State Highway Patrol cars parked across the road. The limo stopped, and at the same time, Brenda received a call from Jill.

"Brenda, the road is blocked, and our driveway is packed with trucks and vans from every news network in the world. I tried to run off reporters interviewing Betsy and Caroline. Goddess only knows what the kids are telling them."

"We'll be there as soon as we can get past this roadblock. Meanwhile get the girls in the house."

"I tried, but every time I step outside, a mob surrounds me and sticks microphones in my face. Why are they asking me questions about Loa?"

Brenda looked around at all the cops and chaos. Calling 911 wouldn't do any good. "Keep a tight lip for now."

Jorge lowered his window. "Hey. Get out of our way."

"Sorry sir. We've been ordered to keep traffic to a minimum out here. Neighbors are complaining. Public access to the beach is blocked. You'll have to wait here or turn around and go back where you came from."

Jackie let herself out the back door. She had a way of making a leggy approach that demanded the cop's attention. "We came from that mansion, officer." She pointed to The Ranch. "So let us pass or you'll be trading your patrol career for a job writing parking tickets."

"Oh my God. You're Jackie O'Neal." He bent to look through the limo's tinted windows. "Is Brenda Ayler in there too? You're the hottest topic in the country right now."

"Tell your boys to open the road for us, and while you're at it, get all that junk out of our driveway."

As it turned out, clearing a path for the limo was easier said than done. With fifty yards to go, Jorge hugged the shoulder and shut off the engine. "Ladies, I'm sorry, but we'll have to walk from here."

He led the way, pushing through the mob, the girls behind him in a tight formation. They stopped long enough to corral Caroline and Betsy and carry them across the portico to the front doors. Jorge hustled the sisters inside while Brenda and Jackie took up defensive positions on the porch to address the mob of reporters and journalists.

"Silence," Brenda shouted. "Everyone calm down. We know you all have questions, and we're happy to answer them, but please, contain your enthusiasm and conduct yourselves in an orderly fashion."

"We don't have much time," Jackie added. "The police have been ordered to clear you all off my driveway. If you don't want your vehicles towed, your heads billy-clubbed, and your asses arrested, calm down."

As the crowd settled and Jackie was answering a question about the late senator James Hoffman, Brenda was reading the minds of the news mob.

What a gorgeous redhead. I'd do her. This came from a woman reporter with blond hair and pouty lips. Brenda wanted to shout out, "I'd do you too."

This dynamic duo would make a big splash in the White House. They've got this election in the bag." How about that? A man who wasn't thinking about sex. Refreshing.

Another woman reporter with the looks of a dark-haired Spanish maiden had her big browns focused on Jackie. *I love her Soft as Silk Facial Scrub. I feel as if I've known her all my life. LZF has my vote.*

Yeah. Loa's blessed sand was doing the trick.

That redhead has great tits. Now there was a typical man. Brenda had the urge to cram that microphone down his womanizing throat.

"Jackie, Liberty University News here. Your little girls told us about a giant meat grinder in your garage. And you have a dog that likes balls. And there's a goddess who lives in the greenhouse out back. Is there any truth to these claims or just the musings of little girls?"

Brenda took this question. "Absolutely true. The meat grinder is for making dog food, Girlie Dog loves balls, rubber balls, tennis balls, nerf balls, and our goddess lives everywhere in the universe, so why not in a spooky greenhouse?"

Police paddy wagons and tow trucks arrived on scene to the sound of blowing whistles and clacking nightsticks.

Jackie and Brenda joined hands. "We want to thank you all for coming today." They lifted their clasped hands in the air. "Vote LZF, everyone."

The mob dispersed, no one got arrested, and peace at The Ranch was restored.

But watching from their respective locations, the opposition candidates, the incumbent and the challenger were not happy with the way things played out on television. Every network was singing the praises of the new girls on the block.

The President paced the Oval Office, steaming mad. He picked up the phone. "Get me the Attorney General on the line. I demand an investigation into Brenda Ayler and the LZF Party. Call in the FBI, the CIA, the Marines. Those women are frauds. They're rigging the election. We'll take them all the way to the Supreme Court if we have to. We've got to dig up some dirt on them or we're finished. Finished, you hear?" He slammed down the phone.

In the challenger's campaign headquarters, the entire place was in an uproar. "These women must be stopped. They're not only a threat to our party, but to our opponent's, as well. Call the President. We'll have to team up to defeat this feminist threat to our democracy."

Thus the battlelines were drawn in this war of the sexes.

On Brenda's side, however, they had a few problems to solve before the long arm of the law came snooping. The Sisterhood met in the kitchen to plot their strategy.

Brenda and Jackie were both of the same mind. Evidence tampering. "We have to get rid of Girlie Dog's dogfood."

"Let's row the mason jars out to sea and empty the contents into the Sound. Max will be a feast for the fishes."

"How ironic," Lilly said. "Pan-fried trout to chum in the water. Oh, dear Max, you were such a fool to come here." Then she asked, "And what are we going to do with the meat grinder? It's swarming with his DNA."

Jackie said, "We can clean it with bleach then run a cow through it. I'll send Jorge to the butcher shop. Then we can fill new mason jars for Girlie Dog's burger-chow."

Just then Betsy and Caroline skipped into the kitchen. "We need a jar of food for Girlie Dog."

"Fresh out, girls. Use the canned dogfood."

"Jackie, Girlie Dog doesn't like food from a can."

"That's too bad, Betsy. She'll have to get used to it or starve to death."

Caroline gave her a stinky-nose. "You and Brenda are so mean sometimes."

"Sorry you think so. Now wipe those frowns off your faces and go get a can from the pantry."

As Brenda and Jackie carried the jars to the boat on the beach, Lilly made a firepit and burned Max's clothing. The sisters sat around it like any old beer party on the beach, stoking the flames and adding more firewood. Pretty soon they were dancing around it naked and whooping it up, as the nymphs normally carried on. Monica and Jill put the boat to the waves and rowed out to sea while Melinda and Donna cleaned the meat grinder with bleach and a lot of elbow grease.

By the time Jorge returned with a side of beef, the fire had dwindled and the party had moved to the pool deck. Monica and Jill, just back from their little boat trip, set to work grinding up the cow and packing the hamburger into new mason jars. Betsy and Caroline put on the dog-burger labels.

Girlie Dog sat close by, tongue dripping drool. It was obvious that she didn't care where the meat came from.

That night, the sisters went to bed without a care in the world.

***

Back in Washington D.C., nobody of a political bent was sleeping. The justice department had already tasked the FBI to look into the affairs of the LZF Party and their candidates, Brenda Ayler and Jackie O'Neal.

Larry Montford, the Deputy Director of the FBI, was on a late-night conference call with the Attorney General, Federal prosecutors, and campaign staffers. "What do you have on Jackie

O'Neal?"

"Squeaky clean. Skin care tycoon. Billionaire. Divorced forty years ago, but she doesn't look a day over twenty-five. Must be her skin cream."

"And Ayler?"

"Hard to say. She's traveled from Denver to Haiti to New York. Her fiancé went missing more than a year ago, her mother died, heart failure, and her uncle, ah...Fred Jensen received one hundred percent of the estate."

"Brenda got nothing?"

"She gave it all to her uncle. A real Mother Teresa type, she is."

Montford groaned. "Come on, you guys. You gotta do better than this."

"They're lesbians. Does that count?"

"Get me a FISA warrant—"

"How? We don't have a stitch of evidence to surveil them."

"Make something up. Pay off a judge. I don't care how you do it. The President won't take no for an answer."

At meeting's end, they were all pretty glum but determined to dig up dirt on the women who would deny them their place on the throne of power.

But they had no idea who they were up against.

***

At Frank and Carrie's house, Frank was just about to take Carrie for a roll in the hay when the landline rang.

"This better not be a telemarketer telling me my car warranty has expired." He picked up the phone. "Hello?"

"Is this Frank Leatherwood?"

"Yeah, what's it to ya?"

Carrie said, "Honey, be nice."

"This is Special Agent Montgomery from the FBI."

"What can I do for you, mister FBI?"

Carrie tugged on his sleeve. "The FBI?"

"What do you know about Brenda Ayler?"

"She's running for President. Where do you live...under a rock?"

"I suggest you cooperate, Mister Leatherwood."

"And I suggest you take a long walk off a short pier." He slammed down the phone. "Prick."

Carrie propped herself up in bed. "What did he want?"

"Information about Brenda. Don't we all?" He gathered Carrie in his arms. "Now where were we?"

***

Back at The Ranch, the Sisterhood was spending time and a lot of money getting together all they needed for LZF Central. Taking time out for breakfast, they watched the national news channels. Brenda and Jackie had become well-known, sought-after celebrities, much to the chagrin of the opposing parties' candidates. Reporters and commentators talked about the investigations underway, a purported illegal FISA warrant coming down the pike, and the desperate quest to find something, anything the conservative and liberal news media could use as a weapon against the LZF newcomers.

It was Lilly who noticed a sister was absent. "Where did Monica go?"

"Joseph picked her up early this morning. She's on her way to the airport to get on Alfons' jet for a quick turnaround trip to Haiti to retrieve the loot Baby Doc embezzled from us."

Jill frowned. "Ever hear of a bank transfer?"

"It's a bit more complicated than that. She's got to recover cash Juan Senior put in a safety deposit box at El Banco Haiti while Baby Doc was on the run."

"But, Brenda, Baby Doc will have a heart attack when he sees Monica."

"It'll be okay. She won't kill him."

Upon arriving at the private airport hangar, Monica found Alfons waiting to see her off. He was decked out in a suit and tie, so she knew he didn't intend to join her on the flight. As he walked up to the limo, confusion tangled her thoughts. Why was he here? Didn't he have better things to do? What was he holding behind his back? *Maybe he wants me to fire him up before the jet engines are fired up.*

She stepped out of the limo and into a light breeze that played with the hem of her dress.

Smiling bigly, he stopped in front of her, shoulders back, and he sucked in his gut, well, he gave it a good try.

"What are you doing here, Alfons?"

Her terse tone didn't put a dent in his demeanor. He presented to her a beautiful bouquet of flowers. "I brought you something."

"They are lovely, Alfons, but you have never brought me flowers before."

He set them in the cradle of her left arm. "I've never asked you to marry me before."

"Say what?"

He got down on one knee, his face solemn as a wedding vow. "I want you to be my wife. Share my life. Share my fortune. Please say yes and make me the happiest man alive."

Touching his cheek, she felt a bit of tears tugging on her eyes. "You are a sweet man, Alfons, but you know I am a lesbian zombie. I am loyal to our Queen Brenda and our Goddess Loa. I love what you and I have together now, but I need to be free to experience other women and other men. Besides, I have no interest in your fortune."

"Monica, I'm not asking you to give up your way of life, the love you have to give others, your sisters and your conquests. You're a great asset to the Sisterhood, your Queen, and your Goddess. I would only ask you to sleep with me a few times a week instead of once every month or so."

She looked at the flowers in the crook of her arm then down at the man on his knee. They'd had a lot of fun times together. She didn't want to just blow him off, especially since his offer was so sincere. "Can I think about it?"

Looking up at her like she was heaven itself, his smile never wavered. "That's a lot better than a no."

"Now get up. You are embarrassing me."

He stood, gave her a hug and a kiss on the cheek. Yeah, kissing on the mouth was still not allowed. Maybe after they were married she'd let him taste those luscious lips. "I better let you get on the plane now, and try not to wreck it like you did my yacht, and lastly don't kill anybody in Haiti."

"I won't. I promise."

As the skyline of New York faded in the distance. Monica

thought of the advantages to being married to Alfons. He was a fantastic lover, and yeah, sometimes their tempers collided like a head-on train wreck, but their relationship always came out unscathed. Still, the matter of a kiss on the lips remained paramount. Right now he was a human male with all his idiosyncrasies and frailties. One kiss on the lips would change him into a subservient slave to the Sisterhood, as was General Taylor, Admiral Kincade, and Charles, Charlie, Mantella of WNN. She'd spent all her time protecting him from Brenda's influence, her seemingly hypnotic control...and through it all, his loyalty was always to a gorgeous Haitian black woman he treasured so dear. It would break her heart if she lost him to the Sisterhood.

Chapter Thirty

The sisters were sitting around the table, eating breakfast and making small talk when the national news broke from their political reports to a breaking story:

"Dateline Las Vegas Nevada."

Brenda said, "Everyone be quiet. I need to hear this."

"A body has been found in the desert," the newscaster said, "off a dirt road five miles west of I-15. Two dirt bikers came upon the skeletal remains of, what appears to be, the victim of a tragic accident. Somehow, from somewhere, a boulder had come down and crushed his skull. There was no ID on the body." An aerial view from a police helicopter showed a heavy police presence, yellow crime-scene tape around a sandy flat of rocks and sagebrush, a ribcage, hip, and limb bones protruding from under a boulder too big for any ten men to lift. "Las Vegas and Nevada State police are investigating."

Lilly said, "So what?"

Brenda pushed a button to pause the broadcast. "I'm the one who killed the two-timing prick. His name was John Marshall."

"Do tell," Lilly pressed.

"Back when I was fat and ugly, he said he loved me. I thought I was the luckiest woman on earth, even though he was no prize either, a slob at best, but we were going to get married, so in preparation for my fairytale life to come, I gave him fifty grand to plan the wedding. He promptly split for Vegas with his ex-wife. When I caught up with them, it wasn't pretty."

Resuming the broadcast presented Brenda with a problem she never could have seen coming. A reporter was standing at the screen door of a familiar house, and sure enough, there was John Marshall's mother, crying into the microphone. "My son's been missing for over a year. He'd gone to Vegas to remarry his ex-wife. Neither have been seen since."

"Yes, ma'am. We found the missing persons report and came to ask if you think the body found in the desert could be his?"

"Oh, dear God...I always hoped they'd gone off on their honeymoon to some faraway place...but if it is John's body, then I know who killed him."

"Who?"

"Brenda Ayler."

"The LZF's Presidential candidate?"

"I don't know. The Brenda I knew hasn't been seen since either." She burst out in tears and closed the door on the reporter.

"There you have it, folks. Though it seems impossible that anyone could lift a heavy boulder and drop it on a man's head, we've got us a murder mystery, and you can bet the FBI is going to jump into the investigation, as well. Stay tuned."

Brenda turned off the TV. "Sisters, for those of you who weren't here for the first Black Friday party, there's something I'd like to show you in the Crystal Shrine."

Jill and Lilly followed close behind Brenda with Chloe, Melinda, and Jackie trailing to the greenhouse shrine. The air inside seemed alive with the aroma of greenery: the sprawling, leafy branches of the Sister Tree of Life, the vines and roots and the damp soil in the Pit of Ages, into which Brenda descended.

"Why's she going down there?" Lilly asked Chloe.

"I don't know."

The girls leaned over the golden railing and saw Brenda lift a human skull from the entanglement of roots and vines.

"Who's that?" Jill asked.

Brenda said, "Catch," and threw Jenny's skull up to them.

The girls jumped back, but it was Jackie's hand that reached out and grabbed the skull in midair. "Wimps. Did you think it was going to bite you? Meet Jenny."

"Where's the rest of her body?"

"Consumed by the Sister Tree of Life."

Brenda climbed out of the pit. "We have to get rid of it."

"How?"

"Smash it to smithereens with a hammer and scatter the crumbled bits on the beach."

"I'm not going to do it," Jill said.

"Me neither," Lilly put in.

"I'll do it." That came from Chloe. "I never liked that traitorous bitch anyway."

"Sold." Jackie tossed Jenny's skull to her. "There's a hammer in the garage by the meat grinder."

"What's the big deal, anyway?" Lilly asked.

"Just in case the FBI comes snooping. Our opponents from the opposing parties would do anything to ruin us, the LZF, and our women's movement. The only way they can win is by coming up with dirt on us."

"On you, Brenda," Chloe stated matter-of-factly. "We didn't kill anyone...and besides...Goddess Loa killed Jenny."

"Try explaining that to the police. We are sisters. We stick together, no matter what."

"Come on, girls. While Chloe makes dust of that skull, we've got to get over to LZF Central. The movers finished up two hours ago. Maria is hanging political swag. We're going to help her get ready for our official opening. Jill, you'll stay here with the kids, and don't let them watch movies all day."

While riding in the limo to LZF Central, Brenda said to Jackie, "I wonder how things are going with Monica."

"Give her a call."

Using speed dial, Brenda was surprised when Juan Senior answered. "Where's Monica?"

"She is in closed meeting with Janice about company books. No interruptions. She give me her phone in case it ring."

"Tell her I'm on the line."

"I don't know. She get mad. Only hear moaning and gasping in office. I think this not a good time."

"Juan Senior. When the meeting is adjourned, tell Monica I put a surprise in her suitcase."

"Si, Miss Brenda. I do for you."

When Monica got the message, she opened her suitcase and found an old flip cell phone and a note with a phone number. She called the number.

Brenda answered. "I see you found your new phone. It's a burner."

"What is up?"

"Just in case the FBI has tapped into our phones under an illegal FISA warrant. I gave my phone to Caroline, and Jill gave hers to Betsy. They even call each other when they're in the same room. We'll use these burners for official business."

"Okay."

"Did you get the cash from the safety deposit box?"

"All accounted for. I'll bring it back on Alfons' jet."

"And the books, how's Janice doing?"

"Perfect. Every dollar accounted for. I will be back tomorrow night."

"See you then."

***

At FBI headquarters, Agent Stephanie Phillips took off her headset and tossed it on the surveillance counter where electronics and monitors were stacked to the ceiling. "This is bullshit." Having earned every one of her gray hairs working for the bureau, she leaned back and folded her arms. "Who gives their phones to little kids?"

Agent Montgomery held up a finger, looked up while listening intently into his headset. "Girlie Dog likes her new dogfood. Damn. They're watching Frozen together again. Why don't they hang up? I'm getting sick of that song."

"And I'm sick of being used as political assassins. The President's got his panties in a wad over the LZF's campaign, and his opponent's on board with all this cloak and dagger shit. Why can't they work together like this in Congress instead of all their one-upmanship and bickering?"

"It's a job, Stephanie, so quit your bitching."

"Give me a good bank robbery, all right?"

"How about a murder investigation?" This came from Deputy Director Larry Montford who'd just walked up behind them. He may have been short and pudgy, but he had high aspirations in the Justice Department. "Las Vegas." He dropped a file on the counter. "John Marshall. Quantico just verified the ID by DNA. Dental records were useless due to the boulder that crushed his skull."

Montgomery, the go-getter he was, grabbed the file. "What's this got to do with our investigation?"

"His last-known girlfriend was Brenda Ayler."

"No shit?" He opened the file, saw the crime scene photo, looked up, astounded. "Since when is a boulder the size of a brick shithouse used as a murder weapon? Looks like an accident to me."

"Just find a way to pin it on Ayler, okay?" The Deputy Director walked away.

Montgomery closed the file. "I'd rather listen to these kids than chase this wild goose."

***

About this time, the Sisterhood had nearly arrived at LZF Central. As Jorge turned the limo onto Maiden Lane, he stopped suddenly, jarring the girls in back.

"What the hell, Jorge?" Jackie demanded.

"Look."

The sisters moved forward in the cabin so they could see out the windshield. The street and sidewalks were packed with women milling around, carrying signs, and chanting, "We want Brenda. We want Jackie. LZF all the way."

"What do I do?" Jorge asked. "I can't run them over."

"Open the sunroof."

"Yes, 'm."

The tinted panel opened, letting sunlight into the cabin. Brenda and Jackie stood in the opening and waved to the crowd. Cheers went up all down the block. Riot police kept the white supremacists and anti-fascists at bay.

"We're going to win this one, ladies," Jackie shouted to the crowd. "With your help."

Brenda threw in, "The days of the White House being a good-old-boys' club is coming to an end. Get out and vote. Absentee, mail-in, or at the polls. The USA is counting on you."

The crowd went crazy, pumping their signs and cheering as they opened a path for the limo to proceed to the headquarters building.

However, those in power and those seeking power were not so enthusiastic. In a secret meeting at Camp David, the two opposition parties were in all-out panic mode. Some were on the phones, calling in favors and begging for donations from their rich friends far and near.

"We need a nationwide television blitz to defeat these upstarts."

"Combine our advertising budgets."

"Anyone know a guy who knows a guy who'll blow these bitches' heads off? Money is no object."

"What's taking the FBI so long to nail those lesbian man-haters?"

Yeah, it was politics as usual, dog eat dog, top dollar gets the prize, the rich didn't care about the common citizen, only their own political aspirations were on the front burners of concern. The women wanted a war, well by golly they got one, and this side was going to play dirty as dirty could be.

***

In New London, while watching the street party on television with Carrie sitting on his lap, cheering for her sisters, Frank felt a grumble in his stomach. Brenda and Jackie were definitely preoccupied, as well as were the other sisters in the limo. How many, he didn't know, but definitely at least one would be at The Ranch to watch over the kids. There'd probably be no better time to take a look around. But first he'd have to get out of the house.

"Carrie. While you were in the shower, I got a call from Navy admin. I have to sign some discharge papers. While you're watching this, would it be okay if I got that out of the way?"

"Today? Do you have to? I want you to share in all the excitement."

"I'm excited. Trust me."

"How about I go with you?"

"You'd just have to wait in the car. Civilians aren't allowed in Administration." He kissed her. "I'll be back before dinner."

She got off his lap with a pout on her lips. "Hurry. I'm getting more pregnant every minute."

He laughed but didn't think it was funny. Driving as fast as he could get away with, Frank pulled up in line for the Cross Sound Ferry. This way he could get to Long Island in an hour and a half. To drive around Long Island Sound, it would take five hours to get to The Ranch. He didn't have that much time to get there and back.

And so it was, that after a pleasant ride on the ferry, and a short jaunt down NY-25, he parked down the block from The Ranch, the home of Brenda Ayler, the Queen of the Sisterhood and soon-to-be President of the United States. The beauty and expanse of the house and grounds amazed him. If money grew on trees, this would be a rainforest.

From the trunk of his Audi, he pulled out the roadside emergency kit, removed a yellow vest, and put it on. This way, to any casual observer driving by, he'd appear to be a utility worker on duty.

He strode around the back of the house where he encountered a high Redstone wall he could barely see over. Pool, potted ferns, a steaming hot tub on a raised platform, deck furniture... "Oh, oh," he murmured as he ogled a naked woman lying facedown on a towel, soaking up the sun. The autumn chill didn't seem to bother her one bit. She must've been the babysitter left behind to watch the kids, and that ball-chomping dog had to be around here somewhere, as well.

He slinked past the wrought-iron gate and across the path that led down to the beach, worked his way around the ocean-side of the house, came to the four-car attached garage. The side door was unlocked so he slipped inside. A Mercedes, mowers, bikes, typical garage stuff, he made out right away, but as his eyes adjusted to the darkness, he saw it plain as day.

A giant meat grinder.

"What the hell?"

And there on the bench, mason jars of ground meat, rib bones, and long bones, and coagulated blood black as tar... He choked back a gag reflex. *Are they human bones?* He wouldn't know; he was a sailor, not a butcher. The blood looked like blood he'd seen on battlefield corpses, but blood was blood to the naked eye, no matter its source, man or animal. Still, if this mess was a human at one time, the Sisterhood was as evil as evil gets. *But what can I do about it? If I say something, they'll know I was snooping. And they have powerful friends everywhere. I could find myself in a whole lot of shit, or maybe even run through this meat grinder... I gotta get out of here.*

As the sun began to set, he arrived back home to his wife's loving arms. His foray to The Ranch left him shaken but no more enlightened about the goings-on of the Sisterhood and their Queen. At the moment, whether from his imagination or his instincts, he was safe, Carrie was safe, and their baby was safe. The flip side: he felt powerless if any of that should change.

***

Back in Port au Prince, Monica was packed for her return trip to New York, clothes, shoes, and a half million in cash. She thought about stopping by the cemetery to commune with her daughter, but one look into her heart told her she couldn't let it be broken again. To go there and not see her, or to see her and have to say goodbye, either way would be a lose, lose situation for her emotions, already strained by Alfons' proposal of marriage. *Wait 'til I tell my sisters. They are going to pee themselves.*

"Thank you, my sweet Goddess. Please hug Maya for me and tell her mamma is doing just fine."

***

As Alfons' jet steaked through the sky toward JFK, the sisters were riding in Jackie's new limo toward The Ranch.

"Good news," Jackie announced. "I got us a venue for our first public pep rally."

The girls cheered.

"We can expect fifty thousand supporters."

Brenda quirked an eyebrow. "Better be a big place."

"Yankee Stadium big enough?"

"I hope to shout."

"Next week we're going to check it out. I've ordered uniforms for all of us, just to keep it real."

The girls cheered.

As Jorge turned onto the road to the house, he noticed a black four-door sedan parked across the street.

Brenda saw it too, and as they drove by, she noticed two men in suits and sunglasses watching them pass. With all the hype that had been on TV regarding the investigations into the LZF, Brenda took a shot of adrenaline to her system. "Jorge, stop."

As the limo rolled to a stop, Jackie and Brenda were already jumping out like buckshot from a double barrel. They paced to the driver-side window. "What are you guys doing here?" Jackie demanded. "Watching my house?"

There was no response. Both men were dialing their cell phones.

"Run down the window or I'll break it out."

The window motored down, and a hairy-knuckled hand presented a billfold he'd opened to show an FBI badge and ID. "Are you Brenda Ayler?"

"No. I'm Lady Godiva."

Brenda nudged her aside. "What do you want with me?"

His partner got out of the car, and with practiced precision, drew a gun from under his jacket and pointed it at her from across the roof. "You're under arrest."

That put a sharp edge on the confrontation.

"On what charge?"

The sisters and Jorge sprang from the limo and protectively surrounded Brenda.

"Murder One."

"Bullshit."

"By the time this gets to court, you'll be kicked off the ballot. You girls are out of business."

"Oh, I get it. You guys are monkeys for the opposition."

"Yeah, you could say that." The agent behind the wheel had his gun aimed at the clutch of beauties. "Just call me King, and call him Kong. Now get on your knees, Brenda, hands on your head. Any of you bozos interfere, you're going down for obstruction of justice."

"What justice?" Jackie shouted. "This is a sham."

Kong said, "Do it and do it now."

King pushed open his door, but Jorge wasn't having it. He kicked the door shut so hard it knocked the gun from King's hand. As it clattered on the pavement, Kong shot Jorge. He went down with an oof. Maria flew over the roof and coldcocked Kong. His sunglasses went flying as he took a dive. Melinda had King by the throat so fast he must've thought he'd upchucked a brick.

"This shit's gonna look really bad on your résumés, boys."

With that said, the entire Sisterhood pounced on the thugs.

Kong found his feet and swung at Maria, but Donna was already on his back, arm clamped around his throat like an illegal police chokehold. Maria kicked him in the nuts so hard everyone heard them crack like chestnuts roasting on an open fire. He went down with two hotties handing him his lunch.

King, unable to inhale a breath, managed to bend down enough to pull a pistol from his boot. That was a bad idea. He got off a shot, all right; right through his foot. Sad part was he couldn't even scream; Melanie's grip on his throat was relentless. She pulled his ass through the open window, slammed him to the ground, and Chloe was the first one there with a spiked heel to his nose. Now that Melinda had released his throat, he could scream bloody murder, and boy did he take advantage of his newfound air.

Brenda and Jackie just stood there and watched their girls make short work of the FBI's finest. Before they could say *J Edgar Hoover*, they were both lying facedown and wearing their own handcuffs. This didn't stop Lilly from cracking a nut for Kong's buddy, King. The way he screamed, make that two nuts.

One could say King got the worst of it, Kong a close second, but Jorge had taken a bullet for the sisters. The funeral would have been tearful...if he hadn't gotten to his feet and brushed himself off. "What did I miss?"

Jackie got on her cell phone and made a call to Larry Evans, the US District Attorney for the state of New York. "You've got two FBI agents in need of medical attention. Yeah. My place. Foolish of them to go for a false arrest. Sure, hang on."

She knelt to whimpering King and held the phone to his ear. "The US District Attorney wants a word with you."

Larry Evans was yelling so loud everyone could hear. "What the hell do you think you're doing?"

"Official...business...sir."

"Get out of my district before I have you busted down to pachyderm poop pick-up patrol at the Bronx Zoo."

"We're in pretty bad shape, sir."

"You let those women beat you up?"

"We didn't have any choice."

"I wouldn't let that get around the squad room. You guys will be laughed out of the bureau."

Jackie took the phone back. "Thank you, Larry."

“Anytime.”

She hung up. “Okay, sisters, take the cuffs off them.”

As the idiots were being released, Jackie noticed a half-dozen cars had stopped, and the drivers were videoing the fracas with their phones. “Hey. Get out of here.”

The cars sped off.

The thumped agents painfully got in their sedan, King and Kong in their respective seats, and King blew a U-ie of blue smoke and peeled away.

“Pricks,” Chloe yelled after them.

Chapter Thirty-One

Back at JFK, Alfons' Learjet whined up to the private hangar. Engines shut down. The APU bumped on. Monica tucked the Cosmopolitan magazine she'd been reading in the seat pouch and unbuckled her safety belt. After some shuffling in the cockpit, Captain Parsons stepped out. "Miss Abelard, I've just received word your limo is en route. You may wait in the executive lounge inside." He released the cabin door, and as it levered to the tarmac, steps unfurled. "And if you know anyone, we're still looking for a flight attendant. Our last one quit, you know."

She strode to the doorway, the money-laden satchel in hand and her purse strap over her shoulder. "I'll keep that in mind." Stepping down, she inhaled the cool autumn air of New York, a refreshing change from the Haitian heat, and smiled up at the gulls circling and swooping above.

A ground crewman rolled her suitcase to her. "Here you go, ma'am."

"Thank you."

The moment she strode into the lounge, she saw a commotion on the flatscreen; her sisters were in a slugfest with two thugs in black suits. Closed captioning read: *FBI AGENTS WERE BIG LOSERS TO LZF CANDIDATES IN ILLEGAL STING GONE BAD*. Mesmerized, she set down her satchel and sat in a plush chair, just as Chloe shoe-spiked a guy in the nose. The rumble looked like prostitution night at the WWF but without a referee.

Downright embarrassing. *What the hell is going on? I leave for three days and miss out on all the fun, but what is this fracas going to do to the campaign?*

Just as Jorge got up from the pavement and brushed himself off, and before she could grasp the true meaning of his actions, a crewman interrupted the show. “Miss, your ride is here.”

“Ah...okay.” She collected her bags and strode outside to a white stretched limo belonging to Alfons. But it wasn’t Joseph who climbed out to open the rear door for her, it was Alfons himself, dressed in a chauffeur’s coat and hat. Always the role-player. He probably wanted to get it on right away, a quick game of passenger and cabbie.

“Did you miss me?” she whispered, breathily.

“Like a dove misses the morning sun.” He took her bags.

She kept her purse, got in and got settled while he put her bags in the trunk. Then, entirely professional, he marched to the driver’s door, executed a perfect military right-face then jumped in like a kid getting on a rollercoaster ride. So much for professional. He looked at her via the rearview mirror. “Where to, Missus Duda?”

“Alfons, please. Not now. Take me to The Ranch.”

“Of course. As you wish.” That sounded more hurt than professional. He accelerated down a row of parked private jets worth billions of bucks, then turned into *Airport Parking*.

“This is not the way to The Ranch,” Monica griped.

“I got a surprise for you.”

She leaned to the divider window. “In your pants, I suppose.”

He slapped the steering wheel. “Damn, Monica. You ruined the surprise.”

The limo dipped into the underground garage and pulled catawampus across several parking spaces. He shut off the engine and joined her in the back cabin. His tented trousers screamed volumes about what he intended.

“Are we not a little old for a backseat banging, Alfons?”

“I gotta know, Monica. Did you think about it, us getting married and all? I’m bustin’ at the seams to hear you say yes.”

She glanced down to his lap. “So I see. Something is going to bust a seam.”

He moved in for a kiss.

She almost didn’t turn her head away in time. “No, Alfons.”

“Ah come on, girl. You’re killin’ me here.”

“I told you—” Her cell phone vibrated.

Buzz, buzz, buzz as in buzz off. That’s how Alfons heard it.

“I have got to get this.” She pulled a dinosaur flip-phone from her purse. "It's Brenda."

"Of course it is." The only banging Alfons did was banging his head on the way out of the cabin. "Don't worry. We'll talk about it later." He repositioned his hat.

"Hello, Brenda."

"Did you see the news?"

"Yes. What was that fight all about?"

"The opposition is getting desperate to knock us out of the race. They're pulling out all the stops. Can you get down here to headquarters?"

"Yeah, one sec. Alfons, LZF Central, please."

"Alfons is driving?"

"Yeah, driving me crazy."

"About what?"

"Tell you later."

The limo accelerated out of the garage as if the ten mile-per-hour speed limit meant nothing. When it arrived on Maiden Lane, Alfons had to inch through a mob of women in order to park in front of the building that housed the LZF.

"Has everyone gone crazy in this town?" he shouted over all the hoopla.

"I'll be back. Don't move." Monica stepped out, only to be greeted by loud sighs and boos from those who had thought they'd get a glimpse of, or even a chance to touch, Brenda Ayler. Not to be dismayed, she pressed through a crowd that funneled into the front doors and formed a line down the hallway. As she pushed and dogged her way through them, she heard comments that, under normal circumstances would have been fighting words.

"Hey, bitch, back of the line."

"No cutting in."

"Who do you think you are, anyway?"

Once she got inside the office, she bobbed and dodged until she found Brenda behind a line of tables decked with political swag. "What in the world is happening?"

Brenda handed her a paper: *Volunteer Application*. "I never imagined we'd get so much support."

"All these women want to help us?"

"And there are more scenes like this in every city across the country. Local women have established political action committees, fundraisers, farmer's markets and carnivals, bakeoffs and chili contests. Jackie's *Soft as Silk Facial Scrub* is selling off the shelves."

"What did the FBI want?"

Brenda pulled Monica into the conference room, away from prying ears. "They came to arrest me on a baseless warrant for a murder in Las Vegas."

Her eyes got big around. "And I know what murder you are talking about."

"They didn't care if I was guilty or not, they have no case, just wanted to tie my hands legally and get me kicked off the ballot."

"How can they get away with that shit?"

"Someone in the FBI is indebted to the President somehow. Once we find out who he is, he'll be the first corrupt son-of-a-bitch to get bounced out on his ear once we take the White House."

"Brenda." Monica said this sternly, using the same tone she would use on a disobedient Caroline. "Your past could come back to haunt you."

"I trust Loa will intervene. She'd never let this women's movement go down on account of John Marshall or Big Bad Brooklyn Daddy."

"I hope you are right."

Monica looked around the room for the first time, noticed the extravagant conference table, the highbacked chairs, and pictures on the walls. One was a six-by-nine montage of women's portraits titled *Women Activists of History.* Some were black and white photos: Susan B. Anthony, Carrie Chapman Catt; some sepia: Elizabeth Cady Stanton, Ida B. Wells; and others more modern: Malala Yousafzai, Justice Ruth Bader Ginsburg, and Brenda Ayler.

"Nice touch."

She strolled to the poster she had designed from Chloe's idea, a Rosie The Riveter type theme but with Brenda flexing her arm muscles and titled, *She Can Do It as Your President*. A warm glow of pride welled inside.

There were LZF logos, as well, with a lightning bolt signifying power in a circle around the letters that signified solidarity among women. Banners read: *Vote LZF. LZF for Women's Equality. LZF all the way.*

"I like what you've done with the place."

"I thought you would." Brenda led Monica back into the fray. Jane Gray and Jackie were taking applications and putting women to work on the phone banks set up on tables alongside the windows. Red white and blue flags and pendants hung everywhere space provided.

"Who is this beautiful woman?" Monica extended a slender hand to the new girl in town. "I'm Monica."

"Oh, my God, Monica, you are absolutely the most stunning black woman I've ever seen. I'm Jane, Jane Gray."

Monica took her hand, more of a hello-touch than a handshake. "You do know, Jane, that once you go black, you never go back."

"I'll take my chances." Jane smiled then asked Brenda, "How do you like the place? Did I earn my commission?"

"Thanks for helping out, Jane. We owe you a lot more gratitude than money can buy, say something more on the line of a hot tub party and some delightful wine to drink?"

Staring at Jane's voluptuous breasts, Jackie asked, "What do you think, Jane? Are you game?"

"Depends."

"Really? On what?"

"If clothes are optional or not."

That got Brenda right where she breathed. "I like the way you think."

"Me too," Jackie added. "We'd love to have you come visit us at The Ranch."

"The ranch? Like with horses and cows?"

Jackie smiled. "Nah...but we do have a dog."

"I love dogs. Is tonight okay?"

Monica jumped in on that. "All right. Tonight it is. Party time." She kissed Brenda's cheek. "I have got to go. Alfons is waiting outside."

"Oh, yeah? What's he driving you crazy about?"

"I'll tell you later." She walked away swaying the sweetest tush north of the Mason-Dixon line, though her sisters would argue that point.

About then, a team of pizza delivery guys worked themselves in through the crowd. They must've had a hundred pizzas. Melinda showed them to the kitchen.

"What's all that?"

"The least we could do was feed our volunteers," Donna said. "Don't worry. I charged it all on your AmEx card."

"Just great—"

"Jackie..." Brenda cut in, "we've got bigger problems than pizza expenses."

"What?"

"Something is going on between Monica and Alfons."

"Something's always going on with them."

"No. This is different. Did you notice how she flirted with Jane?"

"Awe...she's just being nice."

"I think she's scared, overcompensating, looking for a distraction. All hell is going to break loose between her and Alfons."

"Excuse me, ladies."

A man's voice from the application table turned Brenda's attention from Monica's problem to a sudden and unexpected dilemma of her own.

"I be lookin' for Brenda Ayler."

The breath blew out of her lungs, fast and hot as hydrogen from the Hindenburg. She was staring into the familiar face of her uncle from Boulder, Colorado. *Uncle Fred Jensen.*

Brenda was in such a state of shock that she was speechless. However, the same could not be said for Uncle Fred Jensen. "Brenda gotta be 'round here somewhere. This is her campaign office, right? Seen her on the TV, I did. Either she's an imposter, or somethin' bad has happened to my niece. Not seen her in more 'n a year now."

His harping had drawn a lot of attention from nearby volunteers and reporters, so Brenda decided to step up to the table. "Sir, may I help you?"

"Hey, you're that Patti friend of Brenda's. You been sayin' you're Brenda on TV, but you're not. You're Patty."

"Please, sir. Will you step into the conference room with me? We have a nice place to sit and talk, and pizza, if you're hungry."

As he followed her, he yammered on. "Got no hankerin' for food, but if ya all got some hell-fire whiskey, I'll take some o' that."

In the conference room, Brenda closed the door and led Fred to the head of the table. Once seated he looked up at her with stone-cold eyes. "What do you think you're doing, Brenda?"

"Holy Toledo, Fred. For a while there I thought you'd had a stroke or something, the way you were talking like some kind of backwoods—"

"See?" He cut in. "It doesn't feel good to be deceived. Patty, hell. I didn't buy it for a minute, you coming around after your mom died, all full of mystery, but I always thought you'd come home someday."

"Uncle Fred." She pulled up a chair next to him. "This is my home, New York City, and with any luck, the White House is next. I'm on a mission to save the women of the world from the pain I felt when I was powerless against a man."

"He hurt you bad, didn't he, that no-good-for-nothing John Marshall. I get it. Payback. But somehow you've changed from a loving young lady to this...this beautiful shell of a woman with a heart of stone."

She put a hand on his shoulder. "That's not fair, Uncle Fred. My heart is soft and full of love for the women around me, my sisters, and they will want for nothing. It's men that are the problem, present company excluded."

He leaned back and looked her in the eyes. "I should tell you a story about a friend of mine. He had a dog, a mut mostly, but he loved that dog, even after the little guy got old and blind. Then one day he was moving his pickup, thinking the dog was in the house, and when he backed up, he heard the most awful screaming and crying any animal could ever make. He'd run over his beloved dog, and that dog died in his arms, and he cursed God and sold his truck, he could never drive it again, and since that day he's been on a mission to save every dog he can. Eight, ten, twelve dogs in his house and they still didn't heal that hole in his heart, the guilt and grief he carried with him, clear to the day he died."

"Fred. I don't see the relevance."

"Brenda, the old you is like the blind dog that died, and the woman you are now, strong and powerful, you're like my friend, full of grief and guilt to have been so blind to John Marshall's betrayal, that you're now going to save every woman you can. And you blame men, like he blamed the truck. Good God, Brenda, look what's become of you, a bitter Queen of your lesbian Sisterhood."

His words could've been a dagger to her heart, sharp cold steel to muscle and blood. She stood to pace the room, thumbnail to her teeth when a lightning bolt hit her as if thrown by the hand of Loa herself. She turned to Fred swiftly as a lioness turns against the lion to protect her cubs.

"How do you know about the Sisterhood?"

Her sudden angry tone didn't faze him. "I got a call from a young man checking up on you, told me how you're regarded as queen among your followers, lesbians he called the Sisterhood."

"Frank?"

"He didn't say his name. I didn't ask."

"How did he find you?"

"Last year, after you disappeared and before your mom died, we filed a missing persons report. She was so upset her heart failed. She actually died of a broken heart, Brenda, she missed you and worried about you that much."

"I'm so sorry, but I had to leave. I had to fix the mess that I was."

"Only in your mind, honey. We didn't see the faults you saw in yourself."

"I did what I had to do."

"When you finally came home as Patty, I knew you weren't missing, but with funeral arrangements, the estate, and all, I forgot about the report. It's online, you know."

"I didn't, but thanks for the heads up."

"Now you're a beautiful woman running for President...I just don't know how you did it, what happened to you, what's going to become of you."

She got down on her knees at Fred's chair. "What did he want to know, Uncle Fred, this young man with no name?"

"The same thing as me. What made you into this beautiful and powerful woman with such an effect on men that they lose control of their own lives just to please you? I told him I didn't know and flew to New York to ask you myself. Don't blow me off like Patty did. I only look like a fool."

"Fred, I can only tell you that I went to Haiti where something terrible happened, and then something equally as wonderful came next. You don't ask God why he made the sky so beautiful. It just is, as I am beautiful, I just am, and I don't ask why."

He ran a calloused hand down his weathered face. "I can live with that, but if I can give you some advice, let the people in your life be who they are. Let them follow their own dreams, find their own happiness, their own security in this world. Control is only an illusion. My friend couldn't bring back his dog, but he died trying. Don't be the dog, Brenda."

"I'm not, Fred. I'm the truck."

"Then what can I do to help around here? Floors? Windows? I can certainly take out the trash."

She stood and kissed his cheek. "Just go home, Uncle Fred."

"Yeah, suppose you're right." He stood and gave her a hug. "Guess it's best to leave this hootenanny to you."

"I love you, Uncle Fred. No matter what happens, remember that."

"I'm glad I found you, Brenda, but a little sad the old Brenda I knew and loved is gone."

"She's in good hands. Take care of yourself, and don't be talking to strangers, you hear. There are a lot of people out there trying to dig up dirt on me."

"Clean as whistle. That's what I'll tell them. You've got my vote. I'll see myself out."

She opened the door and let in all the noise. "Let me get someone to help you through the crowd."

"Please don't. I'll enjoy bumping into all those women on the way out. Close as I'll get to true love at my age."

Then he melted into the throng of bodies and the voices clamoring for the LZF.

Chapter Thirty-Two

That night at The Ranch, Jane Gray arrived in time for splashdown as naked sisters jumped in the pool and frolicked like sprites in an adult fairytale land. Melinda, wearing only a white maid's apron, showed her back to the pool deck where Brenda and Jackie lay on side-by-side air mattresses. Flickering tiki torches lit their nakedness with a heavenly glow. She heard the girls' giggling and splashing over the soft strains of classical music. As she strode past a cart of expensive bottles of wine that had been opened and left to breathe, little tingles of anticipation excited her in places that had been dormant for so long.

Cued by the sound of high heels tapping on the deck, Brenda and Jackie raised their sunglasses to their foreheads, and though the sun had set an hour ago, they wore them to look cool and mysterious for their guest of honor at tonight's lesbian zombie initiation. "Hello, Jane."

"I seem to be a bit overdressed."

"That is easily rectified." Melinda unzipped the back of Jane's dress and let it slide down her body to the deck. "No bra and panties, Jane? What kind of party did you expect?"

She kicked off her shoes. "God knows I don't know what to expect, but I'm ready for anything."

"I'm happy to hear that." Brenda patted the air mattress. "Come join us."

Jane fell between the two women, felt their warm flesh against hers, and welcomed strange but beautiful hands touch the most sensitive places on her body.

"We have a surprise for you," Jackie breathed. "Look."

From out of the forest of potted ferns and between two tikis strode long-legged Monica onto the deck, naked as the women watching her. Firelight radiated off her ebony body and shimmered with every stride toward them.

"Oh, my," Jane said. "Chocolate is my favorite."

In true lesbian zombie tradition, Jane was treated to the full experience, kissing and caressing, exploring and foreplay, both oral and mechanical, and plenty of wine drinking that finally led to a game of submarine, where all the girls joined together in the hot tub. This was a defining moment in Jane Gray's life of lesbian fantasies and heterosexual failures. She was now a sister of the Sisterhood, a piece of the pie, and a cog in the wheel of the greatest women's movement the world had ever seen.

***

However, there were men in power who would break the Sisterhood's back, strip the cogs from that wheel, and eat the pie themselves. At 5:45am, Admiral Roy Kincade, the newest member of the Joint Chiefs of Staff, got a call from General Lawrence Taylor.

"Roy, sorry to call you so early, but the honchos of the major political parties want to meet with us at Camp David right away. As it's a Navy installation, they said you're handling transportation in and out."

"I'm driving your direction now. A Navy Sikorsky is standing by at Andrews to fly us in. I wonder what those political hacks want with us."

"Shit, Roy, I know what they want, military action against the LZF, the dirty bastards."

"I sure as hell hope not. I'll be there shortly."

***

At Camp David, in the woody hills of the Catoctin Mountains, the Navy helicopter slewed in and settled on the helipad. After the side door slid open, Lawrence and Roy jumped out and were immediately greeted by a Marine MP and a Navy Shore Patrol sailor. "Gentlemen." They exchanged salutes.

"Follow us," the Marine said.

As the turbine engines whined down, the top brass followed their escorts into the Field House where suited mobsters met them with offered handshakes. Turned out they weren't mobsters but national committee chairmen from both parties. They were joined by New York Senator Drew Pearson, and Alabama Rep Paul Simpson, each from a different party and both members of the Armed Services Committee.

"Right this way."

They were led into a conference room where everyone seated themselves around a long table. The door was closed and all cell phones were collected and put in a box. "There'll be no record that this meeting ever took place, gentlemen, under the order of the President.

"What's going on here?" Taylor asked to get the ball rolling.

"Yeah," Kinkade added. "I don't like the smell of this place."

"We have a problem we hope you can help us with. You're both familiar with the LZF debacle—"

"Women's equality is not a debacle," Taylor interjected. "It's been a long time coming."

"Look," Pearson said, feathers looking a bit ruffled. "Those women have this entire country in a stew. It's time to fight back with the full force of the United States Military. If not, the President could lose this election to a bunch of broads."

Simpson added, "And our challenger is feeling squeezed out of this race, a race we usually run together, against each other, as it's been since the Civil War."

"This threat to our democracy cannot go unchallenged."

"It must be stopped."

Taylor grumped. "What do you want us to do, nuke them?"

"Could you?" This came from the President's handmaiden, Pearson. "I mean, is it possible?"

"Get real," Kincade kicked in. "You're going to lose because you're all a bunch of pricks."

"Call us what you like, but the firm handle we've had on the legislative branch is in jeopardy."

"You guys hate each other, can't get nothing done. The only thing you handle is your interns."

"We know what we're doing. If the right pork for the right project isn't included in the right bill, we're going to fight for our special interest groups, on both sides of the aisle. Without them, we wouldn't have our jobs. And without the LZF we just might keep our jobs. Polls predict we're going to lose the majority in both chambers to those lesbian communists."

Simpson added, "It's time for you boys to do your duty, step up and protect this country from the threat."

If Taylor could've spit across the table, he would have, but his mouth was full of the shit these guys were feeding him. "So I'll ask again. What do you clowns expect us to do about it?"

"General Taylor, send in the troops, seize The Ranch, and arrest those bitches. Admiral Kincade, put them on the Carmick, steam them out to sea, and make them walk the plank."

"And be sure you're in shark-infested waters."

The idiots laughed.

Lawrence wasn't laughing. "You want us to kill those women for you? Hell, we'd all wind up in Leavenworth for life. You guys don't know shit about the power you're up against. You'd have better luck lassoing a tornado."

"We came to you two because you are patriots, and you know these women personally. Tell them to back off. Drop out of the race. Maybe they'll listen to you. If not, feed them to the sharks."

Lawrence stood. "Maybe you should listen to me. If I were you, I'd kiss up to those young women."

"Yeah." Kincade stood too. "This country is going to belong to them."

"Ready to go, Roy?"

"Yeah. We better not get close to these ass-wipes. Their shit might rub off on us."

"My boots are already full." Taylor snatched their phones from the collection box, and tossed Roy his cell.

Pearson wouldn't shut up. "At least tell them the FBI is on to them."

"The same FBI that tried to arrest Brenda? How did that go for them?" Now Taylor laughed.

"Those guys went rogue. The real McCoy is going to nail them to a prison wall."

"You wish."

After they turned their backs on the homicidal senators and party committee chairs, Taylor threw open the door, and Kincade slammed it shut. "I can't believe those bastards." Roy spit on the helipad.

The chopper engines were already whining up.

"Never corner a coward," Lawrence said. "He'll come out fighting mad."

"Yeah. I've heard that before."

They ducked the downdraft and climbed into the vibrating Sikorsky.

Buckled in, General Taylor felt a chill that came from his core. *I wonder what those bastards are going to throw at us next.*

***

At eleven in the morning, the sisters had eaten their breakfasts and gotten dressed for the day, only to have Brenda, Jackie, and Jane bound down the stairs, wearing black pinstriped uniforms with the black NY logo embroidered over their boobs. A quick spin showed off their names on the backs, as well. They were wearing exact replicas of New York Yankees uniforms, direct from China.

Caroline and Betsy stole a glance at each other then shouted in unison, "That's so cool."

Melinda, similarly dressed, brought in an armful of boxes and set them on the kitchen table. "Here you go, girls."

The sisters were all giggles as they found their respective uniforms, it wasn't hard, their names were on the shirt-backs.

Betsy and Caroline found theirs quicker because their boxes were the smallest. Clothes went flying as the girls disrobed and donned their infamous garments.

Maria stood straight, legs spread, and with her arms in a position as if she were holding an imaginary bat, she swung. "Crack...home run."

Her sisters started jumping around like overjoyed cheerleaders.

With Caroline and Betsy present, Maria couldn't say aloud what she was thinking. *I saw a picture of Pedro Palo, the short stop. He's a Mexican like me and gorgeous. I would let him bang me all day and all night, and then come back for more after breakfast.*

A horn honked from the driveway. The sisters ran to the window to see an authentic Yankees bus idling outside, the folding rider door opened for passengers.

"Come on, ladies," Jackie said. "Let's get aboard." Everyone streamed out the door, jumping around like real baseball players entering the field.

Riding to the stadium, the sisters were all excited but none of them could match the enthusiasm of Betsy and Caroline. As soon as the bus stopped, they were out the door like it was the last day of school. Hand in hand, they ran toward the main gate.

Jill stepped off the bus and yelled, "You two wait right there."

They didn't bother to listen, ducked under the turnstile, and kept going until they were out on the field, running the bases and laughing to beat all get-out.

Unbeknownst to the Sisterhood, some of the Yankees had heard that the LZN candidates would arrive this afternoon to check the facilities for an upcoming rally. So, just as the sisters stepped on the field, five players jogged out from the dugout like they were about to play a real game. The shocker was on them, though. They'd never before seen angels wearing baseball uniforms, and these were worn so beautifully.

The girls stopped running bases, dead in their tracks as the five ballplayers lined up along the first-base line. They were all good looking, but none were Pedro Palo. A disappointed Maria, along with the other sisters, strode over to meet them. Caroline and Betsy fell in behind.

Maria thought he probably had a hundred girlfriends.

Just then, Pedro came running out on the field, "Sorry, I'm late. Good lord. This must be the Miss America Contest."

Maria couldn't take her eyes off him. He was a good six feet tall and solid muscle. Dark brown eyes and slicked back black hair...and goddess, that infectious smile. Being a lesbian, and so near to her teen idol, conflicting emotions flooded her libido. As much as she'd love the bragging rights, she knew he wasn't interested, busy as he was shaking hands with his teammates. *He's probably gay.*

The sisters walked down the line, shaking hands, and nothing close to sexual tension bloomed until Maria stood in front of Pedro. She was speechless.

He looked a bit starry-eyed. "Te ves bien con see uniforme.

Me gustaría verte desnuda."

"You think I look good in this uniform but you would like to see me naked?"

"Si. You know Spanish."

"I was born in Mexico. You still want to see me naked?"

"I would love to."

Maria leaned to his ear and whispered, "Ask your buddies to cover for you then meet me in your locker room in five minutes."

"Si, senorita."

His Spanish accent set her heart ablaze. She rushed to Brenda. "I have to go pee."

The bullshit wasn't lost on Chloe. "Come on, Maria. He's going to think you're some kind of whore."

"You girls have fun playing with that baseball. I'm going to play with two balls, and a bat, and there's going to be one hell of a home run." She took off for the locker room.

Pedro got there a couple of minutes later to find Maria completely naked and leaning back against his locker. Her legs were spread and she was looking damn fine.

"You like?"

"Si."

"I found your locker." She pointed to the nameplate above her head: *Pedro Palo*. "Wanna play ball?"

"Okay. I take one for the team." He started kissing her lips, worked his tongue in for a Mexican hat dance with hers, while using his free hands to drop his pants. He kissed her nipples and grabbed her ass with both hands. Their breathing got hot and heavy. It was the bottom of the ninth when he put it to her as if he were sliding in to home plate. That got her going, like a wave in the stands, and each thrust banged her backside into the locker, making a terrific racket, and in the same time it took him to run the bases, it all came to a double header with a ♪*da-da-da-dat-da-da*♪. *HOME RUN* flashed on the scoreboard in his brain. He'd delivered the winning pitch, no hits, no runs, no errors. Maria, on the other hand, had to head for the showers.

Out on the field, Donald Larson was pitching underhand to Lilly who, after swinging and missing five pitches in a row, finally hit a ball to second base. That got her a standing ovation from the boys in the dugout.

Then Brenda stepped up to bat. She had been reading Larson's mind and knew he was bored. *Women can't play baseball. That's why they invented the softball*."

She gave the bat a practice swing. "Hey, Donald, give me an overhand as fast as you can burn it in here."

"You asked for it, lady."

The ball came in at ninety-two miles per hour. With vision like a Falcon and the strength of ten men, she hit the ball with a mighty swing. The bat exploded in her hands, but the ball took an arc high above the center field scoreboard and made a beeline for the fence. Open-mouthed, the Yankee players watched as if for the first time in their lives they'd seen a space shuttle launch. The ball was last seen passing the 408-foot marker as it rocketed out of the ballpark. WNN got it all on tape in their preview show for the upcoming LZF Party rally taking place in a few days.

Brenda tossed the splintered bat handle aside. "Still think women can't play baseball?" she shouted to Donald, probably the most bewildered pitcher in baseball history.

Beyond everyone's point of view, in the parking lot outside the stadium, the ball struck pavement, bobbled, then rolled toward a curb sewer where it would be gone forever, if not for a boy's tennis shoe that stopped it dead.

When the video hit the airways, twelve-year-old Tommy Bartlett was sitting on his couch with his dad, tossing his precious find up a few inches and catching it again. Tom Senior saw the video broadcast, heard about the ten-thousand-dollar award to the finder who returns the infamous baseball relic, and looked at his son. "Where did you get that ball?"

"It flew out of the stadium, landed right in front of me, and I stopped it with my foot. Why?"

"Let me see it." The ball had a miniscule dent in it, but mostly he noticed tiny wood splinters embedded in the skin at the point of impact with the bat. The broken bat. "This is that ball they're talking about on TV, son. You just found the Golden Ticket."

"The check for ten grand will be available to the person who returns the ball during the LZF rally on Saturday."

"We're going to a political rally, son."

"It's my ball, dad. I found it."

"I'll get you another one."

Ninety percent of the male population of the United States bought into it, just like Tom Senior. They wanted to believe their baseball could pass for the ball on everyone's radar. Closets were dug through, dusty trunks were opened, sporting goods stores across the country sold out of authentic Major League baseballs in less than an hour. Brenda's plot was sure to pack Yankee Stadium on Saturday.

Chapter Thirty-Three

Back at The Ranch, home of the lesbian zombie Sisterhood, they felt safe, but still, like most American families, they had security cameras and a computer full of video surveillance that usually got ignored. However, these days, with all the reporters and cops snooping around, Brenda made it a point to check the recordings every two days or so. Tonight, after a bat-busting, and if she counted Maria, ball-breaking day at Yankee Stadium, Brenda sat at the monitor in the sitting room and scanned through the security footage before dinner.

Not much to see while they'd been gone to the stadium, but the day before, while they were at LZF Central, a utility worker had come around for some reason, yellow vest and all. He just appeared out of the blue, walked around back, looked over the pool deck wall, yup, there was Jill soaking up the rays. Then the worker moved around the house to the garage. When he went inside, Brenda felt her nape hairs bristle. "What the hell?"

Jackie stepped up behind her. "Something wrong?"

She switched to the cameras inside the garage. The worker looked at the car and glanced toward the lawn equipment. That's when they saw a face they recognized.

Jackie reacted the loudest. "Frank?"

He walked up to the meat grinder. The camera picked up the terror on his face, as if he'd been staring at a dead body.

Brenda's heart sank. "This is not good."

"Brenda. It's just a meat grinder. I'll have the girls clean up the mess tomorrow."

"I told them to leave it bloody, cow bones and chunks of meat. There's also a few jars of hamburger for Girlie Dog. If it was spick and span, a snoopy cop might suspect something nefarious and take a closer a look."

"Okay, Brenda, I get it. It's not good that Frank invaded our privacy, violated the sanctity of our home. He might have gotten inside if not for Jill, the girls, and Girlie Dog being home. We'll talk to him, set him straight."

"It's not that easy. There's more." She turned away from the monitor to face Jackie. "Remember the old guy who came into the office?"

"Yeah, ah, Fred. You said he was your uncle."

"It was Frank who contacted him, got the number through a missing persons website, asked him about me, which motivated Fred to come ask me for himself."

"Oh, dear." Jackie plopped down in a chair. "We'll have to kill him, and my goddess, that will break Carrie's heart."

"Everything I've done was for her, so she could be with the man she loves, have a baby, a family, as near to a normal life as possible for a lesbian zombie. And this is the way Frank repays us...by snooping around like some kind of hotshot detective."

"And he takes our goodwill as an intrusion...meddling."

"Worse than any mother-in-law."

"Hell, Brenda, if we don't kill him, then we've got to tell him who we are, who he is, who his wife really is, not only a zombie, but a lesbian to boot."

"I worry he won't stick around."

"Then his love for Carrie isn't as strong as she thinks it is. We have to tell him, put their love to the ultimate test."

"Let's invite him to dinner, Carrie, too, and Robert, Maggie, and Zoey. Make it a family affair, then air out our dirty laundry and see what he does from there."

"If he doesn't let up on his stupid detective work, you know what has to be done."

"Look at you getting all homicidal."

"You're not the only one trying to protect this Sisterhood."

A few minutes later, Maggie answered her cell as she watched Robert tickling Zoey's tummy, making her laugh and flail her arms and legs.

"Sure, Brenda. We'd love to, and yes, we'll bring Carrie and Frank with us. See you then."

Robert looked up. "What now?

"We're invited to The Ranch for dinner and drinks tonight, and we have to bring Carrie and Frank with us, even if you have to put him in the car with one arm twisted behind his back."

"I better call Frank."

At 8:30pm, Robert drove his Range Rover up the drive at The Ranch and parked under the portico. The front door flew open, and they were immediately greeted by a barking Girlie Dog and a dual blast of cheers from Caroline and Betsy. By the time they'd gotten out of the car, the entire Sisterhood surrounded them. Frank was quick to notice that Brenda wasn't present.

Once inside, more mayhem followed as Carrie's sisters scurried about setting the table while Maggie got Zoey and all her stuff settled in: diaper bag, bottles, baby blankets, formula...the list went on and on. Frank cringed. With Girlie Dog barking and Zoey bawling and women yakking, it was a recipe for a major headache.

Jackie handed Frank an opened bottle of beer, Corona light, like this was some kind of special occasion. "Frank, do me a big favor. Brenda is out back in the greenhouse. Would you please tell her that dinner will be ready shortly."

"Gladly." He wasn't lying. It was a great excuse to get out of this madhouse. After ducking out the back door, he could see a dim light flickering in the greenhouse, not fifty feet from him, but oddly, even in the dark, the glass panels weren't clear, but frosted somehow. As he walked toward the double doors, he hoped it wouldn't be cold inside.

To his delight, it wasn't cold...but a little spooky. A single candle on a small table gave off the only light. And instead of rows of potted plants, there was only one big ass tree. And a golden railing. He paced the golden tiles to the railing and looked down into a pit.

"Don't lean on that railing."

Brenda's voice startled him. He spun around, damn near dropped the beer bottle, but didn't see her. "Brenda?"

"Don't be alarmed. I just wanted to talk to you in private."

A spotlight blinked on, illuminating the tree, and then he saw her sitting on branches that formed a chair of sorts, maybe a throne with high back arches. He choked down a gasp. The light made her red hair look aflame, and her eyes reflected that light, as if she weren't human, more like an animal with night vision, a dog, a cat, or a deer in the headlights. It took all his military training to keep a cool head. "What are you doing up there?"

"I've got to know, Frank, do you hate me?"

"Of course not."

"Do you have something against Jackie?"

He frowned. "No."

"Do you not trust us?"

"What do you want, Brenda?"

"I know you've been snooping around our home, even snuck into our garage. I want to know why, Frank. What were you looking for?"

"I don't know...just wondering about this place."

"I know it was you who contacted my Uncle Fred. You called him with questions about me. Why, Frank? Why didn't you just ask me, man to woman?"

"Damn, Brenda. You're scaring the shit out of me right now. What's this all about?"

"Haven't we given you a perfect life? A perfect wife? A perfect home?"

He took a long hard pull on his Corona. "That's just it. You've given Carrie and me these things, a home, a job. I didn't have to work for them. I didn't have to earn them. Just poof...here you go, Frank, just in case you're not man enough to take care of your family on your own. It's all so weird to me, being a Stepford Wife. I just wanted to know how you have so much power to control my life, Carrie's life, and everyone else's lives around here."

Brenda stepped down from the throne as if walking on steps of air. As she glided toward him, he gripped the beer bottle tightly and resisted the urge to step back.

"Okay, Frank, I'll tell you about me, about us, about you too, Frank, but after I do, either you *will* embrace the Sisterhood, accept Carrie's sisters as your own, and Robert as your brother, or you'll run from us as fast as you can, but sadly, even the Arabian Sea won't be far enough or deep enough to escape the truth about who you really are."

"Me? I know who I am."

"No you don't. Think back, Frank. That first kiss with Carrie in your arms. Three days of bliss. You haven't been the same since, so madly in love you turned your life upside down, even walked away from the Navy, not for me, Frank, but for her. And you want to know why you did all those things beyond your control? I can clear that all up for you, Frank, tell you the truth, right here and now."

For the first time in his life, Frank felt afraid, really afraid, deep down to the bones, the guts, and the soul afraid. The fear wrenched him so badly, he had to shake free of its grip on his throat before it strangled him to death. "Brenda, I'm really sorry I pried, but right now, I don't think I can handle the truth. So please, can we go inside and have a nice family dinner, forget all this spooky shit?"

She hooked her arm in his. "Apology accepted. When you're ready to hear the truth, let me know. Until then, come to me with your questions."

"Brenda, you can count on that."

They walked together, arm in arm to the house, and once inside, they found the sisters celebrating with wine, women, and song.

"What's going on?"

"It's all over the news," Jackie said. "The ball you hit out of the park, some kid named Tommy Bartlett found it. The league verified its authenticity. He and his dad, Tom Senior, will be at the rally to accept the reward money."

"That certainly is good news, and ten grand is cheap publicity."

"You're a household name now, Brenda, on account of one baseball. Brilliant strategy."

Frank held Brenda's chair then sat next to her. She looked him in the eye. "Any questions, Frank?"

"Nah. I'm good. Can someone pass me the potatoes?"

***

The next morning at LZF Central, the sisters were busy tracking online ticket giveaways for the big rally. To add even more excitement to the big event, the Yankees and the Pirates had agreed to play an exhibition game after the political show. This was arranged by Pedro Palo as a thank you gesture to the LZF

Party, but everyone in the Sisterhood knew it was gratitude for Maria's performance in the locker room. In two and a half hours, all 50,000-plus seats were filled.

Jackie's cell rang. She looked at the caller I.D. "It's Charles Mantella from WNN, girls. Let's have a little quiet." She answered in a smooth, sexy tone. "Charlie, what's up?"

"What can I do for you, Jackie? That baseball stunt you pulled put us over the top on the ratings chart. What else you cooking up under that strawberry blond hairdo?"

"Well, now that you mention it, do you remember Tom Caldone from the Black Friday party?"

"Yes, the movie guy with the cave women bonanza."

"He's currently producing three ads for us, you know, dirty politics stuff against the President and the two opposition parties."

"Excellent."

"And seeing as how you own the most influential network in the country, with the largest audience ever, thanks to Brenda's swinging arm, I'd like you to run those commercials coast to coast in all the primetime slots. I know it won't be cheap—"

"On the house, Brenda. The least I can do for all you've done for me."

"How sweet of you, Charlie. Tom will have the ads to you next week."

"Knock 'em dead, Jackie." He hung up.

***

Saturday morning came to The Ranch with more fanfare than the end of World War II. As *Take Me Out to the Ball Game* blared from the sound system, the girls hurriedly donned their Yankees uniforms and caps then gulped down breakfast. Not a one of them could shut up or stop giggling. Girlie Dog bounced among the girls and barked to beat the band.

Brenda paced the front room practicing her speech. "We have come to a turning point for the women in this country. A bend in the road long blocked by men of power, in both political and business enterprises."

Jackie popped her head in. "Come on. Jorge is out front."

With everyone in the limo, the mood couldn't have been

more joyous on Prom Night. Though they'd arrived at the stadium early, the parking lot was jammed with LZF fans. Jorge let them out at the back gate.

The home-team locker room had been converted to an event launching pad where everyone gathered before the show. Brenda was happy to meet Tommy Bartlett and his father, Tom Senior. By golly they looked excited enough to pee their pants.

On monitors around the room, Brenda could see the stadium manager's crew had set up a platform and podium at home plate. Old Glory flew from eagle-topped poles planted all down the first-base line, and red white and blue pennants encircled the arena. A high school marching band was on the field, performing precision maneuvers to *America the Beautiful*. They'd created the LZF logo and marched from right field to left field and back.

The stadium seats bristled with color and celebration, fans waving LZF pennants and huge hands with pointing index fingers. All around the third deck, television cameras from every network panned the crowd. Of course, the WNN crews were at ground level to broadcast the biggest political event in history.

When the band marched off the field, the stadium manager came into the locker room. "Hello, ladies. I am Ricardo Hernandez, the manager of this ball park. It is my pleasure to assist you. Brenda, you are up. Follow me, please."

Maria's heart about stopped when she recognized the man. She grabbed Brenda's arm and whispered, "He is not Ricardo Hernandez. His real name is Ricky El Paco, the brother of the cartel boss who killed my family in Mexico City after I fled the country. I will kill him, here in this stadium. It's so noisy, no one will hear him scream."

"Whoa there, Maria. This is not the time or place for a murder. Relax. You'll get your chance."

The Sisterhood followed the imposter down a tunnel filled with echoes to the dugout and out to the sundrenched field. Jackie and Brenda led the girls up the platform steps to the podium and waved to the crowd in all directions, even turning to those behind them. From all the noise, one would swear Babe Ruth himself had just hit a home run.

After the sisters got seated in folding chairs along the back of the platform, Jackie stepped up to the microphone but had to wait for the crowd to settle down before she could say a word. She raised both arms to hurry the process then tapped the mic. "Ladies and gentlemen, before I introduce the next President of the United States, I want to ask Tommy Bartlett and his dad, Tom Senior, to please come up to the podium."

Brenda stepped back to make room for their special guests.

Once situated, Jackie removed the microphone from the stand and bent to Tommy's eyelevel. "I understand you have found something you want to trade me for ten thousand dollars. Is that right, Tommy?" She pointed the microphone at him.

"Yes, ma'am. I have the ball Brenda hit out of the park." He produced it from his coat pocket and handed it to her. "See the splinters from the broken bat?"

Jackie held it up, and the crowd went nuts. "Now I have something for you."

The stadium manager approached with a giant check, big as any Publishers Clearing House prop, and handed it to Betsy and Caroline.

"Here's my part of the deal, Tommy, a check for ten-thousand dollars."

The girls presented the check. Tommy and his dad held each end for pictures of them with their big award. Then Jackie asked, "What are you going to do with all this money?"

"My dad said we're going to Disneyland."

"Of course you are. Let's hear it one more time for Tommy."

The fans applauded, not so raucously as before, as many of them were disappointed that they didn't have that Golden Ticket baseball, after all.

Jackie reseated the mic in the stand. "It's now my great privilege to present to you the next President and my best friend Brenda Ayler."

The enthusiastic response returned as Brenda took center stage. She waved. "Thank you, everyone. Let me start by saying thank you to the New York Yankees for hosting this rally today."

While the crowd settled again, she unfolded her speech. "We have come to a turning point for the women in this country. A bend in the road long blocked by men of power, in both political and business enterprises."

But some men across the United States and around the world

had a different point of view. "We ain't going to put up with this shit. That bitch is going to be President over my dead body."

If the lesbian zombies had heard their chauvinistic retorts, they would have said, "If that's the way you want it, we'll be glad to oblige you."

The sisters sat through Brenda's speech, crossing their legs, primping their hair, and clapping at the appropriate times. Yeah, they wore the best looking Yankee uniforms in the stadium, and they knew it.

"For you ladies out there, let me close with this reminder. Look for Jackie O'Neal's Soft as Silk Facial Scrub at a store near you."

She stepped back. A high school girl stepped up. "I'm here to sing a song for you, Brenda."

This was news to her. "By all means, young lady. The stage is yours."

As she adjusted the microphone, the stadium quieted. One could have heard a pin drop.

She started with a single note that resonated around the stadium as if a Siren of the Sea was singing into the microphone, then: *"A year of nights, a year of days. Moonshine turning into rays. There never was, but there could be, a place in heaven, for a goddess like me. I start my journey when the stars expand, and lay my legacy in a woman's hand."*

Brenda calmed her heart with the palm of her hand. It was as if Loa herself were singing a salute to her, to her sisters, and to the women of the world.

The song ended, and while the crowd cheered their praises, the girl turned to smile at Brenda. "Thank you for making this a better world for girls like me who'll one day grow to be women like you." She descended the steps and was gone.

The stadium manager, Ricardo Hernandez—aka Ricky El Paco, took the stage. "Folks, have we got a treat for you. As you know the Yankees and the Pirates are going to play three exhibition innings, but what you don't know is that Brenda Ayler is going to throw out the first pitch."

She was stunned to hear this, but how could she say no? The crowd was on their feet waving pennants and fingers.

The sisters cleared the stage, Brenda followed them and

Ricardo, and then a crew of men swooped in to move the platform and all the flags down the first-base line. The Pirates ran out on the field to an orchestra of boos, followed by the Yankees and cheering. The teams lined up and shook hands, after which the pitcher led Brenda to the mound and gave her a baseball. “Good luck, kid.”

Padro Palo stepped up to bat with a shit-eating grin on his face. A couple of practice swings, then he set the bat on his shoulder. The catcher moved into position, squatted, and smacked his glove with his fist.

Brenda wound up and let ‘er rip.

What happened next would be talked about on sports shows and written about in sports journals for years to come. Had the radar failed at the same exact second the ball was pitched, or did the ball go by so fast it was undetectable by radar? One thing that couldn’t be disputed, the hole burned through the catcher’s glove.

Brenda walked off the mound, swiping her hands together. Her first-pitch would go down in history as the one that opened the doors for women in Major League Baseball.

***

As great as all that sounded, Maria was not impressed. She’d been sitting in the dugout, glaring at the stadium manager, Ricardo, Ricky El Paco, as he paced the sideline. Even before the third and final exhibition inning ended, he fast-stepped off the field, ducked into the dugout, and took the tunnel to the locker room. Maria, with murder in her heart, got up and followed him.

In the locker room, he was counting baseballs in a wire bucket. She slinked up behind him, wishing she had a knife to stick him in the kidney. “Ricardo?”

He turned around, wide-eyed shaken out of his wits. “Jesus, girl, you frightened the pants off me. Who are you?”

Sounding sweet, she spoke softly, “I’m Pablo’s friend, Maria. He told me all about you.”

“Okay.” Completely having lost count, he dropped the armful of balls back into the bucket. “What do you want?”

“I would love to get together with you...” she fiddled with his tie, “see how you measure up to Pablo.”

"Are you high?"

"He probably told you about our locker room escapade."

"Yeah, he told the whole team, and looking at you, I can see why."

"I know you are a busy man, but I was hoping we might go out, you know, for pizza or something. Maybe tonight?" She slipped a card in his shirt pocket. "Call me if you can."

"No I can't. I'm a happily married man."

"Oh yeah?" She pulled on his tie, drew his face to hers and gave him a kiss to die for...tongue and all. Sure, he tried to pull back, but that tie was as strong as any hangman's noose. When she let him go, he looked a bit starry-eyed.

"Maria, you say?"

"I like my pizza with pepperoni." She turned and sauntered out, down the tunnel, and back into the dugout to join her sisters still watching the exhibition game.

Brenda grabbed Maria's arm. "What were you doing in there?"

"I had to pee."

"Like hell. You followed Ricky in there."

"So what?"

"Did you kill him?"

"I put a spell on him, you could say."

"You can't do it, Maria. You'd put the Sisterhood in peril. The campaign. The cops will know you did it in five minutes."

"His family killed my family."

"Keep your voice down." Brenda looked around for loose ears.

"One of them slit little Jose's throat, thought it was funny, gave him a Band-Aid. He was still clutching it in his hand, long after he died. He was only ten. I've kept the Band-Aid in my chest of drawers, and I would look at it most every morning. I'd hold it in my hand and pray to Loa to let me avenge my wonderful little brother. It was Ricky, I tell you. He did it. I now have my chance to slit his throat in return."

"We have an election to win. After that, you can kill him all you want."

Chapter Thirty-Four

Little did they know, there were other forces at work planning vengeance upon the Sisterhood, right now in Karachi, Pakistan, for the Taliban brother of the late Imam, Mohammed Abdullah Abadi. This plan didn't involve the simple slitting of a pretty throat, no, it would be an all-out Jihad on the sisters of sin. A spy had already been dispatched to verify the target's location.

Aqib Asad Abadi, in a rant on the very spot where his late brother perished, spoke to his loyal terrorist brothers gathered in the village square. "I have it all planned out, my brothers. On a Saturday very soon in September, we will be anchored off the coast of Long Island, America, in a ship provided by our Iranian jihadist friends. Our army for Allah will transfer to small rubber boats and go to shore to begin the attack on eight infidel whores who dwell in sin against Allah. We will first rape them and then behead them and then leave the bodies for the birds. Islamic justice will be served. We will prevail because the great Mohammad (peace be upon his holy name)will be with us.

The terrorists stood, thrust their rifles in the air, and shouted, "Allahu Akbar. Allahu Akbar. Allahu Akbar!"

***

But on this night in early September, the sisters slept in peace, though Brenda dreamed about Mohammed Abadi and the moment Monica dispatched that murdering Imam pedophile to hell. *I wish that I could have been standing in front of little twelve-year-old Jasmine when those bearded brothers started throwing stones at her. She would be alive today, and they would have been dead.*

Around ten in the morning, the sisters, one at a time, slugged down the stairs, still exhausted from a day at the ballpark, and soon they started arguing as to whose turn it was to fix breakfast. Jill solved the problem when she called Jorge. “Please drive to the donut shop and get four dozen glazed.”

By the time he arrived, they could have cooked bacon and eggs. Everyone was starving. As soon as he set the boxes on the kitchen counter, Caroline and Betsy made a beeline for the sweets. But goddess forbid there were no rainbow-sprinkle donuts.

After they opened every box, Betsy yelled the loudest. “What the hell?”

Jill spoke up, “Betsy, I didn’t raise you to talk like that.”

Caroline sprang to her defense. “You guys cuss all the time.”

Just then the door bell rang, and Caroline, Betsy, and the dog ran to answer it. When she opened the door, Girlie Dog barked at a sawed-off, five-foot-nothin’ *A-hab the A-rab type guy,* complete with a headwrap, standing on the porch.

“Hay-low, little girls, is dis the Sisterhood lives here?”

“Yeah. What’s it to you?”

“Sorry I bother to you.”

“Your English sucks,” Betsy chimed in.

Caroline crossed her arms like a prison guard. “Now get your camel-loving ass off our property.”

“Have good a day.” Walking off he thought, *this where is they live, all right. I will to report our leader.*

Back in the dining room, Jackie asked Caroline, “Who was it?”

“Some foreigner from Arabia somewhere. He asked if this is where the Sisterhood lived. I told him to get lost. But when I read his mind, he was thinking he would report to his leader.”

Jackie cocked a brow. *Arab? Leader? Taliban. On our front porch?* “Caroline, you may have just saved our lives.” After flipping open her burner cell, she punched in Jorge’s number. “Get back to the donut shop and buy every rainbow-sprinkle donut in the place.”

“Yes, ‘m.”

Caroline and Betsy were all smiles as each sister gave each girl a hug, and when they were through, Jorge came in with the sprinkle donuts, and the girls dug in and gave one to Girlie Dog, too.

Brenda was on the phone with Lawrence. “I believe that the Taliban in Pakistan are out for revenge. They may attack us here at The Ranch.”

“Are you sure?”

“One of their spies was just here, on our porch, asking about the Sisterhood. Of course, Caroline blabbed everything.”

“Brenda, we will check into it, and if your hunch is credible, we will stop them.”

“I don’t want you to stop them. I want them to attack us so we can kill them.”

“Brenda, you are our Queen. We can’t have you in danger. I’ll call Roy and have him get Navy intelligence focused on suspicious ships crossing the Arabian Sea or any Iranian ships docked in Pakistani harbors. It’ll have to be a big ship to get here from the Middle East. Meanwhile, I’ll get a platoon together and en route to secure The Ranch, and I’ll get NORAD satellites on the hunt in the next thirty minutes.”

“Do this for us and you and Roy will be in for an all-nighter with me and Jackie.”

“Brenda, that’s not necessary. We would do it for you, anyway. How about breakfast? Our treat.”

“You’re on.” When she got off the phone, she heard the girls arguing in the sitting room. She ducked in to see what the beef was all about, found Maria swearing up and down. “Goddess damn right. I’m going to kill that SOB, and no one can stop me.”

“Shut up,” Lilly shouted. “I don’t want to hear about Ricky anymore.”

Brenda jumped in. “You heard her, Maria. Nobody is killing anyone, understand?”

She got all puffy-faced then stormed out.

It wasn’t ten minutes later when they heard the garage door go up and the Mercedes back out. They ran to investigate and saw Maria behind the wheel, spinning a donut and roaring off down the drive.

“She’s going to kill him.”

“Jackie, we have to hope a miracle occurs and she doesn’t do anything we’ll all regret.”

“I don’t know why I just thought of this, but it was in Greek mythology that the Goddess Pandora opened a box and let hope fly out. Let's hope Loa can slam the lid on this box."

***

Maria pulled in to one of Jackie's pizza franchises, twenty-seven miles from The Ranch, to get her promised pepperoni pizza. Before she got out of the Mercedes, she checked the jackknife in her back pocket to make sure it was out of sight.

She met Ricky at a back table with two beers waiting. Unfortunately the place was packed with patrons and noisy conversations. *I've got to kill him where there aren't any witnesses.*

Ricky held her chair like a perfect gentleman. Once seated next to her, he made small talk. "Pedro Palo told me you are from Mexico City. I too am from Mexico City. Does your family live there?"

They did, you prick. "I had two brothers and a sister. *They were murdered.* My mother was a great cook, *raped and murdered,* and my dad, in my eyes, was a saint...*all the way to his last breath.* We sang in a mariachi band...and I was almost raped by my dad's best friend...*whose loyalties were to drug dealers and murderers like you.* I was sixteen years old when I fled my home, drunk, scared, and alone. How about your family, Ricardo?"

"Mexico is a tough place. I am happy to know you got out of there okay. I know this sounds terrible, but my father was no saint, not like yours. He ran a cartel pushing dope to the United States. Times got hard with law enforcement and rival cartels. I was afraid I'd get sucked into the family business of drugs and murders, so I got a visa and went to Texas University."

"You want me to believe you didn't kill anyone?"

"Why wouldn't you believe that...or did you kill someone?"

Yes, you lying prick. I killed your father, well, with the help of a diamondback rattler, but still, I won't tell him that until the moment before I slit his throat.

"This is your story, Ricardo, not mine."

He took a gulp of beer. "I made up stories about my Padre being a doctor and my Madre a nurse. I told friends I was an only child. I didn't want to let on that I came from a family of murderers. I think even today, if someone walked up to me and said my family killed someone in his family, and now he's going to kill me, I would say go ahead. I don't blame you."

"So...when did you go to Texas University?"

"Let's see...that would be seven...eight years ago. I graduated with a bachelors in business management."

If he speaks the truth, that means he wasn't in Mexico when my family was killed. "So you weren't there during the El Paco murders."

His face turned white, which was a lot of pallor for a Mexican. "El Paco, no..." He set down his beer glass and looked at her with terror in his eyes. "I fear you know more about me than you let on."

"Yes, I do, Ricky El Paco." The jackknife made a click under the table. "You slit my brother's throat, and I'm going to gut you like a fish."

His eyes didn't leave her eyes for a second. "I feared my past would catch up with me someday, but you have to believe me when I say I had no part in any killing. But kill me if you must. I don't blame you."

"Do you have any contact with your family?"

"No. They are all dead. I think it was another cartel that killed Padre. The Bendoso Brothers...got him and his buddy Pedro with rattlesnakes. Terrible way to die." He glanced to the aisle. "Oh good. Here comes our pizza. Pepperoni you said."

The server set down the pizza.

"I don't get it, Ricky. I've got a knife at your gut, and you're all happy because the pizza is here?"

He dished her up a slice, then one for himself. "I've lived a good life, by God's law, been blessed with a good job, good wife and two growing kids. God knows I am innocent of any killings, so he will welcome me into heaven with open arms. Of course, if you do gut me like a fish, I will miss my family, and I know they will be devastated if I didn't come home. But know this before you strike, I am very sorry for your brother, what happened, but I wasn't there."

Maria took a bite of pepperoni. *What am I going to do?* He looked content munching on his pizza, a man with no guilty conscience. Damn. If I hadn't given him that kiss I could be reading his mind right now. She folded the jackknife and put it away. Now she had both hands free to tackle her pizza.

I'm glad I didn't kill him. He's a victim of his family, just like I was, before I fled to Haiti where I accidentally killed Brenda on the operating table. Even under the worst of situations, things had worked out.

"I have to say..." Ricky swallowed, "I don't cheat on my wife. I don't really know why I am here with you, but I must ask if this date is one and done, or will I see you again?"

Yeah, that kiss may take a while to wear off, then his affections will return to his wife, so I'll have to let him down easy. "This might feel like a date to you, but in a few days, you'll forget all about me."

"I am sure my wife will appreciate that."

"So let's enjoy the pizza and forget about Mexico City."

"Si." He chomped on another slice. "Gotta love those Yankees."

Chapter Thirty-Five

Jackie, relieved Maria had come to her senses, was about to turn in for the night when her burner phone vibrated. *At this time of night? It better be something important and not some bullshit.* "Janice, do you realize what time it is?"

"LeRoy is here...in Port au Prince, sure as bigfoot—"

"Did you tell him where you are?"

"Hell no. He sends money here every week. Put two and twenty together."

"What does he want?"

"Me."

"You?"

She sighed. "The big lug wants me to come back with him, to the church, the televised sermons, the good life we had before the lesbian zombies screwed up his life."

"And...what did you tell him?"

"Something along the lines of go jump in a lake, but he's not taking no for an answer. You've got to help me get rid of him."

"Are Reinhard and Albert around?"

"They're sleeping. What else do you expect they'd be doing this time of night?"

Jackie rolled her eyes. "Get Reinhard on the phone." By now Jackie had made it into the bedroom and was sitting next to a sleeping Brenda. "Wake up." She gave her redheaded lover's beautiful shoulder a shake.

"What?"

"You've got to hear this. LeRoy is back in town, Haiti, that is."

Brenda blinked sleep from her eyes and sat up. "I swear that guy is brain dead."

"Janice," Jackie said into the phone. "I'm going to put you on speaker."

"Here he comes now."

There was a bit of shuffling before a gruff voice said, "Do you guys know what time it is?" He yawned...the wannabe Nazi henchman for the lesbian zombies actually yawned.

"Reinhard, if I was there right now, I'd slap your happy ass into next Tuesday."

"Sorry, Jackie."

Brenda said, "I told LeRoy, that if he ever bothered Janice again, that would be the day that he died."

"Easy. We kill him."

Jackie took it from there. "This is what I want you all to do. Janice, tell him yes, that you'll meet him at the old burned-down clinic, 9am tomorrow, and you'll even bring some pilfered cash, to sweeten the pot, so to say. Reinhard, you and Albert will lie in wait for him to arrive. Make sure Aurora's truck is there and filled with gas."

"Yeah, his...I mean her truck is there."

"Good. When shithead shows up to get Janice, give him a knockout punch, gag him, then put him in the back of the truck—"

"Just like Dr. Gomez did me," Brenda put in.

"And cover him up with cow-shit manure from the park."

"Just like he did me."

"Really?" Reinhard said. "That's disgusting."

"I was dead," Brenda assured him.

Jackie went on, "If the cops stop you, they might check under a tarp, but they wouldn't dig through a pile of shit to see what's in it."

"My Queen, what do we do then?"

"Drive into the Forest of Fear, find the Pit of Ages, and dump him in it, and don't leave until his fat ass has been consumed by the roots and vines. If he's conscious, all the better."

"Yes, my Queen. You ladies must really hate this guy."

"We do."

"Get on it, boys, and no screwups, you hear?"

She hung up.

Brenda looked at her with admiration. "I kinda like your homicidal streak, Jackie. Must say it turns me on."

Jackie leaned in and kissed Brenda's soft as silk cheek. "But, sweetheart, when it comes to personally removing creeps from this earth, you're way meaner than me. That's why, my dear, we make such a great team."

Brenda's burner cell vibrated. She looked at the screen. Jane was calling.

"You're working late tonight."

"Brenda, we almost missed the deadline to get LZF on the ballot in every state before the absentee ballots and mail-ins were printed. According to the polls, we should get sixty percent of the votes."

"Who did you get to run for Hoffman's Senate seat?"

"Brenda, you'd said you wanted a lesbian zombie to represent New York, so I took the liberty to put my name in as the LZF candidate. The women who are loyal to you will also vote for me and any other women on the ballot."

"Good call, Jane. You are really efficient."

"I try."

"See you in the morning."

"Wait. One more thing. Agent Stephanie Phillips contacted me from the FBI. She was assigned to execute an illegal FISA warrant and listen in on your cell phone calls. When all she heard was a bunch of nonsense from two little girls, Deputy Director Larry Montford ordered her to make something up to nail you."

"Did you tell her thanks for the heads-up?"

"She told me she loves Jackie's *Soft as Silk Facial Scrub*."

Brenda and Jackie shared conspiratorial glances.

***

The next morning, somewhere in the jungles of Haiti, a lone Toyota pickup, beaten by age and impossible roads, bounced and jerked toward the Forest of Fear, so named because of the many mud bogs, seemingly bottomless pits, and vermin of every kind, including notorious army ants that devoured every living thing it their paths.

In the bed of this pickup, a pile of manure joggled, under which lay the brainless LeRoy Parker, unaware of his fortunes and shortfalls. A jerry can of gas, a shovel, and a broom kept him company. In the driver's seat, Reinhard, the tattooed ex-neo-Nazi, wrestled the steering wheel, while his equally decorated partner in crime, Albert, rode shotgun and hung on for dear life. Anyone who happened by these guys out here in the middle of nowhere would have known they were totally lost.

"The Forest of Fear has to be around here somewhere," Reinhard said, barely able to keep from biting his tongue.

"Pit of Ages?" Albert added as he clung to his balls. "Let's just find any old pit and get the hell out of here."

As if the heat and sweat and bugs weren't enough, they just ran out of road. The only way to proceed was to take a cow-path into the underbrush. Trees, shrubs, ferns, and the kitchen sink scraped truck paint down to raw metal, but he finally found an opening in the foliage.

Bouncing into sunlight, a very curious sight presented itself, a towering column of dirt that protruded from a pit, probably the result of a subterrain collapse during one of Haiti's most recent earthquake. However, these city boys from Brooklyn didn't know an ant hill from a hole in the ground.

Reinhard stopped the truck, wiped his brow, and glanced at Albert. "Looks like the Pit of Ages to me."

"Let's do it."

Reinhard backed the truck up to the edge of the pit. Both thugs got out and climbed into the truck bed to man the shovel and broom to dig LeRoy out of the shit.

He coughed and spit and shook like a wet dog.

Albert looked down at him and laughed. "Hey, mon. You no smell so good." His Haitian accent sucked.

They stood him up and took off his gag. "Where am I?" He looked around. "Where's my wife?" It was then that he realized he was standing on the tailgate of a truck, backed up to a pit, and when he looked down, he had to ask. "Why does the ground move?"

Reinhard and Albert bent forward to look, as well.

"Ants," Albert shouted.

LeRoy tried to jump back, but the Nazi bangers held him fast. "Let me go, goddamn it."

Reinhard said, "Brenda wanted vines and roots to consume the body...why not ants, same thing, right?"

"Beats me, mon."

"Look...I don't know who you guys are, but...I've got money...I'm rich...and I drive nice cars and eat the best food. I just wanted my wife back."

"Doesn't love beat all," Albert quipped.

Reinhard's face turned bullish. "Brenda told you to never bother Janice again, and if you did, you would surely die that day. We are your angels of death."

"No. For God's sake. Don't do this."

"Too late, man."

They shoved him off the tailgate and into the pit. He screamed all the way down to the bottom, which wasn't far but it was loud.

Reinhard looked down. "Albert? Ever see a pig stuck in a wallow?"

"No."

"Me neither, but I got a feeling this is what it would look like."

Ants swarmed over big bad LeRoy's brown-stained pants. Even as he twisted and flailed, the ants held on, in spite of all the screaming. Once he found his feet, he clawed at the crumbling pit wall, scrabbling like a crazy man, but he was slipping on all the mud and ants. Dirt and ants got in his boots, down his pants, and he started slapping the shit out of himself. Down he went into the roil of pissed off ants that streamed into his open mouth, choking off his screams, tunneled up his nostrils, cutting off his air, and burrowed in his ears to his brain cavity. Within a minute, he stopped moving.

"Man..." Albert said, "those little buggers were hungry."

The half-inch herculean ants lifted the body and slowly inched it into the opening to their nest, sheering off clothes and meat enough to make it fit.

Reinhard and Albert could not believe their eyes, until the swarm began to climb the pit walls toward the truck.

"Holy Christ on a cross, they're coming after us."

"We gotta go. We gotta go."

However, the ants had already surrounded the truck and formed ladders with their bodies to give their fellow raiders access to the frame and the fenders. Solid ropes of ants were worming their way up the tires.

"We can't jump down. We're trapped." Albert started shoveling manure over the side in an attempt to bury the little suckers. Reinhard grabbed the spare gas can and started splashing gas on the ground all round the truck.

Then Reinhard's cell vibrated. "Oh shit. It's Brenda." He answered. "It's not a good time. We're in deep shit here. I'll call you later." He hung up.

Albert, fighting for his life, had to say, "You forgot to tell her you love her and how much you miss her, you crazy bastard."

Reinhard tossed the nearly empty jerry can into the pit, struck a match and shouted, "Fire in the hole."

Whoosh. The pit went up like Hiroshima on Monday morning.

The first thing they noticed was the nutty aroma of burning ants, then came the blast of heat as the fire flared up on both sides of the truck. They scrambled over the roof, down the hood, to the ground, then trounced through burning ants to get inside. When Reinhard slammed the tranny in gear and mashed the gas, the truck peeled away in a rolling ball of fire.

Anyone with a brain knew not to light a cat's tail on fire and watch him run. That damn cat sets fire to everything it touches. The same could be said for a burning Toyota pickup as it sped down the cow path and plunged into the underbrush on its desperate race to the open road.

***

Brenda wondered why it was taking so long for Reinhard to call her back. She didn't say anything to her sisters about the deep shit he'd gotten himself into. Probably best to get the facts first, but something definitely had gone wrong.

She sat in her LazyGirl and watched TV with the sisters as if nothing were amiss. Betsy and Caroline were upstairs playing roughhouse with Girlie Dog. Brenda had just finished her second cup of coffee when their cooking show was interrupted by: *BREAKING NEWS*. A jungle fire was raging across Haiti.

"Those stupid clowns."

The sisters looked at Brenda, and before they could ask what she meant by that, she rousted Jackie from the couch. "Let's go for a walk."

Chloe said, "Sisters, it's top secret time again."

"I want the rest of you to get dressed. We're going to LZF Central in an hour, so no goofing off."

Walking down the path to the beach, and as they crossed over the sand berm, she told Jackie about the panic in Reinhard's voice when she'd called him earlier. "It was a simple job. Take LeRoy to the pit, toss him in, and let Loa take care of the rest. I'll bet those guys set the jungle on fire."

Jackie pulled her burner phone from her panties. *Never know when someone might call.* "I'll give Janice a ring and see if she has heard anything."

She got a busy signal followed by, *All lines are busy. Please try your call again later,* followed by a busy signal.

"Shit. I can't get through." She tucked the phone back into her panties. "We'll just have to wait."

Brenda was checking her messages and found a voice mail:

"Brenda, this is Bob Mason with the National Conservative Commission on Election Integrity. I would love to meet with you, as I believe cooperation and coordination between our organizations would be very beneficial to both. Let's say the White House at 1pm tomorrow? I hope to hear from you soon."

"Jackie, listen to this." She replayed the voice mail. "The dumbasses either think, number one, we're just stupid women, or two, they have something on us that can be detrimental to our chances of winning, or three, they'll propose to back the LZF in four years, because their incumbent can't run for a third term."

Jackie sat on the bow of the rowboat, now grounded on the berm, and rubbed the sand off her feet. "I think they're afraid of us. Hell, even a report on WNN said both parties are losing women in droves, all switching to join us. Plus the incumbent doesn't have Loa as a secret weapon."

Brenda wriggled her toes in the sand. *Or Loa's blessed sand.* "Let's meet with the pricks. Maybe the President will be there. We can remind him of the fiasco at the Medal of Freedom awards ceremony...tell him that he made a big mistake not giving us credit for the successful raid in Baddish."

"You're right. He needs to know the LZF Party is *his* fault."

Brenda gave Bob Mason a call back and left a message. “We’ll be there but no promises.”

Jackie gave Brenda a kiss. Strains of hard-rock music electrified the breeze. “Sounds like our sisters are getting wild and crazy. Let’s get back there.”

From halfway up the path to the back wall they heard gaiety and foolishness coming from the pool. At the back gate, they saw nakedness and depravity in full view of Caroline and Betsy, who didn’t have a stitch of nothing on, either.

Brenda burst through the gate and flew off the handle. “Girls, go inside.”

The nympho sisters stopped cold.

Caroline stomped her foot. “Ah, Brenda—”

“Go.”

“We never getta have any fun,” Betsy complained.

“And put some clothes on.”

They skedaddled inside.

As the sisters scrambled into their bikinis, Chloe pointed an accusing finger at Donna. “She started it.”

“That’s a lie, Chloe. You were the first one out of your panties.”

Monica grinned. “I told you we would get in trouble.” However, she was up to her waist in the water too, and had no business playing holier-than-thou.

Melinda climbed the pool steps to the deck. Water cascaded from her long wet hair and trickled down her sensuous curves. The other sisters’ hairdos were dry, which meant Melinda had been the lucky diver in a game of submarine. She slipped into a sundress and stood there as happy as a Meadowlark in springtime.

Lilly and Maria had damn near polished off a bottle of wine. They were giggling away as if their mischief was funny.

“You were supposed to be getting dressed.”

Jackie decided to throw water on the fire. “Hug time, sisters.” The girls gathered around her, but as they formed the hug circle, Jill said, “Wait a minute,” and then rushed to the back door. “Caroline and Betsy, you too.”

They bounded out the door, jumping up and down with Girlie Dog close behind. They’d put on shorts and blouses in short order.

Now in a tight circle with arms around their waists and Girlie

Dog running around them, all happy-tailed, the sisters recited the lesbian zombie prayer to Loa: "Thank you, our sweet Goddess Lord of All. We will never turn our backs on you, as we know you will never abandon us. Keep us safe, keep us together, as we keep you in our hearts." With that said, they broke the circle, exchanged hugs and kisses for all, rushed inside, got dressed, and proceeded about the day's business at LZF Central.

***

The next morning, after a relatively short trip to D.C. on Alfons' jet, and a quick jaunt to the White House by Uber, Brenda and Jackie found themselves waiting at the gate for Bob Mason to escort them in. He was surprisingly young, clean shaven, hair coiffed in a 50's wave. "Ladies." He led them through security to the Oval Office where they found the Vice President sitting behind the resolute desk. He stood and greeted them with cordial respect.

"Where's the President?" Brenda asked.

"He doesn't have time for this nonsense."

"We'll see about that." Brenda was pissed already, and the meeting hadn't even started.

Everyone got seated on plush couches facing each other in the center of the room. Mason kept looking at his watch as if waiting for a bus.

An intern standing off to the side stepped forward. "Anyone want something to drink? Coffee? Tea?"

Brenda said, "No thank you." The others waved him off as she turned to Mason sitting beside her. "Well. We're here. What's on your mind?"

"We're waiting for one more official. He's clearing security right now."

"Fine. We'll give him five minutes."

Jackie glanced around and took in the gilded décor of straight-seemed gold curtains, ceiling to floor, purple carpet, wall to wall, and the Presidential seal everywhere she looked. "Tacky," she muttered.

Two minutes later, a short-fat-and-ugly walked in. "Sorry I'm late. Been chasing bad guys all morning." He strode to Brenda and offered her a handshake. "I'm Larry Montford, the Deputy

Director of the FBI. So pleased you could meet with us today." He sat across from Bob Mason.

Brenda, staring at his fat cheeks and mottled complexion, read his mind: *Goddamned Secret Service. Metal detectors. Pat downs. I think they just like screwing with me.*

"Problems with the Secret Service, Larry?" she asked just to rattle him further.

She read my mind? No way. Just guessing.

Brenda turned to Jackie. "I'm just guessing the Secret Service harassed him, something beyond metal detectors and pat-downs." Both women laughed.

What the hell? These ladies better get with the program, play ball, or some serious shit is going to hit the fan.

"We know your game, Larry, and we're not playing ball with you. One of your agents told us. She found loyalty to the truth more acceptable than building a case against us based on lies. Hope you don't end up like your boys. They didn't fair too well when they took us on. It must have been embarrassing to know the whole country watched them get their asses kicked by a bunch of girls. Now...what the hell do you want?"

Larry felt like he'd just been mind-raped. He shook off the feeling and got down to business. "Do you know a couple of thugs named Reinhard and Albert?"

"Why do you want to know?" Jackie scowled.

Brenda spoke up. "Yeah. Brooklyn skinheads. They work security for us in Port au Prince. I'm sure you already know that, so what's with the third degree?"

"You know they are felons, right?"

"Our background checks are rather lax, and frankly, we don't care. We didn't hire them to be goody-two-shoes."

"Having them on your payroll is going to be a black eye for your campaign, and we fully intend to leak this disgrace to the media." He leaned forward with his elbows on his knees. "However, the FBI is prepared to look the other way, leave them to their shenanigans in Haiti, as long as you drop out of your run for the White House."

"It's in your best interest, ladies," the VP said. "Our great President has much unfinished business—"

"His business is finished, you morons." Brenda couldn't

make it any clearer. Yeah, she was steamed and Jackie hoped they'd get out of there without wearing Secret Service handcuffs, though they could never restrain a lesbian zombie for more than a half a second. Still, the publicity would look bad if they had to break out of the White House. She decided to keep her cool. "If you think you're going to scare us, intimidate us because we're lowly women, well, boys, it ain't gonna happen that way."

Brenda cut in, wagging a finger at Bob Mason. "You should be ashamed of yourself, inviting us here on false pretenses to be bushwhacked by the FBI."

"I get it," Jackie went on. "You geniuses aren't happy that Larry Evans, the District Attorney General of New York, has banned the FISA court from hearing any more of your bullshit pleas to surveil our campaign, so your President has ordered you to resort to schoolyard bullying to get us to quit. It's gotta be embarrassing, professionals as you are, to stoop so low. So go ahead. Leak all you want. We can take the heat."

Brenda wasn't finished. "What are you going to try next, Montford, break our front door down at three in the morning, blast us full of holes, and claim it was a justifiable FBI shooting?"

"Calm down." Jackie patted Brenda's knee. "We've got Girlie Dog, remember? She'll tear them to shreds before they can get off a shot."

Montford, in all his official capacity, had run out of options. He stood. "When we meet again, ladies, your situation will be dire, and you'll then wish you had cooperated with this administration." He turned to the VP. "I'll see my way out."

The intern opened the door for him and he stormed out.

Bob Mason stood. "That went well."

"I wish we could say that it has been a pleasure, but it wasn't. Ready to go, Brenda? We have a private jet waiting to take us back to New York."

They stood and headed for the door, but Jackie stopped suddenly and turned around. "When we move in here, we're going to redecorate the entire room. These colors really suck. Reminds me of the décor in a Turkish bathhouse. Smells like one too."

Brenda chuckled. "I have some flower-print ideas for the curtains, with a nice lace trim."

The VP looked like he might puke.

"My goddess..." Jackie added. "I almost forgot." She dug her cellphone out of her bra and finger-punched the screen. "I had my recording app on. Check WNN tonight. The American people will love hearing what Dick Director Montford had to say." Then they left the two men in a state of shock.

Bob Mason summed it up nicely. "We are so screwed."

Chapter Thirty-Six

Back at LZF Central, Monica and Jane were busy supervising the volunteers on the phones and handing out free jars of Jackie O'Neal's *Soft as Silk Facial Scrub* to women who came in to voice their support for the women's movement.

At the Ranch, Jill had been left to take care of Caroline and Betsy, and to pass the time, they worked on flash cards and cursive writing.

On the flight back from D.C., Jackie and Brenda were lounging in luxury and comfort on Alfons' Learjet when Brenda's burner cell ringed in. It was Janice.

"Things didn't go exactly as planned, but LeRoy is history. Reinhard and Albert came back, seared, but none the worse for wear. The fire in the jungle they started is the biggest problem, now that they've got the phone lines back up and the cell tower going again."

"Janice. I'm truly sorry it had to end this way for LeRoy, but look at the bright side, the roots and vines in the Pit of Ages had a good meal."

A moment of silence drew Brenda's ire. "What aren't you telling me, Janice?"

"They couldn't find the Pit of Ages, so LeRoy ended up in a pit of army ants. Now he's fodder for the next generation of jungle raiders."

"Oh, that must've been painful."

"Then the ants attacked Reinhard and Albert. They barely escaped with their lives."

"Those guys could screw up a wet dream." She looked at Jackie and shook her head. "We're about to land at JFK, then we're headed for a WNN press conference. No rest for the weary."

“Have fun...and thanks for getting LeRoy out of my life for good.”

“You’re welcome, sister.” She hung up.

At JFK, the ever-dutiful Joseph waited in the limo for Brenda and Jackie to descend the steps from the Learjet. It had taxied up a few minutes ago, and the pilots were doing their post flight shutdown before opening the cabin door. Joseph had to get them downtown for their WNN press conference with guest networks from around the country.

As the women finally approached the car, he got out and held open the back door. Jackie was saying, “I’m not looking forward to facing the press. I’m not prepared for it.”

“Relax, honey. Just be yourself and remember, the ones asking the questions have an average IQ of fifty.”

At the home of Lynne and Wesley Miller, she turned on the TV and heard that the news conference would begin shortly. The entire country was slated to watch.

Wes was settled on the couch. “Lynne, I can see why the whole damn country is falling in love with Brenda. She’s lovely. And there’s something magnetic about her personality, but do you think it’s a good idea to have a woman running the country?”

“We’re generally less hotheaded and more nurturing than men.”

“She looks a little familiar. In the heat of battle I can’t be sure, but I think she’s the nurse who bandaged my hand.” He flexed his fingers. “And somehow it magically healed.”

“It probably wasn’t as bad a wound as you thought.”

“It hurt like it was bad.”

“Then it was a miracle.”

“Lynne, you know I don’t believe in miracles, but I thought I saw an angel on the battlefield...I was in shock, I’m sure, yet I think it was Brenda. The red hair, I remember her red hair...and she was among the women who received the Medal of Freedom, I think. I was so wrapped up in the moment when the President singled me out for the job I did, but it’s all like a dream to me now, fuzzy as my recollection is.”

“My recollection is just fine. Brenda is an angel, the way she made me feel better that day I had the cramps and morning sickness.” Lynne sat in the very recliner she’d sat in that day and rubbed her belly. “It’s so hard to believe I’m finally pregnant, not with just one baby but two. If that’s not a miracle, what is?” She sighed. “I can’t imagine what it will feel like when they start kicking and moving around inside me.”

“Funny,” he said. “I’m thinking about two cribs, a double stroller, double diapers, double bottles, double trouble during their terrible twos.”

“Typical man.”

“Get me a beer, will you?”

“I just sat down. Get your own damn beer.”

“When did you cop an attitude?”

“When you got me pregnant, you old fool.”

He got up off the couch. “I’m going down to the officers’ club and drink a beer with my friends. Don’t wait up.”

“We won’t. There are three of us now, remember?"

Wes stopped to think a moment, then knelt at her recliner and leaned in to kiss her tummy. “You’re right. I’ll get my own damn beer.”

In two days, he had to return to Fort Leonard Wood in Missouri where his Rangers trained for any mission that should arise in any hotspot around the globe. It was a general’s job, and he was glad to do it, but with so little time together, there was no sense making war with Lynne.

***

Back in New London, Carrie and Frank had walked across the street to Robert and Maggie’s to watch the news conference together. They got there just as Maggie was laying Zoey down for her nap.

At the Pentagon, the Joint Chiefs of Staff were assembled for the very same reason, along with the Secretary of the Navy, Secretary of the Army, and the Secretary of Defense.

At the White House, the President, Vice President, and the FBI’s ruthless Larry Montford met in the Oval Office to watch the news conference.

Over at the incumbent’s campaign headquarters, Bob Mason called in the Attorney General, the Homeland Security Chief, the Secret Service honcho, and Kentucky Fried Chicken for the show.

Mason couldn't wrap his head around what had occurred in the White House earlier in the day. The nerve of those women defying their authority.

These sleaziest of sleazeball-public-servants were going to watch the news conference in hopes they'd come up with something, anything they could use to slow down the Brenda-and-Jackie steamroller that was about to flatten them.

Over in Karachi, Pakistan, the world's most wanted terrorist, Aqib Asad Abadi was counting down the days until he and his terrorist gang of killers would rid the world of the Sisterhood, and especially Brenda and Jackie.

***

Before the news conference got started, the Sisterhood, including Betsy and Caroline, who were dressed in their Yankee uniforms, gathered in front of the television with popcorn and very expensive wine.

As the girls passed out chocolate chip cookies, Caroline said to Betsy. "No cussing. If our sisters hear one swear word come out of our mouths, they won't let us watch Sponge Bob until we are twenty."

At WNN studios, everyone was in position for the cameras to roll, reporters in their seats and Brenda and Jackie at the podium. They wore matching red business suits, complements of St. Linda's Boutique in Manhattan, and Weitzman-made *Wizard of Oz* ruby stilettos.

Jackie got it started. "We'd normally kick off with a big speech, but wc just got back from a quick trip to the White House, so we'd rather get to your questions. Everybody having a good time so far?"

Some drunk in the back shouted, "You two are dressed the same. Lesbians do that sometimes. Are you two lesbians?"

Jackie answered, "What are you other than an obnoxious asshole."

Brenda cringed. *I thought only Chloe would have an outburst like that.*

Security moved in to haul him away.

The first question came from Rachel of the New York Times.

She stood and flipped her blond pigtails over her shoulder. “I just love your shoes. Do you mind telling us how much they cost?”

“If you have to ask, you can’t afford them.”

“I was just curious.”

“Fair enough. They cost one point six million dollars a pair.” She stepped from behind the podium to give the cameras a good look. “The red are rubies from Sri Lanka, and as you can see, diamonds enhance the sparkle.”

“Good grief. That’s three point two million dollars between the two of you.”

“Your math is excellent, Rachel.” Brenda panned the room. “Next?” Just then she regretted bragging about the price tag on their shoes. Now that’s all the newscasters will be talking about on all the channels and on the editorial pages of every paper. Whispering, with a hand over the mic, Brenda said to Jackie, “I’m sorry what I said.”

“It’s my money to spend, not theirs.”

Rachel raised her hand. “I have a follow up question.”

“Sorry, Rachel. One question per customer.”

A gray-haired lady in the front row didn’t have her hand up like other enthusiastic reporters so Jackie pointed to her.

“You mean me?”

“Yes. What’s your name?”

“Stephanie Phillips. I’m not a reporter, but Charles Mantella said I could sit in because I have an announcement that may interest everyone.”

“Let’s hear it.”

“I resigned from the FBI after twenty-five years of service. Under Deputy Director Larry Montford’s leadership, the bureau has become corrupt as corrupt can be. I was told to find dirt on you two, and if I came up empty, I was ordered to make something up. Everyone needs to know that this administration has corrupted every institution we hold dear. The President’s opponent party has jumped into bed with him to derail your campaign by hook or by crook. Telling you this could get me killed, I realize that, but I refused to go against my oath to defend the constitution from all threats, foreign and domestic.”

Brenda stood there looking at Stephanie. “Rest assured, we are aware of the corruption you’re speaking of, and when we’re elected, heads are going to roll."

"Stephanie..." Jackie clapped her hands. "I applaud your bravery. We need more women like you in the government. Perhaps you'll join our party and run in the midterms."

"I just might do that. Thanks."

The reporters filled the room with their applause.

"As for the FBI," Brenda added, "we told them we wouldn't play ball with them, or anyone, and I'm not talking baseball, although the Yankees have called and asked me to be their designated hitter."

The roar of laughter stopped the questions for a couple of minutes, but back at the White House, no one was laughing in the Oval Office. The President was fuming mad at his FBI Deputy Director Larry Montford. "When are you going to nail that bitch?"

"There's only one option left, Mister President. Pull her out of the game. Kidnap her from The Ranch, take her someplace secluded, like Camp David, and put the fear of God in her."

"Ruthless, but doable." He paced the Oval Office. "I can assign her a Secret Service detail, have them pick her up...bring her in—"

"Sir, they have to be clueless about the real reason for their assignment."

"What are you talking about?" He stopped pacing in front of Montford's chair.

"I believe she can read minds."

"Horsepucky."

He relayed his conversation with her in this very room. "She repeated words I was thinking, more to mock me than rattle me, I'm sure. So to be on the safe side, keep everything on the down-low with the Secret Service. Tell them you want to meet with her to apologize for the dirty politics in this race, face to face."

"I have a few words I'd like to say to her myself, but an apology is not among them."

"She'll be clueless, sir. It's imperative nobody else is privy to our scheme."

"This better not blow back in my face."

"What goes on in Camp David, stays in Camp David."

"Dirty politics," he muttered and picked up the phone to call the Secret Service. "I love this town."

Back at the WNN studio, when everyone settled down, USA Today was up next. “Brenda, Jackie. Thanks for being here. Could you clarify your platform on the homeless? We’ve heard rumors about getting the military involved somehow.”

Jackie took this question. “All around this country we have abandoned military bases. We’ll present a proposal to Congress we call *The Prosperity Act*, whereby these bases will be converted into villages with their own zip codes and Section Eight housing for women. Each village will have its own commissary and a medical facility that will deliver health care, mental wellness, and substance abuse rehabilitation.”

“What about homeless men?”

“What about ‘em?”

“Where do they live?”

“Not with the women and children. It’s mostly men who walk out and leave their wives and families. Not women. I think that’s because women have an instinct to take care of their young. Deadbeat men only want to take care of themselves. Answering your question though, men can sleep in tents wherever they want, but their days of knocking up their girlfriends or wives and then leaving them are over.”

“Aren’t you worried that attitude will make men not vote for you?”

“No. We can get along with the millions of sisters we have out there. Their support will be enough for us to take the White House. Lastly though, men who make babies and then leave the women to support the children all by themselves will be given forced vasectomies.”

“That would be unconstitutional and unlawful.”

“It won’t be when we win. I’ll sign an Executive Order.”

“You’re kidding, right?”

“Of course I’m kidding, just yanking your chain to make a point. Don’t believe everything you hear. Ask questions. Get the facts. Apply common sense to your reporting.”

That got a few nods and murmurs from the media hounds.

A fat reporter from American Pork, sweating like a pig, asked the next question. “Do you believe in Jesus?”

“Do you?” Jackie tossed back at him.

He folded his hands in prayer. “With all my heart and soul.”

"That's all that matters, sir."

Just then, a firetruck and five police cars screamed up and blocked the street. Two firemen and a shitload of cops rushed in. "Everybody out. Now. There's been a bomb threat. We found a suspicious package up against the building. The bomb squad is on the way."

The reporters filed out, lugging their gear, their ranks merging with office workers from upstairs and the production crews: cameras, lighting, and sound. Now that the building was clear and everyone was standing down the block, the bomb exploded in a fireball of smoke and debris. The concussion was like a gut-punch, but everyone was okay.

Men all over the country were calling their pals with the gleeful news of what had just happened. The women had been blown out of the spotlight by some brave bomber willing to fight for man's dominion over women. However, all this act of cowardice did was harden the hearts of the Sisterhood.

Charles Mantella found Jackie and Brenda in the crowd. "Doesn't look too bad, shattered windows, loose bricks and lumber flung about. Nobody hurt."

"The bomb was definitely meant to shut us up without killing anyone. The warning is proof of that."

"Still, you girls better watch your backsides. It may take a week to get opened back up. Sorry your news conference was cut short."

"Yeah. Maybe next time..."

A cop walked by. Brenda read his mind: *The bomber is probably somewhere in this crowd, gloating over the fear he's caused and enjoying the damage his bomb created.* He moved through the crowd, looking here and there.

Her sisters arrived in the limo, piled out and threw their arms around her and Jackie. "We're so glad you're okay."

She huddled everyone together. "Listen up. The bomber might bc somewhere around here. Spread out, read people's thoughts. We might be able to pick him out of the crowd."

After a while of listening to looky-loos, Caroline and Betsy were the first to get a hit. All excited, they ran up to Brenda and pointed at a guy on a mountain bike. He wore a ball cap low over his eyes and a backpack that looked empty. "That's the bad man,"

Caroline said, and Betsy added, “I wish Girlie Dog was here. I’d say sick ‘em Girlie Dog.”

Jackie walked up to him like she was a hooker. “Hi there.”

“This is really exciting, huh?”

“I’m more into partying.” Jackie showed him a very tempting smile. “Would you like to smoke some weed with me?”

“That would be great. I’m fresh out.”

They waded through the crowed, Jackie swinging her tush while the bomber walked his bike, and finally broke loose at an alley, typical for New York City, dumpsters and litter and the harsh smell of urine and rotting garbage. Damn if the sun hadn’t already set, bathing the city in twilight.

“Down there by the blue dumpster.” She reached in her bra as if pulling out a bag of weed, pulled out her cell phone instead, and cupped it in her palm. “Got a light?”

At the dumpster, he dropped the bike, and leaning against the brick wall, he fished a lighter from his pants pocket and flicked the Bic into flame. As the fire momentarily blinded him, Brenda rushed up to the dumpster just as Jackie pushed the bomber between it and the wall. “Hey.”

Brenda shoved the dumpster against the wall, crushing his chest and cracking the bricks all the way up to the second floor. They could hear him wheezing for about a minute, then all went quiet, but for the hum of traffic and patter of pedestrians, all clueless to the murder that had just taken place.

“The trash man will find the body in the morning,” Jackie said as they strolled away from the scene. “But whoever pays the bill will have to pay extra for a special pick up.”

That got them to laughing so hard tears welled in their eyes all the way back to the bomb site and the waiting limo. “Who wants Square Pants t-shirts and Sponge Bob candy?”

Caroline and Betsy started jumping up and down on the expensive limo seats. “We do. We do.”

Monica asked Jackie in a whisper, “Did you catch the guy?”

“He’s smoking dope in hell right now.”

Chapter Thirty-Seven

For the next eight days, while WNN studios were being repaired, the Sisterhood worked at LZF Central, coordinating a new *Soft as Silk Facial Scrub* giveaway drive with Jackie's outlets all around the United States.

It was on the seventh day that Jorge drove up to find there was no place to park. The sidewalks and the street were crowded with people holding signs and placards. The sisters in the limo wished the demonstrators were there in support of the campaign, but in reality, these people were from the Church of the Risen Jesus, proclaiming the LZF were heathens and atheists.

Jorge had to park half a block away, and the sisters had to bull their way through the crowd. Jorge took point, and the girls held hands and shadowed him, much like a clutch of ducklings behind their mother duck. They hadn't made it twenty feet before a guy in his mid twenties and wearing a *Jesus is Lord* t-shirt spit on Jorge. Jorge returned the assault with a right hook to the bastard's mouth, a knuckle sandwich that broke his jaw, and mister Jesus is Lord hit the ground, out cold.

This sparked a riot of rock and bottle throwing, and the sisters were forced to go into defense mode. They each grabbed the nearest rioter by the hair and, using them as shields, dragged them screaming and yelling to the entrance of their headquarters, where they took up defensive positions at the door. "All you born-agains better get back."

Brenda, now standing guard, shoulder to shoulder with her sisters, looked over the crowd of people, their bared teeth, snarled lips, and hate in their eyes. *These shitheads remind me of the late LeRoy Parker and the dumb-asses who followed him. I guess the guy holding the Jesus Loves You sign is their new preacher. His white collar band looks tight enough to choke him. He and his crowd are worshipping the wrong Lord.* She thought to gather up a couple hundred of her volunteers to march on their church with signs proclaiming: *The Goddess* Loa *rules the Universe.*

The new preacher yelled, “Children of God. Remember the teaching of our lord. If you are struck on your cheek then turn your head and let them strike the other side.”

Then again, Brenda thought, *ignorance is bliss. Let them all burn in hell.*

Jorge shouted, “Go home. Read your Bibles. Praise Jesus and practice what you preach.”

He was pelted with rocks and bottles. Sirens cut the morning air, followed by police whistles and barking dogs. Within minutes, the crowd moved down the street, breaking windows, setting fires, and looting stores. Network reporters were on the story like mustard on a hot dog.

As the spitter with the broken jaw was being loaded into an ambulance, three cops came looking for Jorge to hear his side of the story. They determined the *Jesus is Lord* fanatic had assaulted him first, so no charges were levied against Jorge. As they cuffed the prick to the gurney, the sisters cheered their protector, not that lesbian zombies needed protecting. Even Jill and the girls at The Ranch cheered as they watched the riots unfold on TV.

Aqib Asad Abadi also watched the news broadcast as he sat on his haunches in front of an old cathode ray tube television, set up on a rickety table. The floor of his shack in Karachi was only dirt, so to keep from soiling his white thobe, he’d knelt on a dusty goatskin rug. There, from halfway around the world, the fine bodies of Brenda and Jackie appeared before him. Come morning prayers, Allah would forgive him for such licentious thoughts. One of his jihadist brethren brought him a cup of Laban Sobia and commented about the women’s short dresses. “The knees of Satan for all to see.”

“Allahu Akbar,” Abadi recited. “I think that when we go to kill the Sisterhood, we should return here with these two pigs of the earth. I shall make them my wives and fornicate with them nightly.”

“You must avenge your brother, my brother Abadi.”

“But ah, my foolish friend. Death be too good for them. I

shall first cut out their lying tongues. No plague killed my brother. These women brought death in their needles. Nurses from the WHO? Nah." He sipped from his cup of dark spicy brew. "They shall be my sex slaves, to be bound and beaten and shared among my fellows." He imagined them standing before him, naked and afraid, and soon with big bellies filled with babies, to grow to be jihadist fighters, as was their father. "There would be no greater way to honor my departed brother."

"Your plan is a wise one, my exalted leader." He glanced at the grainy image of beauty personified, the redheaded temptress with knees of the devil. "When you tire of this one, I wish to take her for my own to copulate and corrupt before Allah."

"As you ask, but she will not be worth much when I am finished with her. Now go. I wish to dream of the future and masturbate in peace."

***

Back in the USA, the networks had to balance the scales as to what they put on the news and who they would offend. Coverage of the riots was good for ratings, but the predicted landslide victory of the LZF party was becoming old hat. What they needed to keep audiences engaged, were the personal stories of the Sisterhood, human interest stories, but reporters who'd set out to get them came back with nothing, as the sisters were very tightlipped about their personal lives. Network news producers had to keep prying, to keep kissing up to management because they had to be conscious of the big money corporations that paid billions in advertising.

Jackie thought about that too. They were no longer getting requests for political interviews, and none for debates against the other guys. Even Charles, Charlie, Mantella of WNN had requested each sister tell her story on *The Threes*. "Let America fall in love with the Sisterhood."

Yeah, maybe the girls had to make some changes. They could clean up their language, simmer down the sexiness, open up about their families, their struggles before they came to the Sisterhood. Put in some lighthearted stuff...but that in itself was problematic.

This approach could be a total disaster. She could hear Chloe now, telling an interviewer: '*My ex-husband enjoyed sex after beating me. While he was sleeping I put superglue in his dickhole and left him for good. But he found me, begged me to come back. One of my sisters came to my rescue. He fell and broke his neck. We ground him into dogfood for Girlie Dog.'*

Jackie put her index finger to her lips, and in deep thought said to herself, *And what about Monica? 'I was an eighty-year-old woman in Haiti when I blew a guy's head off with a shotgun. Then I went to Paris, kidnapped a bad guy from Haiti and his grandkids, damn near cut his head of with a guillotine, but I changed my mind when he swore on his grandkids' lives that he was innocent in the coverup of the rape and murder of my daughter. When I found out he lied, I went back to kill him for real, but changed my mind when the ghost of my daughter spoke to me at her grave.'* That human interest story would go over like bombers over Berlin.

Donna could tell her story, about her affair with Senator Hoffman behind the back of her lesbian lover, who came to kill her but was shot by police. Caroline could tell how she'd been adopted by the Sisterhood after she survived a fatal disease and then a car crash that killed her parents. Nothing lighthearted about that. Betsy could talk about how she was autistic and bullied by the kids at school before she drank Kool-Aid with Caroline and magically got all better.

Just then, both girls came running in from the front yard. Betsy was out of breath. "Those weirdos that were holding up the signs at your office are in our yard and they chased us."

Then Caroline jumped in. "But Girlie Dog started biting them in the butt. So she chased them out of our yard but one of them took out a gun and shot Girlie Dog but she just stopped and licked where she was shot then went after the bad guy and bit him in the butt and ripped his pants off. So Girlie Dog quit chasing him."

Betsy, looking very serious asked, "Brenda, will Girlie Dog be all right?"

"Yes, sweetie. So don't you worry about her. The person who has to worry is the dumbass that shot Girlie Dog in the first place. The cops will be paying him a visit and they'll introduce him to a pair of handcuffs because he came on our property and fired a gun. He'll be standing before a judge tomorrow."

The next morning, as the Sisterhood arrived at LZF Central,

they were met again by the religious pricks from the Church of the Risen Jesus, chanting Psalms and pumping their signs.

"What is this, Ground Hog Day?" Brenda quipped.

"I see him," Caroline shouted. "That's the guy with the gun who shot Girlie Dog." She pointed out the dipstick-skinny guy with a bushy 'stash and heavy coat.

As the sisters banded together and made their way inside, Jackie called the cops on her cell phone.

Three NYPD cruisers showed up, and four cops made their way to the conference room where Brenda, Jackie, and Jane waited. One officer, Abigail McGill had the sisters' undivided attention. They couldn't take their eyes off her tits, which filled her uniform shirt quite nicely. "So, ladies. You want to report a crime?"

Jane felt comfortable talking to her because she'd met her in an LGBTQ club last month. "There's a guy outside in the mob of morons that was on our property last night protesting, and he fired a shot at our little sisters. The bullet grazed our dog. Now all three are afraid to go outside."

Big and tough looking police lieutenant William Mann asked, "Are the girls here?"

"Yes. Let me call them in." Jackie opened the door and shouted, "Girls, these nice policemen want to speak to you. And no cussing." They walked in like they'd been called to the principal's office. She closed the door.

Lieutenant Mann knelt down to the girls. "Can you point him out so we can arrest him?"

They jumped up and down, all excited. Caroline took his hand and said, "I'll show you the bad man that shot Girlie Dog."

Outside, she pointed to the bad guy.

Knowing the suspect was armed and could possibly be hiding a weapon under that heavy coat, the cops pulled their guns. "Hey you with the coat and the Sonny Bono mustache, hands up."

"What did I do?"

"You're under arrest for assault with a deadly weapon, attempted murder, child endangerment, unlawful discharge of a weapon, trespassing, and animal cruelty."

"Holy shit. Is that all?"

"On your knees. One wrong move and you're dead."

He complied and submitted to a pat down. "Well, well, well," Mann exclaimed like he'd just solved the crime of the month. "What do we have here? You got a permit to carry this Glock 9MM."

"I don't need no stinking permit. It's the United States of America. We have the Second Amendment. Stick your permit up your ass."

"Sorry. Wrong answer. You need a concealed carry permit to terrorize little girls and their puppy." He cleared the weapon and sniffed the barrel. "Yup. It has definitely been fired recently."

"Hey. I was target-shooting last night."

"Sure you were, scumbag. On your feet. I'm adding no CCP to your laundry list of charges. You're looking at ten years on Rikers Island. Officer McGill, get this piece of crap out of here."

Just then the Jesus freak with the white collar strode up like the world revolved around him. "Officer, I can vouch for Arnold. This is all just a misunderstanding."

"Back off, preacher." He knuckled the guy on the chest bone. "You're interfering with lawful police business. You want to join this creep on Rikers? Just give me an argument."

He raised his hands and backed away.

After the commotion settled, the cops and sisters returned to the office where Lieutenant Mann told everyone within hearing range, "Good thing he didn't pull that gun on me. I would have double-tapped that religious fanatic."

Right then, Caroline and Betsy, both wearing big smiles, brought in coffee and donuts. "Would you guys like some refreshments?"

Abigail smiled back. "We would love some."

While the officers munched on donuts and sipped coffee, the girls played *catch me if you can* around the conference table, giggling and laughing like this day was no different than any other.

Abigail set down her paper cup. "Girls, we have to get back to work. It was really nice meeting you. And ladies, you have our votes."

Brenda and Jackie showed them out.

***

Over at WNN, what looked to be a slow news night turned out to be a ratings burner. The lead story was about a religious maniac who took a potshot at two nine-year-old sisters of the Sisterhood but missed and shot their dog. Another network led off with *Dog hater attempts to kill sisters' little pet dog.*

Back at the ranch, Jackie was happy the networks finally got their human interest stories. The LZF was back in the forefront of publicity. There was no way they could lose the affections of an adoring nation.

However, even as the Sisterhood celebrated and the nation cheered, the Iranian trawler Nandoso, flying a Turkish flag, had steamed across the Mediterranean Sea and ploughed into the open Atlantic where the mother of all hurricanes was building its pinwheel of destruction and death. Aboard the trawler, heavily armed Taliban fighters braced themselves for the onslaught of wind and rain and the mountainous waves to come. Though this voyage seemed like a fool's errand, the huge storm would supply cover for their crossing into US territorial waters and blind military satellites as to the ship's exact whereabouts.

Timing was everything. The way Abadi had it figured, the storm would clear the eastern seaboard just as the trawler finished its treacherous voyage, and it would reappear off the coast of Long Island, too late for US forces to stop the assault on the Sisterhood. However, day and night, Abadi would question the wisdom of his plan as the storm washed men and weapons overboard while the trawler chugged along like a slug on a windblown leaf.

Back on her home star of Polaris, in the brightness and glorious heat of the heavens, Loa could see the ship pitching and yawing through the storm. *I'm not going to let it sink, as Brenda had wished to take on the attackers and kill them one-by-one. That woman sure loves a fight, especially against men with ill-intentions toward women.* Such was the fuse John Marshall had lighted, surely as a match to gunpowder. It wasn't Loa's plan to change all of creation, but to plant the seed of reform and let Brenda carry out her goddess's will on earth. For those who would try to stop her, she would have no trouble defeating. *The low-lives will soon stand before me, and one by one, I will curse them to eternal damnation, even as they beg for mercy.*

On all the television channels, the opposing parties ran

commercials, not against each other but against the LZF, stating what a calamity it would be if women ran the country. They already owned fifty-one percent of the population. Men were already in the minority, so it would only be a matter of time before dominatrixes would control the courts, the police, and the prison systems. *Men. Prepare for leather and leashes.*

As appetizing as that sounded, Brenda thought the media was taking women's equality to an all-time low. Snuggled in bed with Jackie, they were watching the lies play out on the big screen TV.

"I wonder..." Jackie said, "if the born-agains have the same take on women leadership. I'll switch to a religious channel. Let's see." She punched the remote until she found the HBC, Halleluiah Broadcast Company, where a commercial was setting the scene, a typical American kitchen with a typical American woman standing at a typical American sink, meaning it was jammed with dirty dishes no man would ever volunteer to wash. A typical American husband steps into the scene and kisses his wife on the cheek. "Honey, when are you going to be finished cleaning up this mess?"

She sighs and holds up two different brand bottles of dish detergent. "I can't decide which one works better to make dishes sparkle. What do you think, dear?"

"You know I don't decide these trivial matters, but I do decide how you must vote in November, and it's not for the LZF Party, you hear? I would be very upset if you did, and you know what happened the last time you got me upset."

Rubbing her butt, she said, "I sure do. Couldn't sit down for a week, so I'm going to vote however you tell me to, dear."

As the typical housewife set about her dutiful chore of washing the dishes, a narrator's voice said, "And the Lord sayeth man shall have dominion over women."

The typical woman's tearful face faded to black.

"Now that's a bunch of bullshit," Brenda blurted out. "The HBC's days are numbered. We'll buy them out and change the format to cooking contest shows."

"Good Goddess. You really let that commercial get to you?"

"I'm so mad I'll never get to sleep."

Jackie shut off the TV and nuzzled Brenda's neck. "So what would you like me to do to make you sleepy?"

Game on.

Chapter Thirty-Eight

The next morning at breakfast, Brenda realized Monica was nowhere around. She'd tried calling her earlier but got no answer. Maria, Donna, and Chloe were in an argument over the best ways to make money, namely using the world's oldest profession. Donna said she wouldn't do it for a hundred bucks, Maria said she'd do it for a dime, and Chloe said she wouldn't do it for a million bucks. The man-hater was true to form this morning. "Any of you girls seen Monica?"

They looked around and shrugged.

Jackie said, "Call Alfons. He might know."

She called him on her burner, just in case the FBI was still listening in, illegal as it would be. When Alfons picked up, it was lucky she didn't have a smart phone with Vid-O-Vision.

"Brenda," he answered. "So good to hear from you. Can you hang on just a second?"

Though he'd tried to muffle the mic, she heard him say, "Quick, pull up my pants then take the rest of the day off."

"Is that Monica, Alfons? I need to speak with her."

"No. It's my new receptionist, April, but trust me, she's good every month of the year. Said so on her employment application."

Brenda sighed and rolled her eyeballs. "So where is she?"

"Who?"

"Monica. She's not answering her phone."

"Brenda, boss of my true love. I don't know where she is."

"I know something is going on between you two. Did you break up?"

"No. I asked her to marry me, and suddenly it's like I got herpes or something."

"Marry you?"

"Honestly, Brenda, us being married wouldn't jeopardize what you all are doing. I just hope I'd see her more often."

"Hmmmm..." she intoned, thinking a marriage into oil money could be beneficial to the Sisterhood. "Are you saying you'd share your oil fortunes with her?"

"She doesn't want the money. She wants her freedom, no matter how good things are between us."

"So you love her?"

"Yes."

"And still you're banging April?"

"Hey, Monica's the lesbian...though sometimes I wonder."

"Trust me, if you'd seen her with Jane the other night, you'd know the true meaning of flamin' gay. There's some other reason..."

"She's a strange one in the sack. She'll bang me 'til the cows come home, but no kissing. It's a rule. Maybe—"

"Wait. No kissing you say?"

"Kinda throws the *you-may-kiss-the-bride* out the window, wouldn't you say?"

"I'll have a talk with her."

"Okay. And if she accepts this hundred thousand dollar rock I bought for her beautiful ring finger, there's a million in it for your LZ Foundation."

"Deal."

***

The Nandoso trawler with its Taliban passengers and Turkish flag got battered by the storm of the century. The good news, what was left of the terrorist raiding party was only two days from the east coast. In two days the storm will have moved into the North Atlantic, though the weather forecast for the assault time called for residual rain and gusty winds.

The ship's captain and navigator were the first to notice a new blip on the radar screen, a large vessel shadowing at a twenty nautical mile distance off the port stern. They had no way to know that it was the mighty destroyer number 33, the *USS Carmick*, dispatched by Admiral Roy Kincade, now a member of the Joint Chiefs of Staff, with full authority to redirect the ship into harm's way.

Navy intelligence had listened in to the chatter going back and forth from Tehran, Karachi, and the Nandoso, but however suspicious, the trawler had every right to sail these international waterways. Once they entered US territorial waters, as their course indicated, that would be a different story. The ship would be subject to legal search and seizure. Everyone on the ship could be arrested and detained, and a terrorist threat to the homeland would be squashed.

If only war were that simple.

***

Even with an approaching hurricane, a woman must get her nails done. That's were Monica was when everyone was looking for her. Now back at The Ranch, all spiffy and sparkly on the fingertips, she couldn't have imagined the conversation that awaited her when Brenda called her into the sitting room.

"What is up?"

"I had a talk with Alfons."

"Just great." Monica plopped down on the leather couch. "I suppose he told you."

"Yes." Brenda sat in her favorite LazyGirl. "The question is, what are you going to tell him?"

"Nothing."

"You can't keep him hanging on like this."

"And you do not understand. From the moment he kisses the bride, he is screwed. His loyalty to me will switch to you, the Sisterhood, Loa, and all this craziness. I do not want to lose him...especially not that way."

"Dear, dear, Monica." Brenda got up and sat next to her on the couch, took her hands, and looked into those dark and sometimes murderous eyes. "Has he ever showed me any attention? Has he ever said, or even thought, that he'd like to take me to the sheets?"

"No, but—"

"But nothing. He's under your spell, not mine. The virus is just going to intensify the love he has for you. And with any luck, he won't have a need for April or any other month of the year."

"April?"

"He turned to her as you turned to Jane, all because you have this silly notion that kissing him will somehow turn the world upside down."

"I fear he will end up like Jorge and General Taylor, and I do not want him to come between me and my sisters. After all, I am a lesbian zombie. My loyalty lies with you, my Queen, and the Sisterhood."

"And therein lies the problem." She squeezed Monica's hands. "Your loyalty isn't compromised by love, and your sisters and I will always love you, married or not. And he's okay with that."

A tear escaped Monica's eye. "He actually offered me an open marriage, but that is easier said than done. Jealousy is a wicked bed partner."

"Have faith in him, in yourself, and in Loa. She wouldn't lead you astray. Follow your heart, Monica. His arms are open. All you have to do is decide, one way or the other. You owe him that much." Brenda hugged the first of her sisters, that fiery Haitian black woman she'd hate to see leave The Ranch to live with Alfons, but it would be a sacrifice for love undenied. And the fact that he was richer than the Vatican helped.

"Thank you, Brenda. You are not only my Queen..." She brushed away the tear. "But my best friend."

"Go get 'em, pussycat."

***

In front of the Empire State Building, Monica got out of the white stretched limo. She thanked Joseph for the ride, then looked up the face of the building. Somewhere up there on the 25th floor, Alfons waited for her to arrive, probably sitting on the very bed in his multi million dollar suite that she would soon call her bedroom...their bedroom, or maybe not at all.

She crossed the lobby and got on his private elevator, and as the door closed she realized her heart was beating a mile a minute. *Goddess, Alfons sure does love me, and he likes the games we play, and he wouldn't be my ball and chain. I don't know why he can't just do me twice a week then ball some other bimbo like April when I'm with my sisters at The Ranch.*

As the elevator rose toward the 25th floor, she had to ask herself a most important question. *Do I love Alfons?* That's when her emotions got complicated, a bit of warmth down below that welled up into her chest and hugged her beating heart. She recalled telling Brenda how she would hate to lose him, and if Brenda had asked why, she would have said she did not want to lose her favorite toy, but deep inside, she knew she loved him for the way he loved her, worshipped her to a fault, gave her everything her heart desired. Her eighty-year-life in Haiti was one of misery and poverty, heartbreak and loss. She had been given a new life, another shot at youth and happiness no other human had ever received. Only a fool would not make the best of it.

The elevator dinged.

And I am no fool.

After stepping off the elevator, she walked the aisles and past the staff, feeling as if she owned the place.

And it felt good.

At Alfons' office, she stepped up to a new receptionist at the desk where the nameplate read: *April Showers*. The jealousy dragon rose in her throat but she didn't let its flaming nostrils show. "Alfons is expecting me."

"Of course. Go right in."

She strode in, chin high like the Queen of Sheba. "I am here, Alfons, with an answer to your question."

He spun around in his desk chair and rose to his feet, all five-foot-four of him trying to look six-foot-six, shoulders back and paunch sucked in. "Monica, please, have a seat." He indicated a plush leather chair usually reserved for oil tycoons and groveling bankers.

She set her curvy backside down and crossed her legs at the knees. "Alfons—"

"Wait. Don't say anything yet. I've got something to show you." He hustled to the door and locked it, and as he turned around, he produced a ring box from his jacket pocket. By the time he got back to the chair and dropped to one knee, he had opened the hinged lid, revealing the most elaborate and brilliant diamond ring ever created by the finest jeweler in New York City.

At a time like this, coy was Monica's middle name. "Alfons,

are you proposing to me again?"

"Yeah, and I ran it past Brenda first, just to be safe. So what do you say?"

"I do not know. I-I have to think about it."

"Are you kidding me? You haven't thought about it since I asked you the first time? Hell. That's all I've been thinking about." Then with a droopy-eyed look that even Lassie would understand, "Monica..." he begged. "I love you with all my heart."

"You do not really know me, Alfons, but before I accept this ring, this very expensive ring, I must tell you who I really am."

"A goddess, the devil, the black voodoo princess of Haiti," he groveled. "I don't care."

"I am a lesbian, as you know, but you do not know I am a zombie."

"Zombie?" He swallowed hard.

"I am eighty years old."

"Eighty?" With a hooked finger he tugged on his shirt collar. Yup. His tie was too tight for this shit.

"And when you kiss me, you will get a dose of the lesbian zombie virus, straight from the Forest of Fear in Haiti, and everything about you is going to be amplified to the moon. I hope that includes your love for me."

"Lesbian zombie virus?"

"Do you still want to marry me?"

He looked at the ring in the open box, still presented to the women he loved, but of course his hand was trembling some now. However, the love he held dear for Monica, the black skinned lesbian zombie from Haiti, overpowered every instinct a normal man would have let loose by now. Running and screaming were the first to come to mind. Instead, he removed the ring, took her left hand, which also was trembling, and slid the promise of his love over her fancy fingernail polish and beautiful knuckles to finally let it rest where lovers profess their undying adoration. He looked up into her tear-filled eyes. "I take that as a yes."

"Yes. Yes. Yes." She threw herself on him, and they tumbled to the floor where lips collided in a passionate kiss long awaited by both, and tongues got acquainted for the first time. As for the rest of the inhabitants of this planet, it was a good thing the door was locked.

Chapter Thirty-Nine

Back on the *USS Carmick*, the CIC (Combat Information Center) was in constant contact with Navel Intelligence who had a direct line to Admiral Kincade who, in turn, forwarded the information to General Taylor. Captain Marquez had Presidential orders to return fire if the phony Turkish ship took any aggressive action against them. Marquez had every intention to send the ship to the bottom of the Atlantic.

Lawrence got a call from Roy. “All indications are the ship we’re tracking is not friendly.”

“I was told it’s a trawler, fishing I assume.”

“The profile fits an Iranian design. The Turkish flag is a ruse, we’re sure. To be safe, I suggest you take the threat on The Ranch seriously until we know otherwise. Mobilize General Miller’s Rangers and notify Jackie of these updates.”

“Will do, Roy. Keep in touch.” Taylor hung up and dialed Jackie O’Neal.

At The Ranch, the sisters were looking at a darkening sky and ominous clouds creeping up from the south. Hurricane Helen was barreling toward New Jersey with 120 mph winds and torrential rain.

“At least the worst is going to miss us,” Jackie said.

“Don’t be so sure.” Melinda was actually the smartest of the bunch. “I’ve seen clouds like these when I lived in North Carolina. Problem is, hurricanes tend to wobble due to the earth’s rotation and the forces put on the storm by high and low pressure gradients. Landfall predictions can be hundreds of miles off course.”

As the daylight faded, it started to rain. Jackie received a call from General Taylor. “Batten down the hatches,” he said. “You’ve got two storms approaching, the hurricane and a boatload of

Taliban. I've mobilized General Miller's forces. They should arrive at dawn."

"Can't you just blow the boat out of the water?"

"That action could be construed as an act of war by Iran. We'd rather surveil them, see if they make any aggressive maneuvers, at least until they cross into US territorial waters. Assuming they will, a Coast Guard cutter is on standby, but the hurricane may curtail any attempts at intercepting the ship due to the high risk of a collision at sea in a storm."

"I see, then, keep me updated." She hung up.

"What did he say?"

"Prepare for war, girls."

The rain began to fall harder, the wind grew more intense, and high waves pounded the beach and crept toward the sand berm as the storm surge heightened.

Monica called to say she had decided to spend the night with Alfons and ride out the storm there, twenty-five stories above the rain-soaked streets of Manhattan. She didn't say a word about agreeing to marry Alfons, and the sisters didn't ask. They were busy boarding up the Crystal Shrine.

What they didn't know was, at the very moment of that call, Monica was not in Manhattan but on Alfons' new jet, a Gulf Stream G550, and they were currently laying a contrail over Nebraska on their way to Las Vegas. Yes, they were to be married in Sin City where dreams were dreamt and fortunes were made and lost. As it turned out, and true to Alfons' nature, he was more interested in their wedding night than high-rolling in the casinos. To him, the libido bump he got from Monica's kiss was money in the bank.

Dawn broke over Long Island, revealing heavy gray skies full of pelting rain and howling winds. The Kraken had arrived with an appetite for destruction and death. It was as if the fist of Satan had slammed down on Long Island. Hurricane Helen wasn't even a near miss on New Jersey. The newly predicted path was to pass right over Long Island Sound and slam into New London.

The sisters were hunkered down, as the weather was too nasty for even lesbian zombies to go out and play. Rain pelted the windows and wind whistled through the eaves. Any time now, General Wes Miller and his Army Rangers were due to arrive and fortify The Ranch against any possible Taliban incursion. Weather reports predicted another twenty-four hours before Helen made landfall on the most densely populated island on earth.

However, there wasn't a drop of rain falling in Las Vegas. The sun-drenched city sweltered at ninety degrees in the shade, but in a suite high atop the Rio, the air-conditioning kept Alfons and Monica Duda cool and comfortable between rolls in the hay and steamy showers. After all, they were newlyweds and acted accordingly.

Brenda decided to call Alfons to see how he and Monica were weathering the storm. She also had an itch to find out how the proposal went over. Monica was feeding money into a silver dollar slot machine when he answered.

"Hello, Alfons. Is the Empire State Building swaying in the wind?"

"Brenda, no it's fine." He signaled Monica with a finger across his throat in hopes she'd get the message that Brenda was on the phone. But no, she kept dropping in coins and pulling the handle, which didn't escape Brenda's keen hearing.

"Alfons? Do you have a casino up there? I hear a lot of dinging and hubbub in the background."

That's when Monica's slot machine hit triple ribbons. Bells went off like a fire alarm and Monica screamed with delight. "Jackpot, Alfons. I hit the jackpot before breakfast."

"What are you two doing in Atlantic City? That hurricane is going to plough the place under—"

"Brenda, we're a little farther west than Atlantic City."

"How far west?"

"Say about two thousand five hundred miles."

"You're not..?"

"We are."

"You didn't..?"

"We did."

Now Brenda let out a squeal. "Congratulations."

All the sisters gathered around, bombarding her with questions. "Who is it?" "What's happening?"

"Monica and Alfons got married in Las Vegas."

Now the sisters started screaming and crying, hell, the hurricane took second seat to all the chaos.

Handing Monica his cell, he said with a smile, “She knows.”

“Is it not exciting?” Monica sang into the phone.

“Well, hey. Thanks for inviting us.”

“I was going to call but it happened so fast.”

“We think it’s wonderful. When are you coming home?”

“Not during a hurricane, I can tell you that much.”

“Have fun.”

Brenda hung up and didn’t know whether to laugh or cry.

***

Back on the *USS Carmick*, the radar operator saw that the Nandoso had changed course to a heading that would put them steaming into Long Island Sound. Less than five minutes later, Lawrence and Roy were notified of the ship’s change in direction. Ten minutes later, General Wesley Miller was on the line. “General Taylor, there’s been a weather delay. Air Traffic Control has shut down or diverted all flights into the hurricane zone. We had to land at Joint Base McGuire-Dix in New Jersey. The weather here is atrocious. They tell us we won’t get back in the air until sometime tomorrow.”

“Shit, that means the girls are on their own.”

“Sorry, sir.”

Taylor had to think fast. “Get a duce and a half from the motor pool. Load up what men and equipment you can and drive to The Ranch.”

“In this storm? We’ll never get through.”

“You will get through and that’s an order.” Taylor slammed down the phone. “Goddess damned weather.” His only hope was that the weather would also deter the Taliban’s assault on The Ranch.

The sisters felt the rain-streaked windows shake under the intense barrage of the howling wind. The storm surge was so bad they could hear the waves crashing over the sand berm. Before long, sharks would be swimming in the pool.

However, that was the least of their worries. Lawrence Taylor called Jackie. “Miller and his bunch are grounded. They’ll be coming by truck, so it’s going to take a while. Until then, you’re on your own.” Phones were ringing in the background. “Gotta go.”

Jackie held the phone as if it had died in her hand. If the Taliban threat were to materialize, there was a good chance the sisters would have to fight for their lives. Sure, bullets were pretty much useless against lesbian zombies, and hand-to-hand combat could be quite fun: knocking out teeth, breaking bones, and busting balls, but headshots were tough to survive, and worse than that, jihadists were notorious for slicing off the heads of infidels. Even a lesbian zombie could not live without a head. A little firepower would come in handy, and for that she thought of Robert and Frank, two of the toughest warriors to ever grace the US military.

As if the phone had sprung back to life in her hand, she punched in Robert's number and filled him in on the problem.

"Yes, I have two AR-15s, a Colt .45, but not much ammunition. I'll check with Frank. We'll be there as fast as we can paddle."

Yeah, paddle was a pun, with the rain, flooding, and storm surge going on, but Jackie didn't find it funny. "Please hurry."

And she had good reason to want him to hurry. The Nandoso had crossed the outer marker, heading toward Long Island Sound. The Coast Guard cutter was unable to leave port to intercept, and the *USS Carmick* was twenty nautical miles out but closing slowly, as the destroyer and its crew were taking a beating.

By the time Robert and Frank got to The Ranch it was close to 10:00pm. Their meager arsenal was more of a joke than anything that could seriously ward off a terrorist attack, but they'd have to make do. Robert reported that Maggie and Carrie and Zoey were hunkered down together to ride out the storm.

The Sisterhood hadn't heard from General Taylor, so they didn't know that the real danger facing them was mere hours away.

No one slept much that night, and daylight only revealed more of Helen's fury: black skies and torrential rain driven by 120 mph winds. The angry surf had climbed the berm where the wind hurled foamy seawater across the lawn in ribbons, gurgling and undulating like some kind of alien had come ashore.

The sisters, dressed for combat in jeans and t-shirts, watched the tempest from the shuddering windows as it went about its destructive nature. The potted ferns had all blown over, the hot tub lid was nowhere to be seen, and the pool had collected a layer of floating leaves, weeds, and branches. The Ranch had seen better days, but one thing lightened the sisters' mood: the Crystal Shrine looked fully intact.

Coffee was being brewed. Everyone had gathered in the dining room where their meager arsenal had been laid out on the long table. Robert and Frank were meticulously checking each handgun and the two AR-15s with two fully loaded clips at the ready.

In Long Island Sound, Abadi and his jihadists were half beat to death, and the calmer waters were of much relief. His prediction that the hurricane would have passed upon the Nandoso's approach was proof positive why he would have been a lousy weatherman. Instead, Helen had lumbered up the east coast at a crawling six miles per hour. He knew of goats that moved faster. However, as Allah would have it, the eye of the hurricane would soon move over the Sound, and conditions for the assault on the infidel women would improve, though time would be limited.

As the forward deck had been piled high with fishing nets, he and his fighters prepared their rubber inflatable boats on the aft deck. Outboards were mounted and fueled and weapons were loaded, leaving just enough room for four fighters on two plank seats and one in the rear to steer the motor. Since he had lost half his men to the storm, he only required ten rafts for those who were left to fight on, and at this very moment, they were being off loaded into the waves.

"Allahu Akbar. Allahu Akbar."

Out on the Atlantic, the *USS Carmick* had crawled within binocular range, and the lookout, strapped to the swaying superstructure, observed a disturbing scene through his pitching round lens. Ten rubber inflatables bobbed in the water around the Nandoso, and he caught glimpses of turban-clad fighters, heavily armed and motoring toward shore. Slightly elevating the binoculars, he caught sight of the storm-battered mansion, and called down a warning to the bridge via his headset. "Captain, the assault has begun."

Just as he said that, fishing nets piled on the Nandoso's forward deck hurled a blast of fire and smoke. "Incoming," he shouted.

Captain Marquez gave the order. "Commence firing."

The cannon blasts from the Carmick's forward battery were

deafening. Each kaboom was followed by a shock of air that threatened to suck the lookout from his post. As the water in the Sound was much calmer than it was out at sea, targeting still proved to be a challenge as the ship pitched and yawed in the waves. Through sheets of driving rain, the lookout watched shell after shell detonate in the water, until finally, one hit home. The Nandoso lit up like a Roman candle as its ammunition stores exploded. Within minutes, the smoking hull rolled to port and plunged bow-first into the depths.

As if Allah himself had opened the heavens to receive his faithful jihadists, the eye of the hurricane made landfall over the Sound. Sunlight revealed the angry eyewall towering above the Carmick, and sunbeams glistened off the sea-swells' frothy lips. Gulls and pelicans soared on the breeze.

Any commander of a sea battle would think peace on earth had arrived in all its glory, but the black rubber boats buzzing toward the beach gave this picturesque scene an ugly stain.

Robert was the first to see them coming. "Frank." He tossed him an AR-15. "Set up a field of fire toward the beach. Use the pool wall for cover. And make every shot count."

Frank ducked out the back door to a sunny pool deck, and though thankful for the lull, he knew Helen's fury would soon return with a one-two punch from the opposite direction.

"Girls..." Robert turned to see the sisters standing shoulder-to-shoulder with mean snarls on their normally pretty faces. "Go to the basement and lock the door."

Damn if it wasn't Donna who broke ranks and grabbed the AR-15 right out of Robert's hands. "You go to the basement. We're here to kick some ass."

"Well, okay then. Betsy, Caroline. Down you go."

"Ah," Caroline complained. "We never get to kill anyone."

"Go."

"Come on, Girlie Dog," Betsy called.

"No. The dog stays up here." Robert knew she'd be an asset in this fight, and by the way she'd handed Butch his balls, the Taliban would likely fall prey to her gnashing jaws.

Jane pulled a Glock from her waistband and chambered a round.

"Where'd you get that gun?"

"Never leave home without it." She joined Frank on the pool deck.

Jackie and Brenda armed themselves with a kitchen cleaver and a rolling pin, Lilly and Melinda, frying pans, while Chloe and Maria got dibs on the remaining handguns. Robert, of course, had his trusty Army-issued Colt .45, the clip shy one bullet that had blown the rapist's brain out.

Three Taliban boats rode the waves to the beach. Fifteen fighters jumped out and pounded sand over the berm. "Allahu Akbar."

This was a battle cry Frank thought he'd never hear. For Robert it was Afghanistan all over again.

Being their first line of defense, Frank and Jane opened up on the invaders. As there was no cover between the berm and the ranch, the pickin's were easy. However, as the second wave hit the beach, they were soon out of ammunition and had to retreat into the house.

Robert and Donna took their places and made short work of the front-running jihadists. With his back to the wall, he slapped another clip into his Colt and looked at Donna.

"I'm out," she said.

A bearded and rag-topped fighter jumped up on the wall, "Allahu Akbar," and lowered his AK-47 at Donna. Robert reached up, grabbed the barrel, and yanked him to the ground. The gun screamed *rat-a-tat-tat*, but with a twist of his arm, Robert aimed the spray of bullets at the fighter who'd just scaled the wall. Bad timing for him. He keeled over, but by the time he hit the pool deck, Robert had disarmed his attacker, and with a quick burst of Russian justice, sent his soul to Allah.

"Thanks," Donna said, breathless.

He handed her the AK-47. "I didn't survive Iraq to get killed by these sand slugs on my home soil." He frisked the dead bodies, came up with four thirty-round clips, then picked up Mohammad Bad Timer's dropped weapon just as three more fighters topped the wall. Donna quickly dispatched them to heaven to meet their maker.

By now, Frank had reloaded, Jane too, and as they rushed to back up Robert and Donna at the wall, a kamikaze jihadist blew the front door off its hinges and charged in through the smoke, only to be met head-on by Melinda's frying pan. He hit the foyer floor just as five other fighters trampled him as they rushed in, AKs ablaze. "Allahu Akbar." They were met with a volley of bullets from Frank, Jane, Chloe, and Maria.

As the smoke cleared, Jackie spotted a camel jockey kneeling in the street beyond the portico with a rocket propelled grenade launcher propped on his shoulder. She threw the eight-inch cleaver with the power of a lumberjack and the accuracy of stinger missile. As the knife blade found his heart, he keeled over sideways and pulled the trigger. The unleashed rocket propelled grenade took out six fighters staged at the berm for a third assault.

The sisters gave each other high-fives and smiles.

The jubilation didn't last long. As a good general knows, in a battle he must guard his flanks, right and left, and his rear, even as he attacks from the front. With no one watching their left flank, the door to the Crystal Shrine stood unguarded. Shattering glass announced their fortifications had been breached. Two terrorists stormed through the dining room, shooting up chandeliers and blasting china to smithereens.

For one of them, the battle turned south when Girlie Dog ran up behind him and latched onto his ass. Oh how he screamed to the sound of ripping flesh and trousers. His buddy spun around and put a bullet in Girlie Dog, but that didn't faze her a bit. While his brain tried to fathom a bulletproof dog, Brenda bashed him with the rolling pin. The crack of cranial bones reminded her of the baseball she'd knocked out of the ballpark.

Abadi charged into battle with the last wave. The back wall of the mansion was heavily defended so he waved five of his men to assault the boarded-up greenhouse. Already the dirty side of the storm was bearing down upon them. Time was running out, maybe only twenty minutes before they got socked by Helen again.

Of the five men who entered the greenhouse, none had come out, and he'd heard no gunfire from within, so he scrambled low and ducked inside, rifle locked and loaded.

The light was bad on account of all the boarded-up glass panels, but it wasn't bad enough that he couldn't make out the sprawling branches of a tree from which hung by their feet the decapitated bodies of his fellow fighters, blood still dripping to the floor.

His throat felt the strangling grip of Satan himself. “What kind of unholy abomination is this?”

Fear ploughed through his chest. He turned to flee, but blocking his way to the door shimmered the ghostly image of a sweet little girl wearing a long blood-stained dress with frilly shoulder sleeves, a sin in Allah’s eyes.

“My name is Jasmine al-Hakim.” Her voice was hollow and distant.

“No.”

“Remember the stones you threw in your brother’s bidding as I lay in the street, screaming for Allah to save me?”

“You lie.” He let loose the AK to bring her down, but the bullets...they passed right through her body as the wind passes through the air.

She rushed him with a snarl and pushed him over the railing, and down into the pit he fell, landing on his back, the air knocked from his lungs. The vines and roots whipped their chorded laces around him, gathered him together like a mummy, and crushed him in their hungry embrace. Yes, that was the end of Aqib Asad Abadi. Only now did he learn the truth of death, of Allah and heaven and hell, along with the true value of his righteousness over women and beasts. None of it was worth a plug nickel.

As the shuttered panels again shuddered in the rising wind, the Sister Tree of Life consumed the bodies of the wicked until no trace of what had happened here remained. Jasmine, sweet Jasmine, faded into the shadows to once again reside with Loa in the universe.

Just before Helen blew her mighty breath across Long Island again, a duce and a half rattled up the drive. It stopped under the portico where Rangers jumped out and, rifles in hand, set up a perimeter defense so others could unload the armament and rations.

General Wesley Miller stepped out of the cab, not unlike General MacArthur’s return to the Philippines, a proud man on a mission of salvation for the people therein. A gust of windblown rain slapped him in the face.

Frank and Robert ran out the blasted front doorway and greeted him with salutes, more a force of habit than any military protocol. “Thank God you’re here, sir.”

Behind them, the jihadist who'd suffered a frying-pan blow to the head stirred.

"Where do we stand with the terrorists?"

Robert gave him the details as he knew them. "Ten boats landed, each with five fighters, maybe fifteen remaining. They're lying low, probably regrouping."

Frank added, "We have a body count, best we can tell, thirty-five—"

A gun blast exploded from the foyer. Frank dropped to the ground, even as Robert whipped around and fired three shots into the jihadist sitting up on the floor."

"Allahu Akbar," he spluttered and fell over dead.

It was then that Robert noticed Frank was down and bleeding. He dropped to his knees. "Frank. Frank."

"Platoon, advance," Miller ordered. "Search and destroy. Kill every last one of these sons-of-bitches."

The Rangers went to work fighting wind and rain and Taliban holdouts. Sporadic gunfire mixed with the rolling thunder of Helen's ferocious return.

"Medic." No one responded. He didn't have a medic, and the man at his feet needed a hospital full of them.

"Frank," Robert shouted. He'd already lifted Frank's head from the ground.

His eyes were jerking around. "Robert...tell Carrie...I love her."

"Hang in there, Frank."

Wind and rain blasted from Helen's bosom as her dirty side unleashed hell on earth.

"There's no getting a medivac chopper in this weather," Miller shouted over the tempest. "He's not going to make it."

"Help me get him inside."

The sisters rushed out and carried Frank into the foyer. They had to step over dead Taliban as they hefted Frank's shuddering body to the couch in the sitting room.

"Where's Brenda? Somebody get Brenda."

"I'm right here, Robert." She got down on her knees beside Frank. "You're bleeding all over my couch, Frank."

"Help me...like you helped...Robert. I don't want to die."

"He looks like a goner to me," General Miller said.

Brenda ripped open his shirt to examine his spurting wound. The bullet had pierced Frank's back, ripped through his spinal cord, and blew out his sternum in a spray of blood and bone splinters. Somewhere along the way, fragments of lead had nicked his aorta, thus the arterial spurting.

"It's bad, Frank. Close your eyes."

"No. I'm afraid...I'll never open them...again."

"Trust me, Frank. And don't move. Don't react, just let me do what I've got to do."

He closed his eyes. She leaned in and kissed him, a full open-mouthed kiss with tongue and all. He didn't move. Not for the entire minute. Then she spit on her hand and rubbed his chest wound.

Before everyone's eyes, the blood stopped spurting between her fingers, and as she lifted her hand, the wound healed over. He sat up, looked at Robert, nodded, then threw his arms around Brenda and whispered in her ear, "Now I'm ready to hear the truth."

Wes was speechless. He looked at his hand, remembered the redheaded angel of the battlefield, looked at Brenda's red hair, all the smiling faces around her, and he suddenly knew he was walking among angels.

***

The dawn brought peace and tranquility to Long Island. Hurricane Helen had whirled off into the North Atlantic, leaving her muddy and debris-strewn footprint behind. Clean up was underway, roads were made passable, and the air was filled with the buzz of chainsaws clearing downed trees.

At The Ranch, General Wesley Miller, still befuddled over the miracles he'd witnessed, directed his troops to body-bag the dead Taliban and collect their weapons for proper disposal. Several of his men were dispatched to the beach to deflate and recover the rafts used for the incursion. By the time they finished, there was no physical evidence that a battle had taken place at The Ranch.

Melinda and Donna and Maria went about the gruesome task of cleaning blood spatter from the walls, floors, and pool deck. Soap, water, bleach, and a lot of lesbian zombie elbow grease would soon make the mansion shine. Yeah, there were hundreds of bullet holes to repair, and several windows, too, for which contractors would be hired in the coming days. The shattered chandeliers in the dining room would take longer to replace. They'd have to come all the way from France.

Robert and Frank helped Chloe and Lilly take the boards down from the Crystal Shrine. Not a single crack was found in any of the crystalline panels. Brenda and Jackie noticed something different about the Sister Tree of Life. Its branches and broad leaves seemed aglow with vibrant color, as if it had been recently fed fresh fertilizer or some other form of nutrients. It was there, as the sun shone through, that Brenda told Frank the truth about the Sisterhood, Carrie, and himself, and how Loa had bestowed upon them a child who would one day grow to become a lovely lesbian zombie herself.

Not long after Frank left, Caroline and Betsy stormed into the Crystal Shrine, yelling, "Those bad Taliban shot our dolls off the top of our dresser."

"They're all full of holes," Betsy added.

"If we can find those terrorists, we're going to kill them again."

"Easy, girls." Brenda gathered them into her arms. "We can always buy new dolls."

"But they're our favorites."

"Okay. Maybe we can fix them. Go play nurses and bandage them up, for now."

"Come on, Betsy." Caroline grabbed her best friend's hand. "I know where the Band-Aids are." And off they ran on a new mission for the Sisterhood.

General Miller and his troops loaded the duce and a half with their grisly cargo and headed off down the road. He would soon be back in the arms of a very proud Lynne. They drove past a horde of news vehicles heading for The Ranch with satellite antennas and cameras at the ready.

Brenda let the reporter from WNN on to The Ranch. "Hello, everyone. This is Thad Harper reporting from ground zero of the Taliban terrorist attack on the United States." While he got the exclusive scoop, Girlie Dog chased the other reporters away.

Once again, the sisters made worldwide news, but not

everyone was praising them for their Alamo-like stand against the terrorists. The Supreme Leadership Authority, the Grand Ayatollah himself, denied any involvement nor took ownership of the Nandoso, sunk by the *USS Carmick* in US territorial waters.

The President, in his Oval Office, was walking around in circles, screaming to his FBI director, "Why didn't General Taylor get my permission for a military operation to aid those bitches? I would have told them no, and hell no. Now Brenda Ayler has another bow in her bonnet, got the whole damn country calling her a national hero again."

"But, sir, let me remind you, the Secret Service has recruited two rookie agents to wrangle Brenda."

"What's taking so long?"

"We are remodeling the Presidential safe room for your unsuspecting guest at Camp David. You haven't lost this election yet, sir."

For Brenda and her sisters, the long day at The Ranch had turned to night. They gathered in the sitting room to watch TV and enjoy each other's company, thankful no one was lost to the Taliban's evil retribution. Yes, they had lived through it all and now basked in praise from news anchors and lighthearted fun from late-night comedians.

Chapter Forty

On the Comedy Central's nightly special, the guest host, Bill Mayer, was drinking a bottle of Brenda's favorite beer from Haiti, Prestige, and he suggested a great use for the Sisterhood. "Hell, if we have to fight a war in the Middle East, don't send in the Army. Just send the Sisterhood. They will shoot the hell out of everything in sight. Damn war would be over in a week."

The audience laughed.

"The National Rifle Association presented each sister with their very own pink AR-15, even engraved their names on the stocks, and added 20,000 rounds of ammunition so they'd never again have to fight the Taliban with kitchen knives and rolling pins."

As the laughter resonated from a television in New London, Carrie was fixing stew for dinner. Frank, good as new, stepped up behind her and slipped his arms around her waist and clasped his hands under her ever-growing stomach. "You knew what you and your sisters were all along, lesbian zombies, and you didn't tell me. Why?"

Turning around, spoon in hand, she slipped her arms around his neck. "Would you have believed me?"

"Well, maybe not, but I'm convinced now."

"You gave my sisters quite a scare, you know."

"I was sure I was going to die, but I remembered how Brenda had helped Robert when he was paralyzed, so in a leap of faith, I asked her to do the same for me. I had no idea her kiss was so potent."

"It's Loa, the Goddess of the Universe who gave her that power."

"Brenda told me the truth, and that I too am protected by

Loa's virus now. That makes me one of you...like your sisters... And Jorge. I asked her why that bullet damn near killed me, since I've been sleeping with you, and she said your kiss isn't as potent as hers because you're pregnant. And Robert, he knows all about the Sisterhood, but he's not protected like me because Maggie isn't a lesbian zombie. She's immune to the virus because of the medication she was on...like an antidote, she said, and Robert took the antidote for a while after Brenda kissed him to save his life. And Loa has a lot to do with all of us being the way we are."

"Frank, I'm happy you're not running for the hills after hearing the truth about us."

"And miss all this fun? No way."

"Promise me one thing."

"Anything."

"I want our baby to be dedicated to Loa, too."

"I promise. Now give me a kiss."

***

Meanwhile, back at The Ranch, while Jackie and Brenda were planning their next event on WNN, Chloe, Donna, Maria, Lilly, and Melinda were bored out of their minds. Chloe said, "Let's drive down to that Biker tits-and-ass bar, drink some beer, play some pool, get a little wild and crazy."

The sisters cheered the idea.

Maria, deliberately being obnoxious, smiled at Brenda. "Mommy, can we go out and play with the bikers?"

"Sure. Take the Mercedes and behave like ladies. The last thing we need is bad publicity."

The sisters all yelled, "You can count on us, Mother."

"Yeah. That's what I'm afraid of."

Forty-five minutes later, the dressed-to-kill sisters stepped out of the car and strutted their stuff past a neat row of parked Harley-Davidson motorcycles, some chopped, some expensive touring models, all the pride and joy of some man inside.

After making their grand entrance and turning more than a few heads, Chloe spotted Tammy and two other girls, Captain Kathy and Sue, from *Three Sheets to the Wind.* They were sitting at a table with two bikers, one black, one white, and both looked like they'd escaped from a tattoo parlor. Braving the smokey haze, the sisters paraded to the table, which immediately erupted in screams, squeals, and laughter.

The looks on the bikers' faces were priceless, like they'd just won the lottery of let's-get-laid. Donna was the first to break their bubbles. "Get lost, boys."

The black dude said, "Hey, we were here first."

"Take a hike."

He stood up, all big and bad in his leather vest of patches and pins. "We ain't goin' nowhere, bitch."

"Yeah, you are." She grabbed him by the balls and squeezed. Her grip wasn't like any other woman's grip: it was a lesbian zombie grip, much like a real nutcracker.

He bent over and let out a yell that drew the attention of everyone in the place. "Let me go, lady, please. I want to have kids someday."

The white biker shot out of his chair, big and bad too, but before he could jump in to help his black friend, Chloe wagged a finger at him. "I wouldn't if I were you."

The big and burly bouncer bounded over. "What's the problem here?"

Chloe released her grip on the biker's gonads. "No problem, sir. Just a little misunderstanding over some family jewels."

"Both you clowns..." the bouncer bellowed, "find something better to do than harass these poor ladies."

The white badass helped the black badass limp to the far side of the bar, well out of harm's way.

Wood scraped hardwood as the sisters collected spare chairs from other tables and got seated with their sailor girlfriends. "Beers all around," Melinda called to the bartender. Hugs and cheek-kisses lip-smacked back and forth. Now that the sisters had the yacht crew to themselves, the girls started to make up for lost time.

Chloe said to Tammy, "We've missed you guys. What brings you to Long Island?"

"We sailed Alfons' new yacht out of the Brooklyn Docks and moored it at Strong's Marina not far from here. A guy there specializes in upgrading sound systems. Alfons wants to rock the world, I guess."

"We sure had some good times together," Sue sang. "Melinda, remember bikini wrestling with me in the volley ball sand pit?"

She laughed. "We were topless in the first thirty seconds."

"That's because you cheated."

They laughed but Captain Kathy looked a little glum all of a sudden. "I sure do miss *Girls' Night Out*. Breaks my heart that she's on the bottom of the Arabian Sea."

"Hey," Tammy said. "*Three Sheets to the Wind* is bitchin' though. You should see the showers."

"Is that an invitation?"

"Yes. We've gotta go sailing again sometime. Bathing suits optional."

They all laughed. The beers were delivered. Donna offered up a toast. "Here's to good times on the high seas."

"Yay." They chugged beers like sailors on shore leave.

"Where's LeeAnne and Joan?" Maria asked. "Those ladies were terrific on submarine patrol."

"Actually, they're on their honeymoon," Tammy said.

Captain Kathy held up her beer. "I married them two weeks ago."

"I'm sure going to miss our threesomes."

"And guess what," Lilly jumped in. "Monica and Alfons got married in Vegas."

"Yes. We heard. Isn't that great?"

"I have trouble thinking of her as Mrs. Duda, though."

"Me too," Maria said sadly.

Chloe slapped her on the shoulder. "Hey, you've always got me."

"Me too," Donna chimed in.

Yes, the lesbians and lesbian zombies were having a wonderful time, but as the nature of the beast often showed its teeth, the bikers just couldn't stay out of it. Many of them thought they were God's gift to women, some had more respect for a worm in the garden, but the drunk at the near-end of the bar had only contempt for women, like maybe his wife wore the pants in the house, or maybe he preferred bloody noses to goodnight kisses. Whatever the case, when Chloe and Melinda passed by on the way to the restroom, he made the fatal mistake of grabbing Chloe's wrist. "Come sit in my lap, whore."

As he jerked her around, Chloe let loose her rage against men with an elbow to his bearded chin. That could have knocked most men off the barstool, but this bruiser took it with a laugh. She pried his grip from her wrist and broke all four of his fingers, leaving the thumb for him to suck in the hospital.

Melanie grabbed a handful of gray beard and yanked his head back, leaving Chloe a clear shot for a fist to his throat. As he gasped for air, Melanie let go of his beard and spun him around on the stool. Once. Twice. Then coming around on three, his face ran smackdab into Chloe's hard right hook. Now that blow knocked him off the barstool. He wasn't laughing as his three hundred pounds of flab hit the floor, but he didn't feel a thing. He was out cold.

Six other drunk bikers rolled in to avenge their downed brother. This drew the sisters into the fray, joined by six sailors from the Navy's submarine school. Within seconds, a knuckle-busting bar brawl was in full swing. Chairs were broken on backs, and bottles were broken on heads. Fists broke teeth and jaws, black eyes blossomed, and blood spattered.

As the big, burly bouncer jumped in to stop the chaos, the sisters and sailor girls ducked low and dashed outside, where they huddled together, hugging and laughing their asses off.

"Come back to our place," Melinda said. "We can continue the party in our pool."

Tammy batted her eyelashes. "But I don't have my bikini."

"Lucky you." Maria giggled.

"Come on," Lilly cheered. "The Mercedes is over here."

As the girls ran past the row of parked motorcycles, it was man-hater Chloe who stopped long enough to give the first bike a kick. All the others went down like dominoes.

Screaming and cheering, the girls piled into the car, and off they went, speeding on their way to relive old times with hot tub bubbles, wine, and a whole lot of submarine diving.

***

Back at The Ranch, Brenda sat in shock at what she was seeing on the TV. Fists and elbows were flying in an exclusive video from WNN, sailors and bikers duking it out in a biker bar. And sure enough, the sisters were in the middle of the smackdown. The barroom was being reduced to rubble before her eyes. “Goddess dammit,” she grumbled.

The Mercedes pulled up the drive. Cheering and laughing sisters were hanging out the windows like high school girls after a homecoming game. They piled out and headed for the pool, flinging blouses and bras as they ran.

“What a bunch of bean brains.” Brenda stormed out to the pool where the sisters and their guests were already frolicking in the water. “Girls. What the hell happened at the bar?”

“We didn’t start it,” Chloe said with her arm around Tammy’s neck as they bobbed in the deep end.

“You put five bikers and three sailors in the hospital.”

“Boys will be boys.” Lilly laughed.

“You’ve got to stop this nonsense. You know there are cell phone cameras everywhere. And video of you guys raising hell sells for top dollar.”

“Mommy, don’t be mad.” That was babytalk from Maria. “We’ll be good.” She looped an arm around Donna and pulled her into a juicy kiss as proof to how good they could be.

“You’re impossible.” Brenda trounced back into the house.

Jackie was walking around in her housecoat. “What the hell is going on? I was sleeping—”

Brenda’s cell phone chimed in. She checked the display. “Oh, oh. It’s General Taylor.” She answered. “What’s wrong now, Lawrence?”

“I saw the WNN video. Those girls have to be driving you nuts. How about you and Jackie join me and Roy for breakfast at the officers club? They serve up a mean steak and eggs.”

She cupped her hand over the phone. “Jackie, do you want to go to breakfast with Lawrence and Roy?”

“Is that all they want?”

“Yes or no will do.”

“Okay.” She popped a coffee pod into the Keurig. “Yes. I can’t get any sleep around here, anyway, not with those crazy girls partying on the deck.”

Brenda uncovered the phone. “You’re on.”

“Great. We’ll pick you up in Roy’s Sikorsky, say two hours?”

"We'll be ready."

At three forty-five in the morning, under the slap of rotor blades and whine of turbine engines, bright landing lights guided a US Navy Sikorsky to the front lawn at The Ranch.

Jackie and Brenda were already dressed and ready to go. As they dashed from under the portico, toward the idling chopper, the sisters and yacht-crew girls raced around to the front of the house to wave goodbye. All were barefoot and wrapped in beach towels.

An air crewman helped Brenda and Jackie get aboard and get seated. By this time, all the racket woke up Caroline and Betsy. With Girlie Dog at their heels, they ran downstairs and burst out the front door.

"Where are they going?" Caroline asked Maria.

"Breakfast."

"We wanna go," Betsy cried.

With a blast of noise and turbulence, the chopper rose into the dark sky, its navigation lights flashing red and green.

Maria tousled Betsy's hair. "Too bad. Looks like it's Coco Puffs for you guys."

***

One hour and forty five minutes later, as the sun rose over the Atlantic, the Sikorsky landed at Fort Meade, Maryland. Alongside the helipad, an SUV awaited the guests of honor. Lawrence and Roy stepped out to greet Brenda and Jackie. "Good morning, ladies."

"You guys look all spiffy in your uniforms." Brenda kissed Roy on the cheek. "It's so good to get out of that madhouse."

Lawrence hugged Jackie. "You deserve a break."

The officers held the doors, and the top-running candidates for the White House got into the SUV. Lawrence nodded to the driver and got in next to Jackie. After a short drive, they arrived at the Officers Mess for that much-touted breakfast.

The place was already packed, and hummed with the sounds of conversations and cutlery at work. No one was sitting at the table permanently reserved for General Lawrence Taylor and friends. As the foursome entered the vast expanse of tables and serving lines, a bird Colonel jumped to attention. "All ranks, attention. Commanding Chiefs of Staff in the mess hall."

Chairs scraped the shining tile floor as personnel stood to attention. Now Taylor could hear a gnat scratch its ass. "At ease, all ranks."

After sitting down, no one in the hall looked in their direction and continued on as if their meals were never interrupted. Jackie said, "When Brenda is your Commander in Chief, will you stand at attention when she walks in?"

"Yeah. Kind of hard to imagine our friendship turning to military protocol, but rest assured, the appropriate respect will be shown at the appropriate times."

They were seated, and top-brass waitstaff attended to their food orders and stood by for anything they needed. As breakfasts went, it had been a long time since Brenda had one so peaceful. No little girls running around, no dog barking, no sisters whining about this and that, and best of all, no dishes to wash.

After a while, the breakfast rush cleared out, as everyone had hustled off to attend to their daily duties for their country. Now, with a nearly empty mess hall, save for a few stragglers, it was quiet enough for the four to talk business.

Lawrence spoke up first. "As you know, the two political parties opposing you, at this very moment, are conniving ways they think will steal the election from you."

"We got that," Brenda said. "They've already asked us to drop out or they'll muddy our campaign with bullshit leaks about our employees in Haiti."

"Roy and I met with them at Camp David, and they wanted our help to get rid of you."

"Nukes," Roy added. "They really like the idea of us nuking you."

Brenda almost spit out her coffee.

"We told them no, of course, so they suggested we feed you to the sharks."

Jackie chuckled. "That would certainly knock us out of the race."

"Do you think the girls' bar fight hurt us?"

"Hell no. The country has fallen in love with the Sisterhood. You're like Charlie's Angels on steroids. Medal of Freedom honorees, Taliban fighters, and women crusaders. You're bulletproof, and they know it."

"Just the same," Roy added, "Don't let your guard down. Desperate times call for desperate action. No telling how low they'll go to discredit the LZF Party."

Lawrence glanced at Roy then back to Brenda. "So...we don't know if this is one of the President's low blows, but he's ordered joint operational readiness drills in San Diego, and he ordered us to watch over the commanders and rate their performances. We're leaving this afternoon."

"We'll be incommunicado." Roy leaned forward. "We don't know if this is a ploy to get us out of the way or not, but if you ladies need anything while we're gone, contact General Wesley Miller. He's at Joint Base McGuire-Dix." He slid a card to Jackie. "Here's his cell phone number."

"Okay, but we're going to be fine."

"Thanks for the heads-up, guys." Brenda pulled the embroidered Army napkin off her lap. "But you could have called us with this information instead of buying us breakfast."

"I'm not satisfied the FBI has turned off their listening ears, besides, it was good to see you."

"We've had a wonderful time."

"The chopper will take you back to The Ranch."

"Have fun in San Diego."

Lawrence laughed. "I doubt it."

Chapter Forty-One

Later that afternoon, the Sikorsky landed at The Ranch. Jane met Brenda and Jackie as soon as they got off the helicopter. "The polls are off the charts," she shouted over the ascending chopper's fury. "A reporter said, that if the election were held today, the candidates from the LZF Party would likely receive 520 Electoral College votes."

"Sounds like this one is in the bag."

As soon as they got inside, Caroline and Betsy ambushed them. "Where did you go?" "Was it fun to ride in a helicopter?" "What did you have for breakfast?"

The sisters ran in from the pool deck, Donna, Maria, Chloe in the lead. "Why didn't we get to go?" came from Donna, "Why didn't you spend the night?" came from Maria, and "Can Tammy and Sue sleep over?" came from Chloe.

Girlie Dog was jumping up and down and barking like a hound on a racoon's trail.

If lesbian zombies got headaches, this one would be a doozy. "Girls, settle down. Give us a chance to clean up and change our clothes, then we'll tell you all about our trip."

Brenda and Jackie bounded up the stairs.

"I'll be in the library..." Jane announced, "watching the poll numbers come in."

While this was going on, the door chimes rang. Caroline and Betsy ran to see who it was. As soon as they opened the door, two guys, all dressed in black and wearing sunglasses, pushed their way into the foyer, and with one hand in the slat of their suit jackets set about checking rooms. Caroline knew right away they were Secret Service agents looking for Brenda Ayler. Both girls ran for the stairs. "Brenda, Brenda, you better come down here."

Girlie Dog wagged her tail at them, having not sensed anything wrong.

"What's all the fuss?" Brenda and Jackie ran down the stairs, both wearing only their bras and panties. When they saw the strangers in the house, they stopped cold. "What are you doing in my house?" Jackie shouted.

"Ma'am, we don't mean to alarm you." Both agents flipped out their badges. "We're from the Secret Service, looking for Brenda Ayler."

Brenda said, "That's me. What do you want?"

"Brenda Ayler, you're under our protection now."

"We don't need protecting."

"We've been sent to escort you to Camp David for a high-level meeting with the President."

"Bullshit." Brenda read the agent's minds, and low and behold, they were telling the truth. "The President, you say?"

"Yes, ma'am."

Jackie jumped in with, "She's got nothing to say to the President."

"That's not entirely true, Jackie." Brenda recalled how the President had copped out on their last meeting in the Oval Office, stuck them with the worthless VP who coddled up to the FBI like a piglet to a sow's teat. The words she wanted to say to the President were still stuck in her craw. "Fine. Do you mind if I put some clothes on first?"

"Whenever you're ready, ma'am. Our car is waiting outside."

"We're driving all the way to Camp David?"

"Actually, we're taking you on the President's helicopter. He's already there, waiting for you."

Jackie grumped. "Cocky bastard's pretty sure you'd accept his invitation."

"He's not only right, he's damn right."

Back in the bedroom, Jackie looked a little worried. "Brenda, are you sure this is a good idea?"

"They're legit, besides, it's the Secret Service. We'll have to get used to them hanging around." Brenda selected tight-fitting jeans, a frilly blouse, and sandals. No way was she dressing up for that buffoon.

"Should I call General Miller...tell him what's going on?

Wouldn't hurt to be on the safe side."

"I'll be fine, besides, four helicopter rides in one day? Hell, yeah. I'm starting to feel like the President already."

***

The President's helicopter was called Marine One whenever he was aboard, but when transporting the LZF candidate, Brenda Ayler, it was just another Sikorsky. The pilot was cleared to enter Camp David airspace, and within five minutes, she was on the ground. Two sharp Marines, proper as the US Honor Guard, escorted her to a bulletproof limo, commonly known as The Cadillac Beast, and the driver, courteous as could be, opened the back door and let her in. As she enjoyed the luxurious interior of fine leather and LED lighting fit for any nightclub, as was the car-bar, the Marines, along with the Secret Service agents, rode the footboards down tree-lined streets to a rustic lodge. As the driver let her out, she envisioned herself slipping away from the White House on weekends to recharge her fighting spirit in this Presidential retreat.

After stepping across a welcome mat that read *Laurel*, and once inside the squeaky-floored lobby, the Secret Service agents stopped her at a reception desk where an armed guard was posted. The sign on the counter read: *NO RECORDING DEVICES OR CELL PHONES BEYOND THIS POINT*. "Security, ma'am," he said and held out his open palm. She read his mind and discovered he was absolutely correct. The President was here and all precautions were taken to insure his privacy.

She surrendered her phone, stepped through a metal detector, and got a green light to enter the lodge. The agents escorted her to a dining room, where male dignitaries were seated and enjoying a fabulous fare befitting the most lavish of royal tables. Lively conversations died the moment she stepped into the room. To her surprise, she was led to the head of the table, and when her escorts pulled out a chair for her, the diners stood like their seats were suddenly set on fire. A quick scan of faces did not reveal the jowly features of the President.

She nodded to the men of governments from around the world, and everyone went back to their own meals and affairs. It took her a moment to get comfortable. *I'm being treated like a queen, and that's a welcomed relief.*

After she finished a plate of prime-rib, garlic potatoes, and asparagus tips, a chocolate moose was served with rich whipped cream and French port. It was easy to imagine her sisters here, joyously lavishing these luxuries on the taxpayers' dime. The Secret Service agents standing at parade-rest to her left and to her right, those she could do without.

As the hour latened, the diners thinned out and the conversations faded. She stood and addressed the SS agents. "I came to see the President at his invitation. Where the hell is he?"

"He's retired for the evening, ma'am. We've a very nice room for you for the night. Tomorrow, the two of you will be refreshed for your high-level meeting after breakfast."

"Could you follow me?" the other asked.

Why not? It's been a long day.

He led her down a long hallway where the eyes of former Presidents and famous guests looked out from gilded lighted frames like ghosts from the past: Dwight D. Eisenhour, John Fitzgerald Kennedy, Marilyn Monroe. The agent stopped at a door and punched a code into a keypad on the wall. The rhythmic beeps produced a metallic grating sound that clanked as the door opened. He stepped aside to let her pass.

The room was quite small but elaborately decorated in leafy 70's-style wallpaper, flowery linens, and ancient wooden furniture, a rocker and a nightstand, on which sat a golden ice bucket with an opened bottle of white wine, no doubt perfectly chilled, and a crystal flute beside it. A pushbutton phone, like any motel room might have, gave her a sense of connection to the outside world, now that her cell was in the safe hands of security. She paced to the attached bathroom, scanned the ornate lighting above a framed mirror and modern bowl sink with chrome fixtures. The four legged bath tub looked inviting, and just beyond that was a water closet with a crescent moon on the door. She sampled the aromas of soap, shampoos, and bubble bath crystals.

"Is everything to your liking, ma'am?"

She stepped out of the bathroom and noticed the flatscreen TV on the wall and the remote on the bedspread next to bonbons and a towel folded in the shape of a swan. An armoire made of dark wood stood next to a window with long, flower-print curtains. Curious of the view, she strode toward the window. "This is quite quaint, I'll say. I should be very comfortable here." She peeled back the curtains, saw a lighted courtyard of perfectly trimmed shrubs and benches, and like a bolt of lightning it hit her. Bars...thick steel bars, top to bottom, side to side. "Hey." She turned to the SS agent. "What the hell is this?"

"For your protection, ma'am. We don't want any prowlers getting in."

"Prowlers? This place has more security than Fort Knox."

"Don't be alarmed. Look right below the windowsill, see the lever marked emergency. In case a fire has you trapped in here, just pull the lever and the bars will pivot outward. Open the window and climb out. You're very safe here."

She read his mind and knew he was being honest with her. "That's a relief." She exhaled. "For a second there I thought I was a political prisoner."

He scoffed. "You're our guest, ma'am. Anything you need, just pick up the phone."

"Very well, goodnight then."

"Goodnight."

He backed out and closed the door, which responded with that metal scraping sound and a clank.

As she didn't have any luggage or change of clothes, curiosity drove her to the armoire. She opened the doors and discovered a lacy nightgown, long dresses, elaborate enough for eveningwear, a pantsuit with matching blazer, and two blouses to choose from...apparently in her size. *My size?* Checking the labels, her guess was correct, and as her heartbeat ticked up a notch, she pulled open drawers, leafed through panties and bras, all in her size too.

These bastards are expecting me to stay for a while.

She stormed to the phone, picked up the receiver, and to her horror, there was no dial tone. Even flicking the switch buttons didn't get a response. Seeing red, she slammed down the receiver and stormed to the door. It was locked. Normally, she could rip a door off its hinges, but this door wouldn't budge. Ten men couldn't break it down.

The window. She raced to the windowsill and pulled on the

lever. It snapped off like a dry stick. "Shit. These bastards are going to pay." She shouldered the wall with enough force to bust through any wall, but these walls must've been made of steel-reinforced concrete, both to the outside and to the hallway, neither even as much as creaked when she bulldozed her body into them.

"Dammit." Frustrated and pissed off, she sat on the bed and unwrapped a bonbon. Sooner or later, the sisters were going to suspect something was wrong. Her disappearance would be big news. She popped the bonbon in her mouth and grabbed the remote. No matter how many buttons she pushed, the TV wouldn't turn on. "No. No. No," she spluttered through her mouthful of chocolate. Examining the remote, she found the battery cover, and sure enough, no goddess damned batteries.

That drove her to the wine. To hell with the flute, she chugged right from the bottle. She might have been cut off from the world, but tomorrow was another day, and sooner or later someone was going to open that door, and when they did, they'd learn the true meaning of *no fury like a woman betrayed.*

***

At The Ranch, Jackie was again on the phone with General Wesley Miller. "She's not answering her phone. She would've called by now. It's been three days. Something terrible has happened to her, Wes."

"I've been trying to track her down, getting stonewalled at every turn. Nobody knows a damn thing."

"Camp David. She's gotta be there."

"Rcar Admiral Perkins, he's in charge, says she's not there."

"He's lying. Go see for yourself."

"I can't just walk into a naval facility. I'm an Army general, got no clout with the Navy."

Jackie's frustration was at level red. "I'm sure you can find a helicopter somewhere."

"Camp David security is impenetrable. Air defense batteries will shoot down any unauthorized aircraft within a ten mile radius. I need Admiral Roy Kincade to get in, but he and Taylor have been ferreted away on some phony special assignment. There is no joint training exercise in San Diego. I fear they're in the same deep shit as Brenda, and I'm sure it's the President's doing."

"Okay, Navy, you say." Jackie's wheels were turning now. "Frank was in the Navy. On the USS Carmick. He knows Captain Marquez. He's got a Sikorsky. Let me call you back."

***

Camp David might have been the playground of the government elite, but for Brenda Ayler, as the days to election drew down to a precious few, this place was hell on Earth. Completely cut off from the world was no way for a lesbian zombie to exist. If not for the bubble baths, she might have gone stir-crazy. Three times a day, someone slid food to her through a slot in the door as if she were a hamster. The food was excellent, of course, and her orders for wine were fulfilled, but she'd be damned if anyone would open the door.

It was after lunch on the third day, that, like the Wizard of Oz, the man behind the curtain appeared on the flatscreen, the jowl-faced buffoon known as the President of the United States. He started off with, "I trust you're being treated well."

She sat on the bed and glared at his image on the television. "What the hell's the matter with you? Leader of the free world and you don't have the balls to meet with me face-to-face?"

"You're a powerful woman, Brenda. I needed to knock you down a few pegs before we discuss the upcoming election."

"Oh? The one you're going to lose?"

"I don't take losing well, especially to a couple of broads."

"Broads? Don't you see? It's that very attitude that forced me and Jackie to run against you."

"Women can't run this country—"

"You're a male chauvinist pig. My sisters and I pulled off the assassination of a terrorist, for our own reasons, mind you, but you had the nerve to lay credit on yourself and your military buddies. We didn't want your stinking Medal of Freedom, but you had to make a big show for the media like we were the frosting on your cake. For that you're going to pay, buster. The LZF Party is your fault."

"I see now that you're still up on your high-horse, young lady, but let me be clear. You have three days to drop out of this election with grace and honor. If not, I'll have to take more drastic measures."

"What? You think you're going to kill me?"

"We have a very safe shooting range at Camp David, however, accidents do happen."

"You'll never get away with it."

"What a shame to waste such beauty, but I'll take power over beauty any day."

"That's obvious, you fat bastard."

The screen went black.

Brenda screamed to high heaven.

***

On the *USS Carmick*, while patrolling Long Island Sound after the hurricane, the Sikorsky was being scrambled. Just as the fueling lines were disconnected, the engines fired up and the rotor blades began to lazily rotate. Starboard of the battleship, *Three Sheets to the Wind* coasted alongside awaiting its tender to return, while a lone man ascended the rope netting to the Carmick's deck. Crewman greeted him with a flight suit and helmet.

Captain Marquez was there, as well. "Welcome back, AIRRs First Class Frank Leatherwood."

"Good to be here, Captain." He stepped into the flight suit. "Thanks for doing this."

"I'm glad you called. General Miller is waiting for you at Fort Dix. Have a nice flight."

"Thank you, sir." After zipping up, he donned the helmet and headed for the helipad. Oh how he'd missed the smell of aviation exhaust and deck soap. Jackie had pulled off a miracle. Once aboard the vibrating aircraft, he signaled the pilots with the OK sign. Engines revved to a deafening roar, and the Sikorsky took to the sky like an eagle from her nest.

The one-hundred-sixty-mile flight took less than an hour, and the bird was only on the ground for five minutes, long enough for General Miller to board and ground-crew to top off the fuel tanks for another one-hundred-sixty-mile jaunt to Camp David.

Frank and Wes shook hands, got seated, and strapped in. No words were needed between the two men. They both knew the urgency. They both knew the high stakes. They were both grateful to Brenda for her angelic mercies, and if she could walk on water, they would not have been surprised.

Fifty minutes later, the Navy helicopter was cleared to enter Camp David airspace. The pilot made quick work of the landing. A Marine guard rushed out to clear the aircraft and welcome the Army General.

"Take us to Rear Admiral Perkins."

The Marine frowned. "Do you have an appointment?"

"I don't need an appointment."

Wes and Frank pushed past the Marine, and they'd no sooner stormed into the Field House when two Secret Service agents stopped them. "May we help you, sir?"

"What are you SS boys doing here? The President is at the White House."

"We're here on special assignment."

Wes grumped. "You wouldn't be the two clowns who took Brenda Ayler from her home at The Ranch?"

"Yeah..." The two shared nervous glances. "We were told she had a high-level meeting with the President, but that never took place, yet she's still here, and we're still on her protection detail."

About that time, Rear Admiral Perkins joined the conversation, all dapper in his highly decorated white uniform. "General." He offered a handshake. "What can I do for you?"

"You can get Brenda Ayler out here right now."

He crooked his eyebrows. "The President has given me strict orders to say she's not here."

"Well, I know different now, don't I?"

"She stays where she is."

Frank pushed his way to the front. "You don't understand, sir. She's no ordinary woman. She's a—"

"Big deal," Perkins spouted off. "She's running for President, and it looks like she's going to win. You know what the means? Both the General and I will be working for her."

"Beg to differ, sir. You guys work for me, a citizen of the United States, same as Brenda Ayler when she's sworn in. She too will be working for us."

Perkins balked at that. "I don't know—"

Wes decided to go for broke. "When Frank here said Brenda

is no ordinary woman, he meant to add she's an angel, the Angel of the Battlefield, and twice I've seen her perform a miracle." He showed Perkins his hand. "This hand was shattered by an AK-47 round, and Brenda healed it with a spit...and Frank here, he was shot clean through his chest, and with only seconds to live, Brenda kissed him. One kiss, I tell you...and he was up and walking."

"Good as new," Frank said.

"I saw it with my own eyes, and I couldn't help but think of all the people who'd witnessed the healing power of Jesus Christ, the lepers, the blind, and didn't step up to vouch for him when he was nailed to that Roman cross. Nobody spoke up. We are here to bear witness for Brenda. Don't be Pontius Pilot. Let her go."

"An angel?"

"On Earth as it is in Heaven."

The Rear Admiral was actually sweating now. "The President...I've got to follow his orders. He's my Commander in Chief. I could get court-martialed—"

"In three days, Brenda Ayler will be your Commander in Chief, elect that is. My bet is you'll get a medal."

He shrugged. "Even so, I don't know the code to her room."

"We do," the Secret Service guy said.

"Let's go."

Ten minutes later, they blew through security at Laurel Lodge, setting off alarms in the metal detectors. One SS agent retrieved her cell phone, the other led Perkins, Miller, and Leatherwood to the door to Brenda's room.

"Brenda," Frank yelled to the door. "We've come—"

"She can't hear you. It's sound proof."

"Wanna bet? Brenda. We're coming in."

The door locks scraped and clanked, and when the door swung open, Brenda rushed out and threw her arms around Frank. "Thank goddess you're here. I couldn't stand another night of cheap wine and no TV."

"We had no idea," a Secret Service agent said. "We were duped into believing your trip here was legit."

She hugged them both, then moved on to General Wesley Miller. "Thank you. How's Lynne and the twins?"

"Doing great. Doing great. Now let's get you home. You've got an election to win."

Chapter Forty-Two

As election night rolled in, LZF Central was abuzz with activity: reporters, volunteers, T&A Caterers, all milling about in a stew of expectations as the vote counts came in. Flatscreens around the room relayed the tabulations as each state reported their results. Charles, Charlie, Mantella of WNN, dressed in suit and tie, stood before a map of the country, the states colored in red, blue, and green for their winning party as they racked up electoral college votes. Green dominated the land from sea to shining sea.

Brenda and Jackie waited and watched in the conference room where excitement electrified the air.

At 10:39 pm, Charles Mantella made the announcement everyone was waiting for. "WNN projects the winner. Brenda Ayler and Jackie O'Neal will be the next President and Vice President of the United States."

The place went wild. Confetti blew across the room. Balloons dropped from the ceiling as party favors whistled and popped.

"Speech, speech, speech," the crowd chanted.

Jackie stood and addressed Brenda. "Are you ready, madam President?"

"Let's do it."

They left the conference room, and pressing through the congratulatory crowd, made their way to the podium and the bouquet of microphones set up from networks across the nation. With Jackie on her right, the Sisterhood on her left, and Caroline and Betsy at her knees, Brenda gave her victory speech before a slew of cameras and bright lights.

"Thank you, everyone. Thank you. And we thank the women of this country for standing with us in our fight for women's equality."

Her speech wasn't buggered up with talk of the failings of the now-defunct major political parties or the corruption of the incumbent President, but she spoke of a brighter future for women all around the world. Would history record her speech as the greatest political address of all time? Probably not when compared to the Gettysburg Address or "December 7th, 1941, a date which will live in infamy," or "Ask not what your country can do for you, but what you can do for your country." However, the power of her words came from her heart, the heart of a leader of women, American women who possessed the strongest hearts in the universe.

Afterwards, scenes from the losers' campaign headquarters were broadcast. The despair, the shock, even the anger on the defeated candidates' faces were on display for the world to see. The President was defiant, claimed the election was rigged, and he vowed to get to the bottom of it, even if it meant taking his grievances all the way to the Supreme Court. Yeah, the dog eat dogs were still barking, and defeated men would never let them lie sleeping.

It was later that night, just as midnight chimed in a new beginning for the nation, that the Sisterhood gathered together on the berm in front of The Ranch and watched the fireworks bursting in air. Yes, good-old-Alfons had anchored *Three Sheets to the Wind* offshore, and his all-girl crew was having a ball lighting the rockets from the stern's helicopter pad.

Over the whoosh and kaboom of the brilliant displays, Brenda, hugging Jackie, heard again the siren's lullaby:

♪ *A year of nights, a year of days. Moonshine turning into rays. There never was, but there could be, a place in heaven, for a goddess like me...*♪

Then out of the blackness across the Sound came the overpowering blasts and fireballs from the cannons on the *USS Carmick*, a twenty-one gun salute the likes of which no human ears had ever heard.

As the fireworks lit The Ranch in brilliant displays, the sisters stood side-by-side and arm-in-arm and took in the fanfare with pride. Caroline and Betsy, perched on the shoulders of Monica and Jill, clapped and cheered in all their little girl glee. Girlie Dog, not afraid of man or beast, now cowered behind the Sisterhood's feet in an attempt to escape the booms and bangs.

As the fireworks reached a dazzling crescendo, a song blasted from the newly upgraded sound system on Alfons' yacht. It was the right song at the right time and the right place:

GIRLS JUST WANNA HAVE FUN.

The sisters sang along with the music. Even Jorge and Frank and Robert joined in while pregnant Maggie cradled her firstborn, Zoey, in her arms. They all knew a similar celebration was in full swing at the home of Wesley Miller, a true witness to the miracles of an angel on earth; no one could ever convince him otherwise, and Lynne Miller, the soon-to-be mother of twins who were destined to change the world one day. Loa, the Lesbian Goddess of the Universe, would see to that.

In the grand finale, the fireworks formed a waving flag of stars and stripes high over the water, lighting the beach where General Taylor and Admiral Kincade stood at attention and saluted, along with the two duped Secret Service agents whose duty it was to protect the new President and her entourage of naughty sisters.

The war was over, and so entered a new period in American history, the Reign of the Lesbian Zombies, where women's dominion over men would be firm and fair. However, as was the nature of men in love and war, they would not go quietly into the history books.

A note from the author about the *USS Carmick*

To those readers who are Naval History buffs or warship enthusiasts, please excuse me for taking authorial liberties by using the *USS Carmick* in this story, though the destroyer is no longer in service. My intentions were to breathe life back into the steadfast ship in honor of those who'd served on her during World War II and Korea, including my brother. Named after Major Daniel Carmick (1772–1816), the *USS Carmick* was commissioned on 28 December 1942 and served in the Atlantic, Mediterranean, and Pacific, as a designated destroyer minesweeper DMS-33. She was decommissioned on 13 February 1954 and eventually sold for scrap on 7 August 1972. Farewell great warrior and thank you for your service.

About the Author

George S. Naas is a long-time Colorado resident who owns Golden Publishing Company and writes in a variety of genres. He's an ancient history buff, a military strategist, and a romantic at heart. When he's not writing or working, he enjoys bowling and cross-fit. He lives in Lakewood with his wife Dana.

Look for Other Works by George S. Naas

Invasion of the Lesbian Zombies

God's Assassin

Finding True Love at 35,000 Feet

Anything Goes

Charlie the Cherry

www.ingramcontent.com/pod-product-compliance
Lightning Source LLC
Chambersburg PA
CBHW072307020726
47501CB00002B/424

* 9 7 8 1 7 3 6 2 4 7 8 0 8 *